HAND OF THE MORNINGSTAR

INDOCTRINATION

ZONDERVAN®

Indoctrination
Copyright © 2008 by Lamp Post, Inc.

Requests for information should be addressed to:
Zondervan, *Grand Rapids, Michigan 49530*

CIP applied for
ISBN: 978-0-310-71373-9

This book published in conjunction with Lamp Post, Inc.; 8367 Lemon Avenue, La Mesa, CA 91941

Series Editor: Bud Rogers
Managing Art Director: Merit Alderink

Printed in the United States of America

08 09 10 11 12 • 8 7 6 5 4 3 2 1

GRAPHIC NOVELS

HAND OF THE MORNINGSTAR

INDOCTRINATION

Series Editor: BUD ROGERS
Story by BRETT BURNER
Art by ERIC NINALTOWSKI
Tones by DIEGO CANDIA
Created by BRETT BURNER

ZONDERVAN®

ZONDERVAN.com/
AUTHORTRACKER
follow your favorite authors

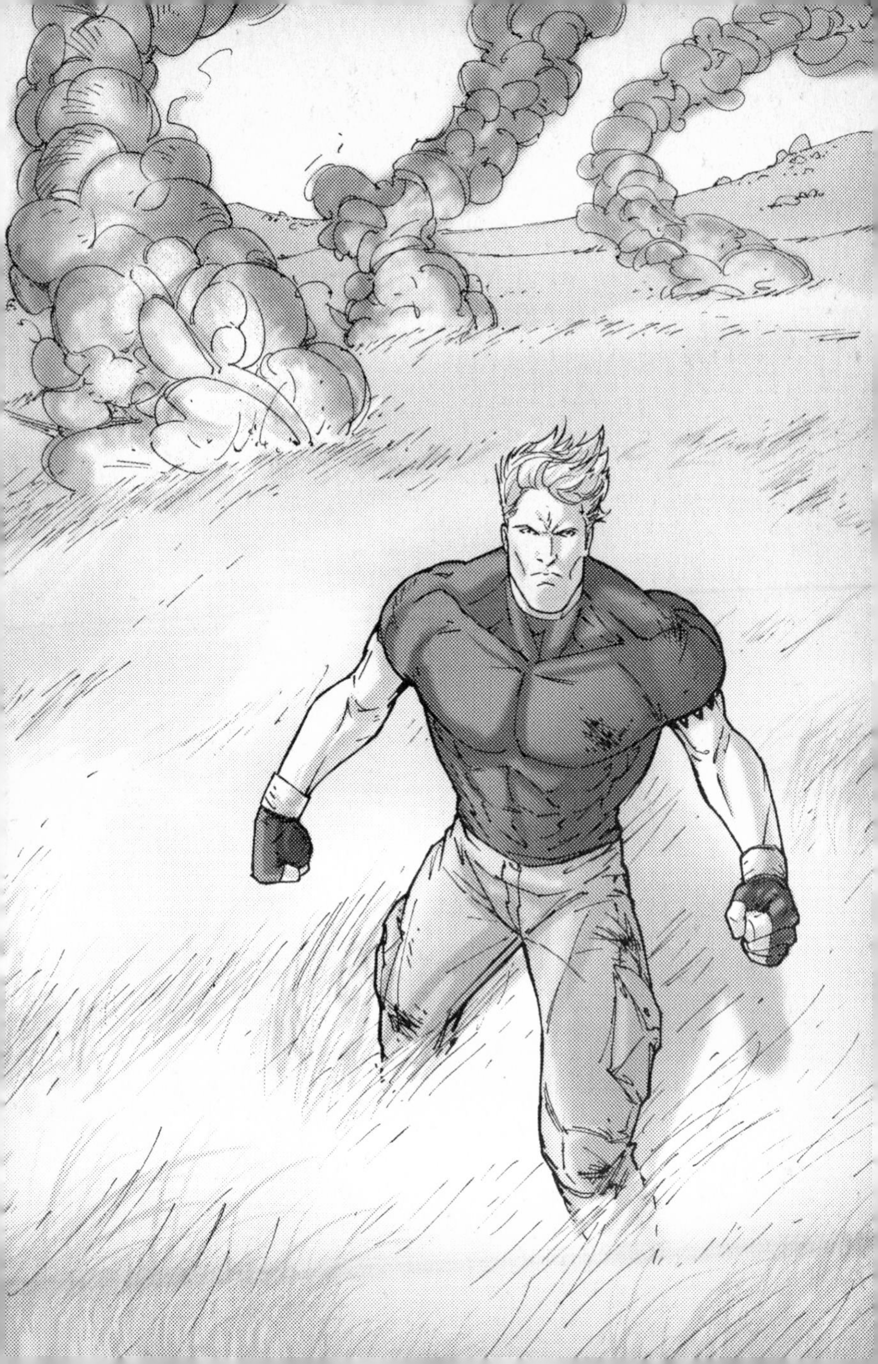

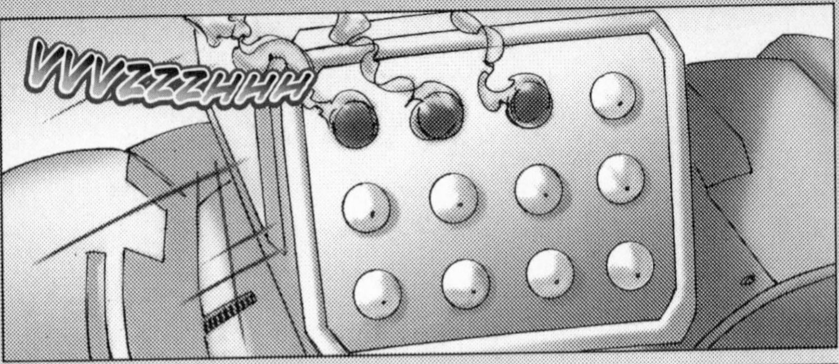
VVVZZZHHH

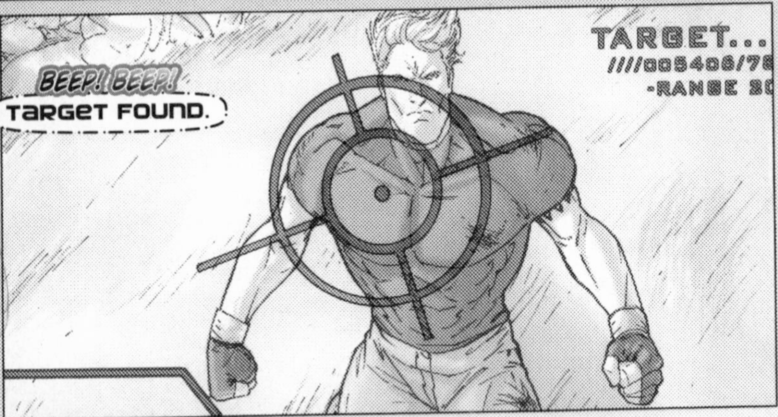
BEEP! BEEP!
TARGET FOUND.
TARGET...
////005406/7
-RANGE 3

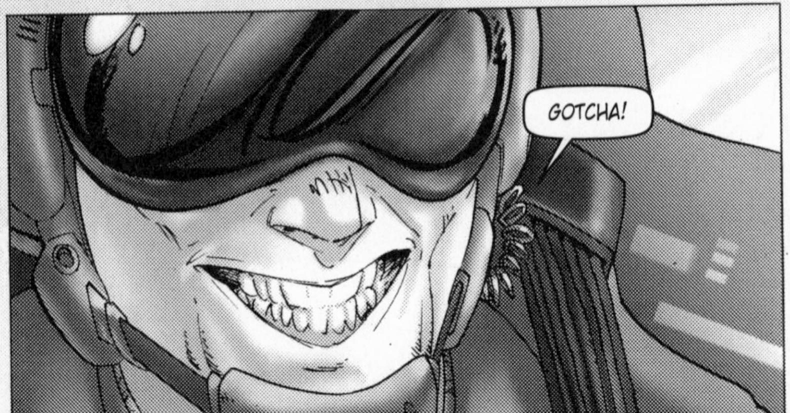
GOTCHA!

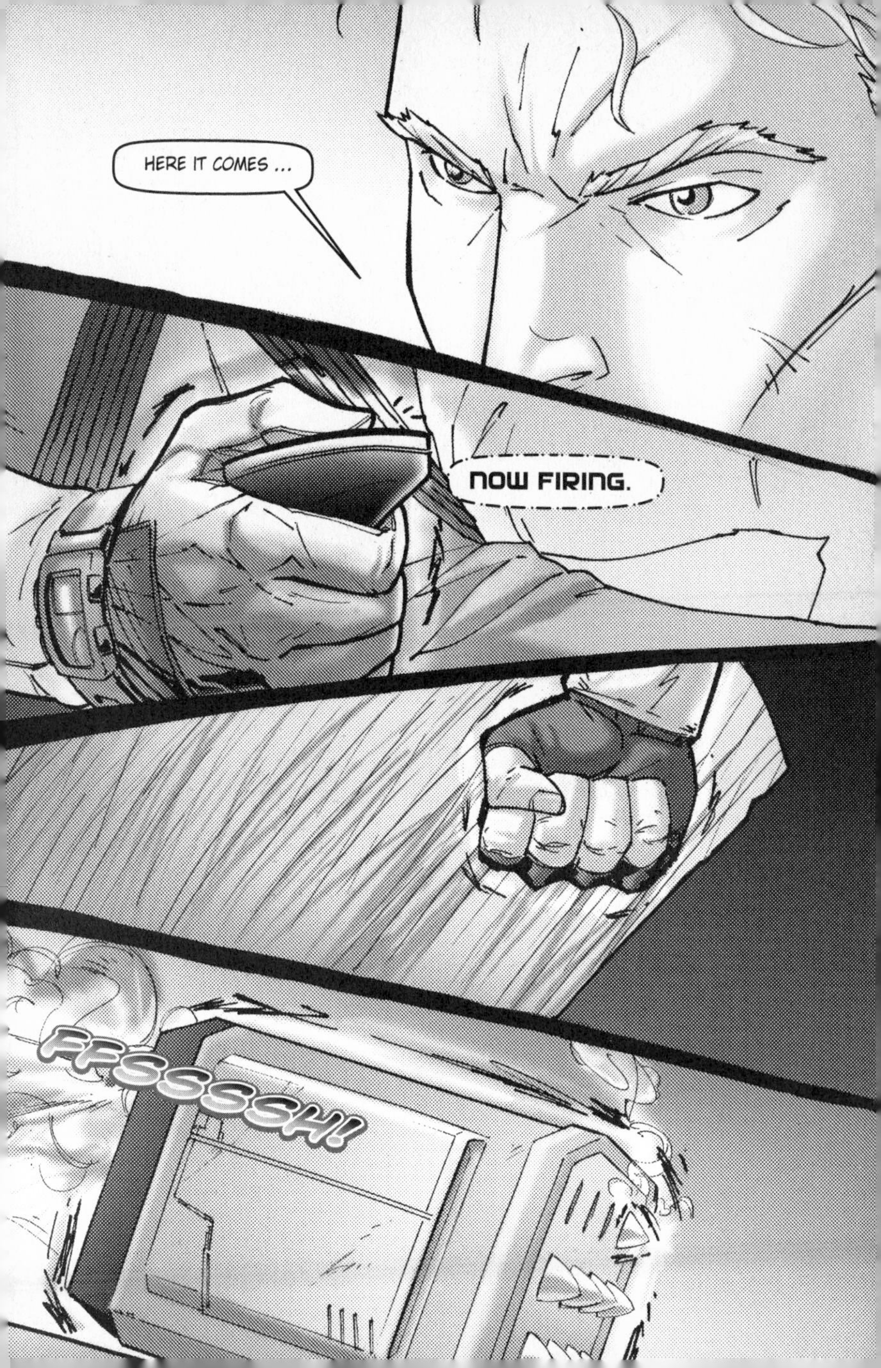
HERE IT COMES ...
NOW FIRING.
FFSSSSSH!!

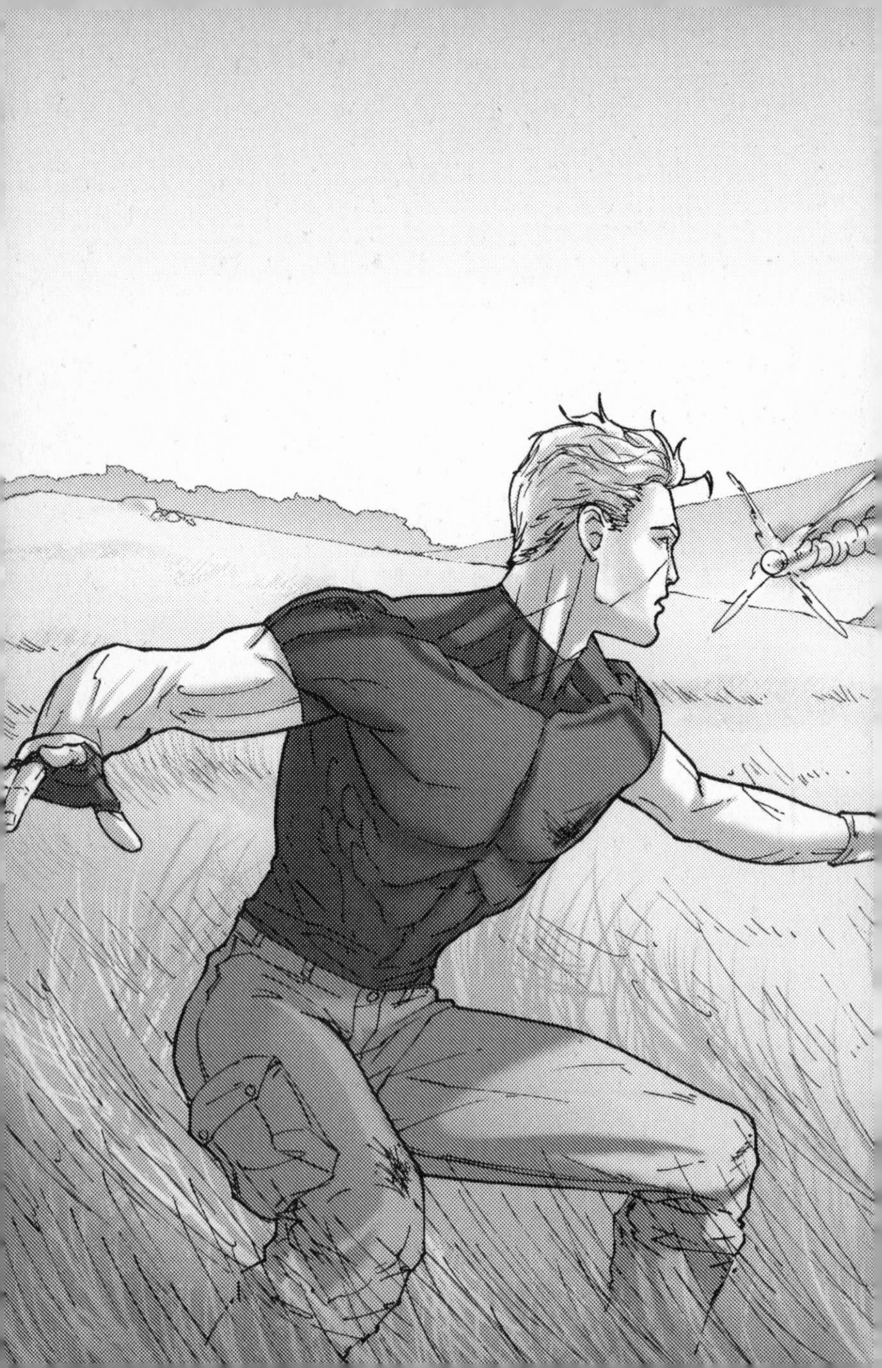

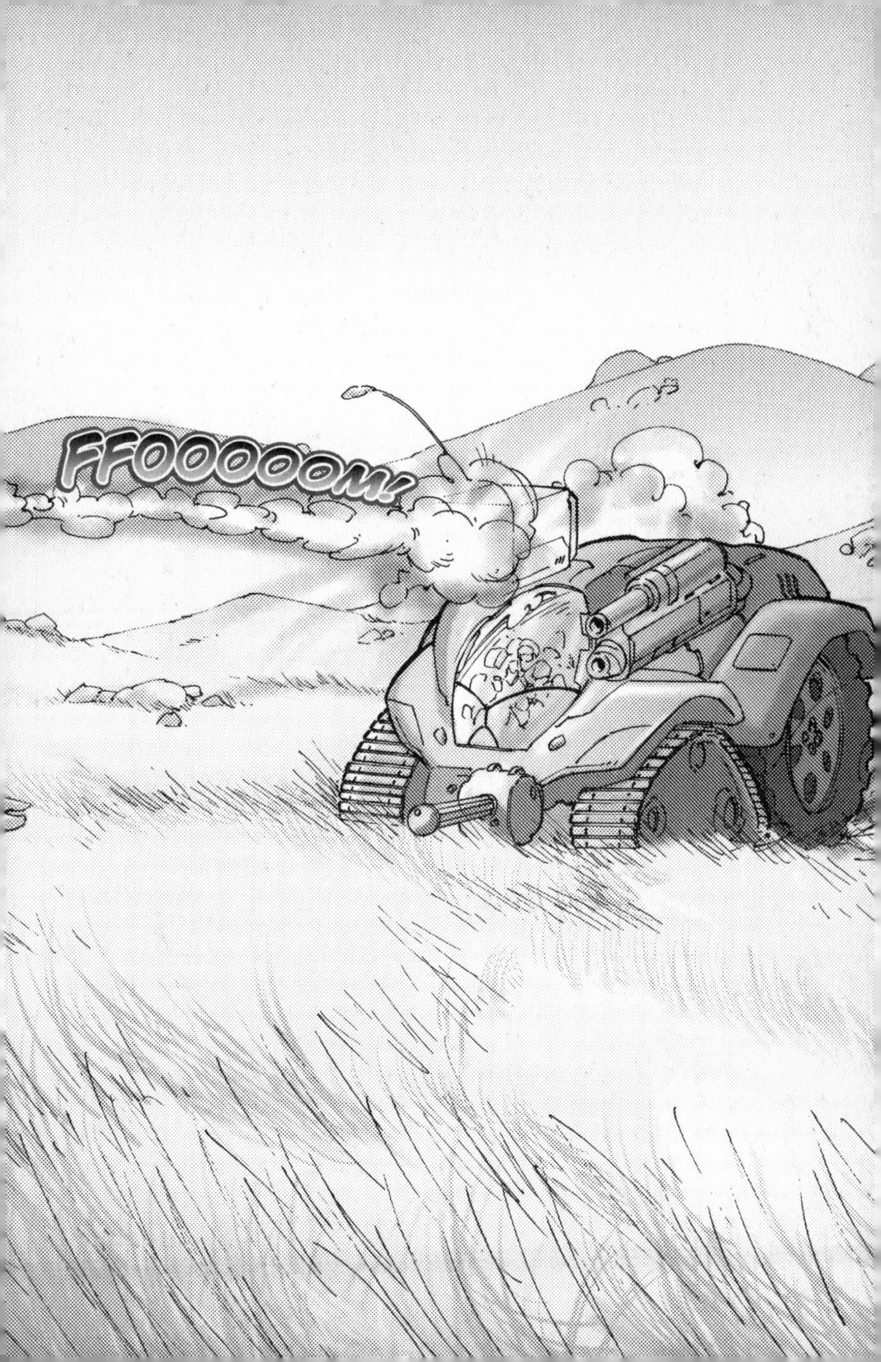
FFOOOOOOM!

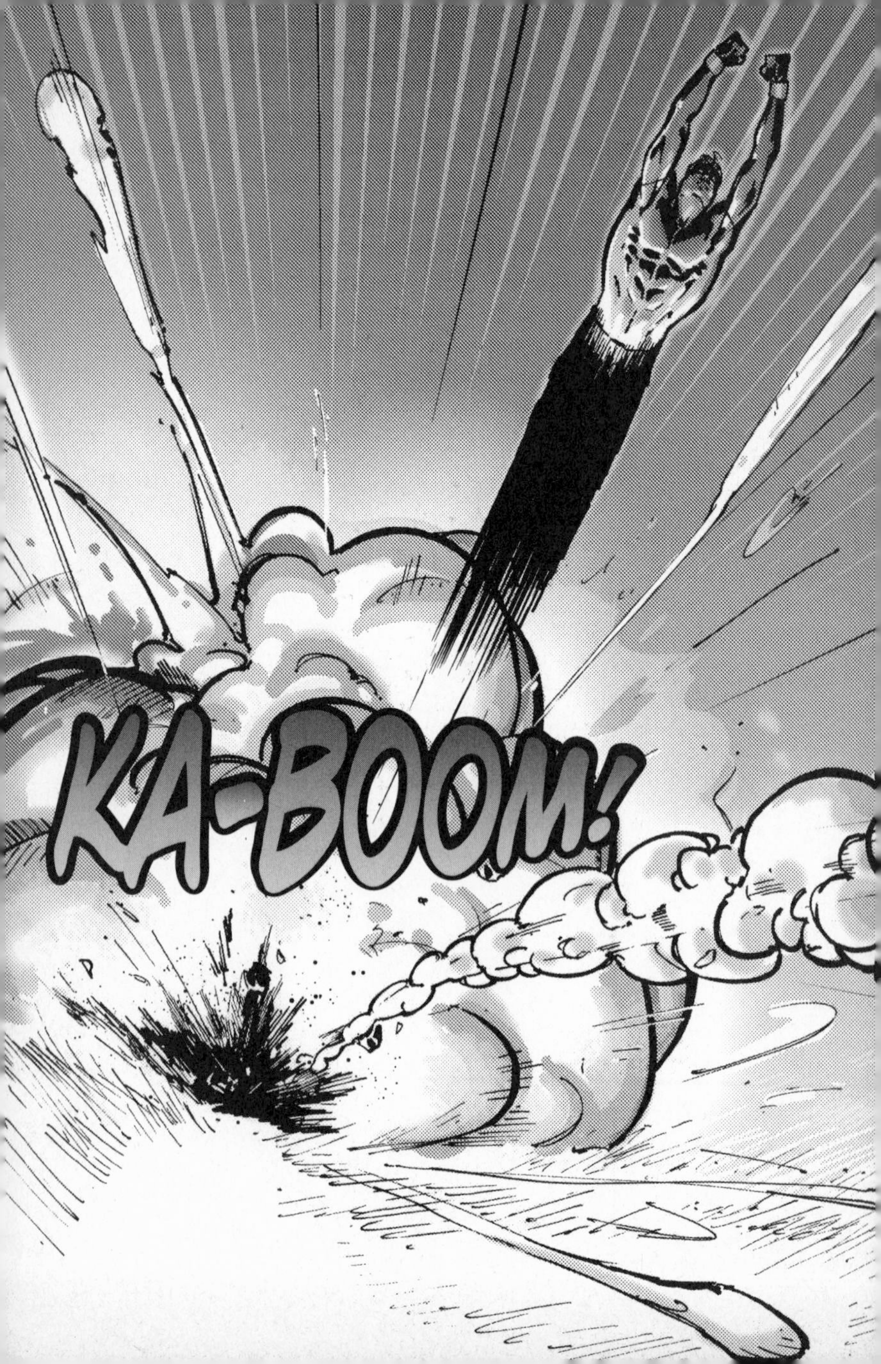
KA-BOOM!

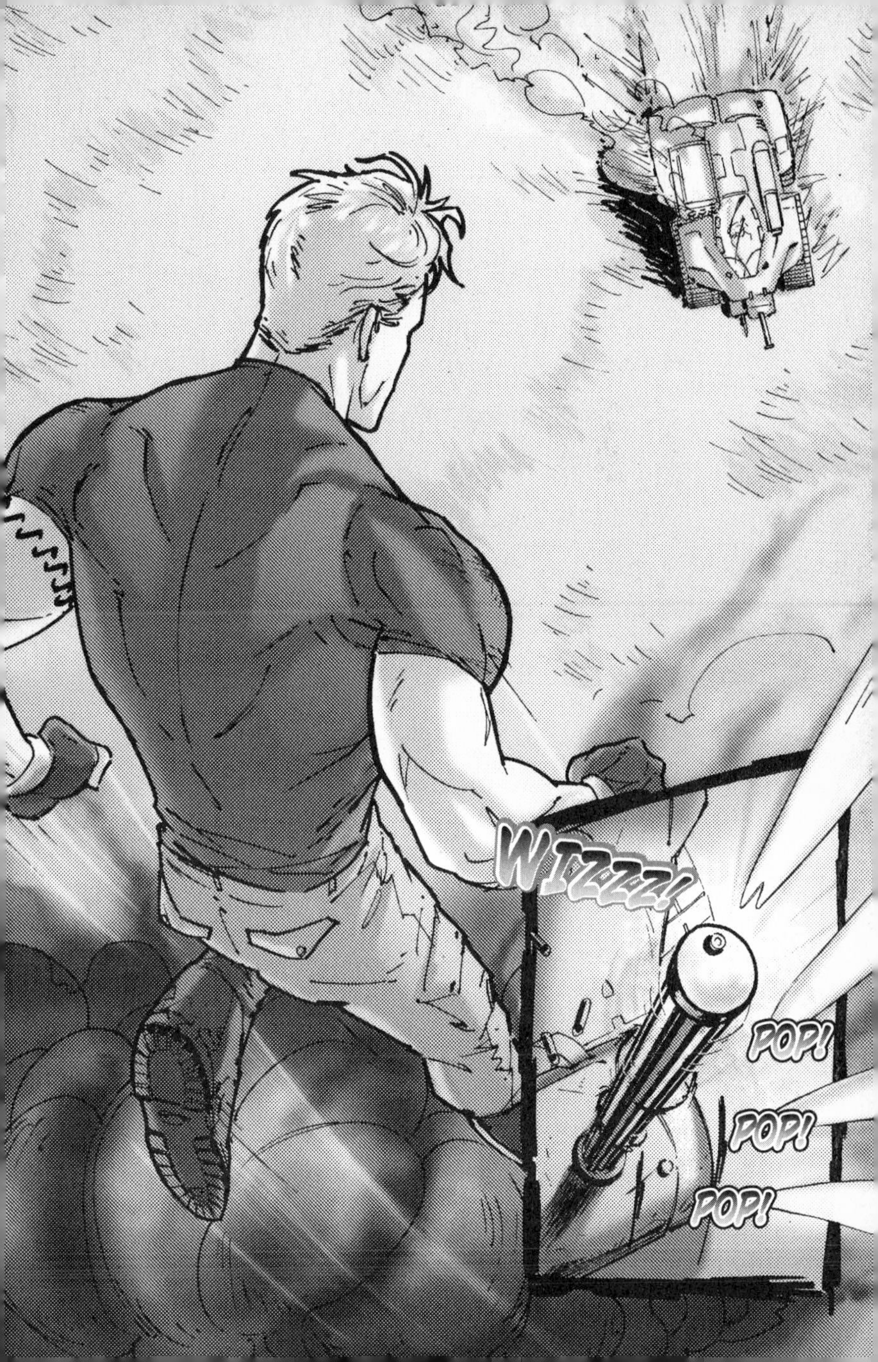
WIZZZ!
POP!
POP!
POP!

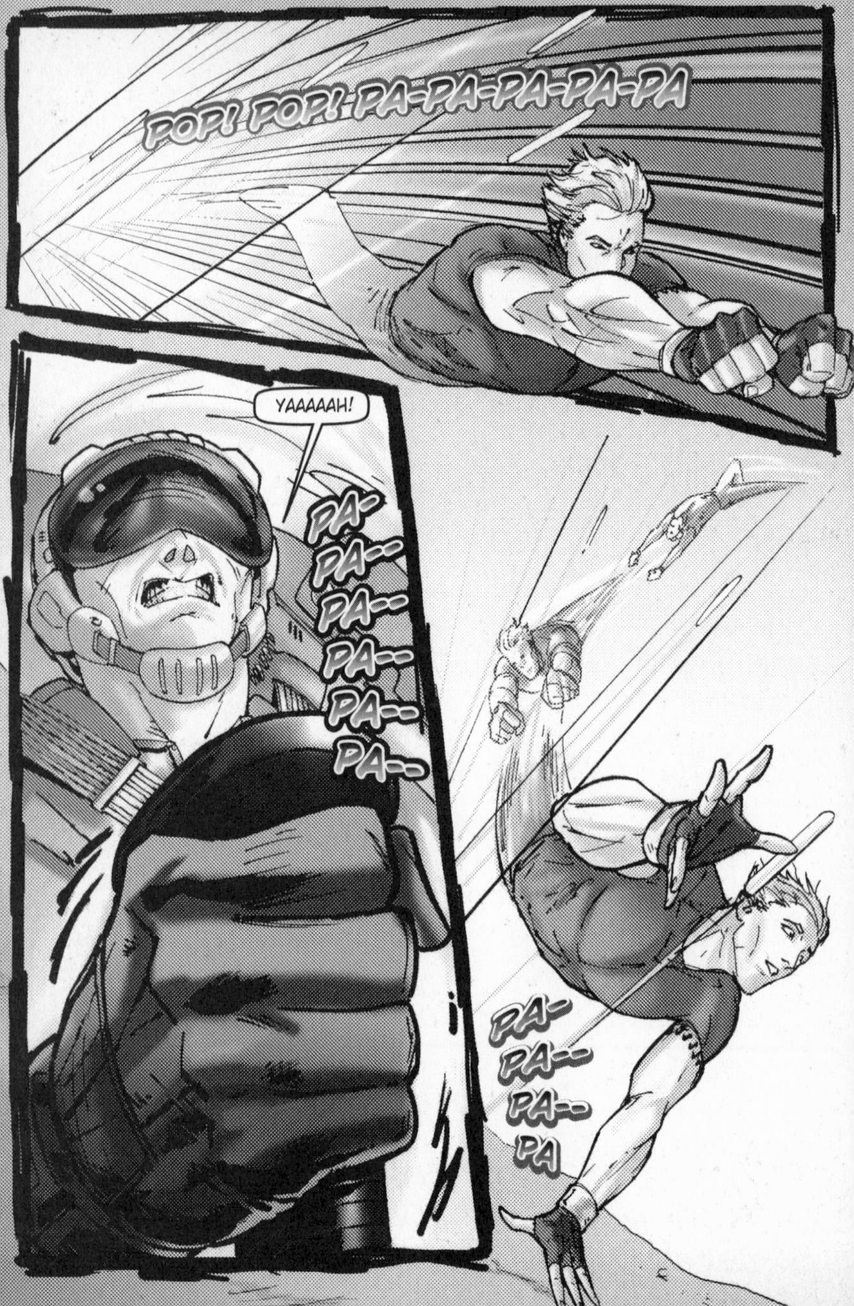
POP! POP! PA-PA-PA-PA-PA
YAAAAAH!
PA-
PA--
PA--
PA--
PA--
PA--
PA-
PA--
PA--
PA

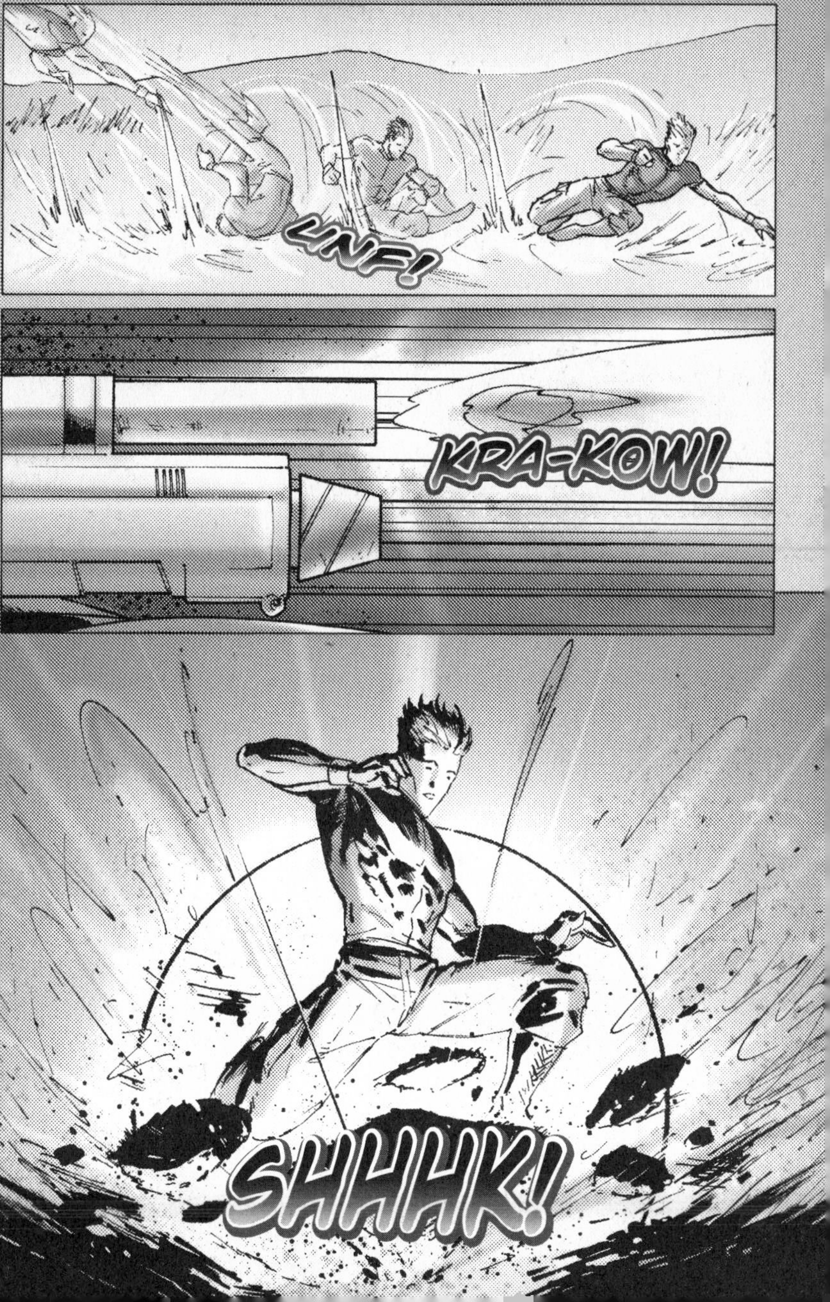
UNF!
KRA-KOW!
SHHHK!

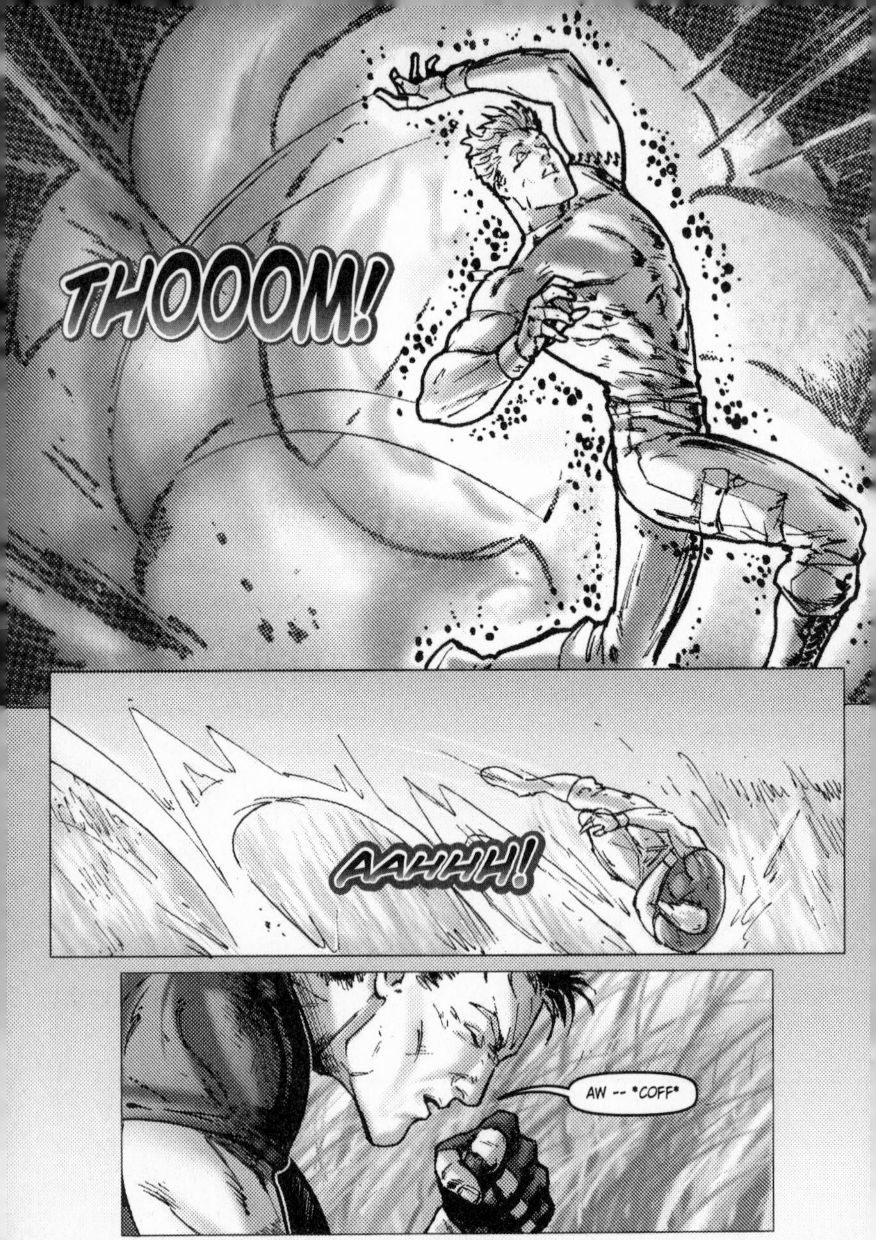
THOOOM!
AAHHH!
AW -- *COFF*

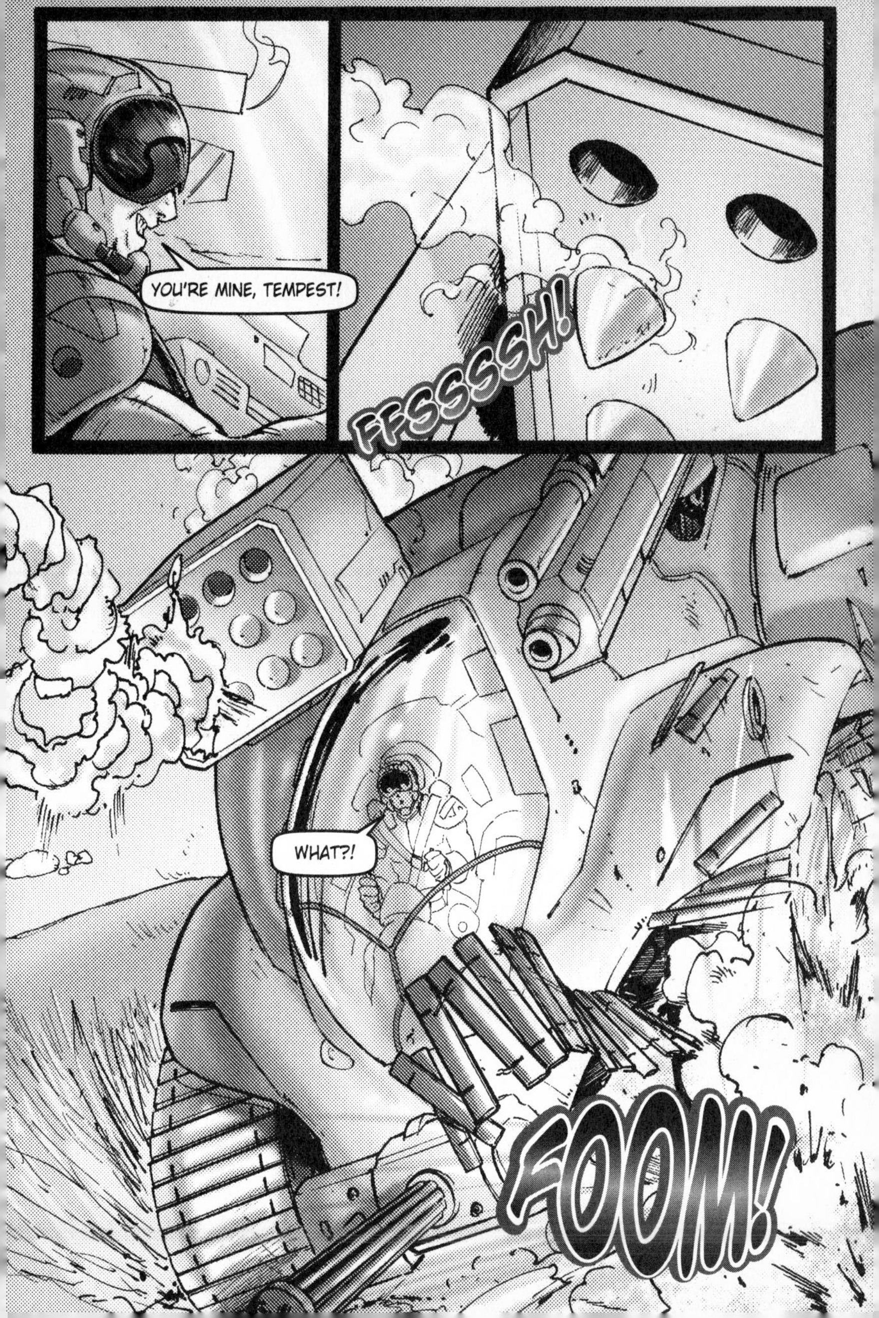
YOU'RE MINE, TEMPEST!
FFSSSSSH!
WHAT?!
FOOM!

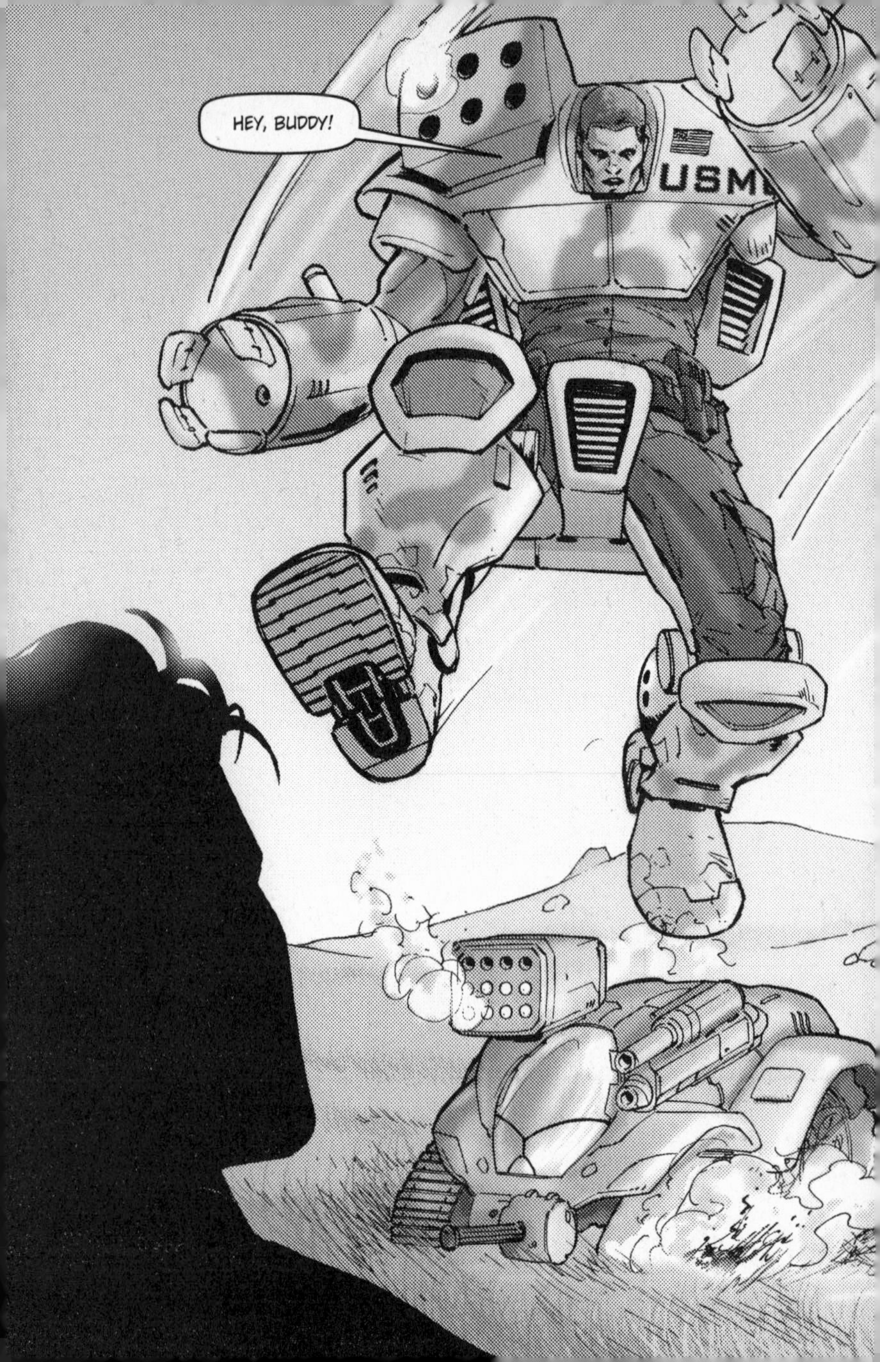
HEY, BUDDY!
USM

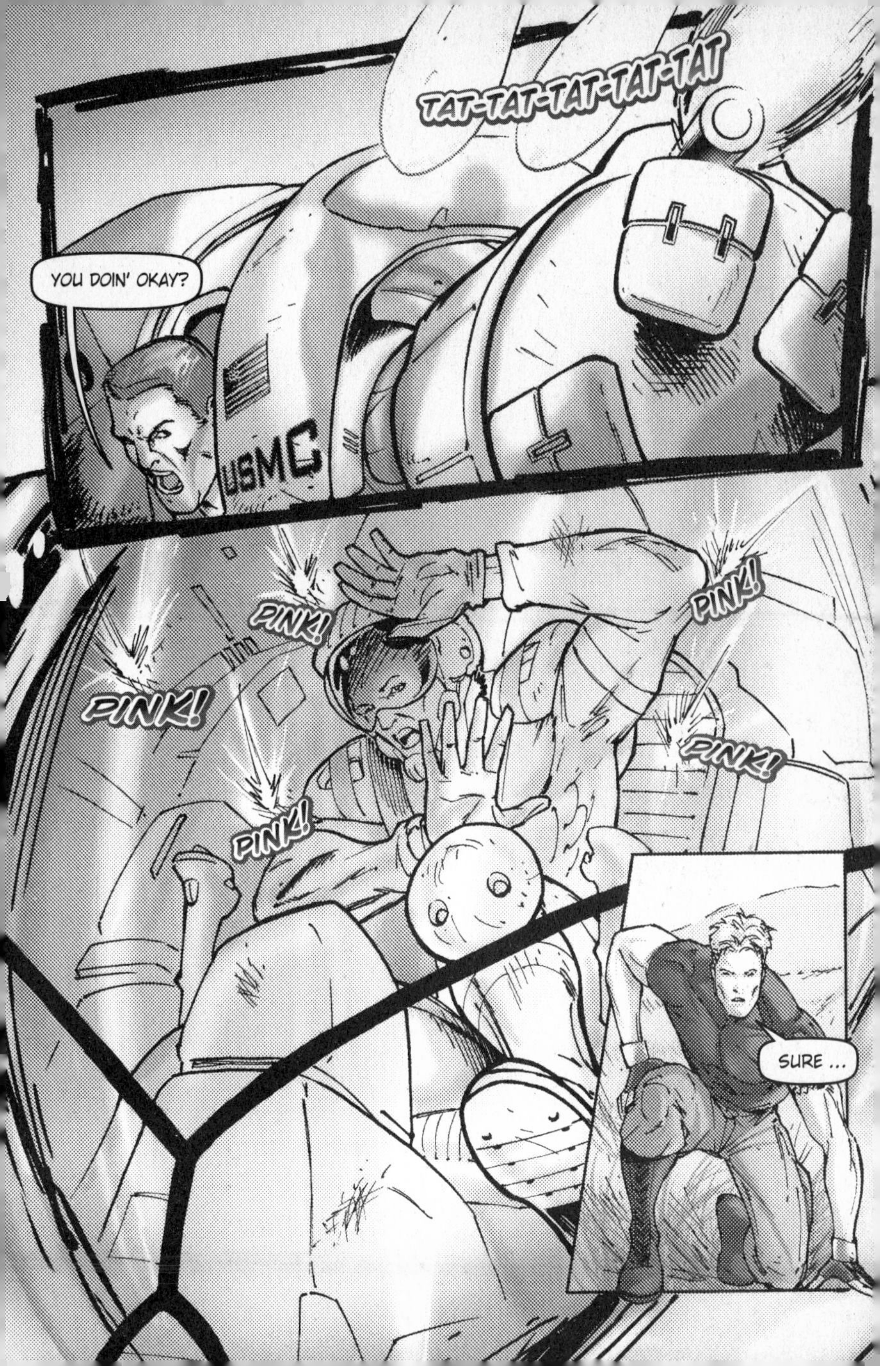
TAT-TAT-TAT-TAT-TAT
YOU DOIN' OKAY?
PINK!
PINK!
PINK!
PINK!
PINK!
SURE ...

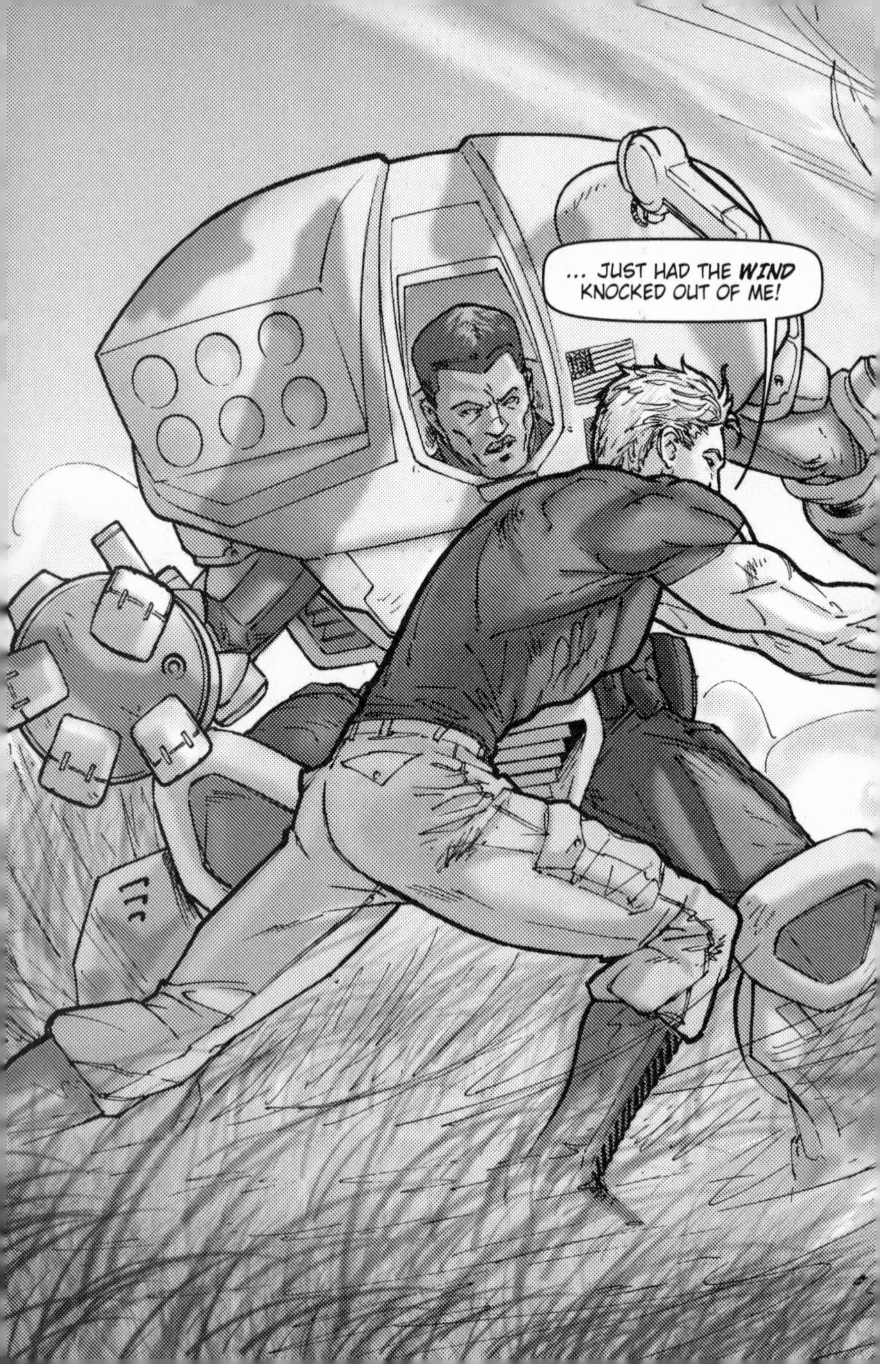
... JUST HAD THE **WIND** KNOCKED OUT OF ME!

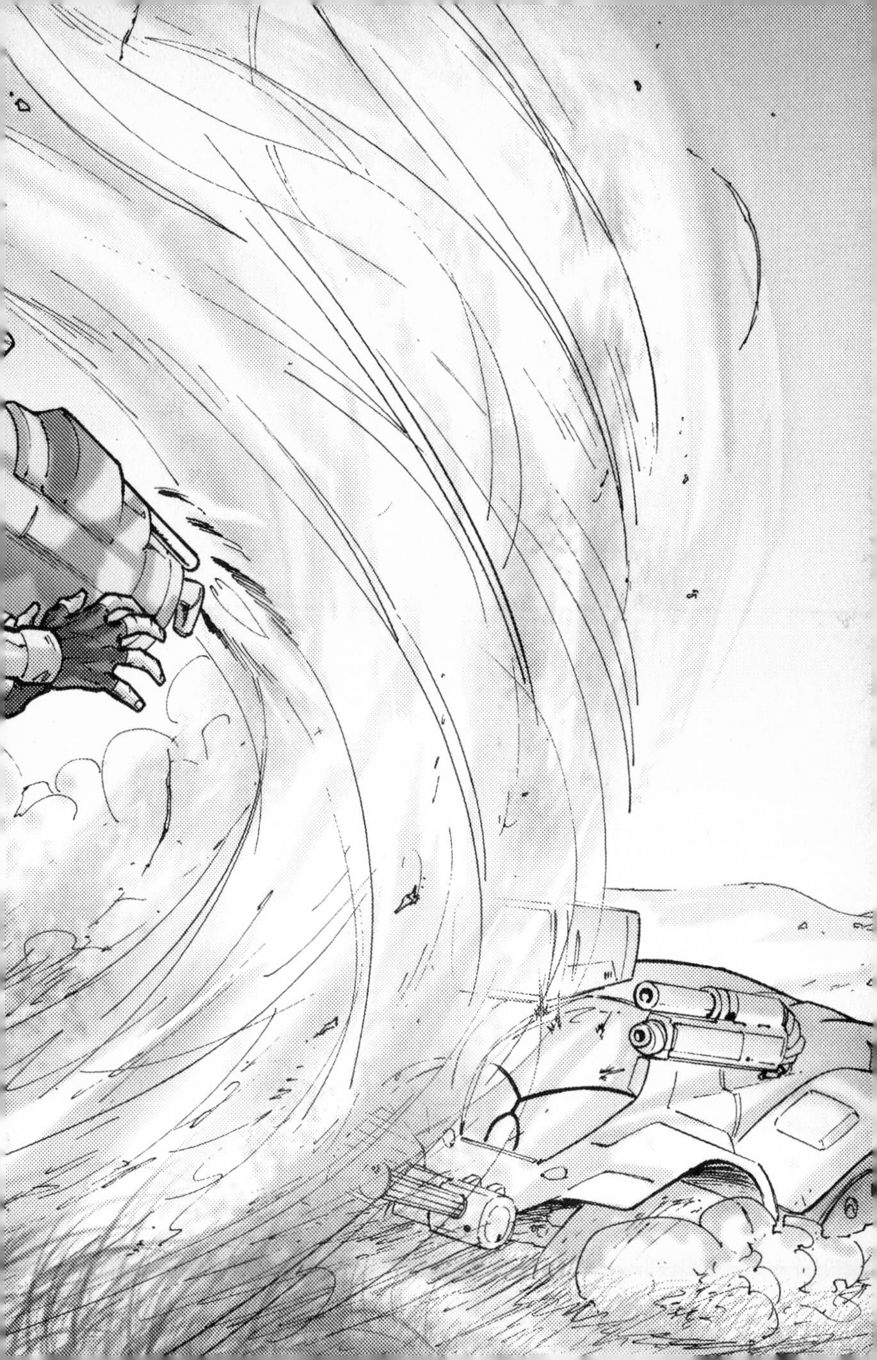

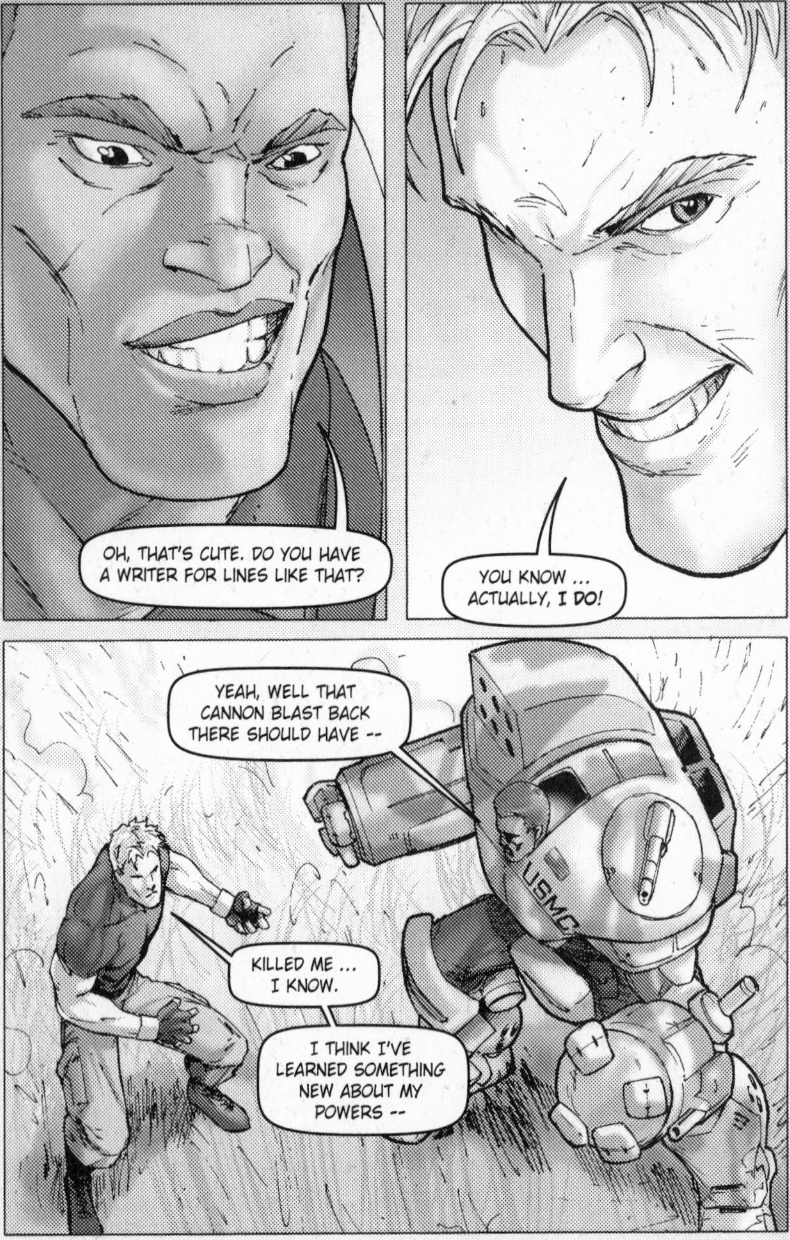
OH, THAT'S CUTE. DO YOU HAVE A WRITER FOR LINES LIKE THAT?
YOU KNOW ... ACTUALLY, I DO!
YEAH, WELL THAT CANNON BLAST BACK THERE SHOULD HAVE --
USMC
KILLED ME ... I KNOW.
I THINK I'VE LEARNED SOMETHING NEW ABOUT MY POWERS --

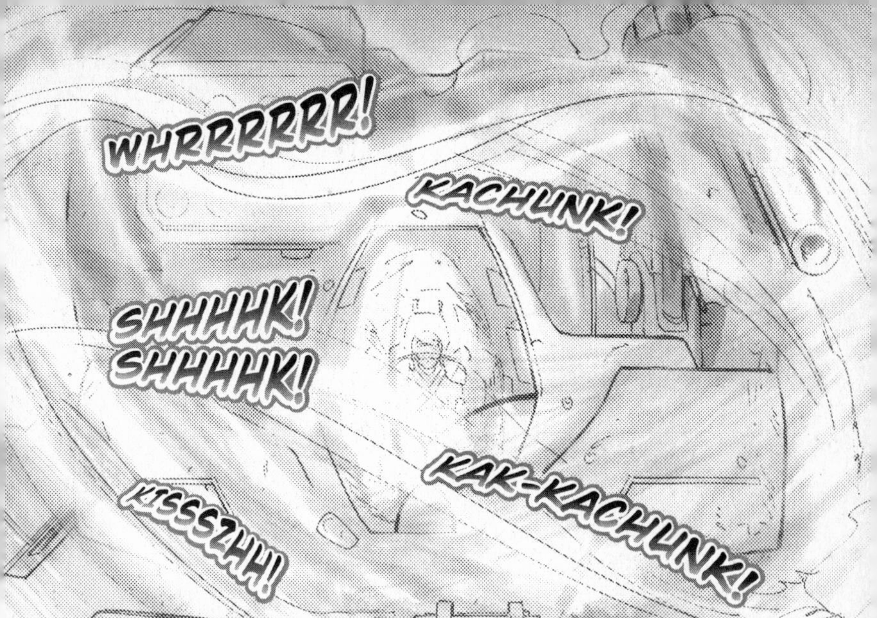
WHRRRRRR!
KACHUNK!
SHHHHK!
SHHHHK!
KAK-KACHUNK!
KISSSZHH!
THUMK!
THUMK!

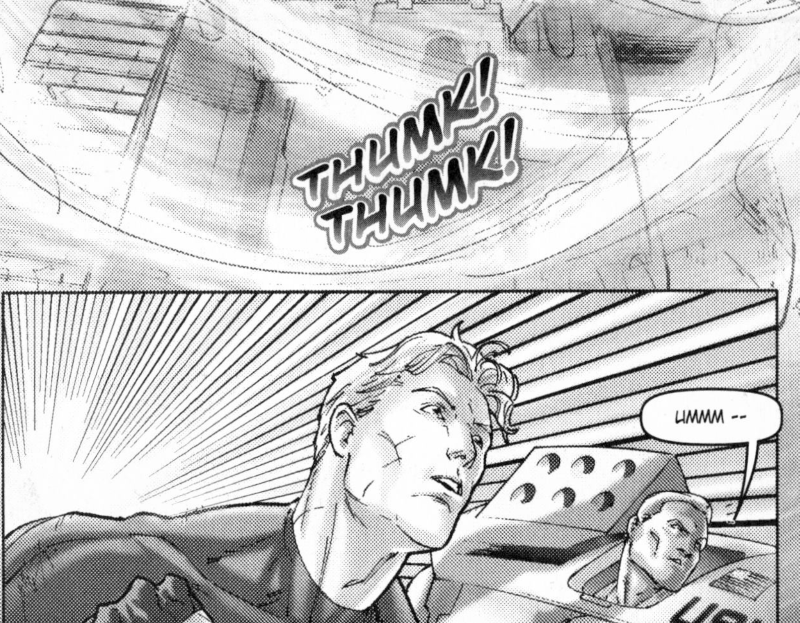
UMMM --
USM

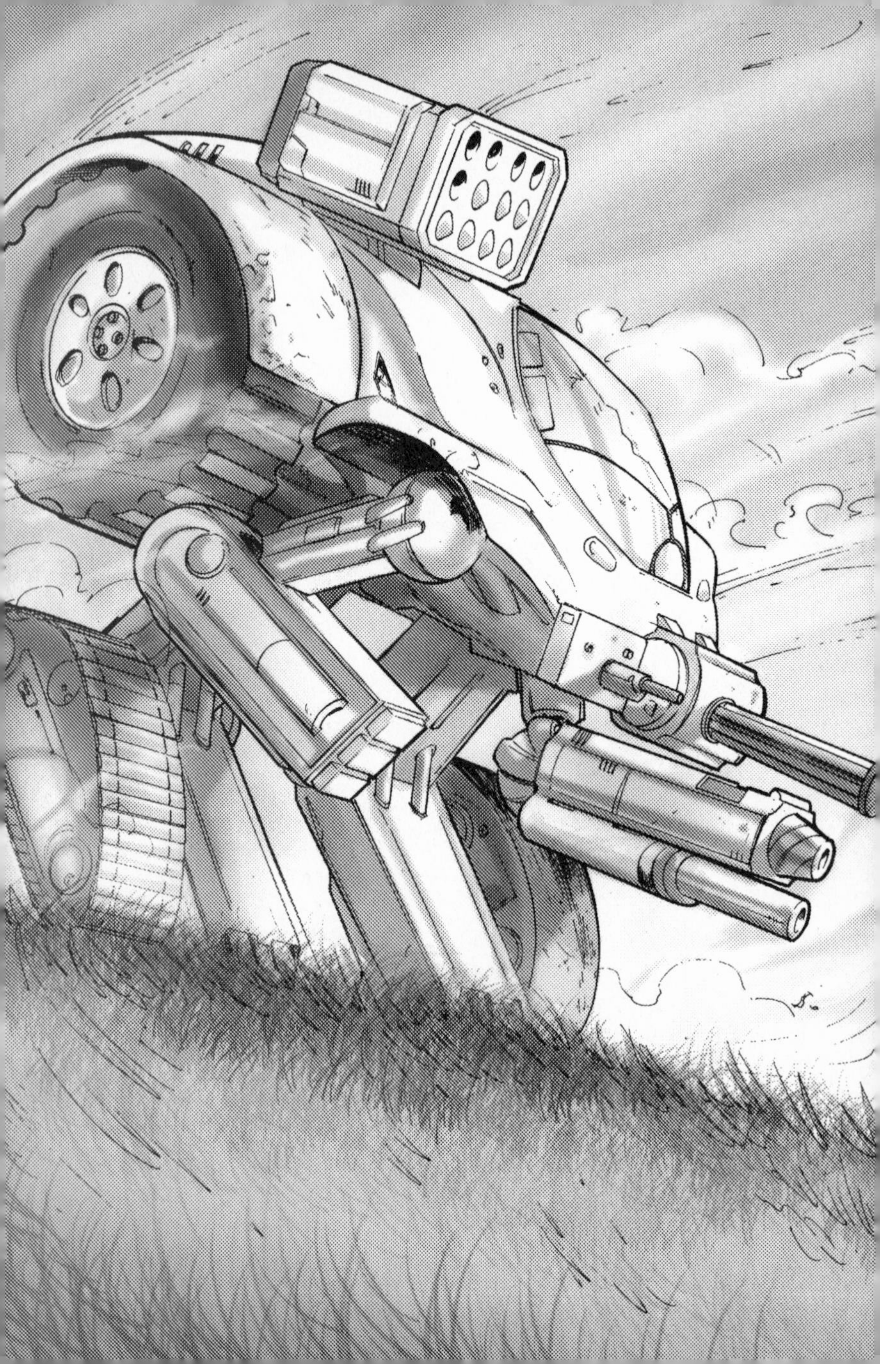

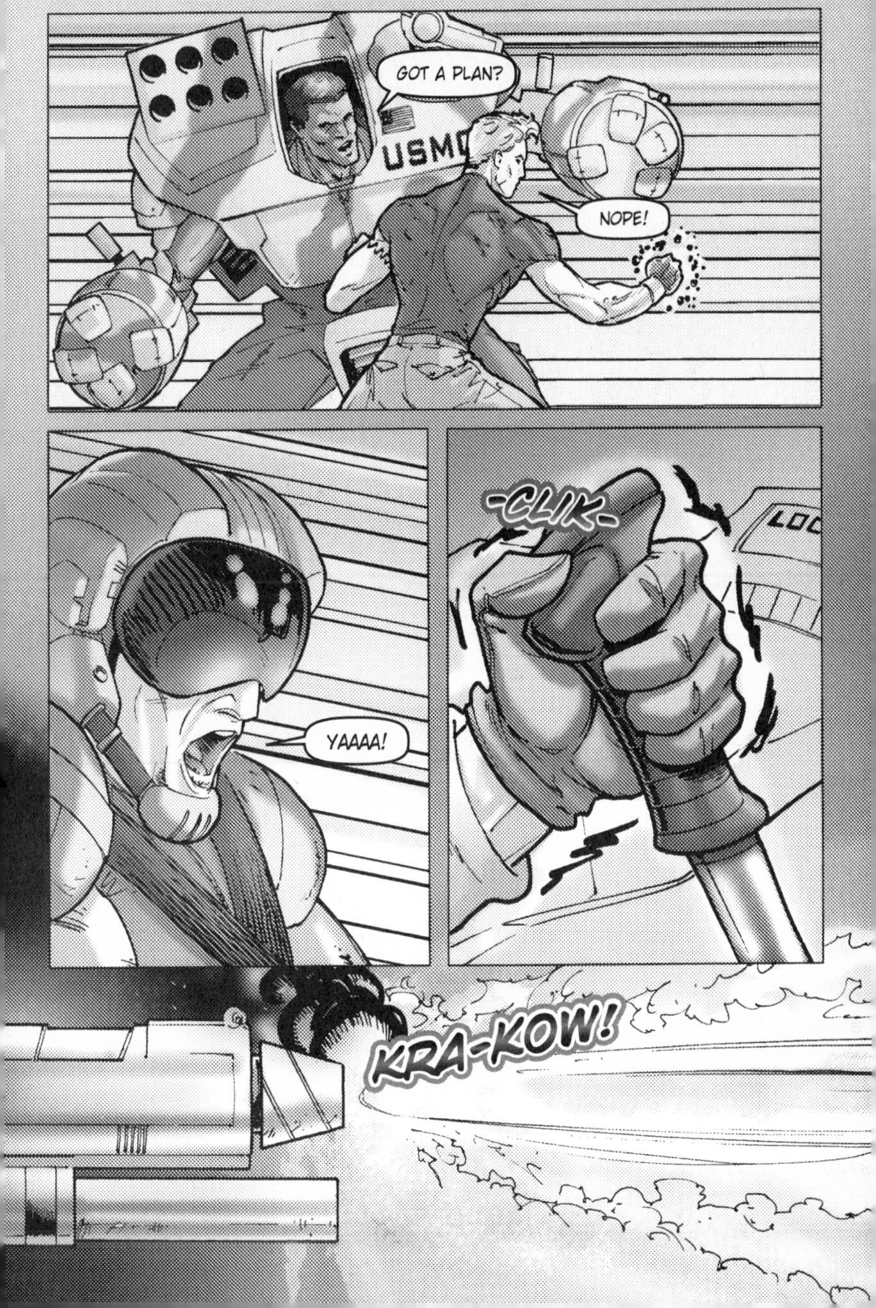
USMC
GOT A PLAN?
NOPE!
YAAAA!
-CLIK-
KRA-KOW!

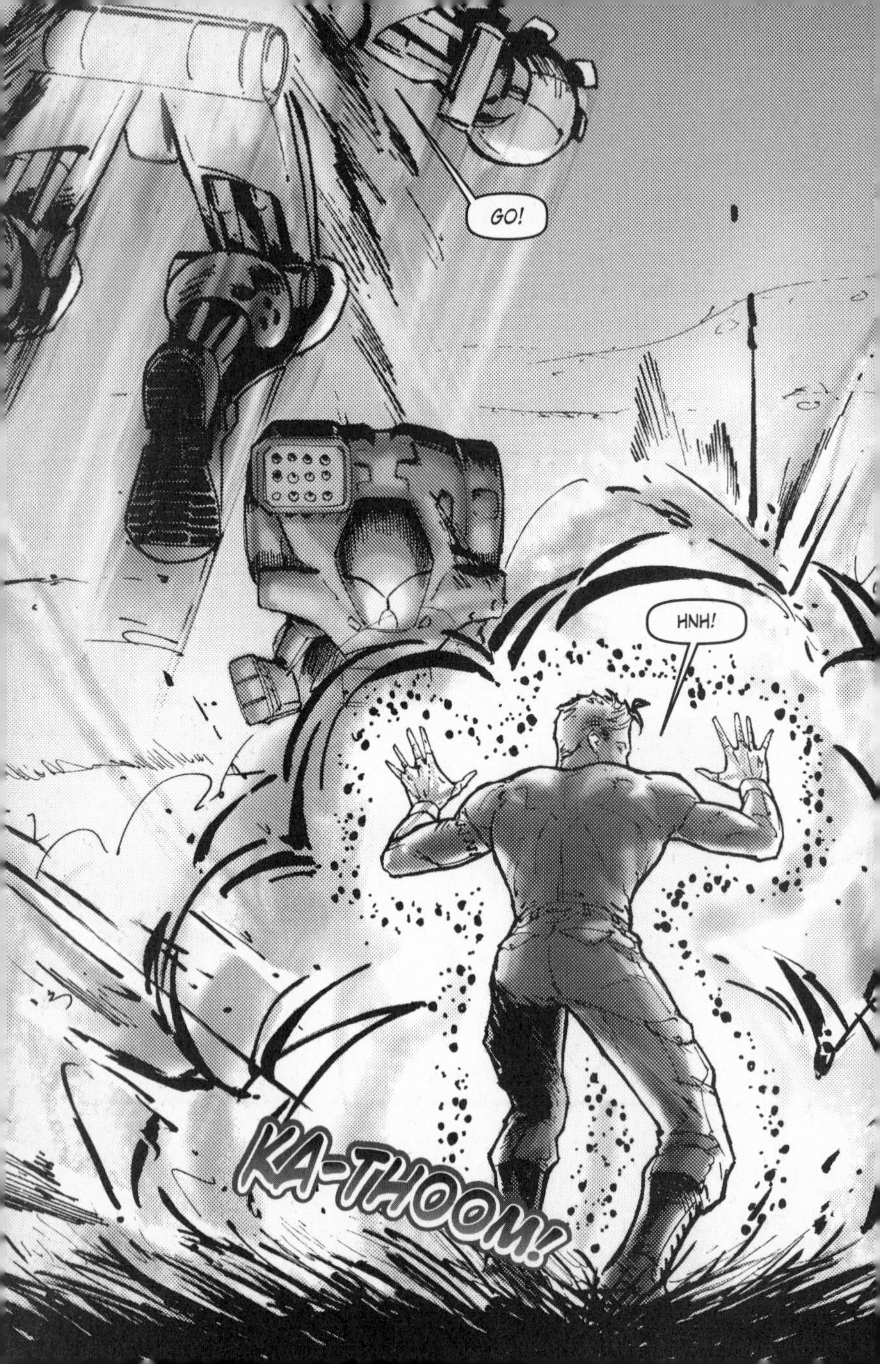
GO!
HNH!
KA-THOOM!

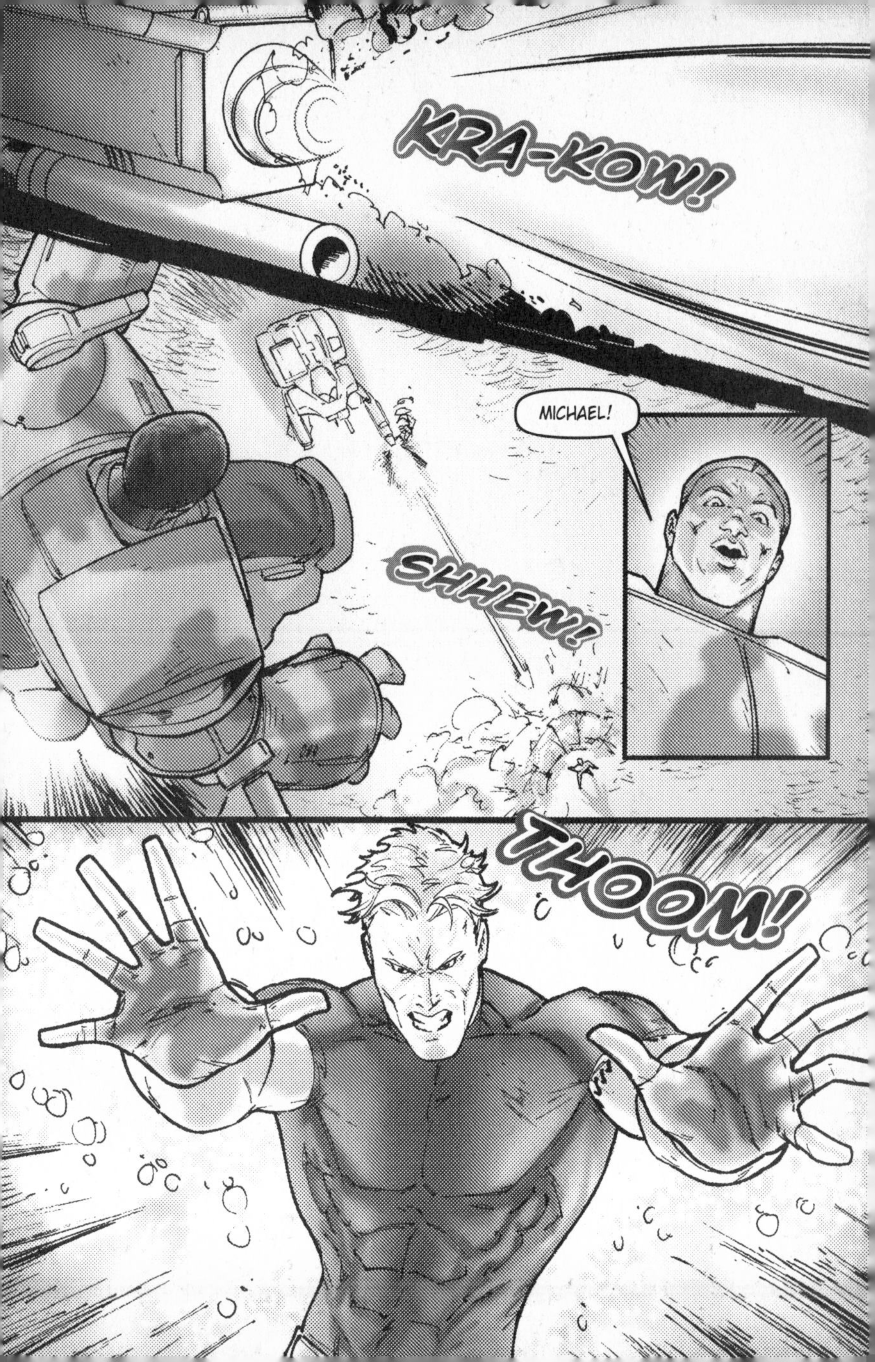
KRA-KOW!
SHHEW!
MICHAEL!
THOOM!

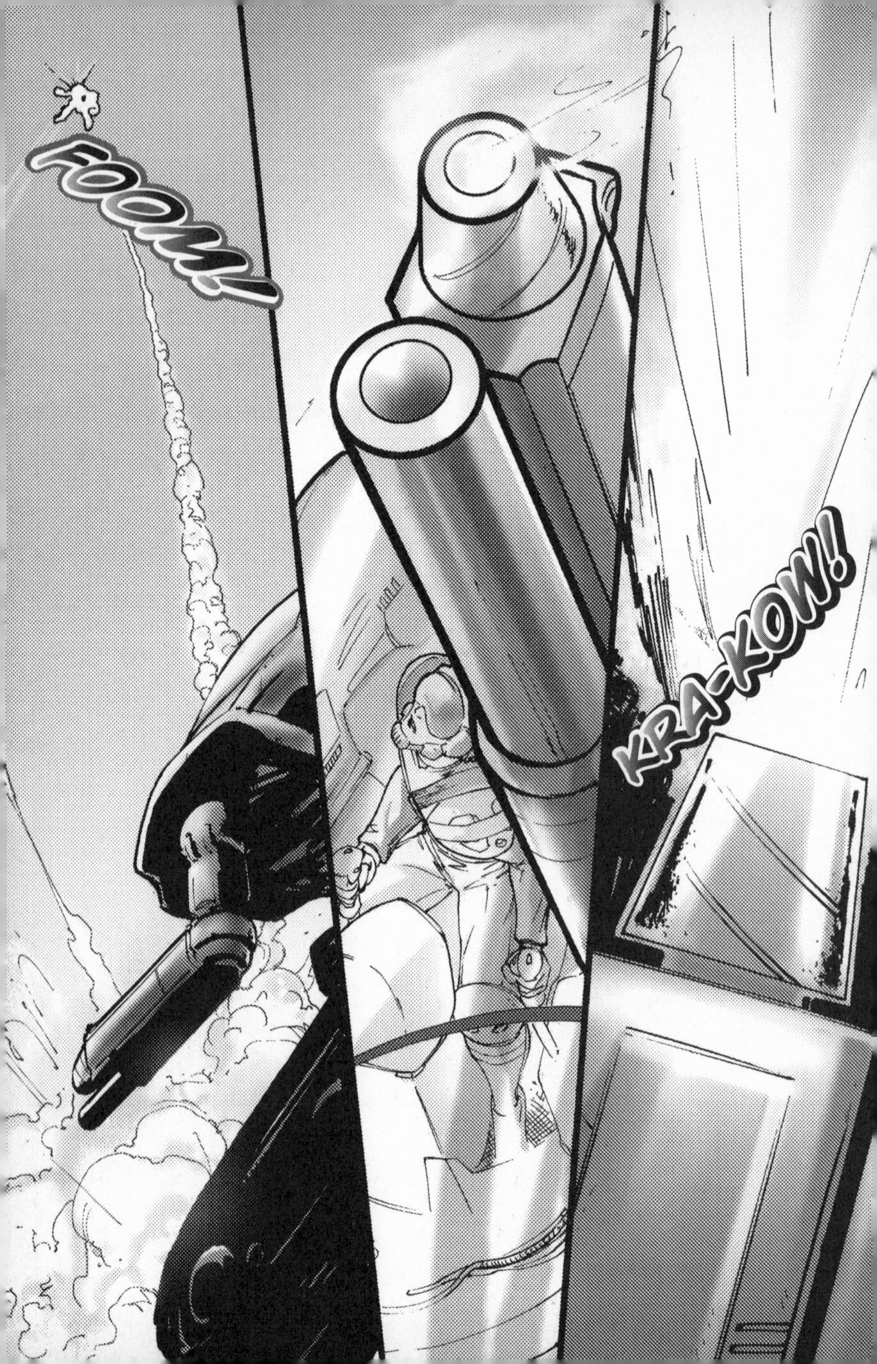
FOOM!
KRA-KOW!

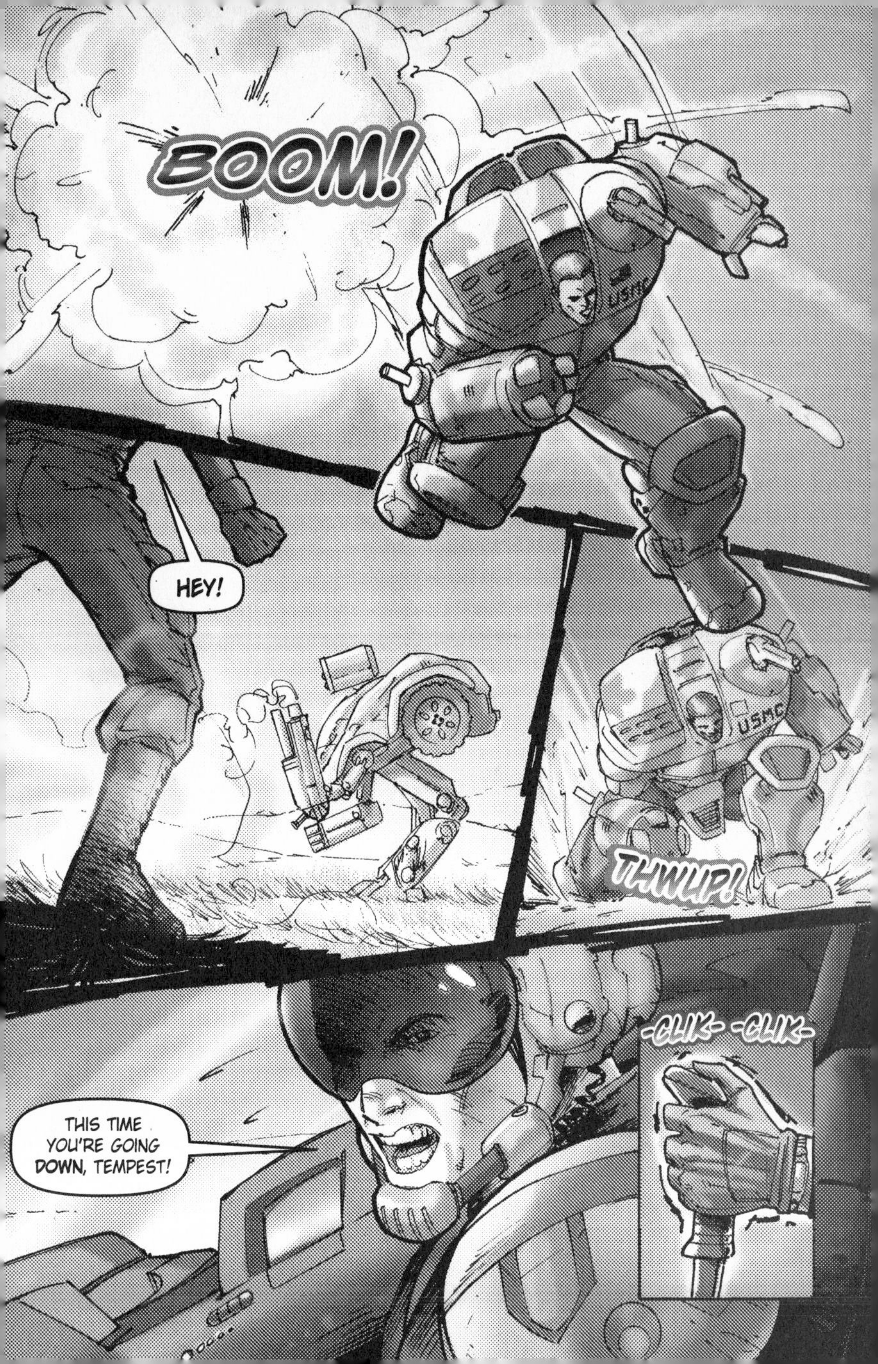
BOOM!
HEY!
THWUP!
THIS TIME YOU'RE GOING DOWN, TEMPEST!
-CLIK- -CLIK-

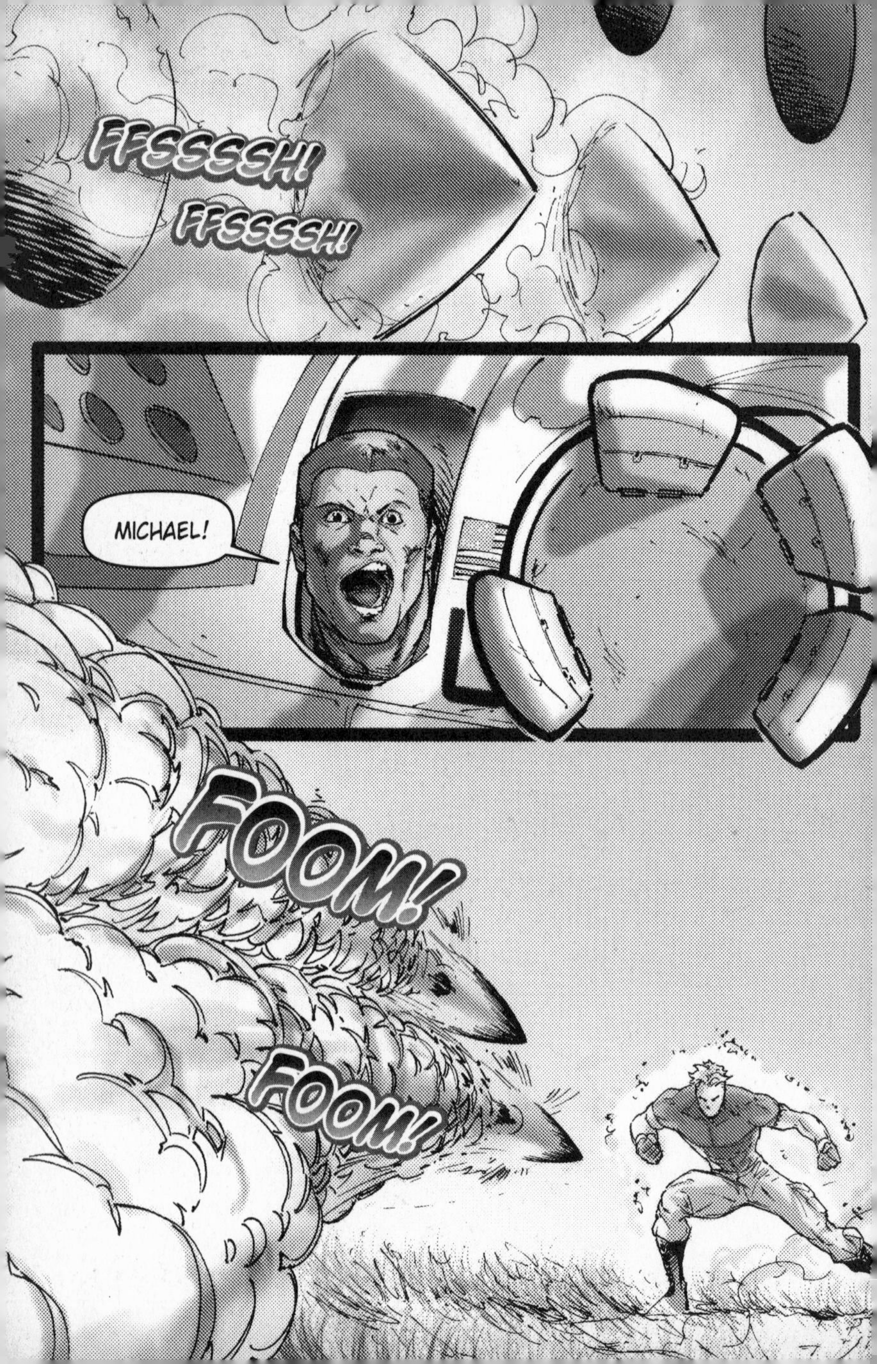
FFSSSSSH!
FFSSSSSH!
MICHAEL!
FOOM!
FOOM!

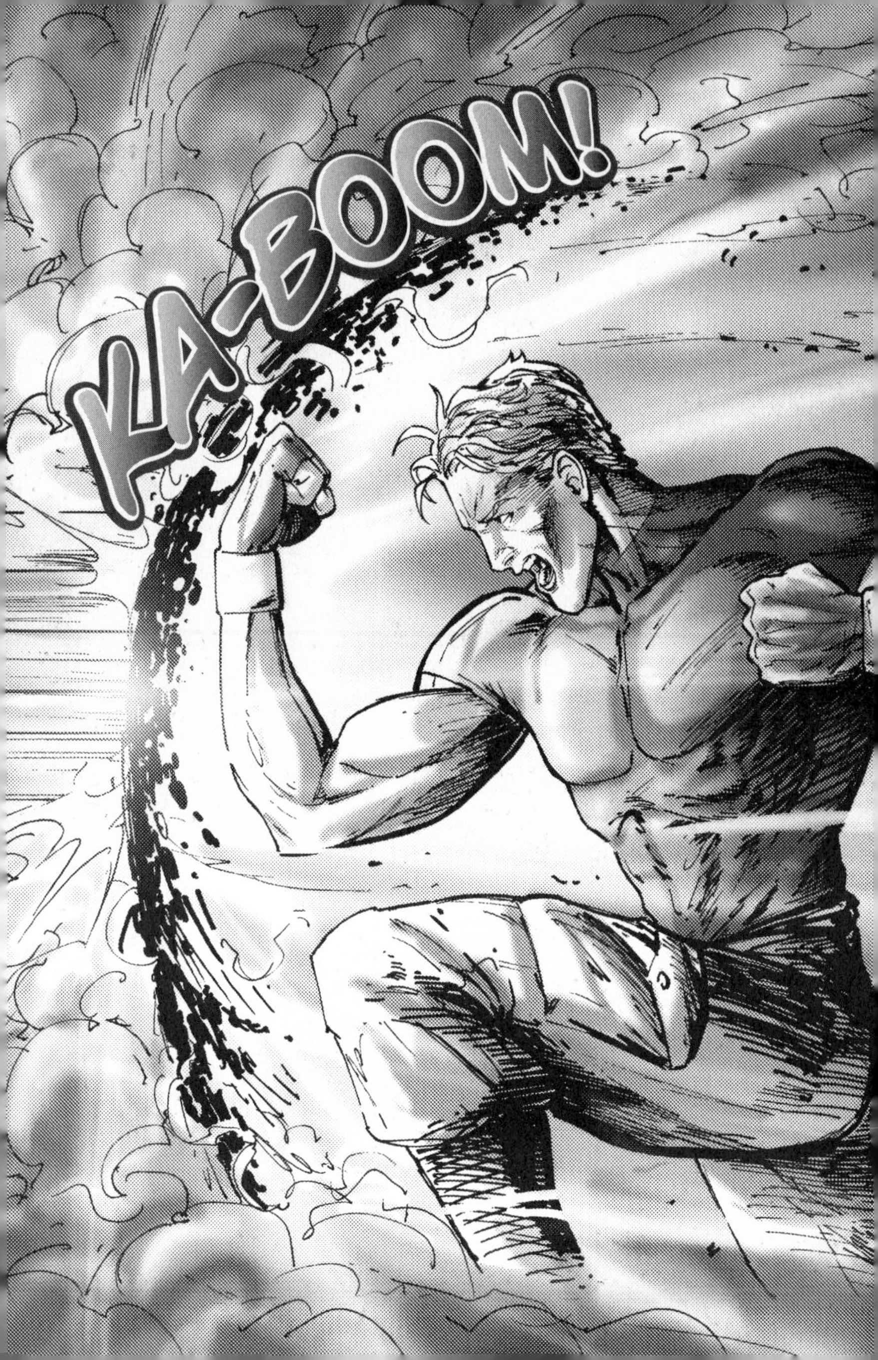
KA-BOOM!

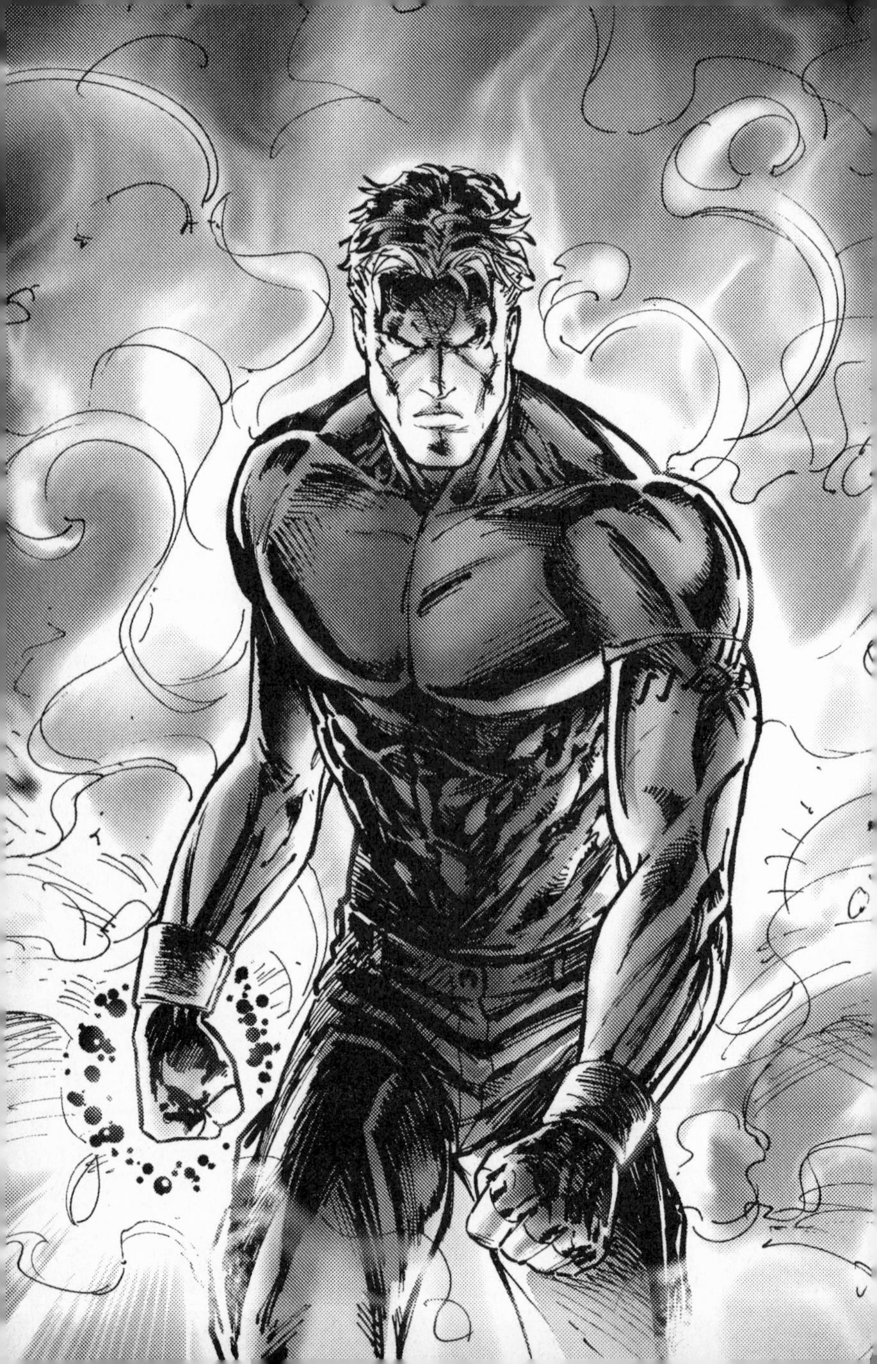

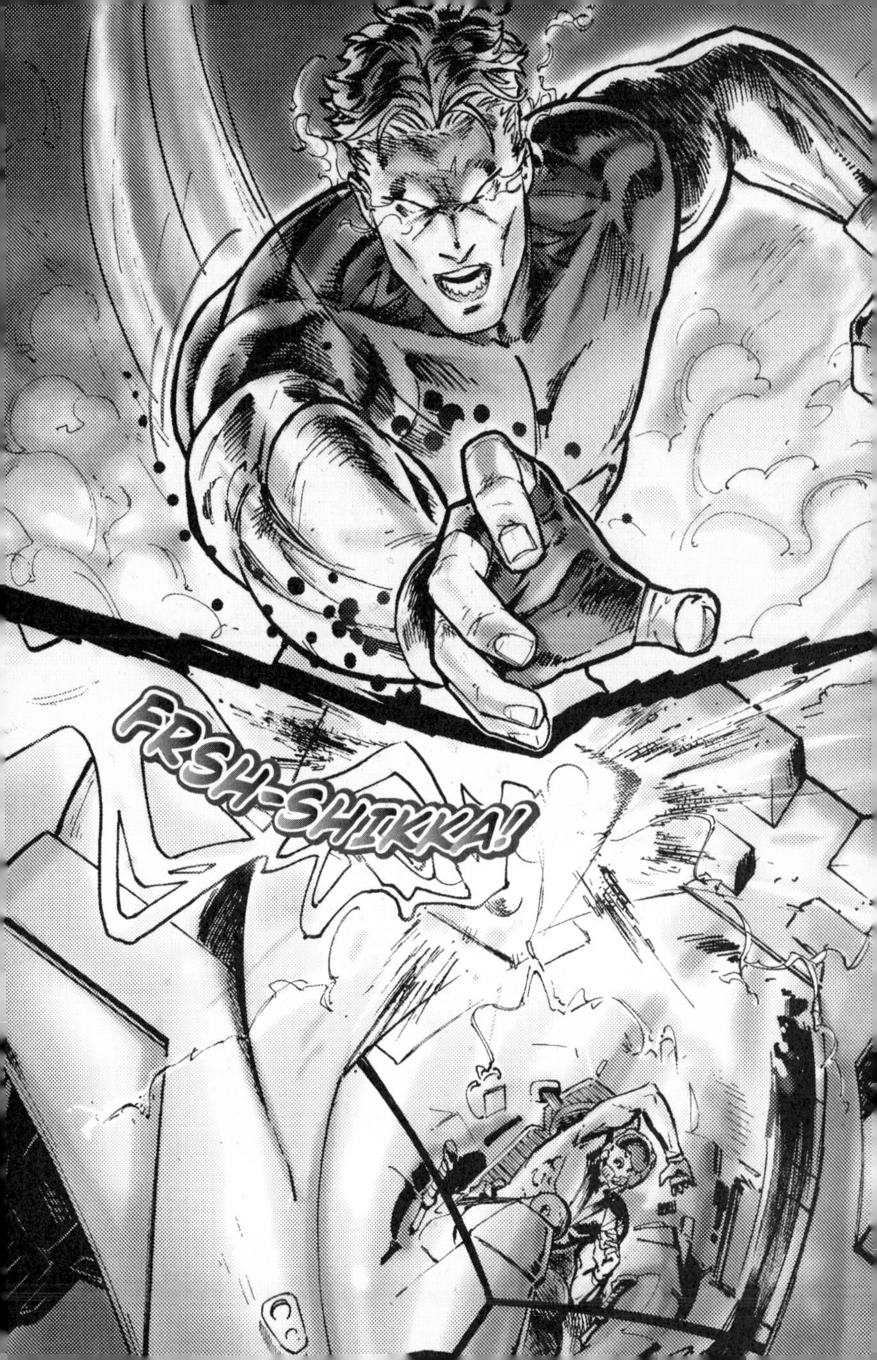
FRSH-SHIKKA!

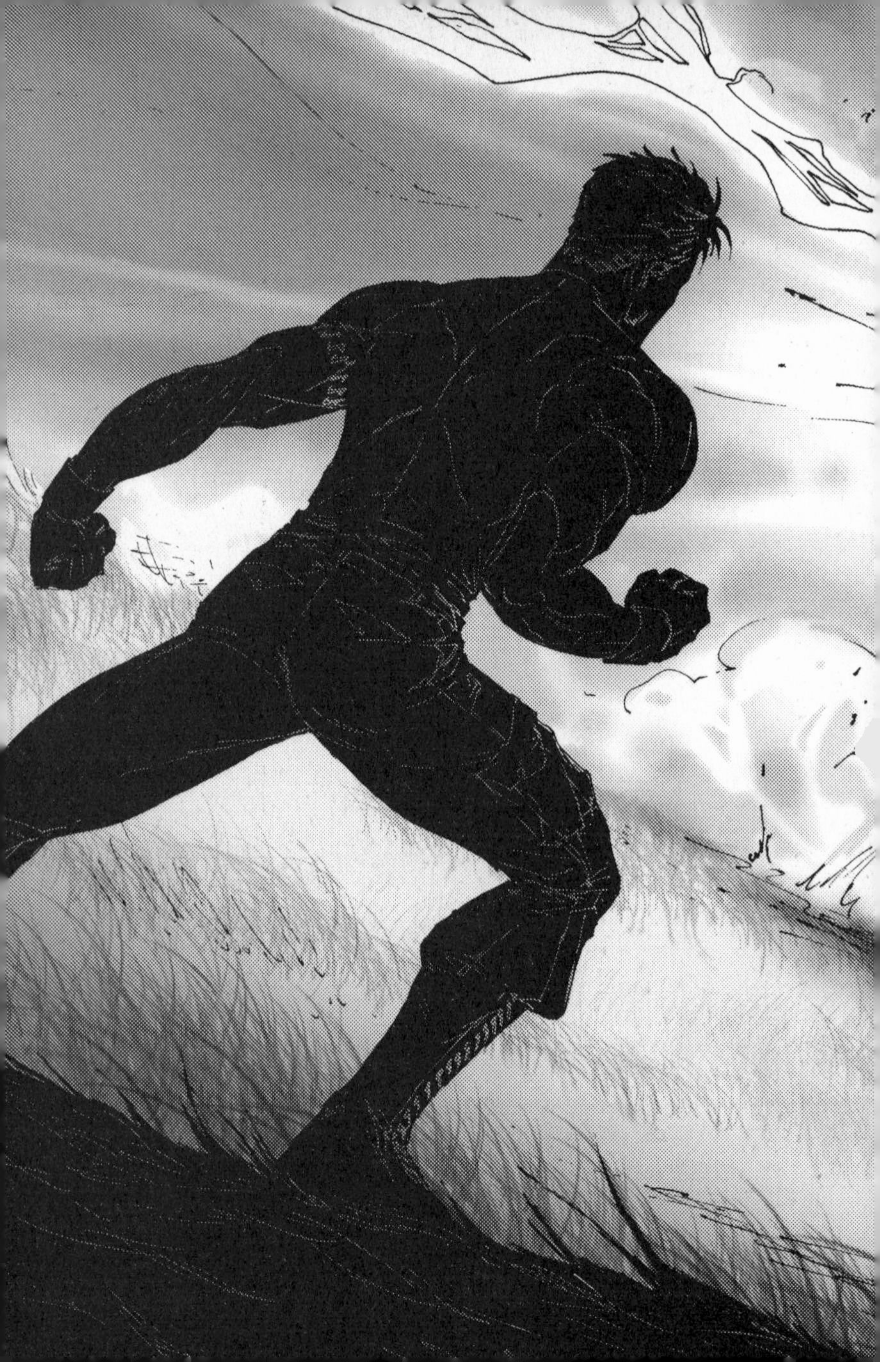

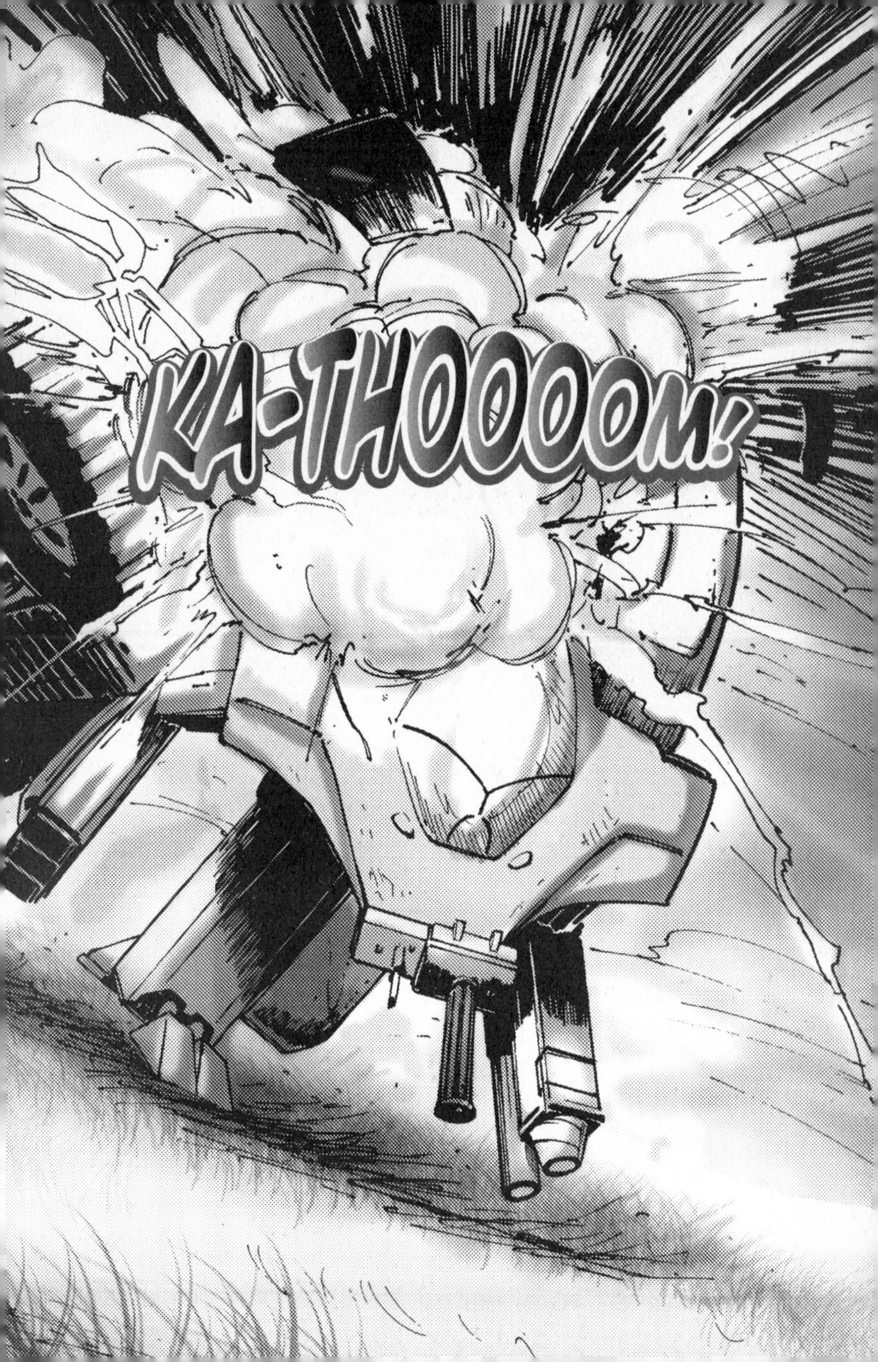
KA-THOOOOM!

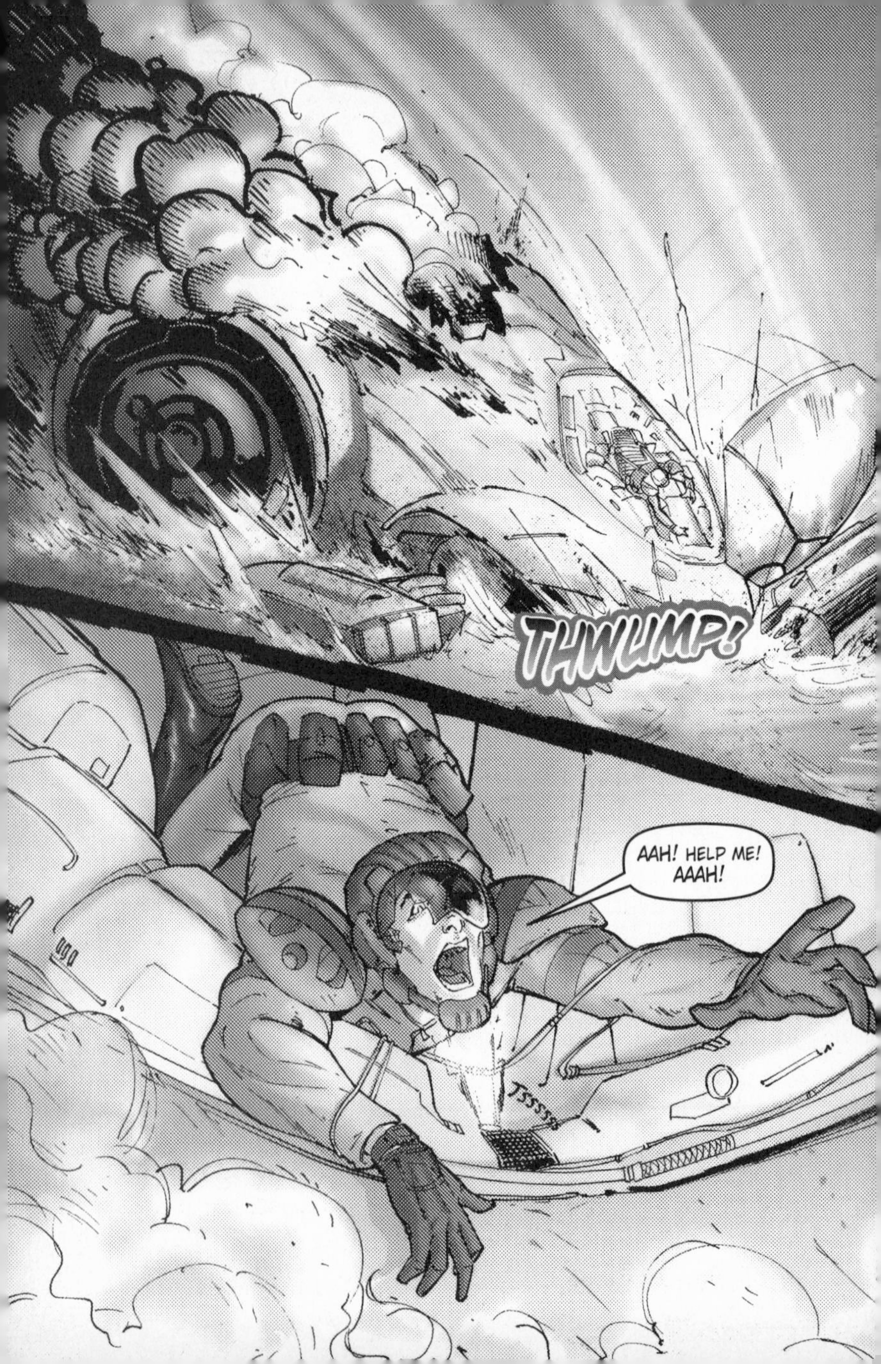
THWUMP!
AAH! HELP ME! AAAH!
TSSSSS

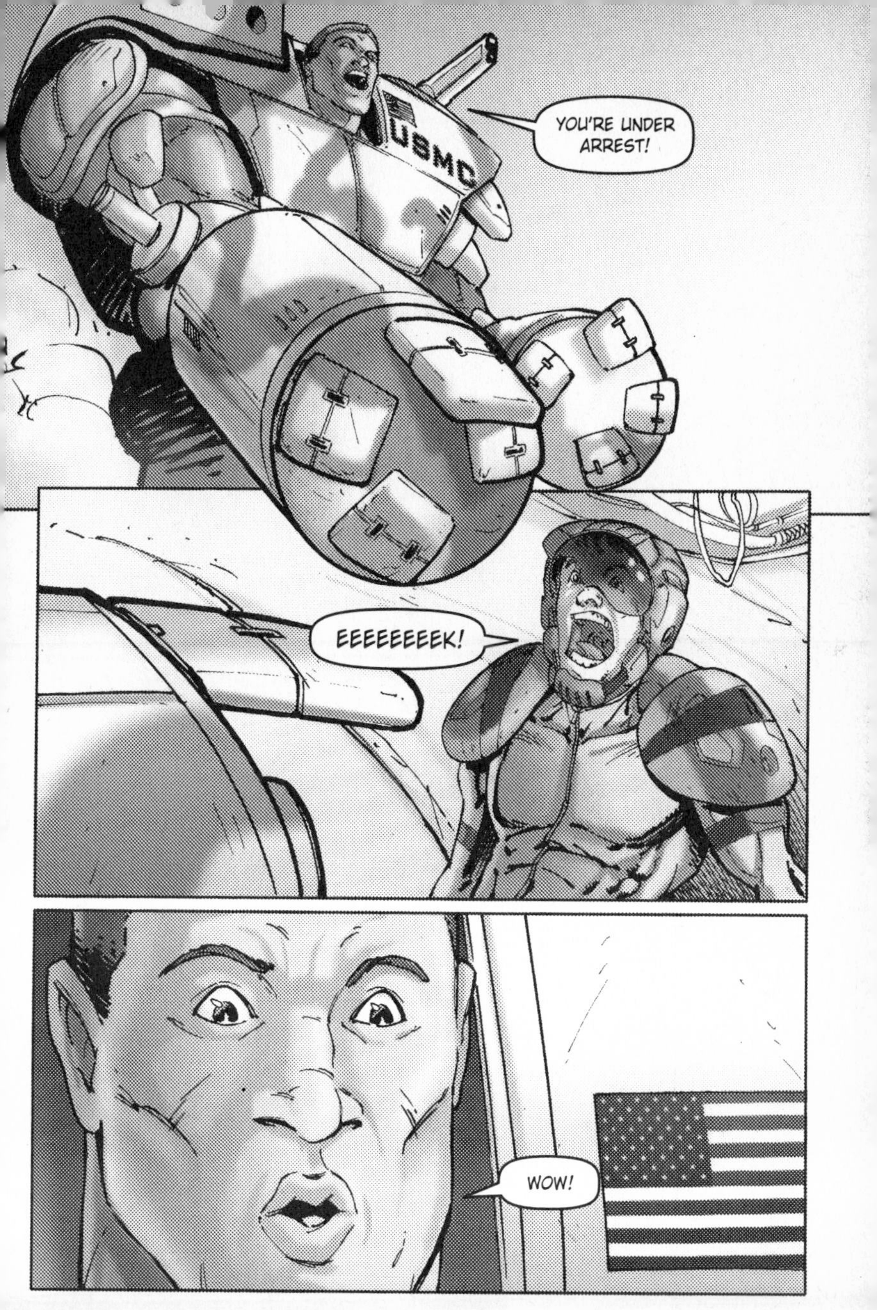
YOU'RE UNDER ARREST!
USMC
EEEEEEEEEK!
WOW!

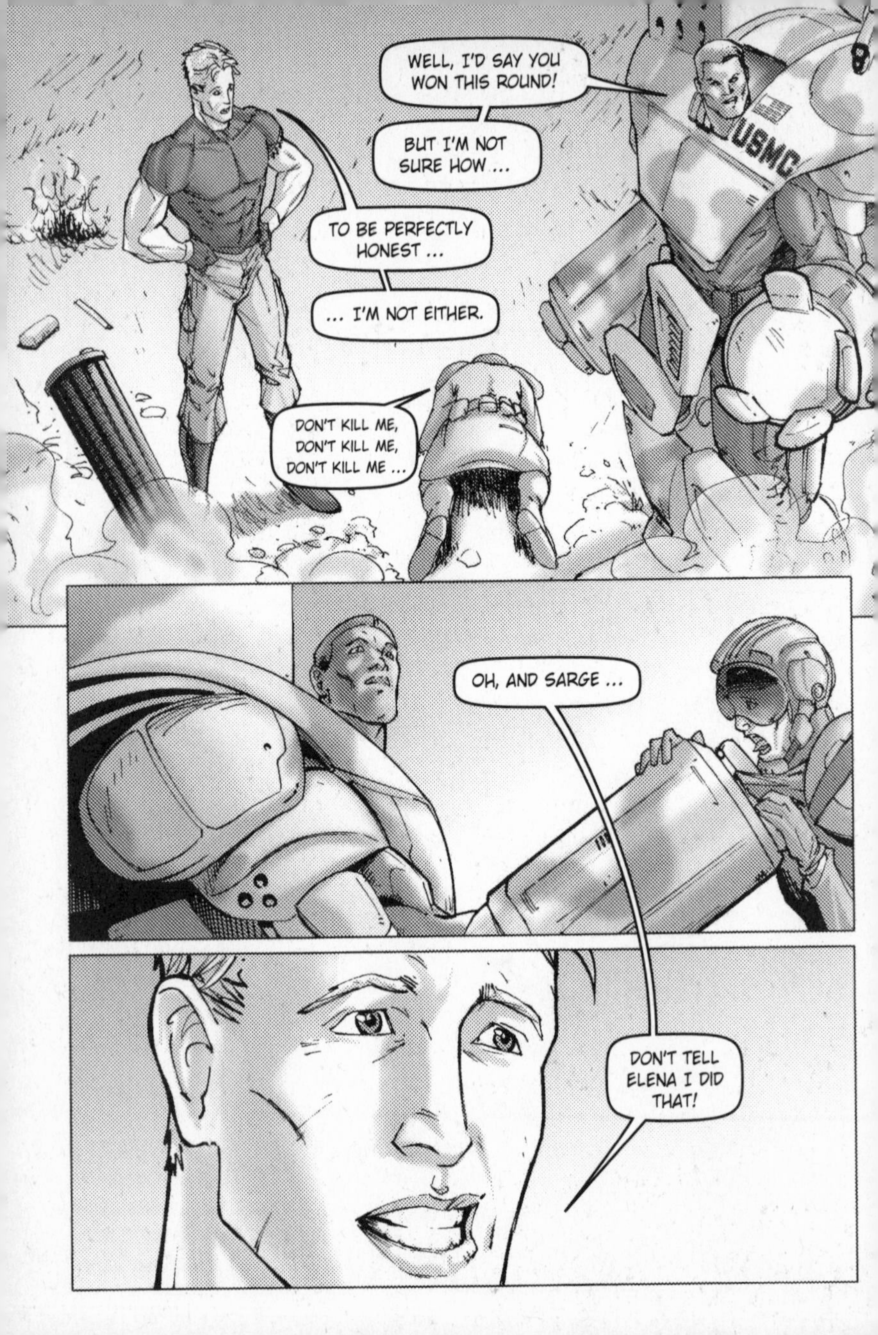
WELL, I'D SAY YOU WON THIS ROUND!
BUT I'M NOT SURE HOW ...
TO BE PERFECTLY HONEST ...
... I'M NOT EITHER.
DON'T KILL ME, DON'T KILL ME, DON'T KILL ME ...
USMC
OH, AND SARGE ...
DON'T TELL ELENA I DID THAT!

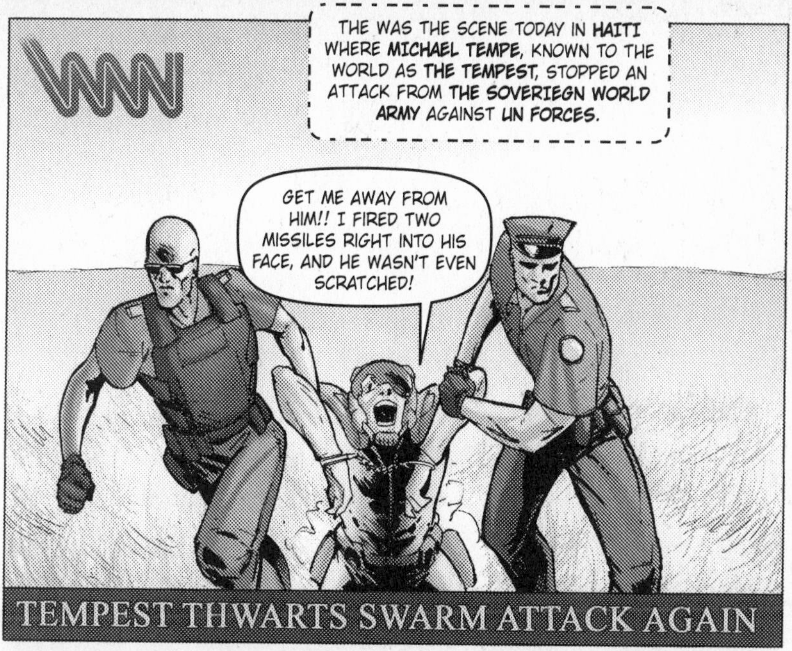
THE WAS THE SCENE TODAY IN HAITI WHERE MICHAEL TEMPE, KNOWN TO THE WORLD AS THE TEMPEST, STOPPED AN ATTACK FROM THE SOVERIEGN WORLD ARMY AGAINST UN FORCES.
GET ME AWAY FROM HIM!! I FIRED TWO MISSILES RIGHT INTO HIS FACE, AND HE WASN'T EVEN SCRATCHED!
TEMPEST THWARTS SWARM ATTACK AGAIN

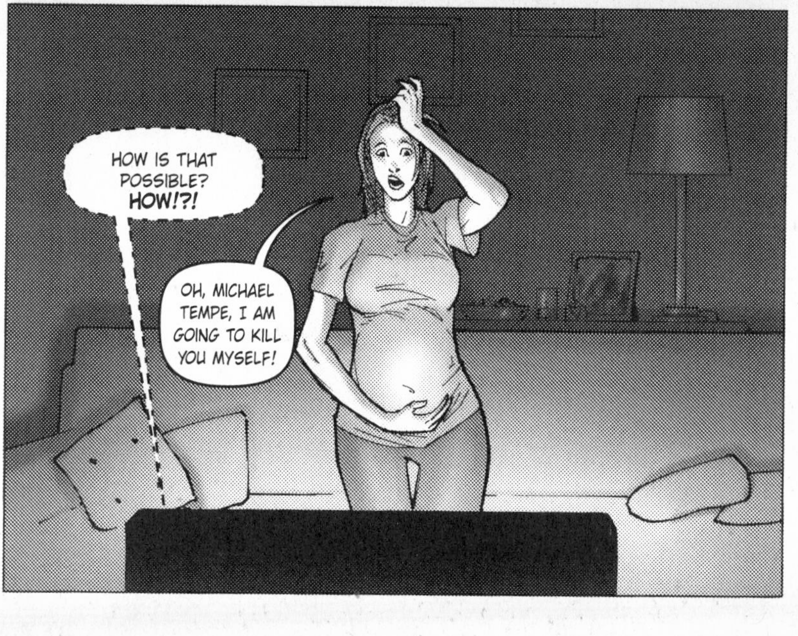
HOW IS THAT POSSIBLE? HOW!?!
OH, MICHAEL TEMPE, I AM GOING TO KILL YOU MYSELF!

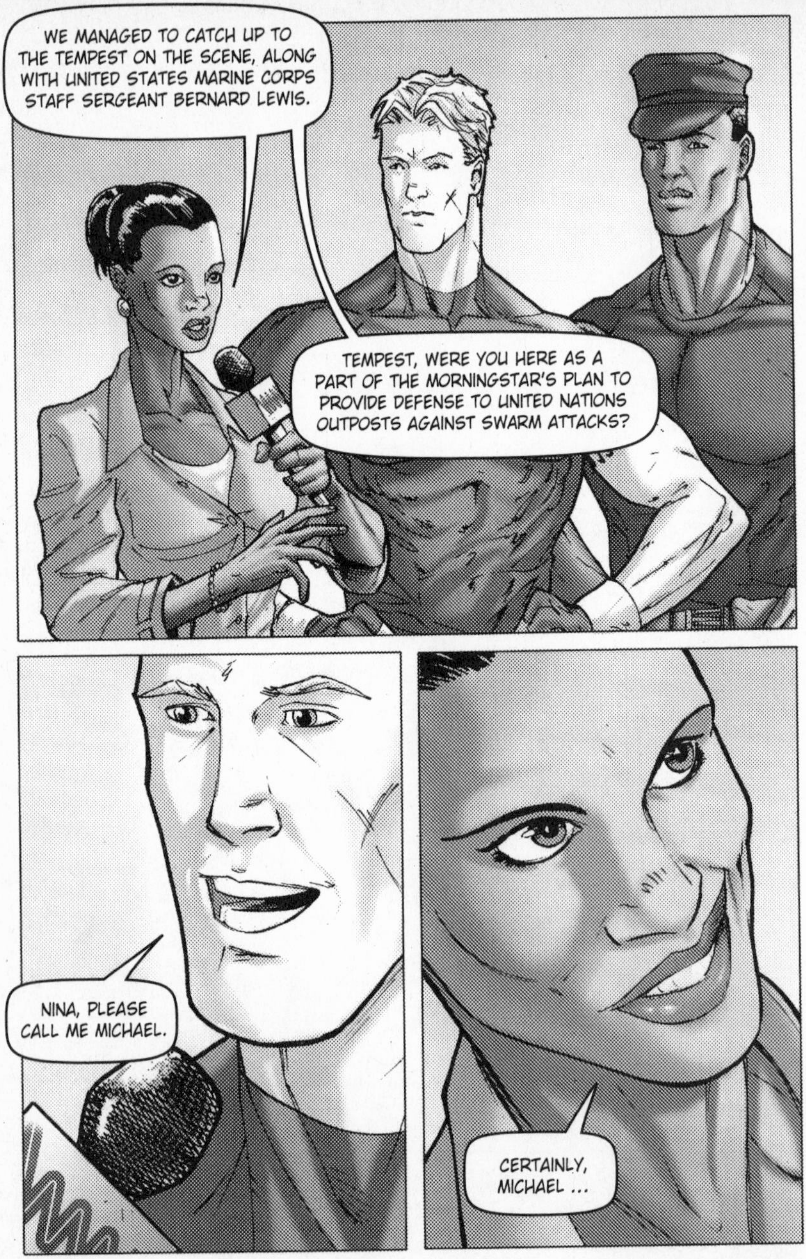
WE MANAGED TO CATCH UP TO THE TEMPEST ON THE SCENE, ALONG WITH UNITED STATES MARINE CORPS STAFF SERGEANT BERNARD LEWIS.
TEMPEST, WERE YOU HERE AS A PART OF THE MORNINGSTAR'S PLAN TO PROVIDE DEFENSE TO UNITED NATIONS OUTPOSTS AGAINST SWARM ATTACKS?
NINA, PLEASE CALL ME MICHAEL.
CERTAINLY, MICHAEL ...

WATCH IT, GIRL ...

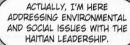

ACTUALLY, I'M HERE ADDRESSING ENVIRONMENTAL AND SOCIAL ISSUES WITH THE HAITIAN LEADERSHIP.

ENVIRONMENTAL **AND** SOCIAL?

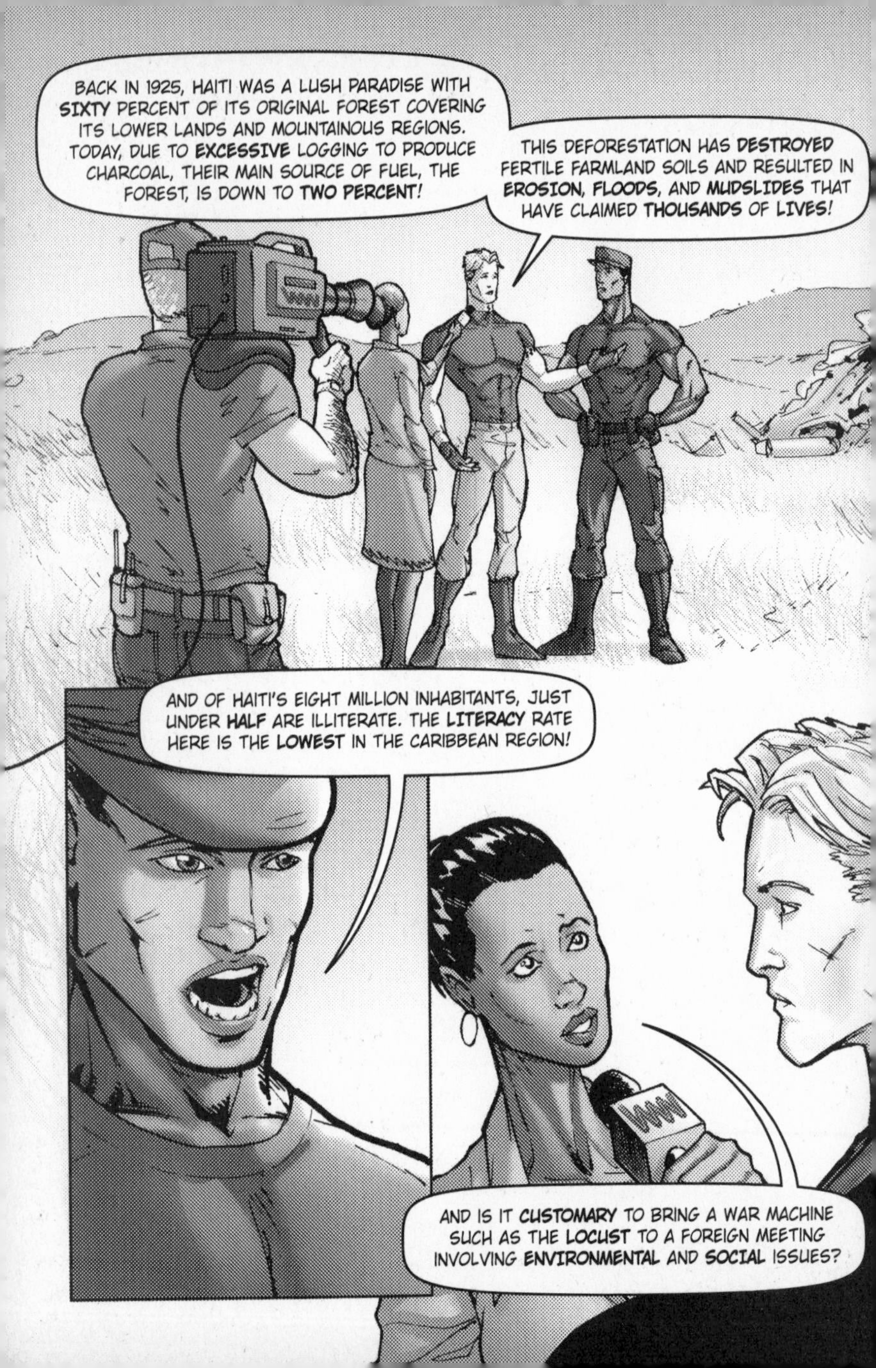
BACK IN 1925, HAITI WAS A LUSH PARADISE WITH SIXTY PERCENT OF ITS ORIGINAL FOREST COVERING ITS LOWER LANDS AND MOUNTAINOUS REGIONS. TODAY, DUE TO EXCESSIVE LOGGING TO PRODUCE CHARCOAL, THEIR MAIN SOURCE OF FUEL, THE FOREST, IS DOWN TO TWO PERCENT!
THIS DEFORESTATION HAS DESTROYED FERTILE FARMLAND SOILS AND RESULTED IN EROSION, FLOODS, AND MUDSLIDES THAT HAVE CLAIMED THOUSANDS OF LIVES!
AND OF HAITI'S EIGHT MILLION INHABITANTS, JUST UNDER HALF ARE ILLITERATE. THE LITERACY RATE HERE IS THE LOWEST IN THE CARIBBEAN REGION!
AND IS IT CUSTOMARY TO BRING A WAR MACHINE SUCH AS THE LOCUST TO A FOREIGN MEETING INVOLVING ENVIRONMENTAL AND SOCIAL ISSUES?

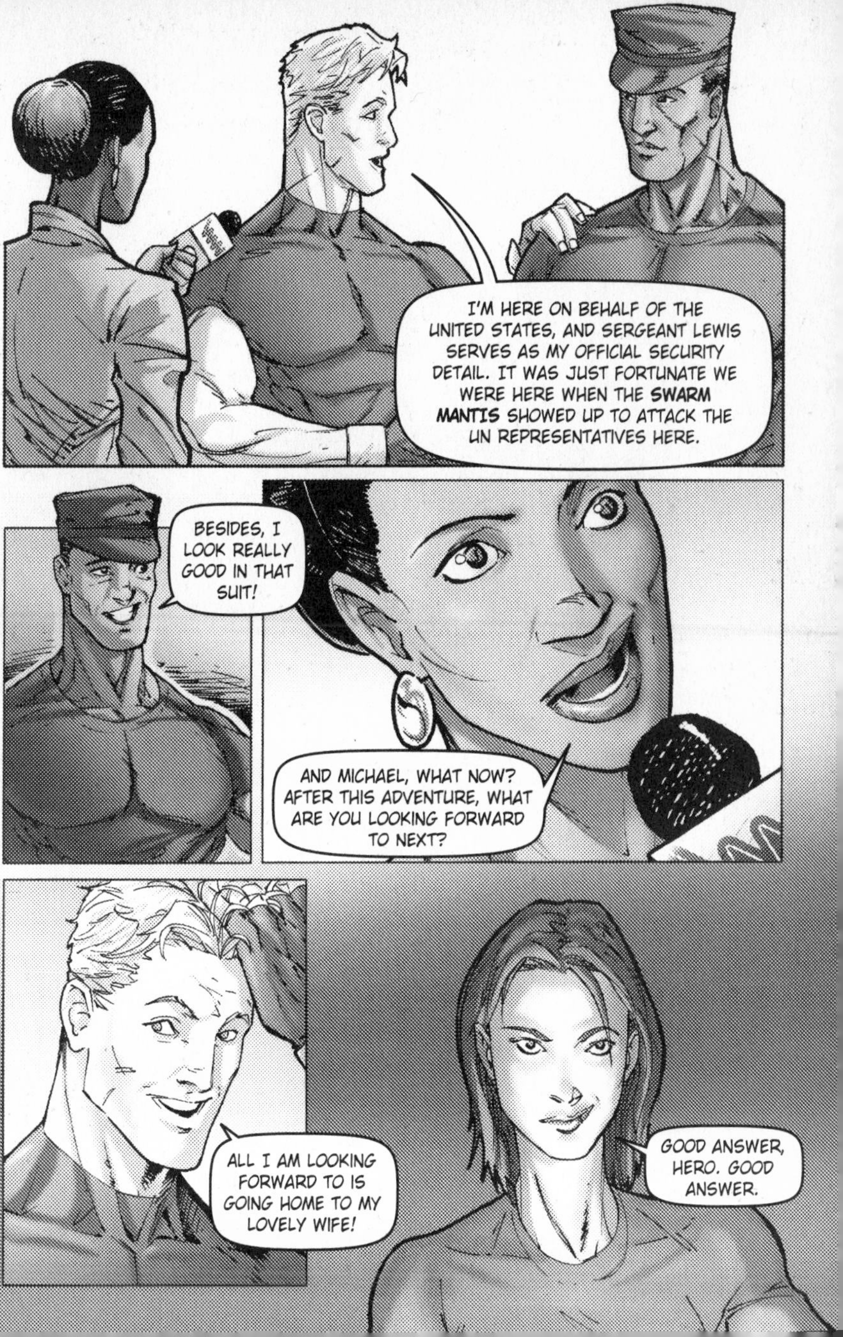
I'M HERE ON BEHALF OF THE UNITED STATES, AND SERGEANT LEWIS SERVES AS MY OFFICIAL SECURITY DETAIL. IT WAS JUST FORTUNATE WE WERE HERE WHEN THE **SWARM MANTIS** SHOWED UP TO ATTACK THE UN REPRESENTATIVES HERE.
BESIDES, I LOOK REALLY GOOD IN THAT SUIT!
AND MICHAEL, WHAT NOW? AFTER THIS ADVENTURE, WHAT ARE YOU LOOKING FORWARD TO NEXT?
ALL I AM LOOKING FORWARD TO IS GOING HOME TO MY LOVELY WIFE!
GOOD ANSWER, HERO. GOOD ANSWER.

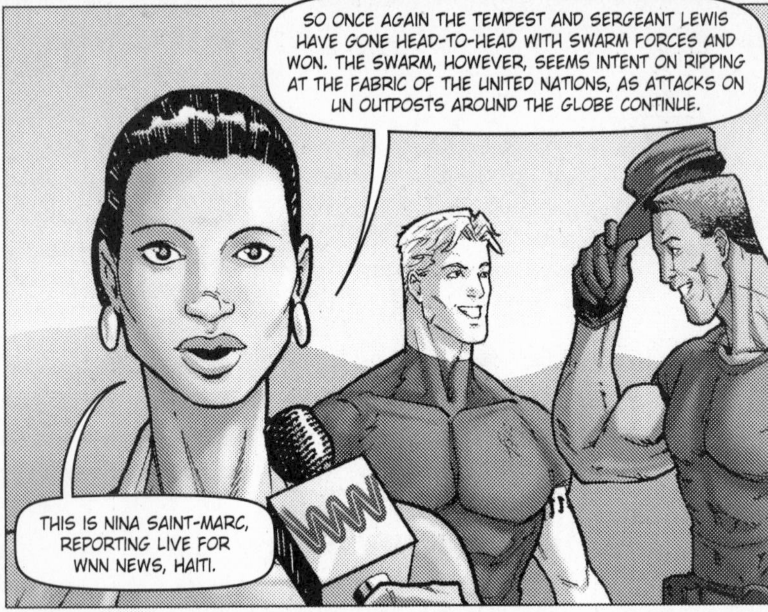
SO ONCE AGAIN THE TEMPEST AND SERGEANT LEWIS HAVE GONE HEAD-TO-HEAD WITH SWARM FORCES AND WON. THE SWARM, HOWEVER, SEEMS INTENT ON RIPPING AT THE FABRIC OF THE UNITED NATIONS, AS ATTACKS ON UN OUTPOSTS AROUND THE GLOBE CONTINUE.
THIS IS NINA SAINT-MARC, REPORTING LIVE FOR WNN NEWS, HAITI.
WNN

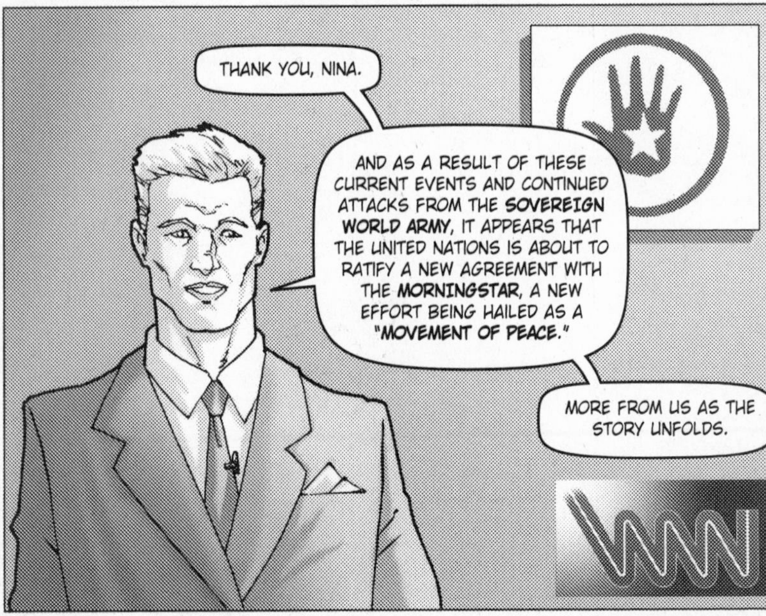
THANK YOU, NINA.
AND AS A RESULT OF THESE CURRENT EVENTS AND CONTINUED ATTACKS FROM THE **SOVEREIGN WORLD ARMY**, IT APPEARS THAT THE UNITED NATIONS IS ABOUT TO RATIFY A NEW AGREEMENT WITH THE **MORNINGSTAR**, A NEW EFFORT BEING HAILED AS A "**MOVEMENT OF PEACE.**"
MORE FROM US AS THE STORY UNFOLDS.
WNN

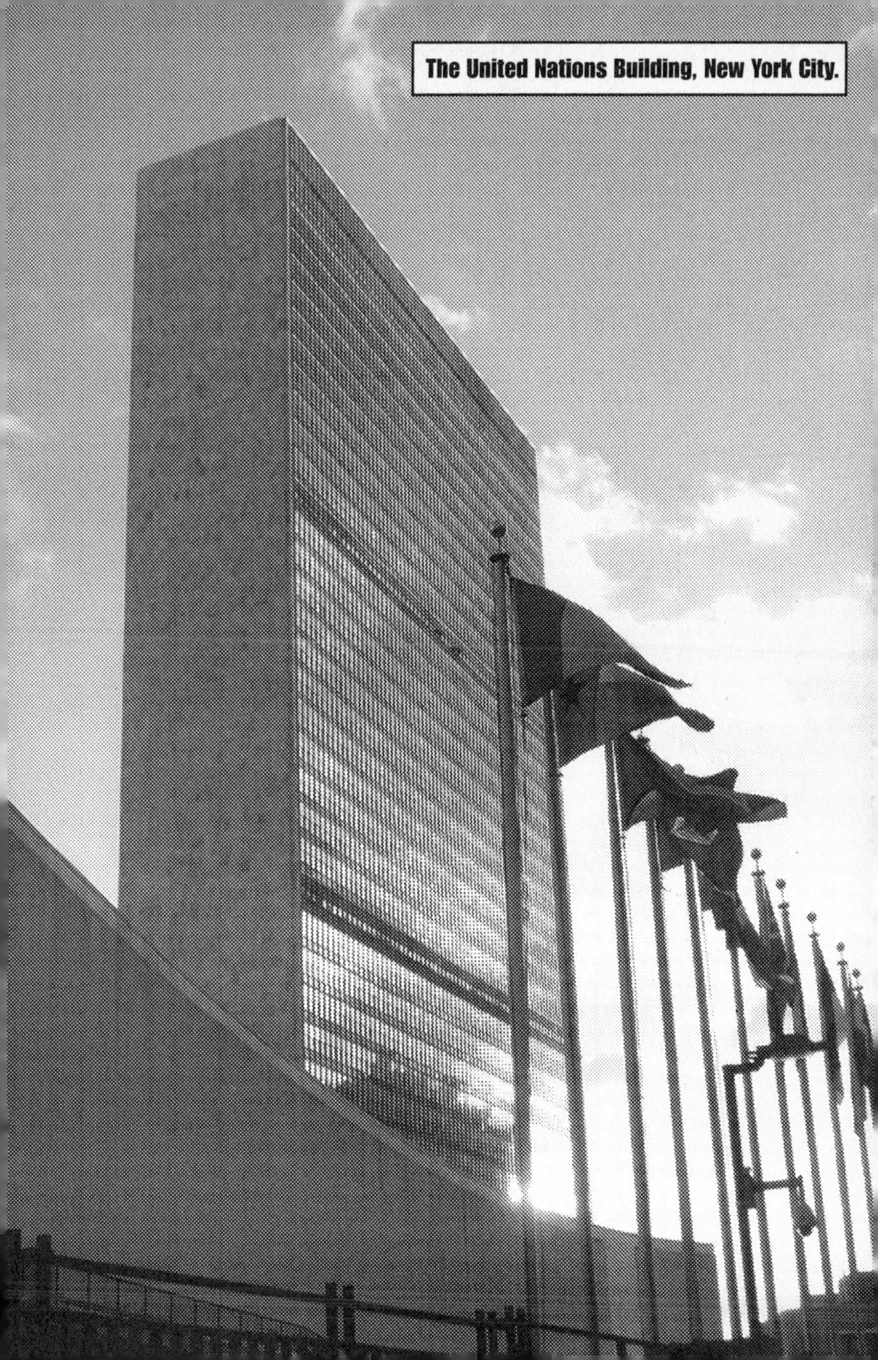
The United Nations Building, New York City.

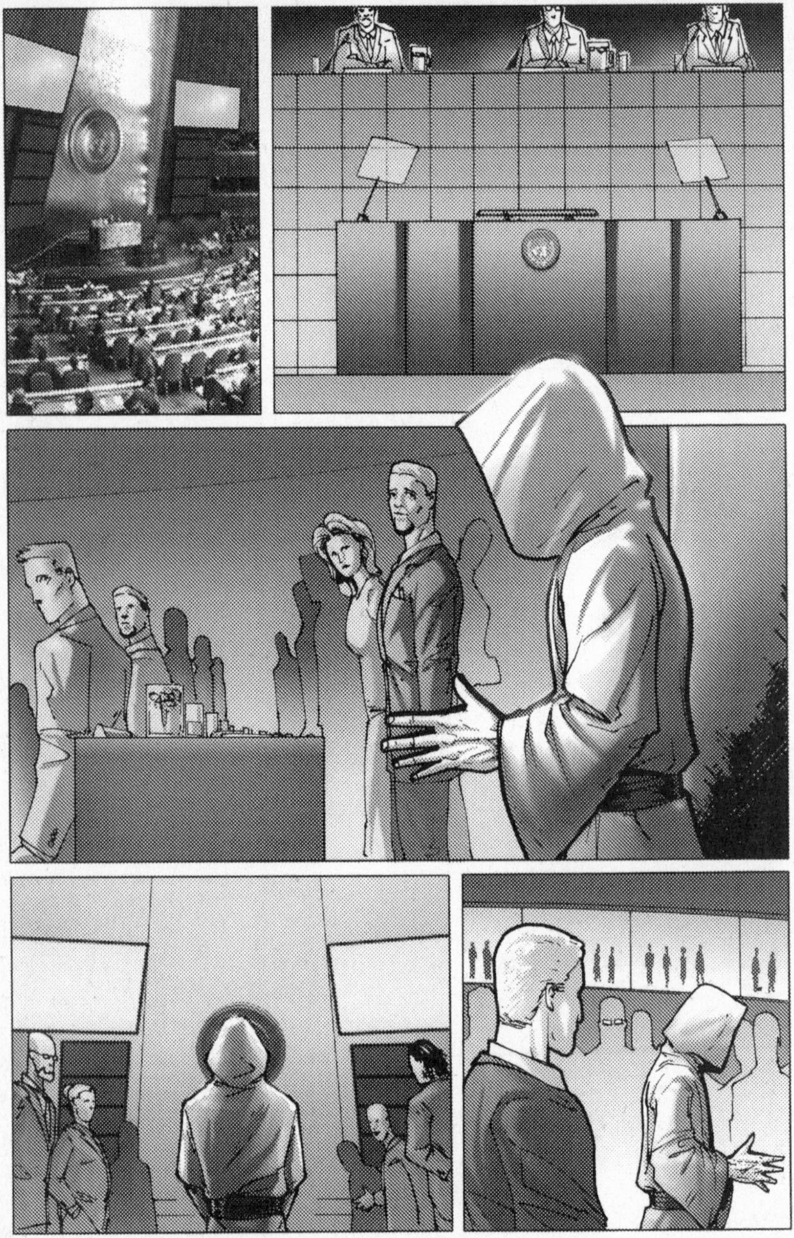

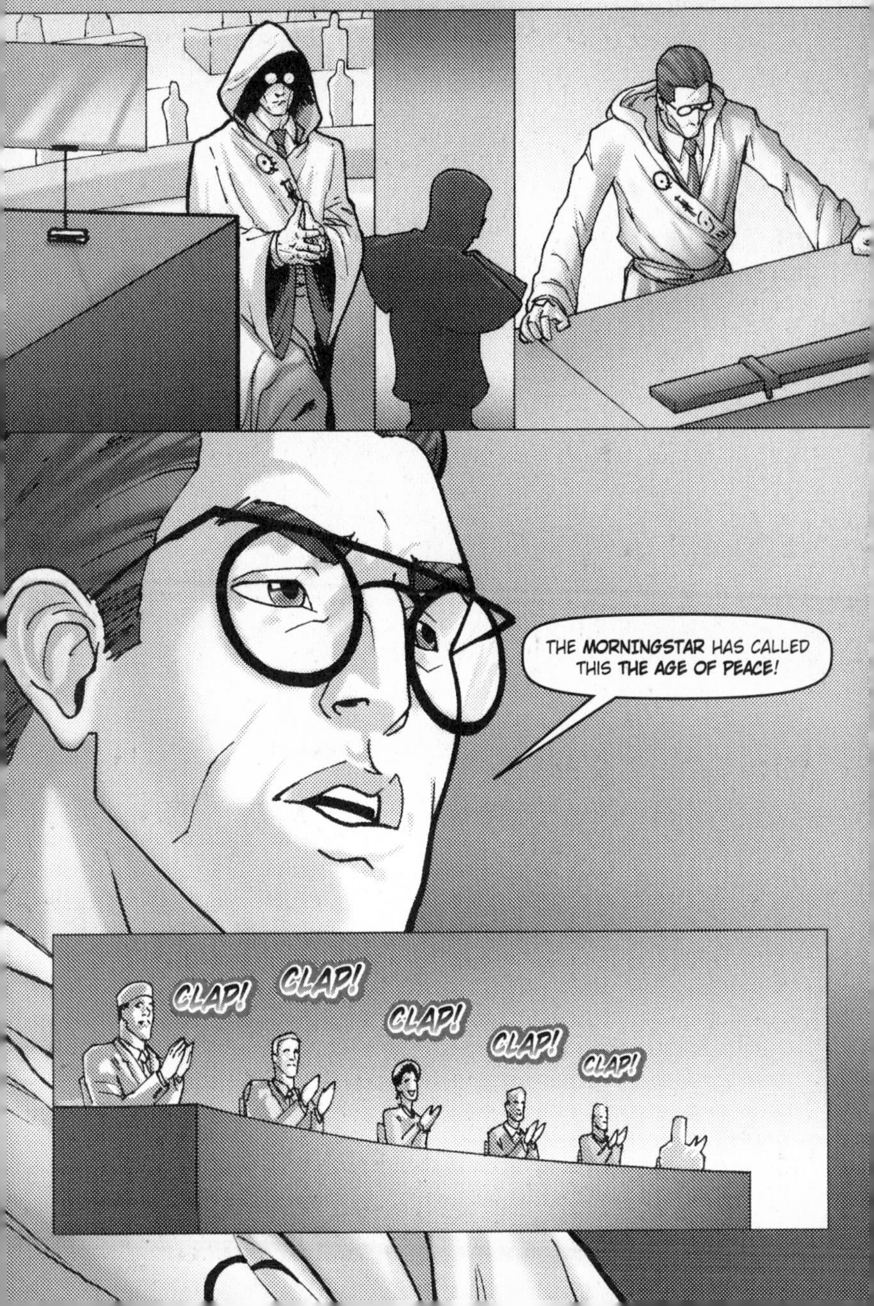
THE MORNINGSTAR HAS CALLED THIS THE AGE OF PEACE!
CLAP!
CLAP!
CLAP!
CLAP!
CLAP!

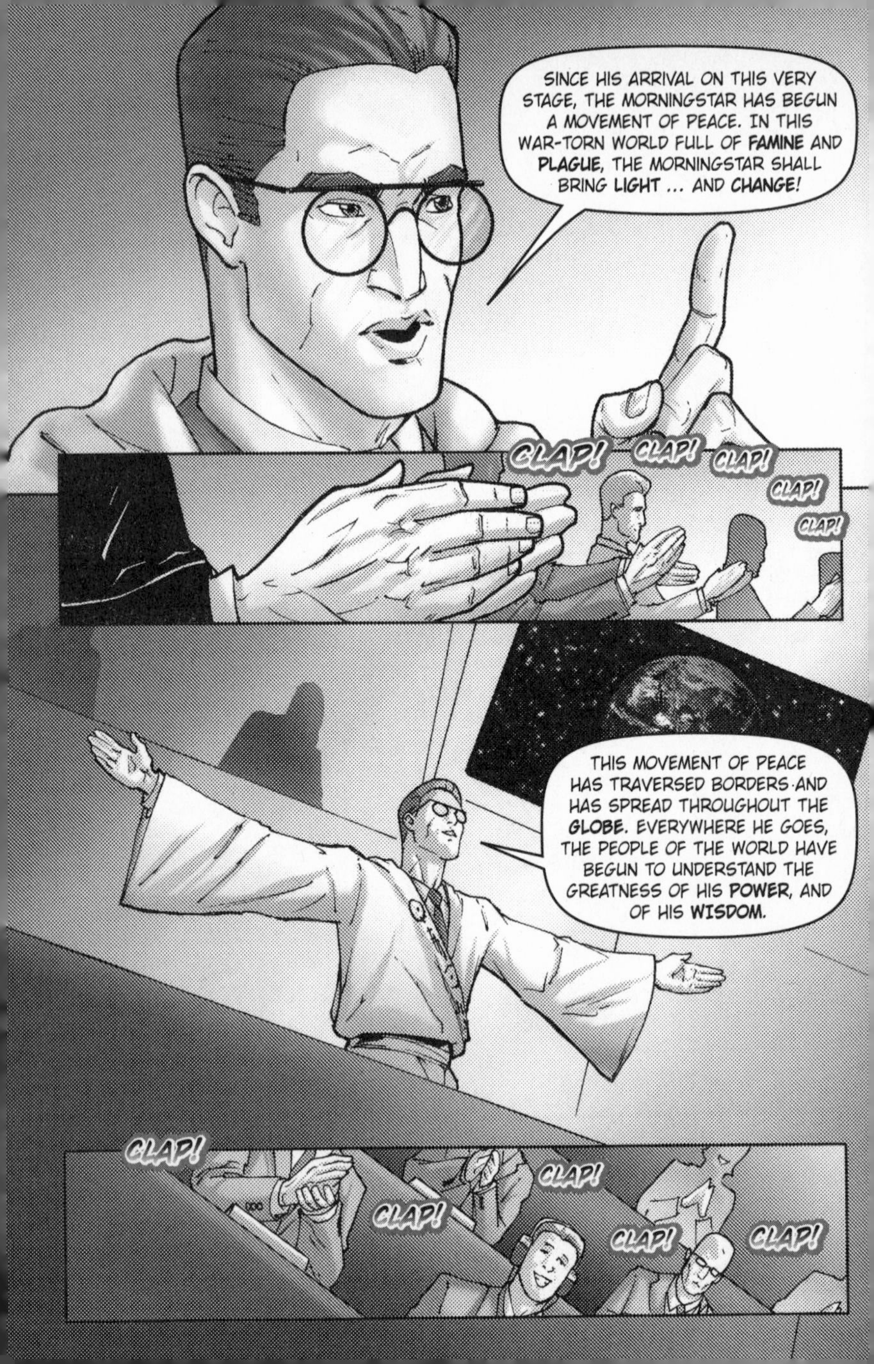
SINCE HIS ARRIVAL ON THIS VERY STAGE, THE MORNINGSTAR HAS BEGUN A MOVEMENT OF PEACE. IN THIS WAR-TORN WORLD FULL OF FAMINE AND PLAGUE, THE MORNINGSTAR SHALL BRING LIGHT ... AND CHANGE!
CLAP! CLAP! CLAP! CLAP! CLAP!
THIS MOVEMENT OF PEACE HAS TRAVERSED BORDERS AND HAS SPREAD THROUGHOUT THE GLOBE. EVERYWHERE HE GOES, THE PEOPLE OF THE WORLD HAVE BEGUN TO UNDERSTAND THE GREATNESS OF HIS POWER, AND OF HIS WISDOM.
CLAP! CLAP! CLAP! CLAP! CLAP!

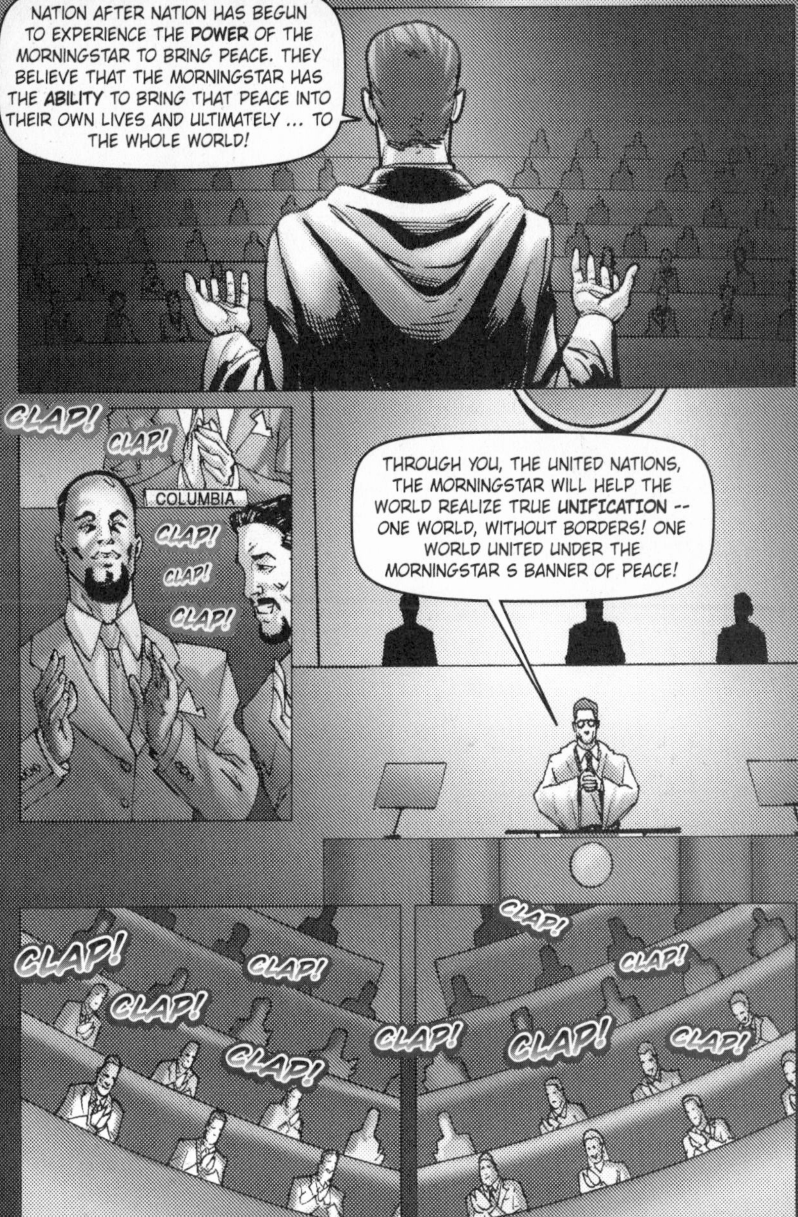
NATION AFTER NATION HAS BEGUN TO EXPERIENCE THE **POWER** OF THE MORNINGSTAR TO BRING PEACE. THEY BELIEVE THAT THE MORNINGSTAR HAS THE **ABILITY** TO BRING THAT PEACE INTO THEIR OWN LIVES AND ULTIMATELY ... TO THE WHOLE WORLD!
CLAP!
CLAP!
COLUMBIA
CLAP!
CLAP!
CLAP!
THROUGH YOU, THE UNITED NATIONS, THE MORNINGSTAR WILL HELP THE WORLD REALIZE TRUE **UNIFICATION** -- ONE WORLD, WITHOUT BORDERS! ONE WORLD UNITED UNDER THE MORNINGSTAR S BANNER OF PEACE!
CLAP!
CLAP!
CLAP!
CLAP!
CLAP!
CLAP!
CLAP!
CLAP!
CLAP!

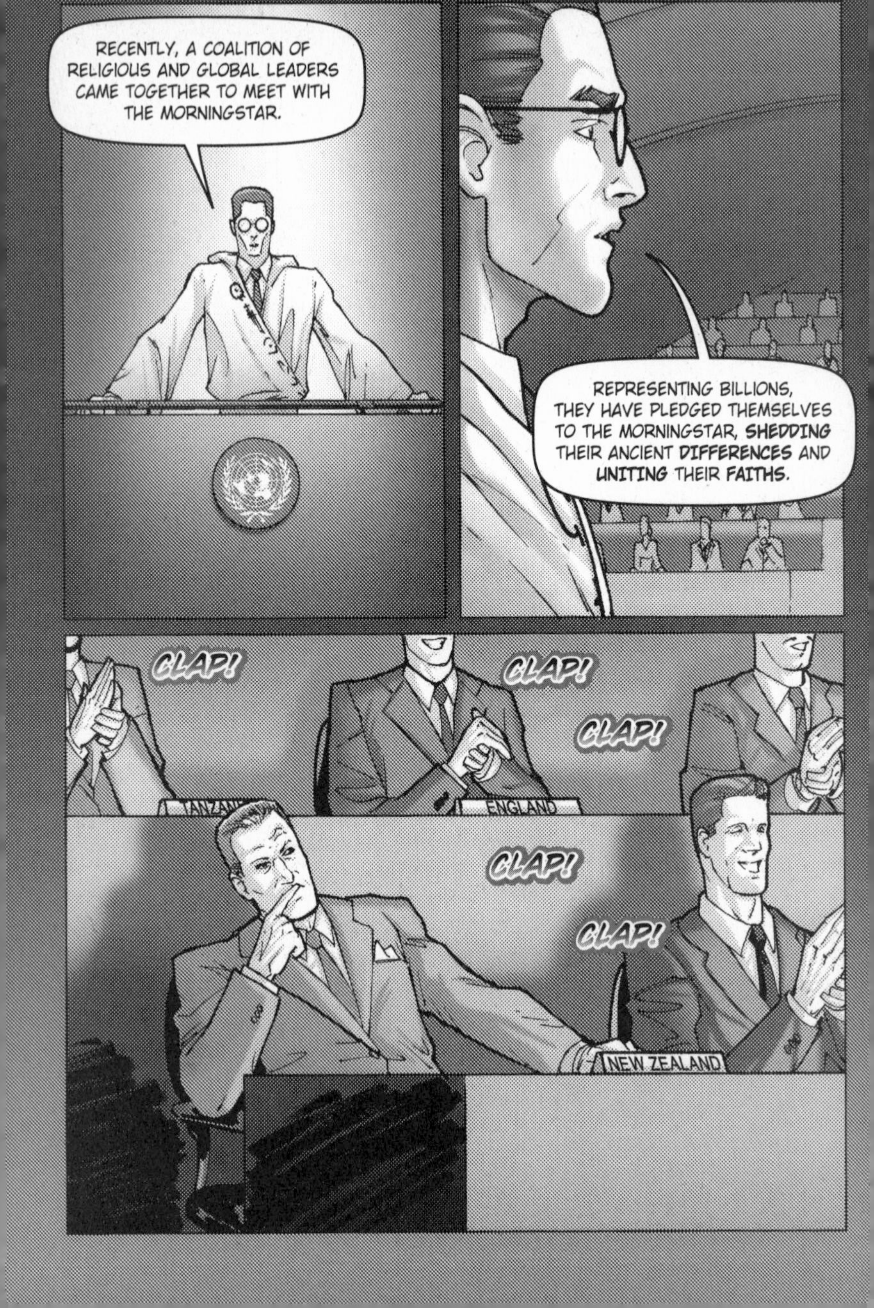
RECENTLY, A COALITION OF RELIGIOUS AND GLOBAL LEADERS CAME TOGETHER TO MEET WITH THE MORNINGSTAR.
REPRESENTING BILLIONS, THEY HAVE PLEDGED THEMSELVES TO THE MORNINGSTAR, **SHEDDING** THEIR ANCIENT **DIFFERENCES** AND **UNITING** THEIR **FAITHS**.
CLAP!
CLAP!
CLAP!
ENGLAND
CLAP!
CLAP!
NEW ZEALAND

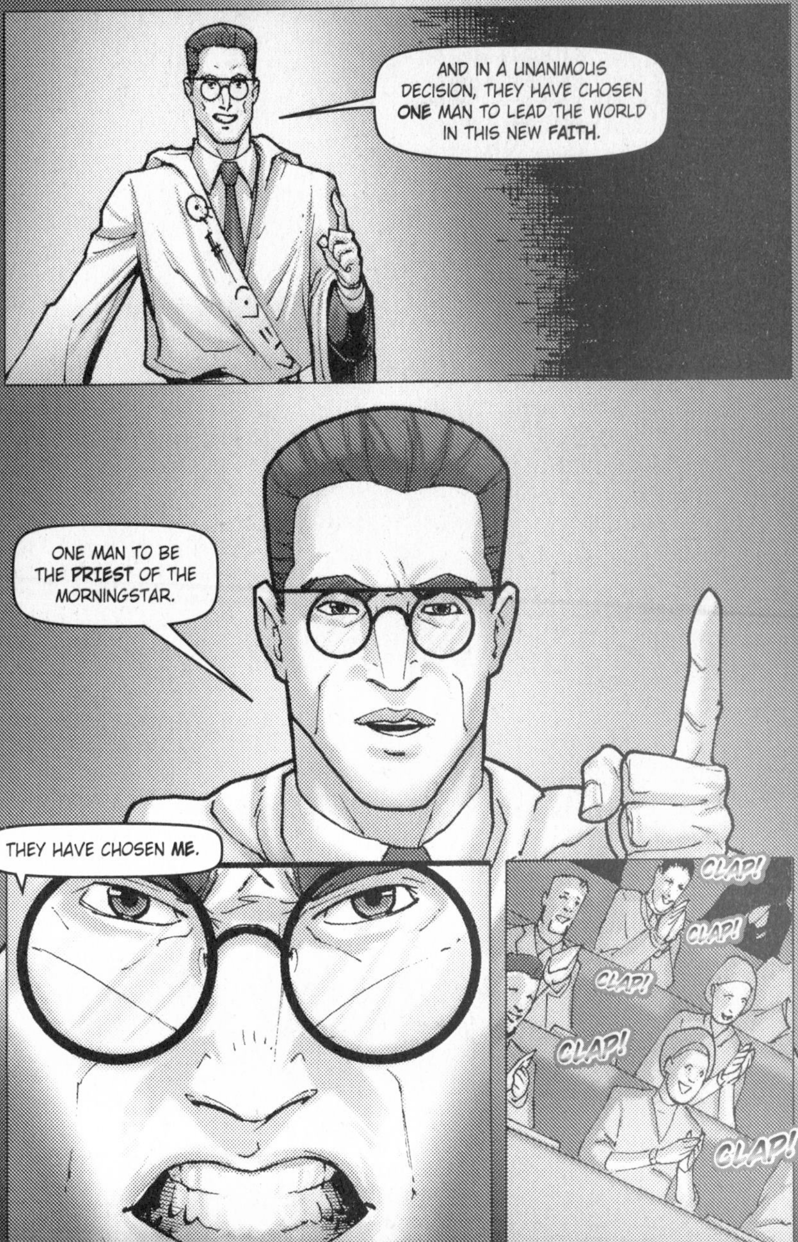
AND IN A UNANIMOUS DECISION, THEY HAVE CHOSEN ONE MAN TO LEAD THE WORLD IN THIS NEW FAITH.
ONE MAN TO BE THE PRIEST OF THE MORNINGSTAR.
THEY HAVE CHOSEN ME.
CLAP!
CLAP!
CLAP!
CLAP!
CLAP!

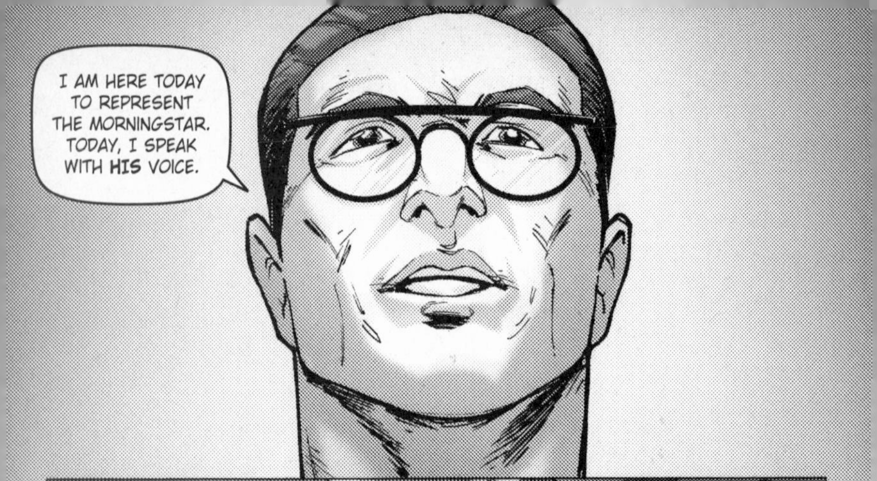
I AM HERE TODAY TO REPRESENT THE MORNINGSTAR. TODAY, I SPEAK WITH **HIS** VOICE.

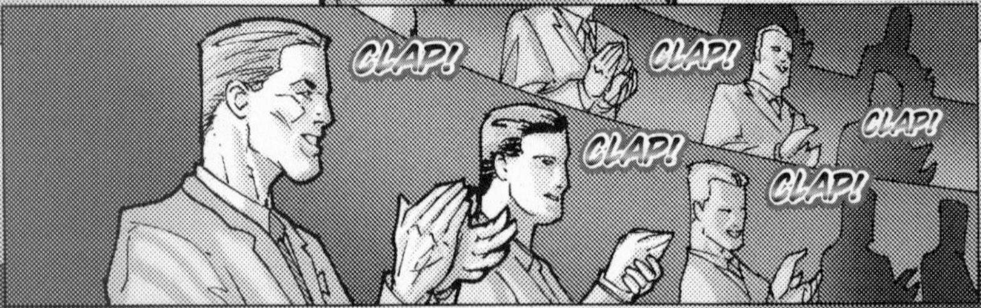
CLAP!
CLAP!
CLAP!
CLAP!
CLAP!

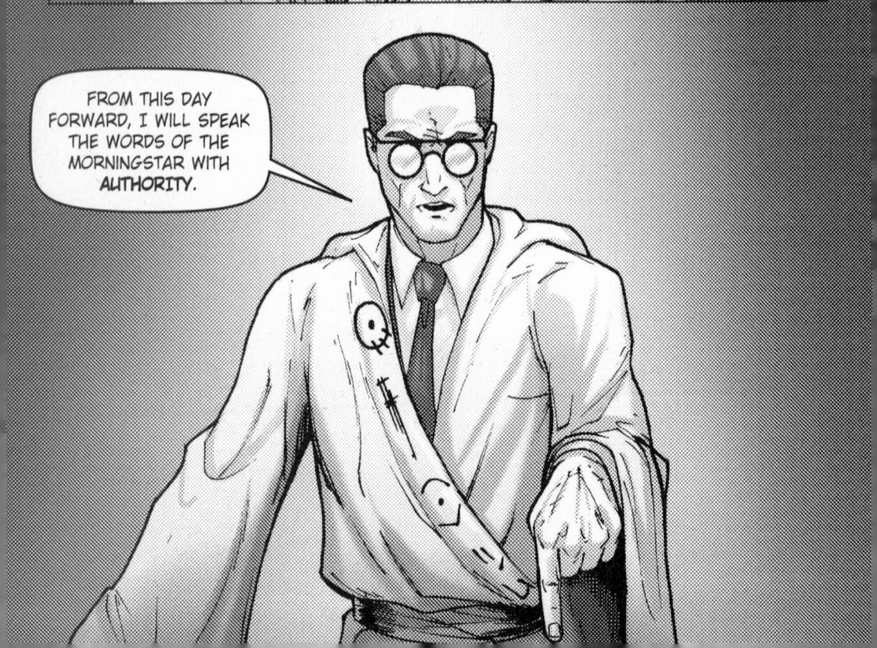
FROM THIS DAY FORWARD, I WILL SPEAK THE WORDS OF THE MORNINGSTAR WITH **AUTHORITY**.

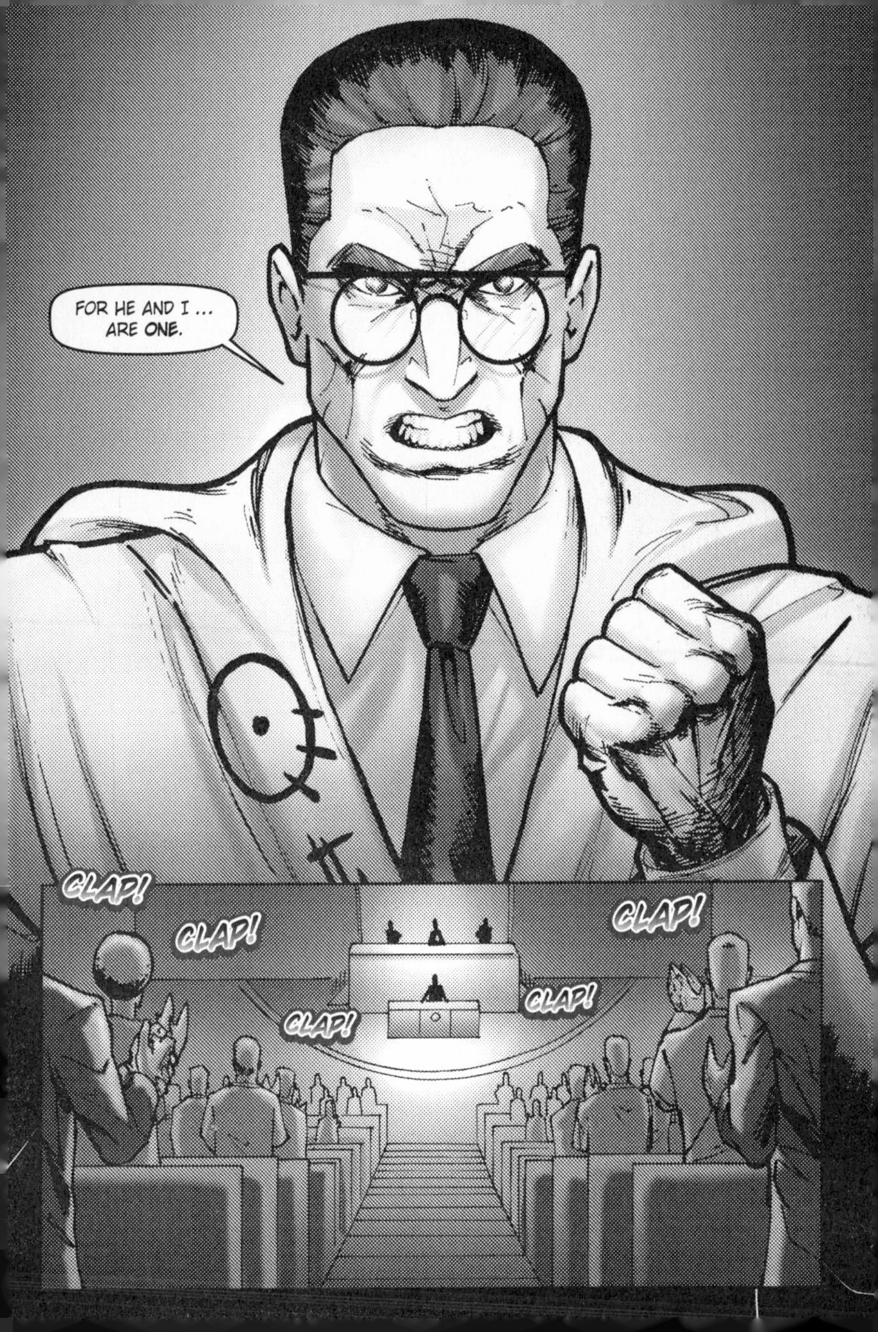
FOR HE AND I ... ARE ONE.
CLAP!
CLAP!
CLAP!
CLAP!
CLAP!

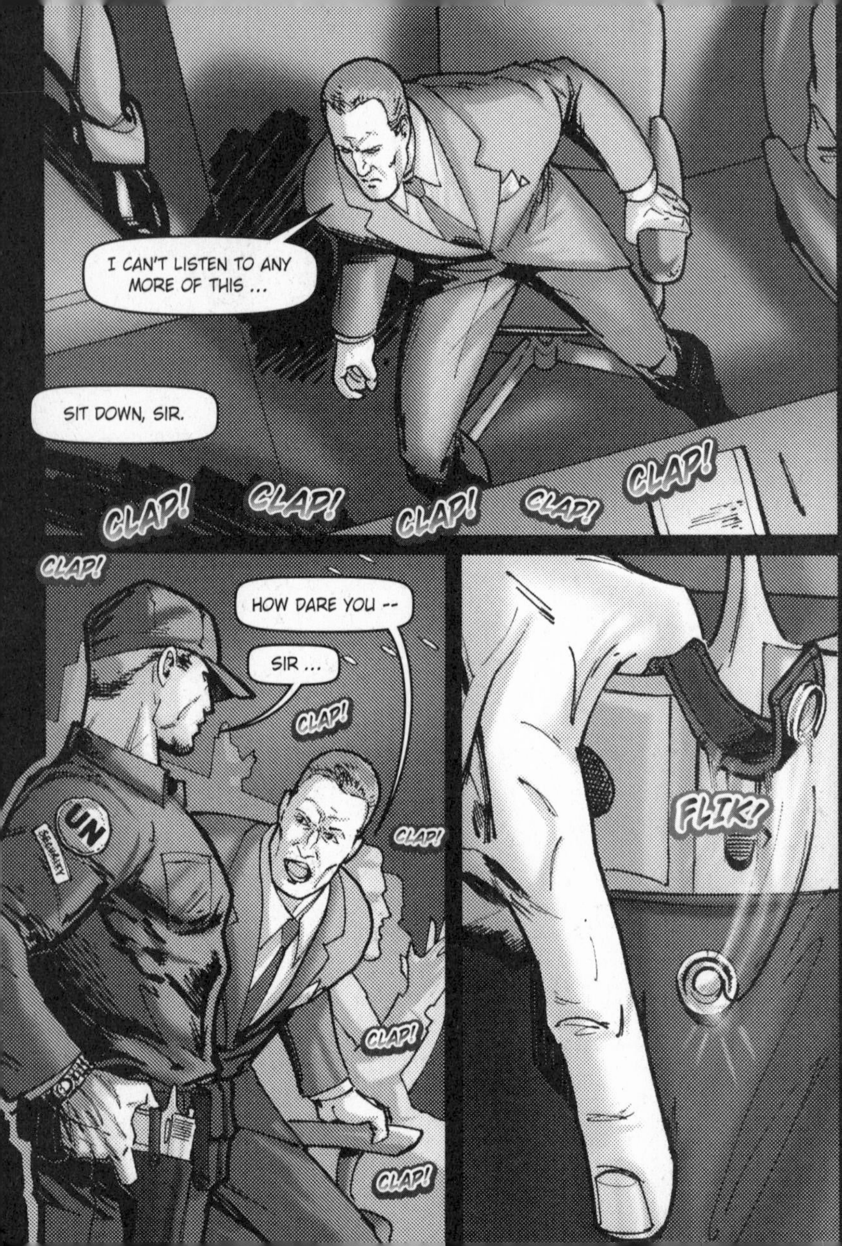
I CAN'T LISTEN TO ANY MORE OF THIS ...
SIT DOWN, SIR.
CLAP!
CLAP!
CLAP!
CLAP!
CLAP!
CLAP!
HOW DARE YOU --
SIR ...
CLAP!
UN
CLAP!
CLAP!
CLAP!
FLIK!

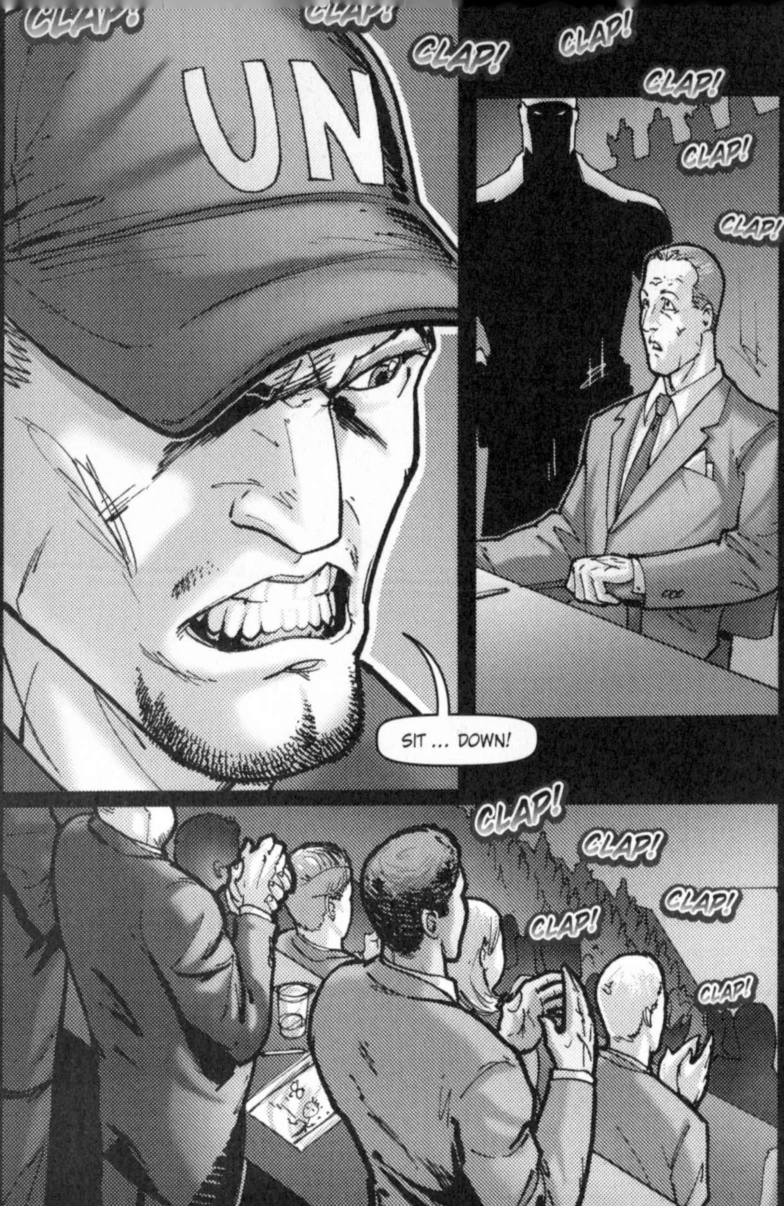
CLAP!
CLAP!
CLAP!
SIT ... DOWN!
CLAP!
CLAP!
CLAP!
CLAP!
CLAP!
CLAP!
CLAP!
CLAP!
CLAP!

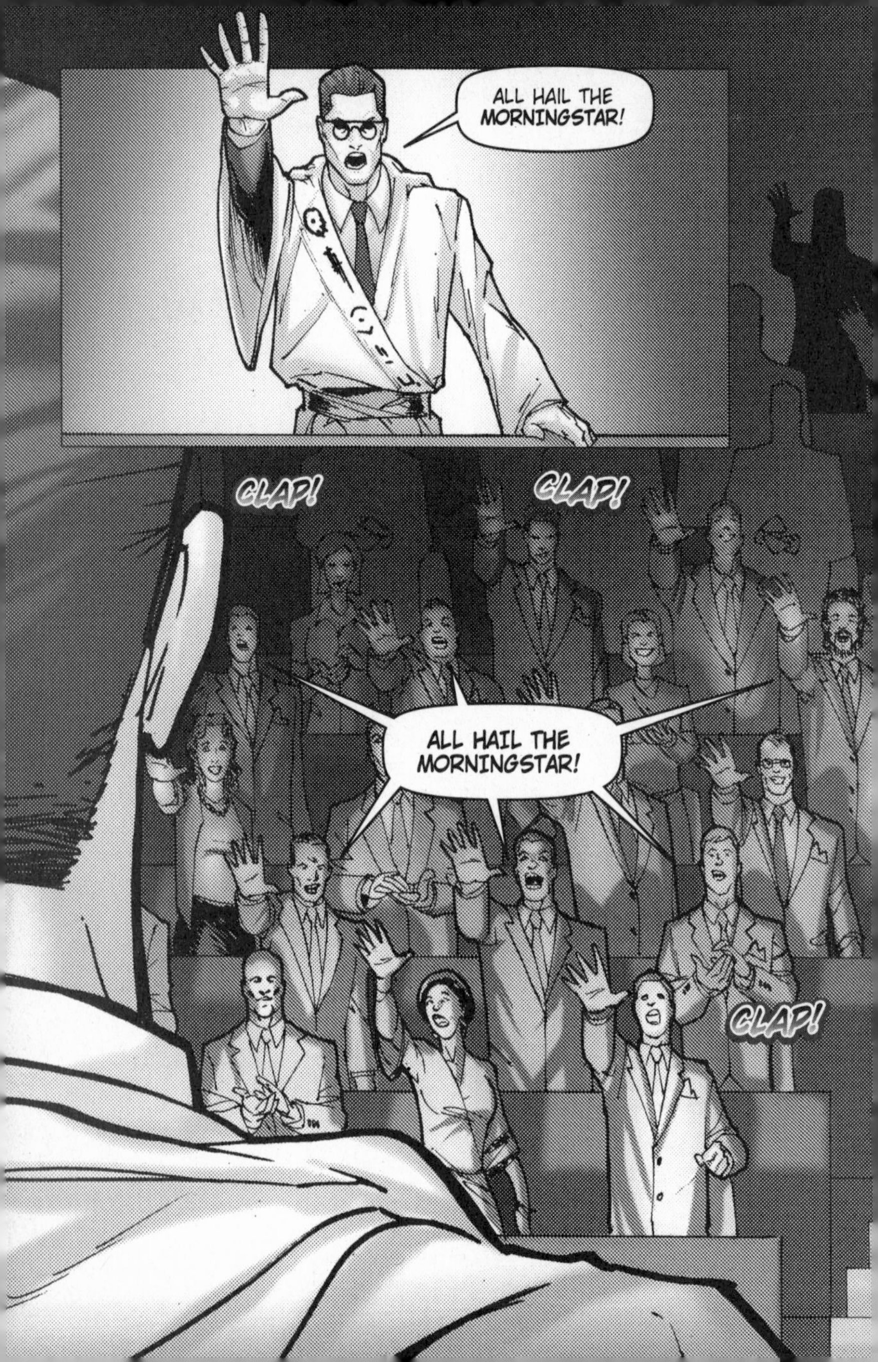
ALL HAIL THE MORNINGSTAR!
CLAP!
CLAP!
ALL HAIL THE MORNINGSTAR!
CLAP!

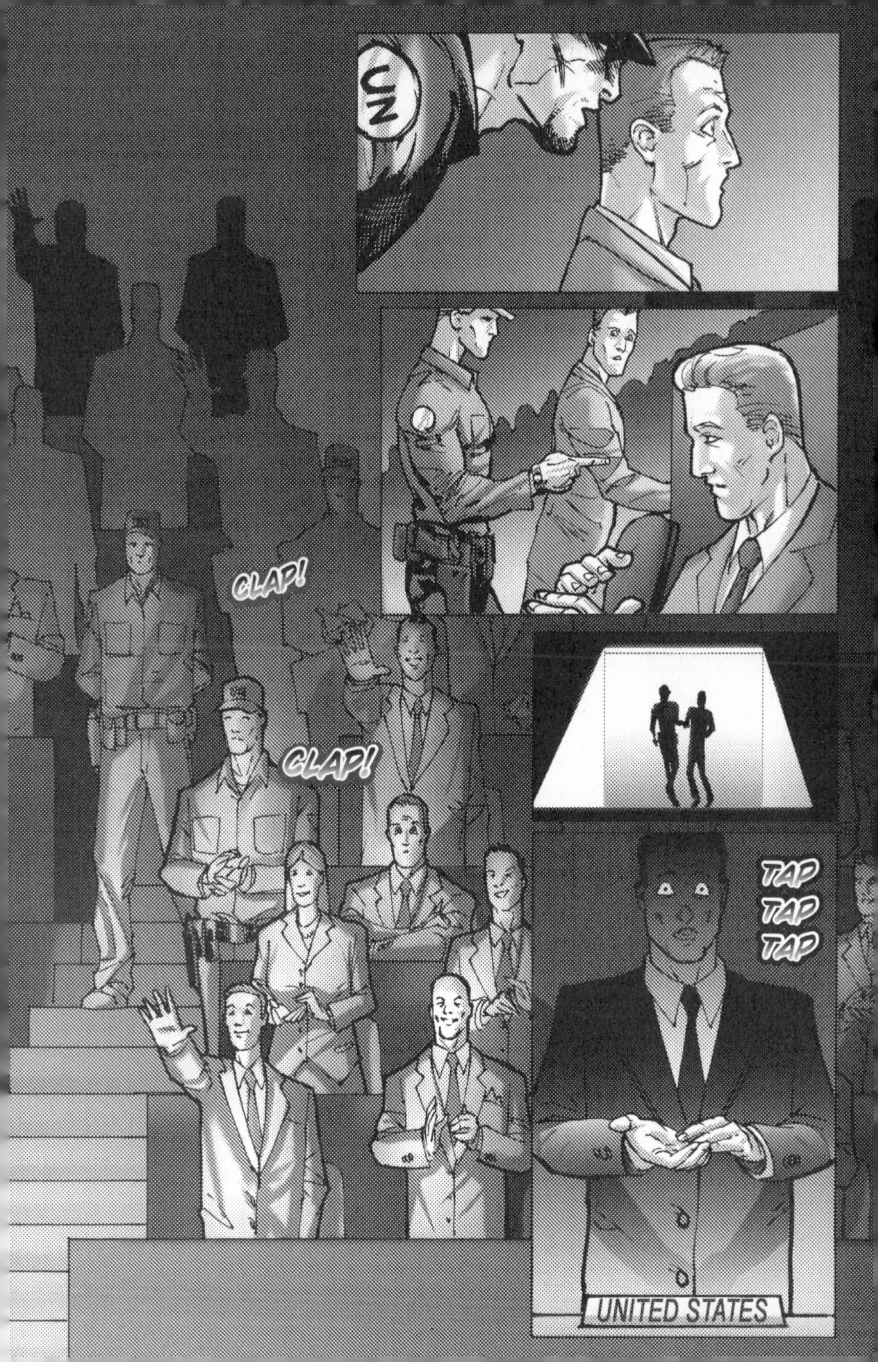
CLAP!
CLAP!
UN
TAP
TAP
TAP
UNITED STATES

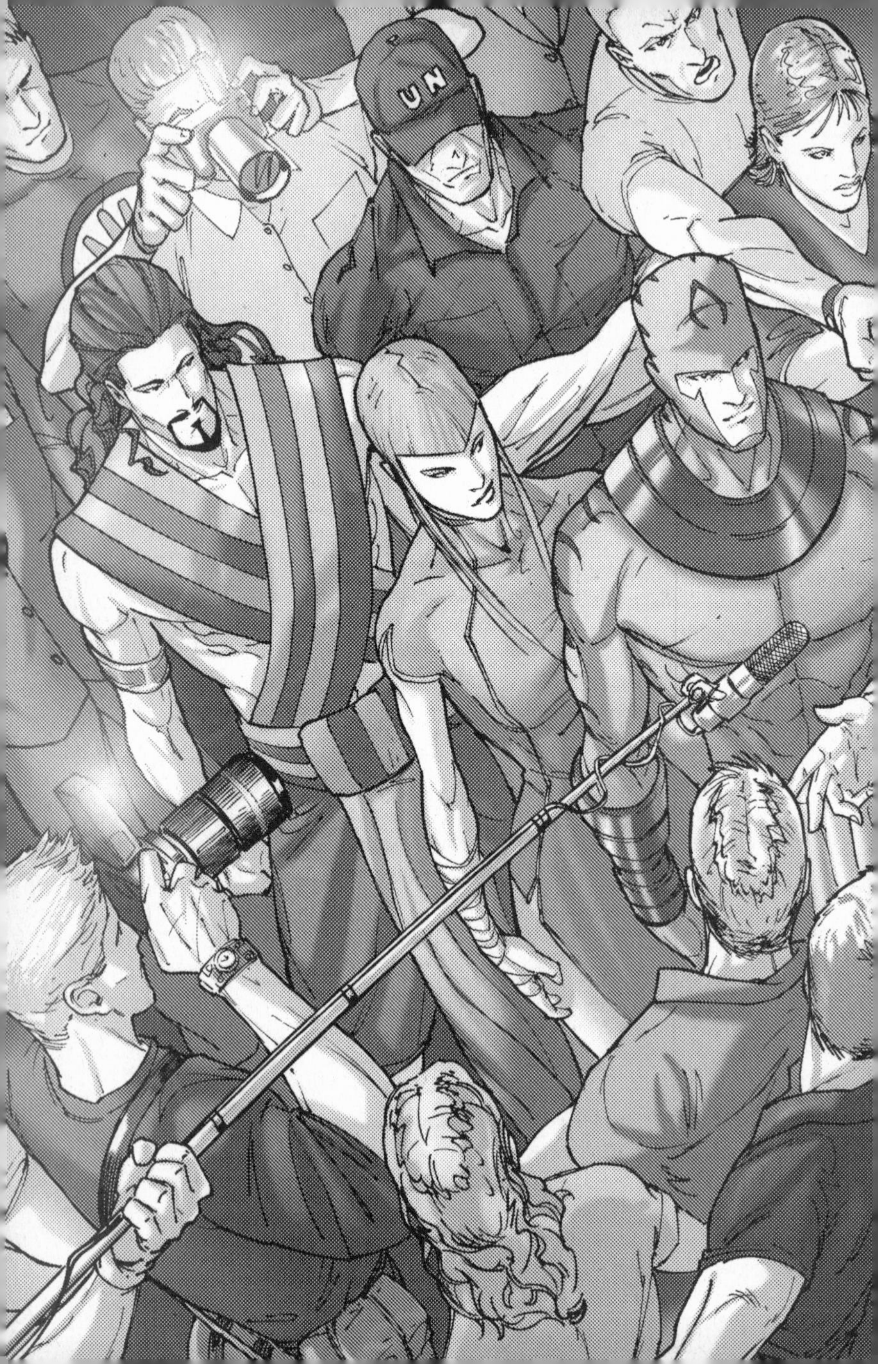
UN

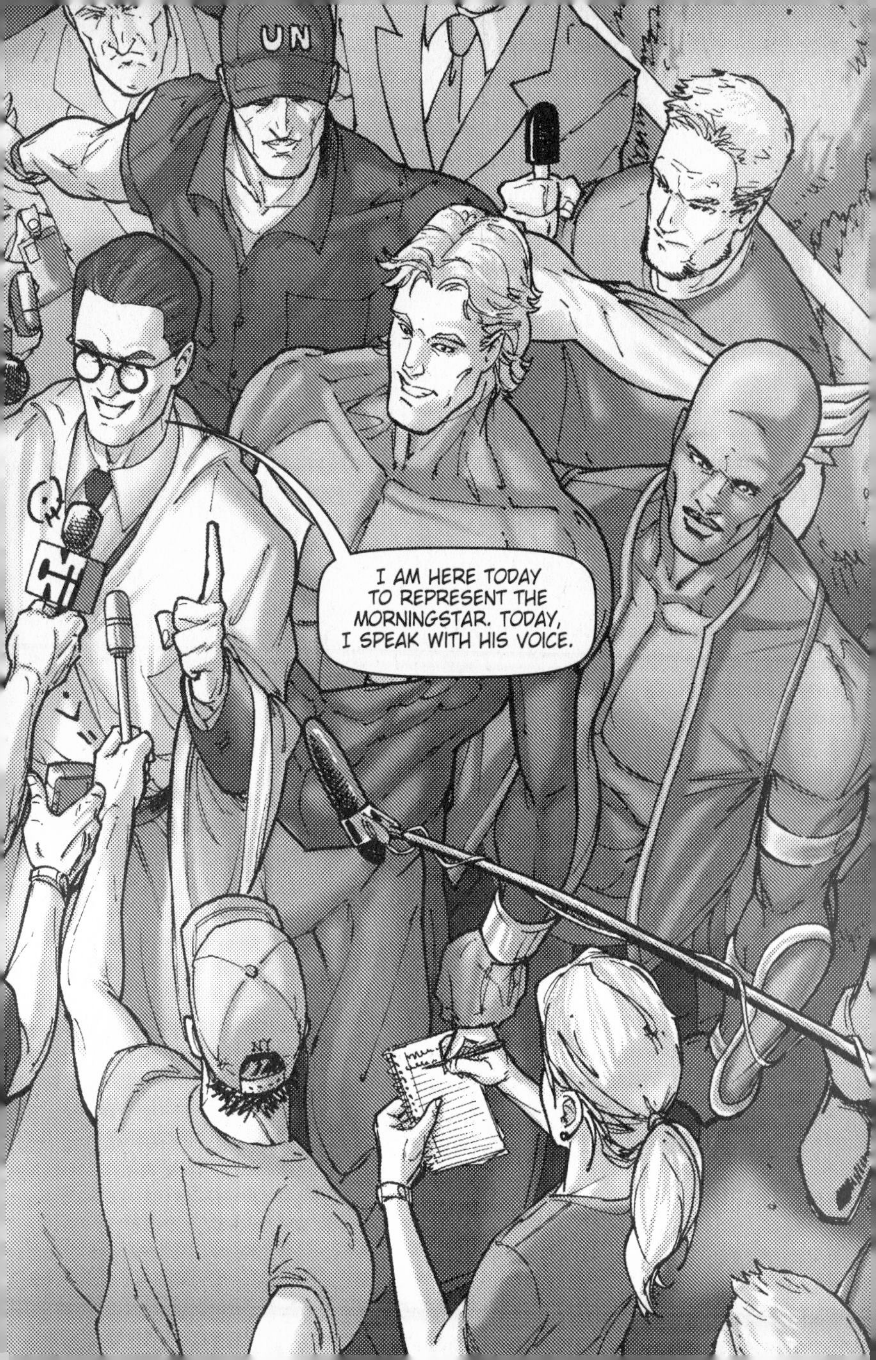

UN
I AM HERE TODAY TO REPRESENT THE MORNINGSTAR. TODAY, I SPEAK WITH HIS VOICE.

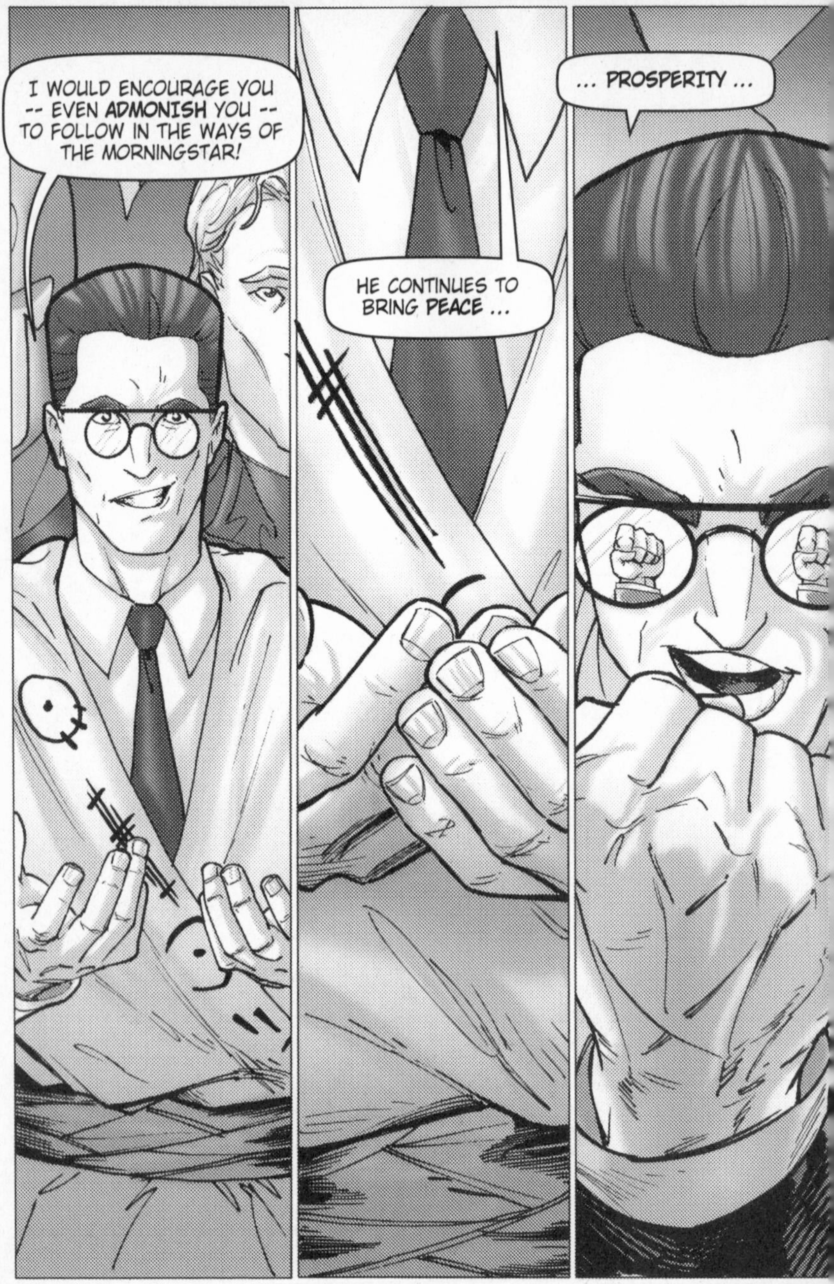
I WOULD ENCOURAGE YOU -- EVEN ADMONISH YOU -- TO FOLLOW IN THE WAYS OF THE MORNINGSTAR!
HE CONTINUES TO BRING PEACE ...
... PROSPERITY ...

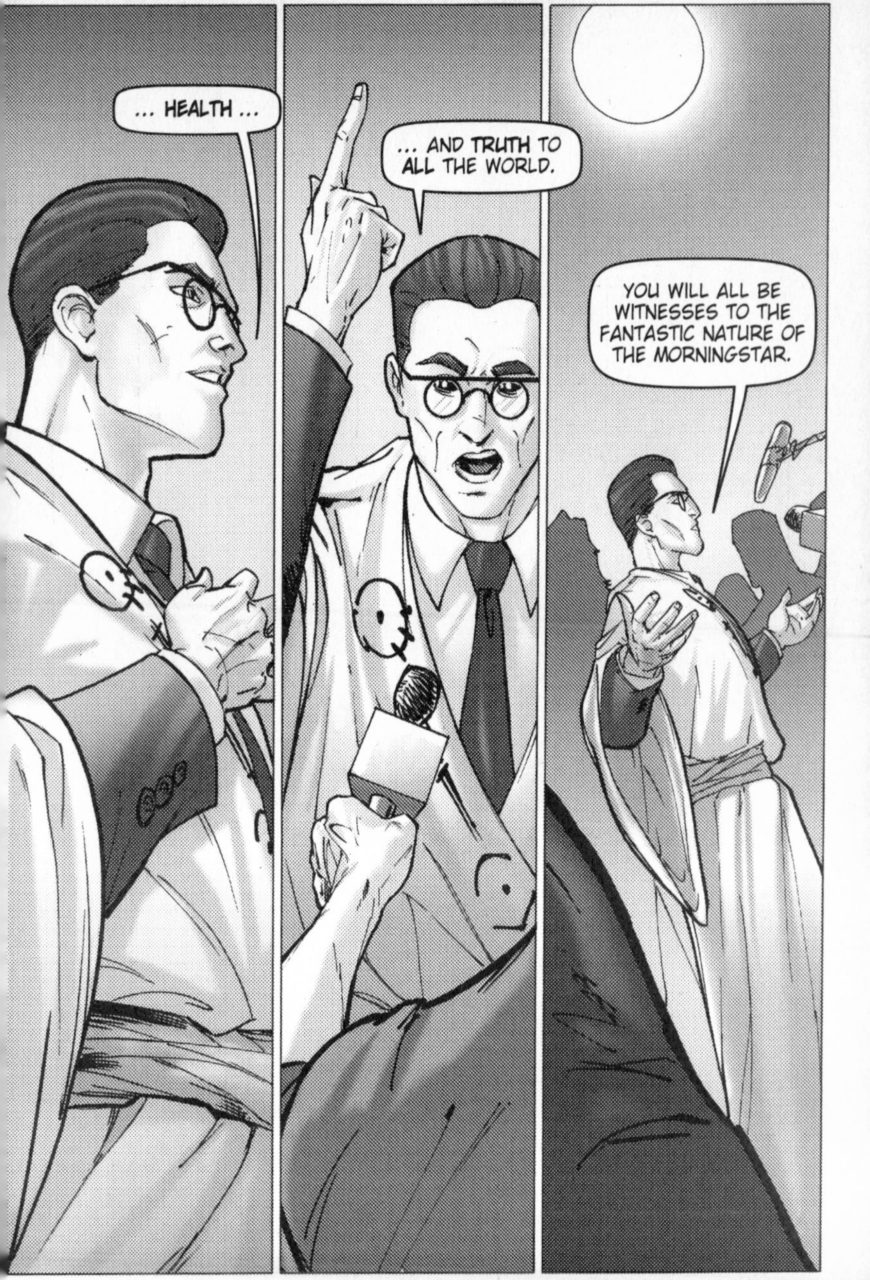
... HEALTH ...
... AND TRUTH TO ALL THE WORLD.
YOU WILL ALL BE WITNESSES TO THE FANTASTIC NATURE OF THE MORNINGSTAR.

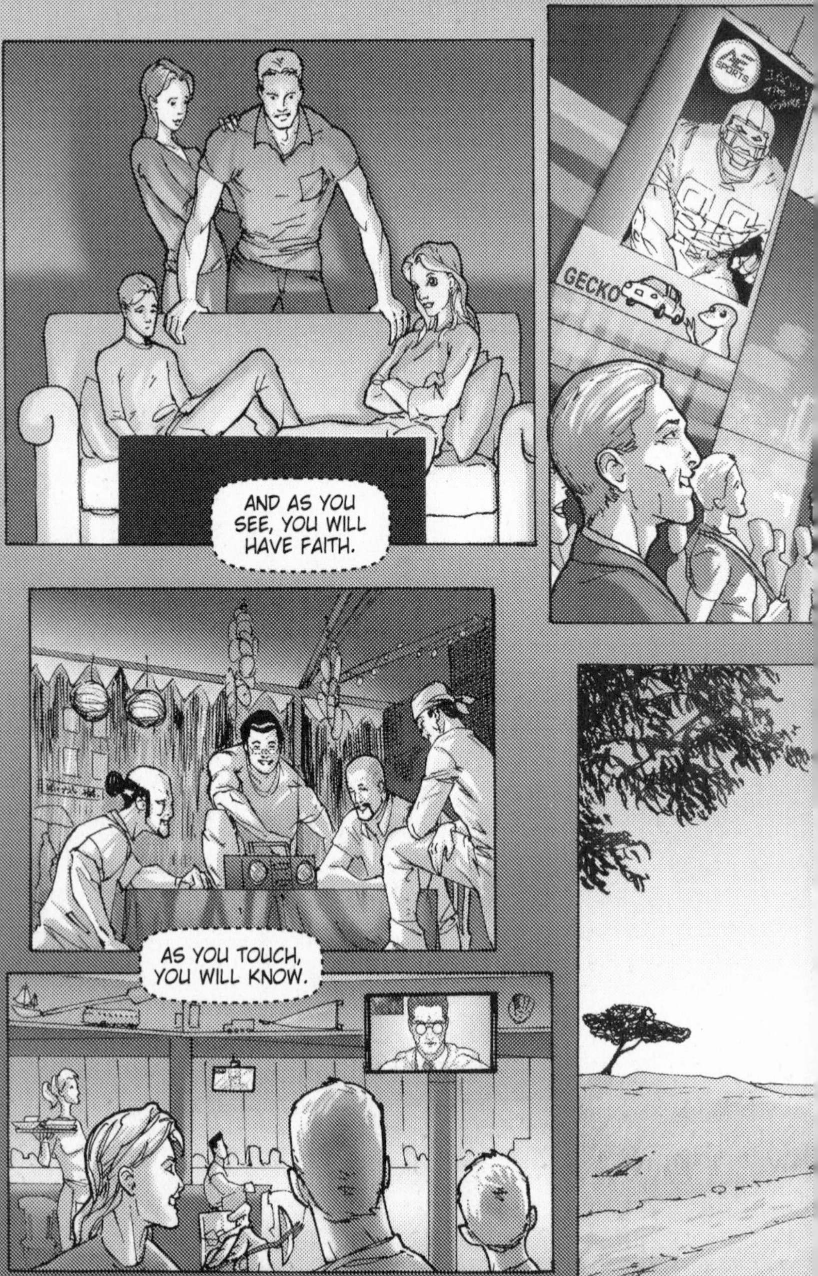
AND AS YOU SEE, YOU WILL HAVE FAITH.
SPORTS
GECKO
AS YOU TOUCH, YOU WILL KNOW.

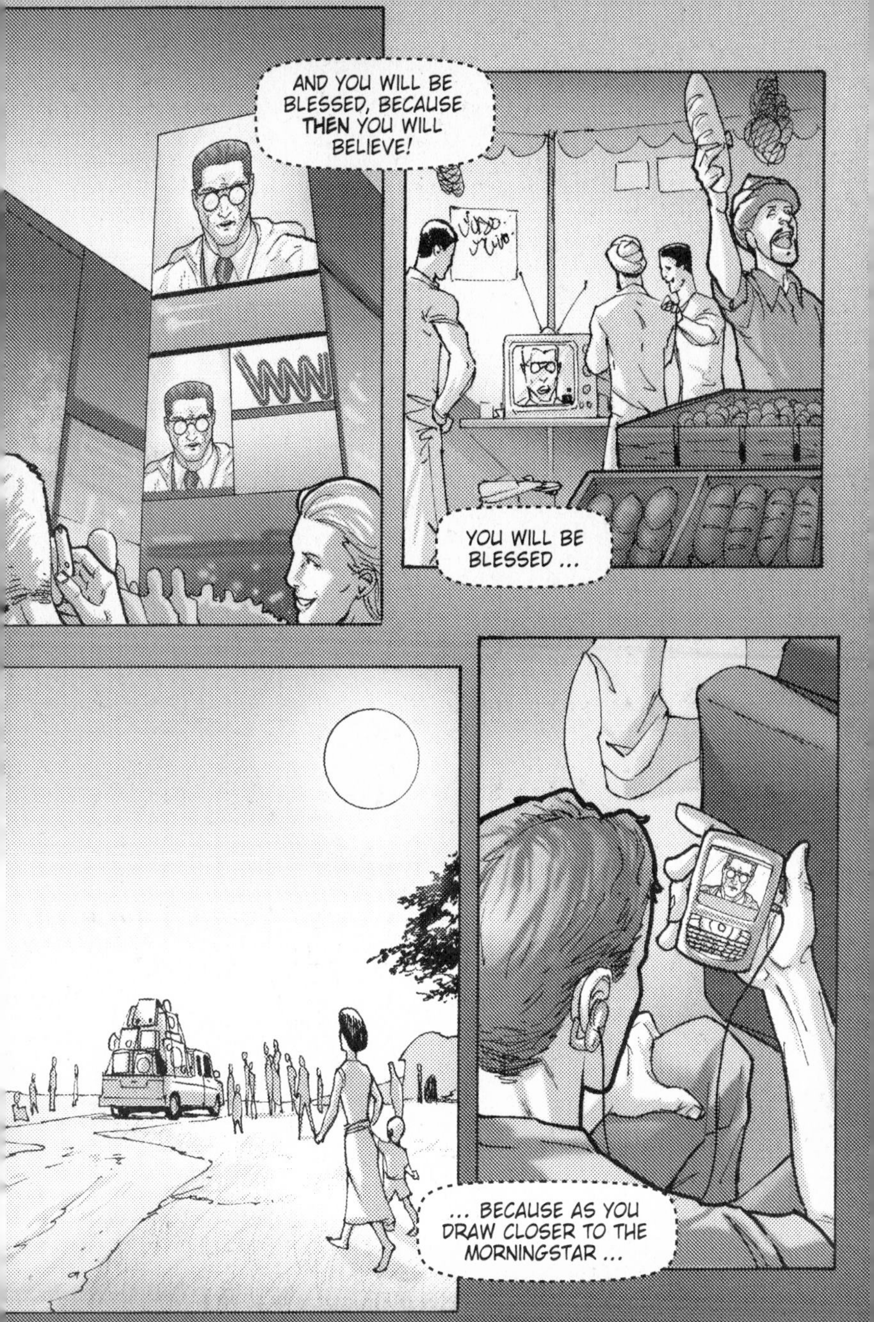
AND YOU WILL BE BLESSED, BECAUSE THEN YOU WILL BELIEVE!
YOU WILL BE BLESSED ...
... BECAUSE AS YOU DRAW CLOSER TO THE MORNINGSTAR ...

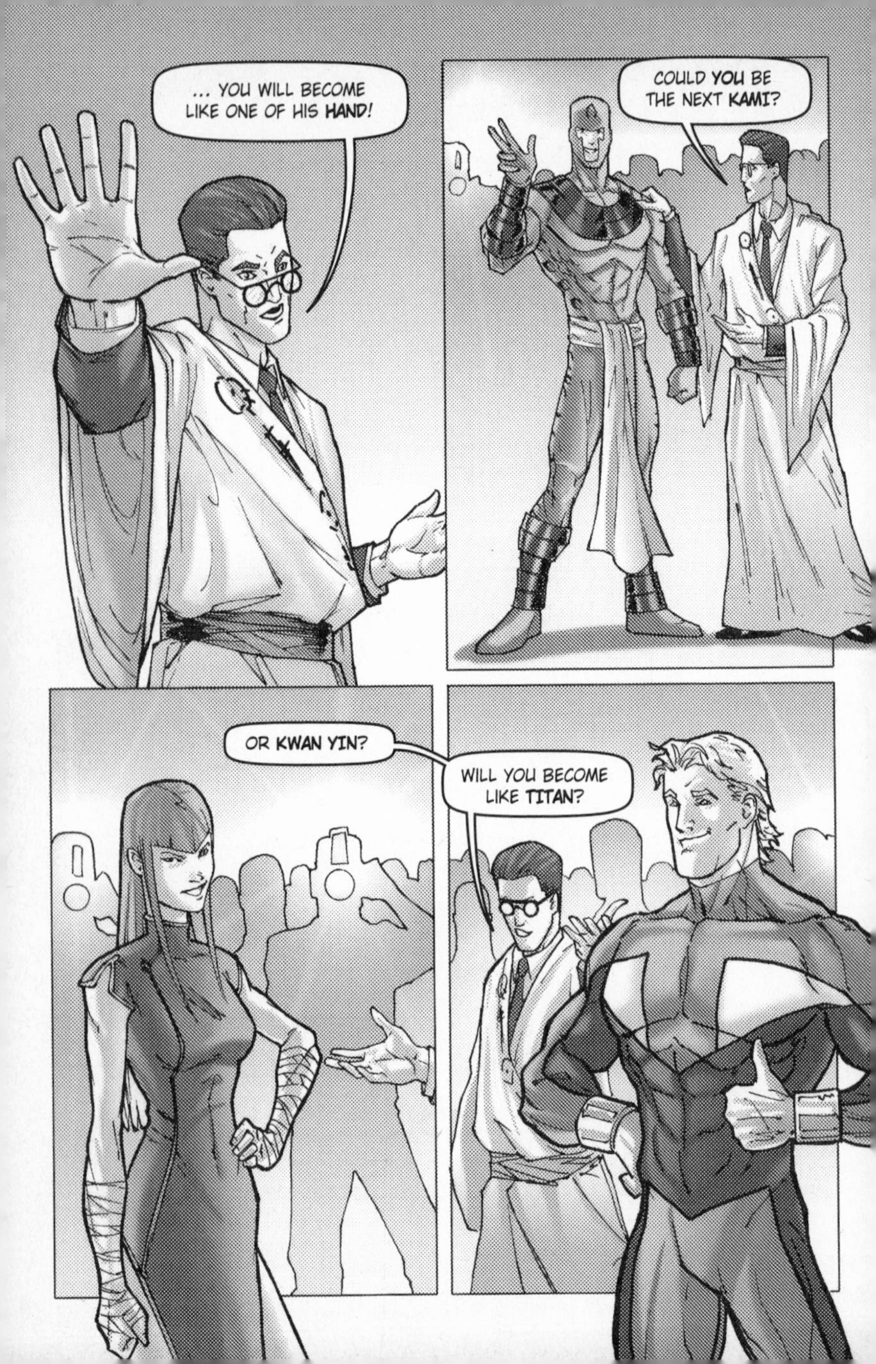
... YOU WILL BECOME LIKE ONE OF HIS HAND!
COULD YOU BE THE NEXT KAMI?
OR KWAN YIN?
WILL YOU BECOME LIKE TITAN?

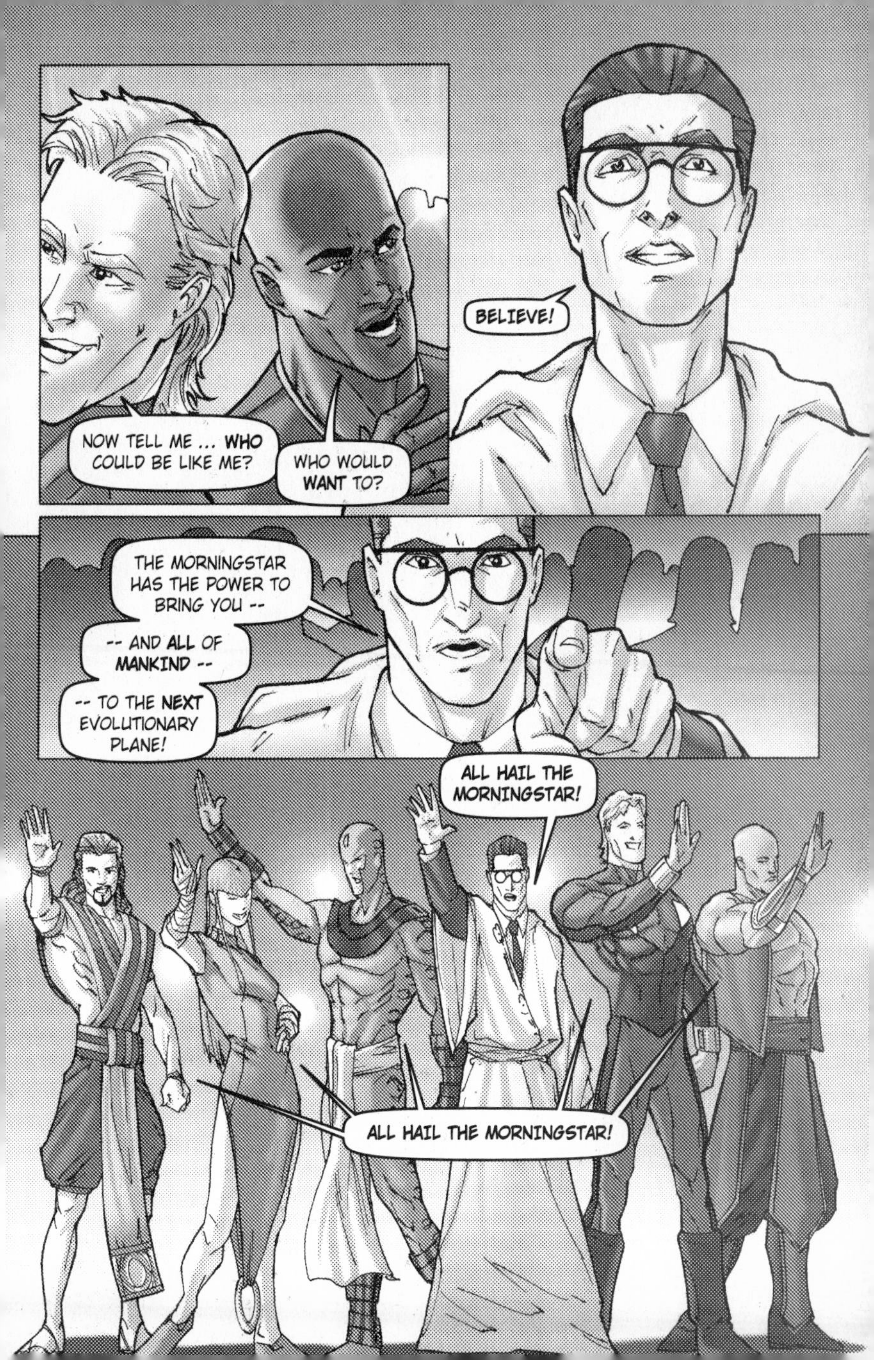
NOW TELL ME ... WHO COULD BE LIKE ME?
WHO WOULD WANT TO?
BELIEVE!
THE MORNINGSTAR HAS THE POWER TO BRING YOU --
-- AND ALL OF MANKIND --
-- TO THE NEXT EVOLUTIONARY PLANE!
ALL HAIL THE MORNINGSTAR!
ALL HAIL THE MORNINGSTAR!

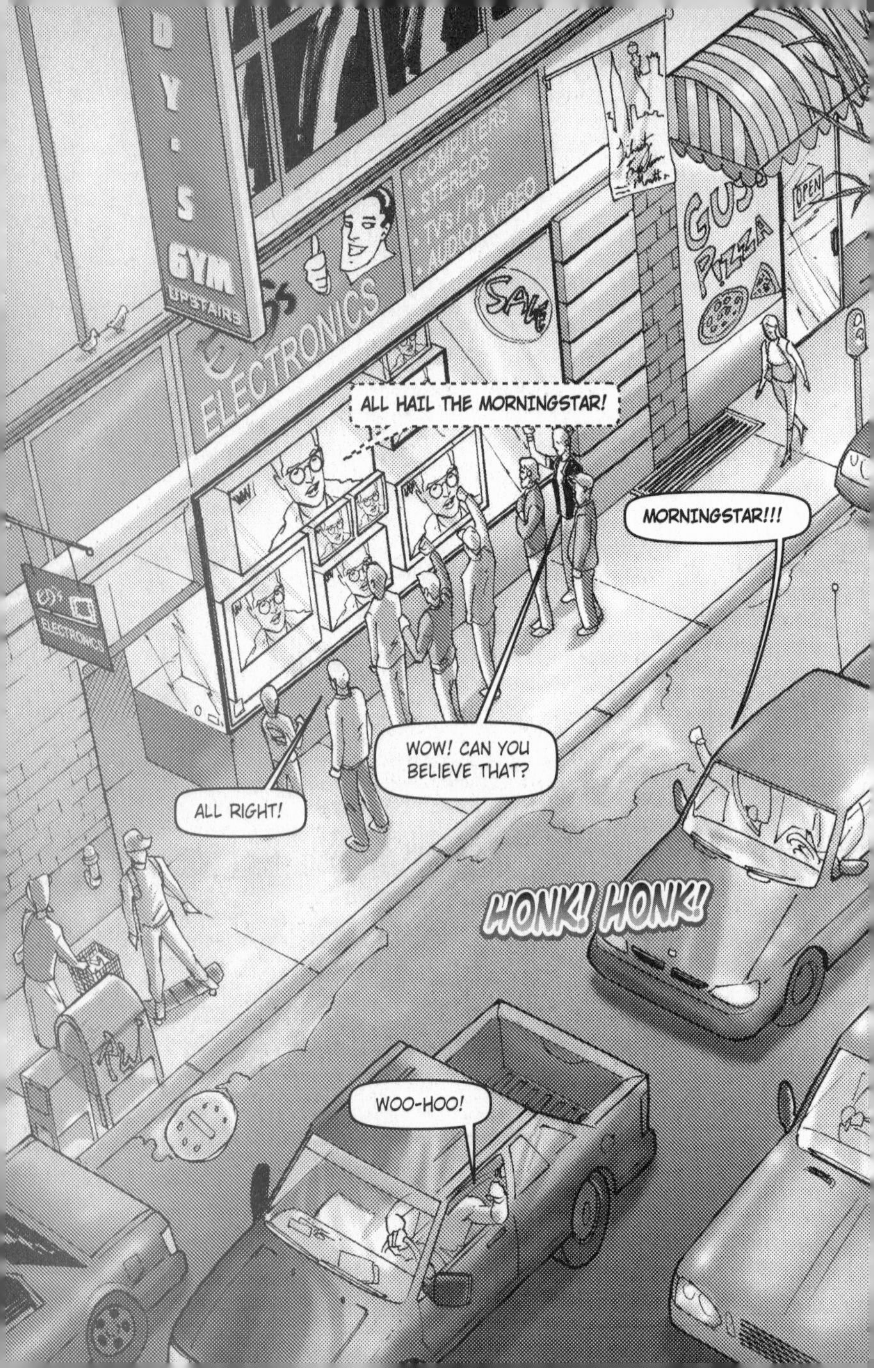
GYM
UPSTAIRS
ELECTRONICS
COMPUTERS
STEREOS
TVS 4 HD
AUDIO & VIDEO
GUS PIZZA
OPEN
ALL HAIL THE MORNINGSTAR!
MORNINGSTAR!!!
WOW! CAN YOU BELIEVE THAT?
ALL RIGHT!
HONK! HONK!
WOO-HOO!

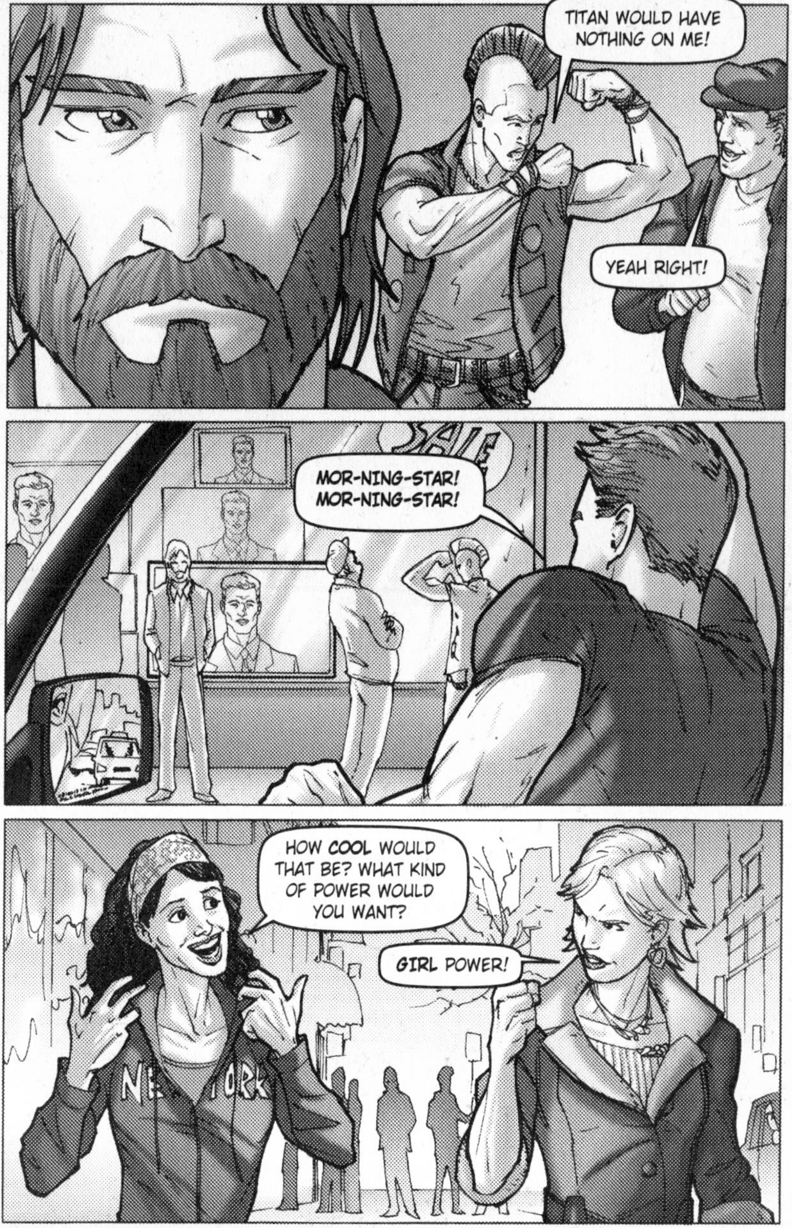
TITAN WOULD HAVE NOTHING ON ME!
YEAH RIGHT!
MOR-NING-STAR! MOR-NING-STAR!
HOW COOL WOULD THAT BE? WHAT KIND OF POWER WOULD YOU WANT?
GIRL POWER!

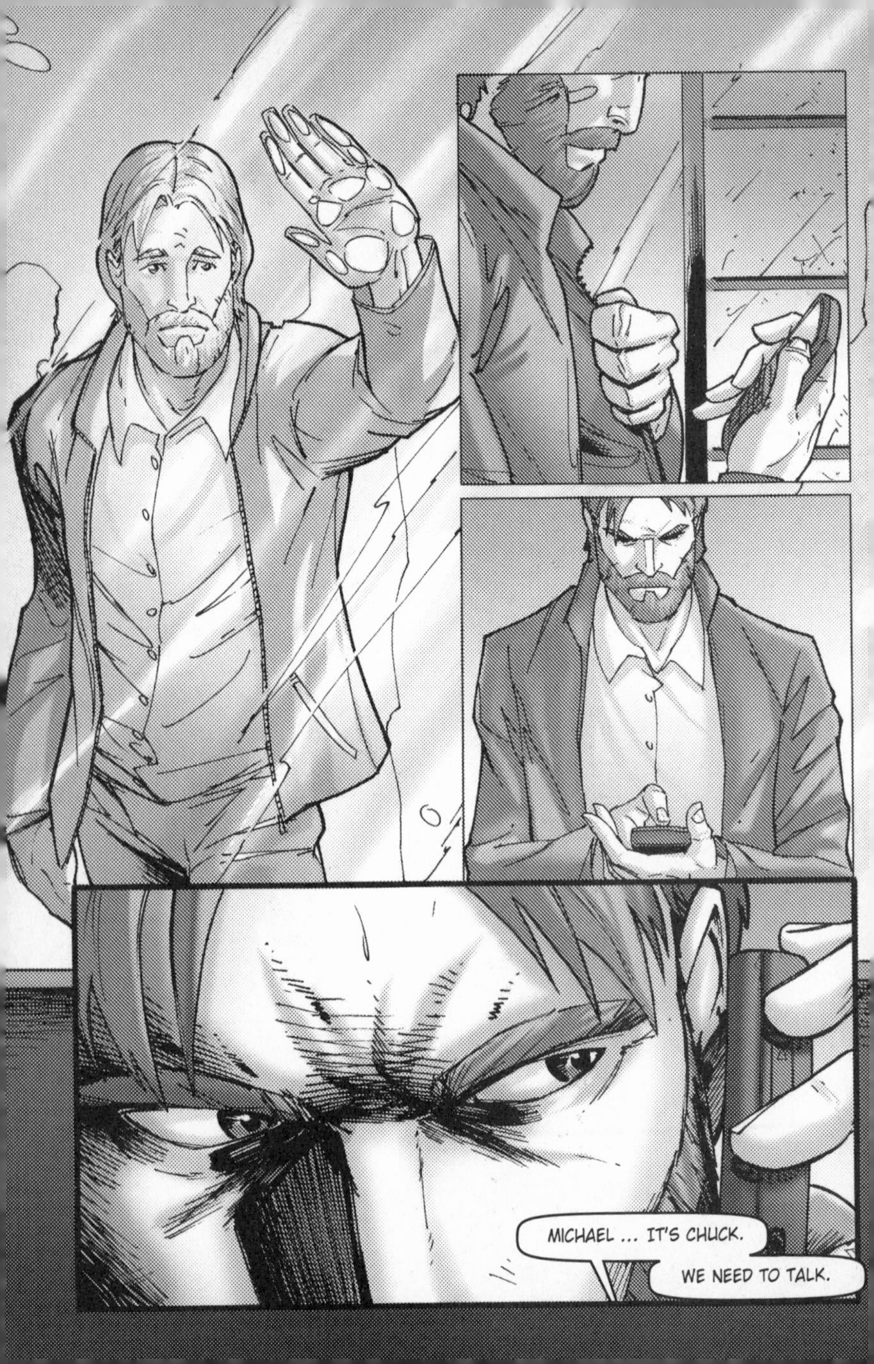
MICHAEL ... IT'S CHUCK.
WE NEED TO TALK.

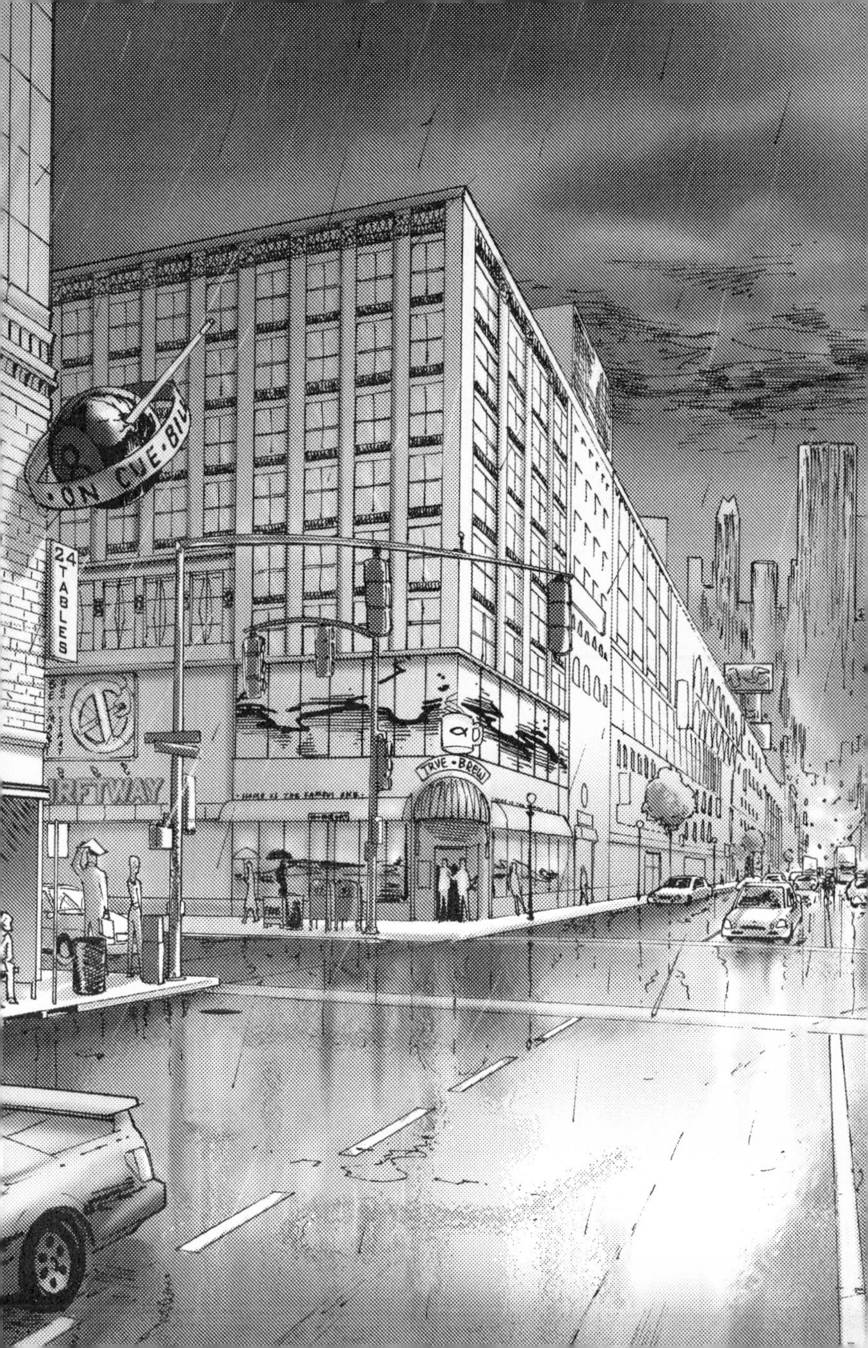

ON CUE
24 TABLES
TRVE • BREW

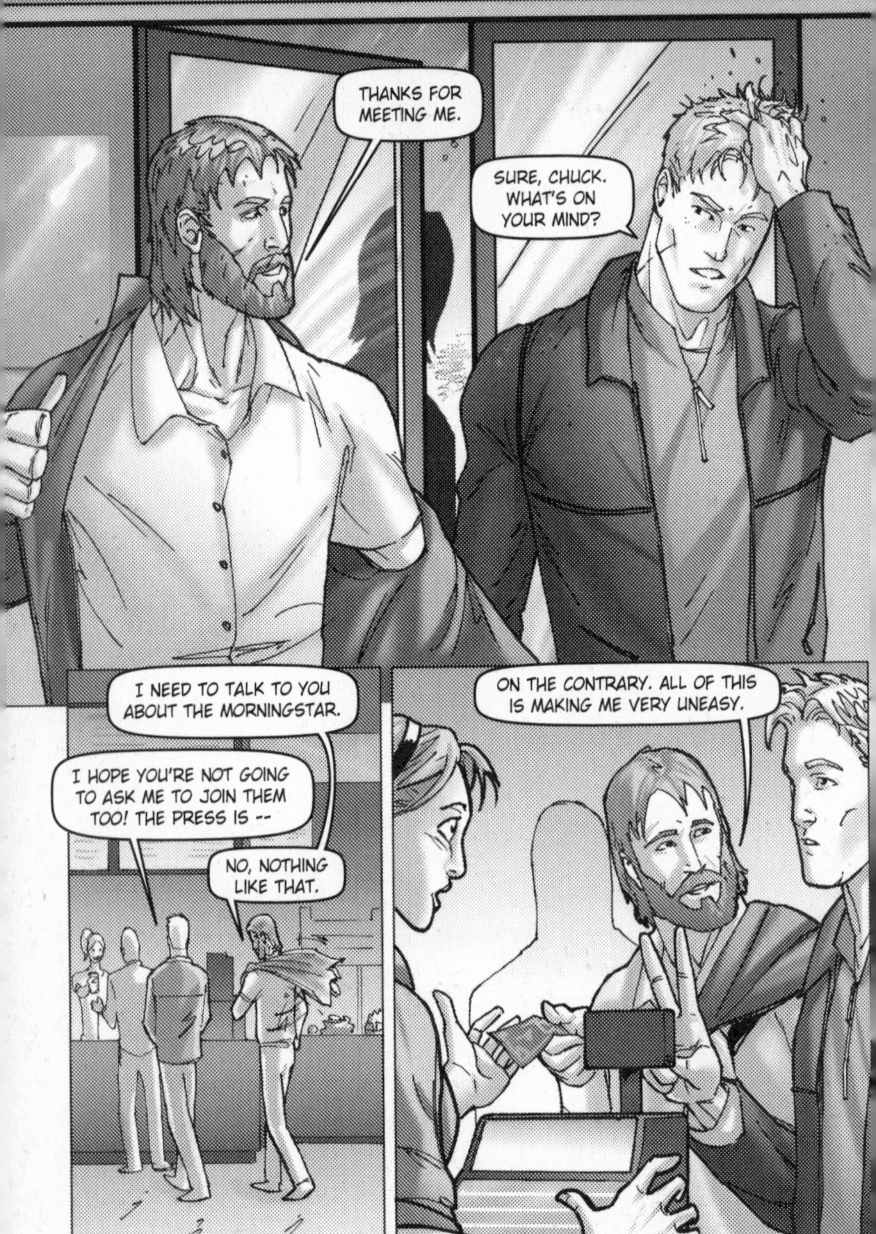
THANKS FOR MEETING ME.
SURE, CHUCK. WHAT'S ON YOUR MIND?
I NEED TO TALK TO YOU ABOUT THE MORNINGSTAR.
I HOPE YOU'RE NOT GOING TO ASK ME TO JOIN THEM TOO! THE PRESS IS --
NO, NOTHING LIKE THAT.
ON THE CONTRARY. ALL OF THIS IS MAKING ME VERY UNEASY.

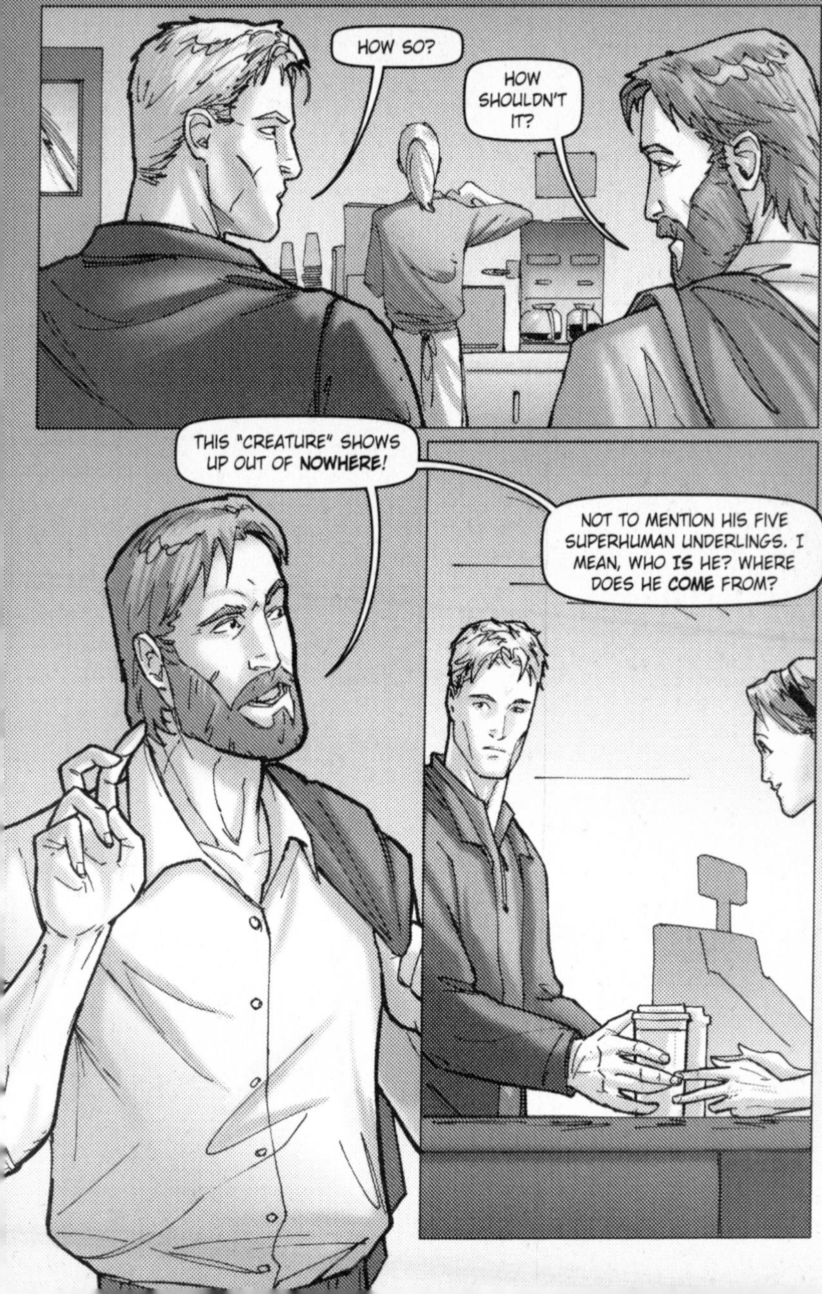
HOW SO?
HOW SHOULDN'T IT?
THIS "CREATURE" SHOWS UP OUT OF **NOWHERE!**
NOT TO MENTION HIS FIVE SUPERHUMAN UNDERLINGS. I MEAN, WHO **IS** HE? WHERE DOES HE **COME** FROM?

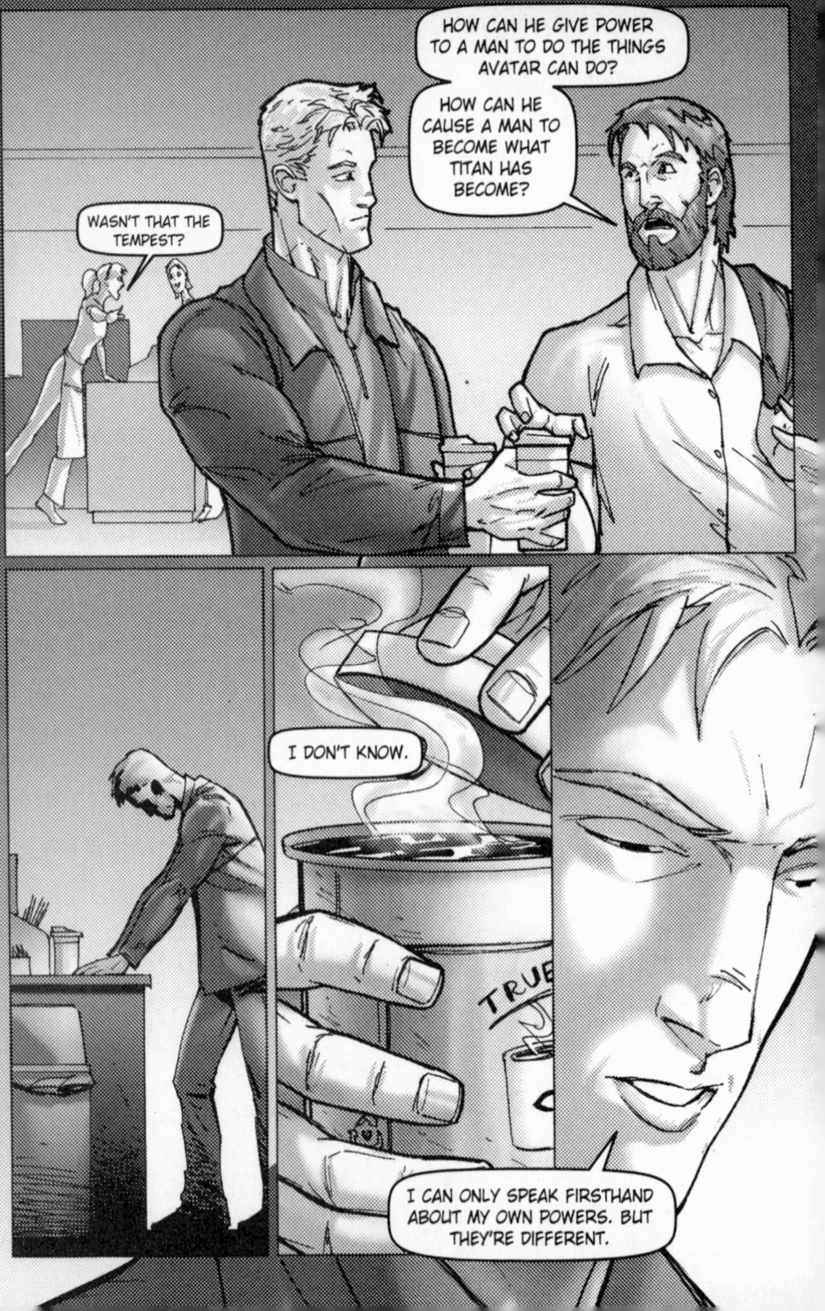
HOW CAN HE GIVE POWER TO A MAN TO DO THE THINGS AVATAR CAN DO?
HOW CAN HE CAUSE A MAN TO BECOME WHAT TITAN HAS BECOME?
WASN'T THAT THE TEMPEST?
I DON'T KNOW.
TRUE
I CAN ONLY SPEAK FIRSTHAND ABOUT MY OWN POWERS. BUT THEY'RE DIFFERENT.

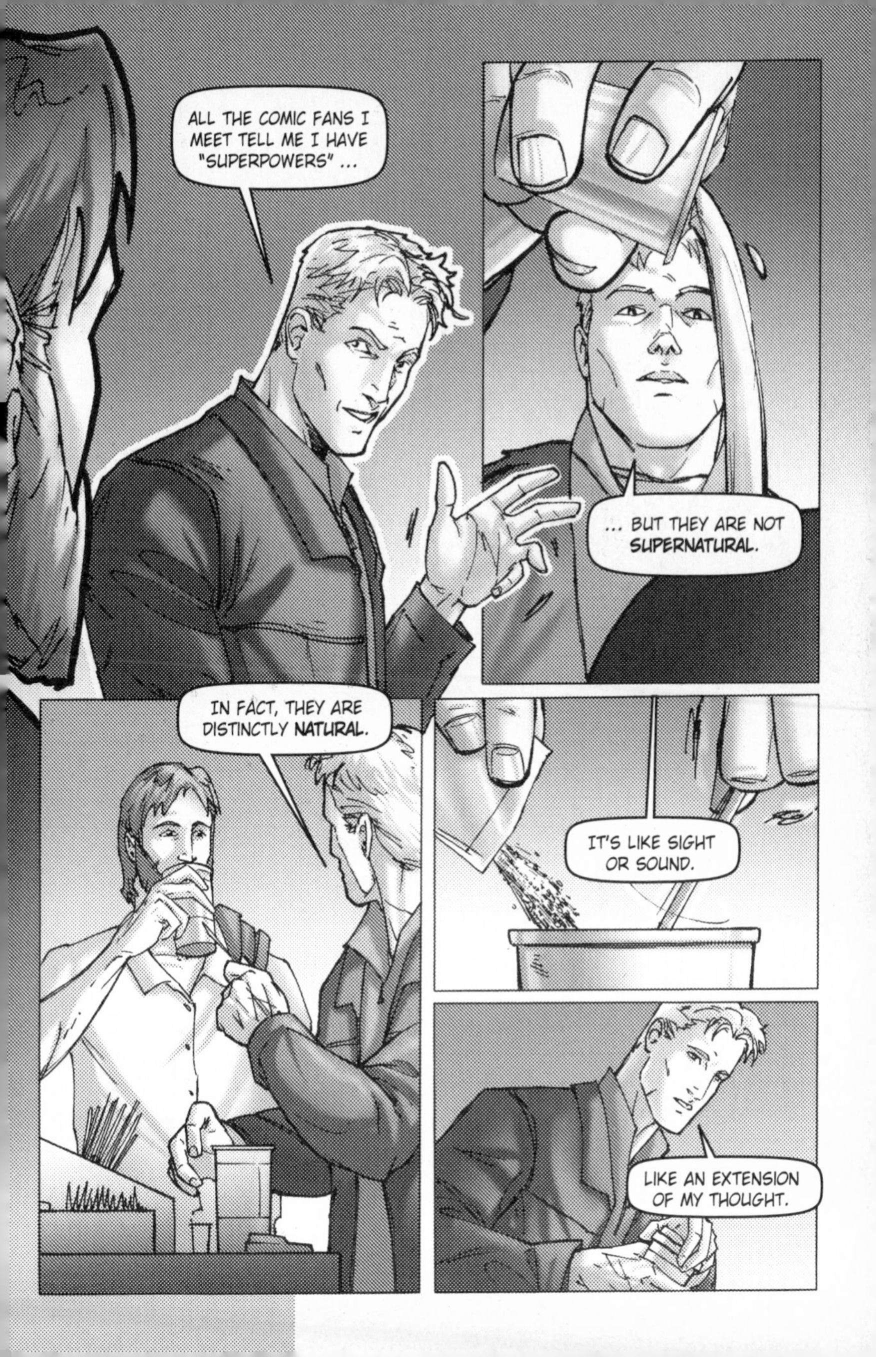
ALL THE COMIC FANS I MEET TELL ME I HAVE "SUPERPOWERS" ...
... BUT THEY ARE NOT **SUPERNATURAL.**
IN FACT, THEY ARE DISTINCTLY **NATURAL.**
IT'S LIKE SIGHT OR SOUND.
LIKE AN EXTENSION OF MY THOUGHT.

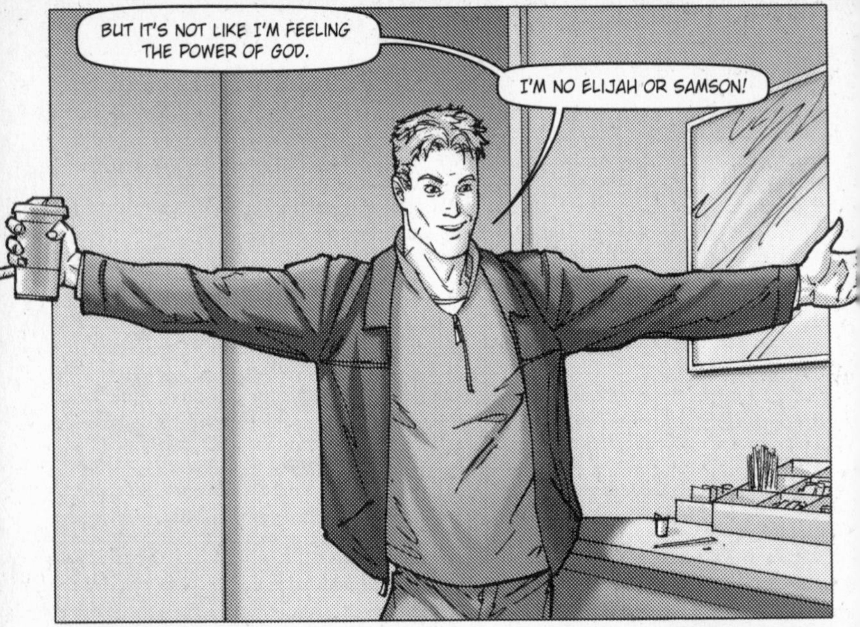
BUT IT'S NOT LIKE I'M FEELING THE POWER OF GOD.
I'M NO ELIJAH OR SAMSON!

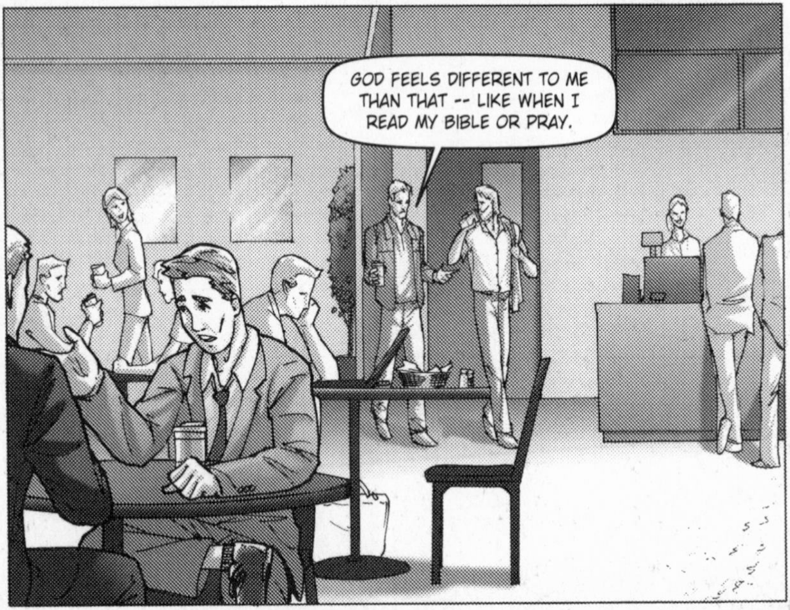
GOD FEELS DIFFERENT TO ME THAN THAT -- LIKE WHEN I READ MY BIBLE OR PRAY.

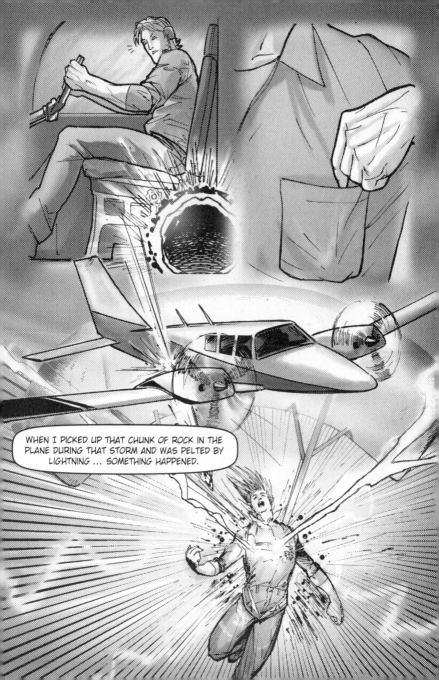

WHEN I PICKED UP THAT CHUNK OF ROCK IN THE PLANE DURING THAT STORM AND WAS PELTED BY LIGHTNING ... SOMETHING HAPPENED.

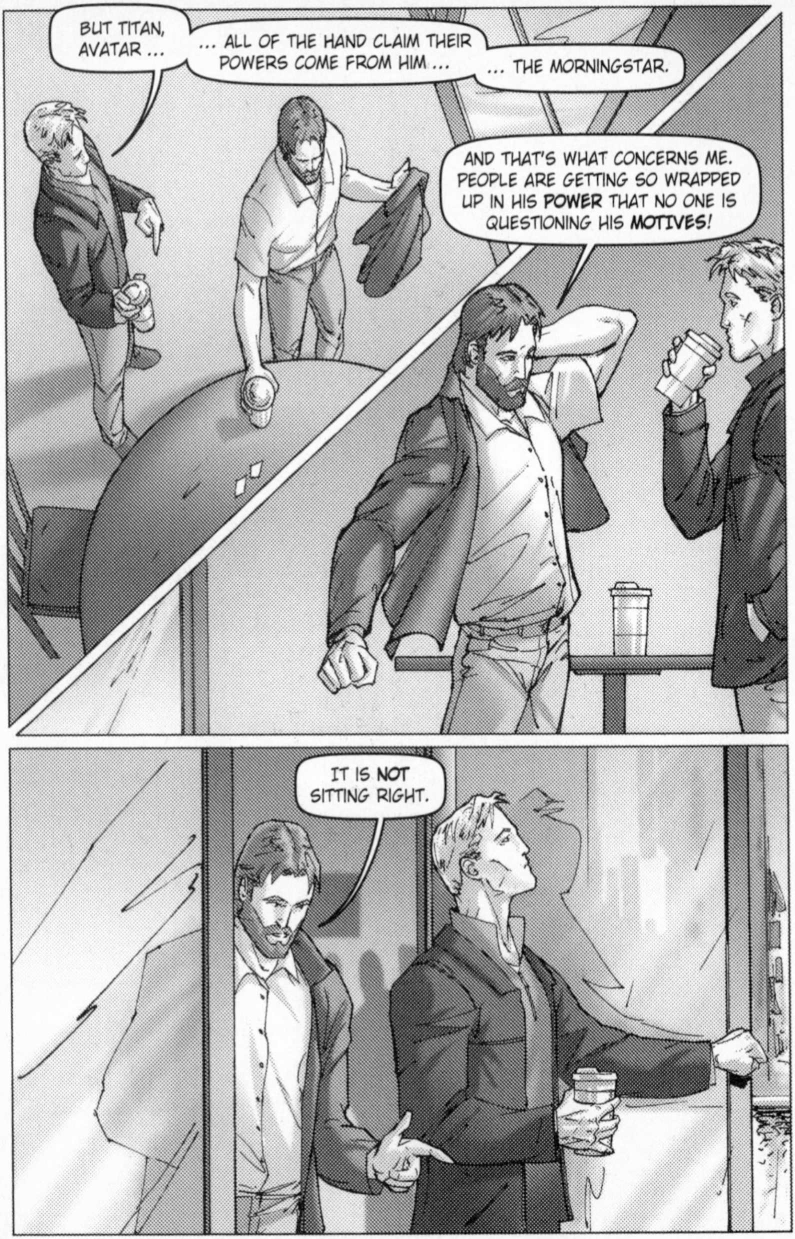
BUT TITAN, AVATAR ...
... ALL OF THE HAND CLAIM THEIR POWERS COME FROM HIM ...
... THE MORNINGSTAR.
AND THAT'S WHAT CONCERNS ME. PEOPLE ARE GETTING SO WRAPPED UP IN HIS **POWER** THAT NO ONE IS QUESTIONING HIS **MOTIVES**!
IT IS **NOT** SITTING RIGHT.

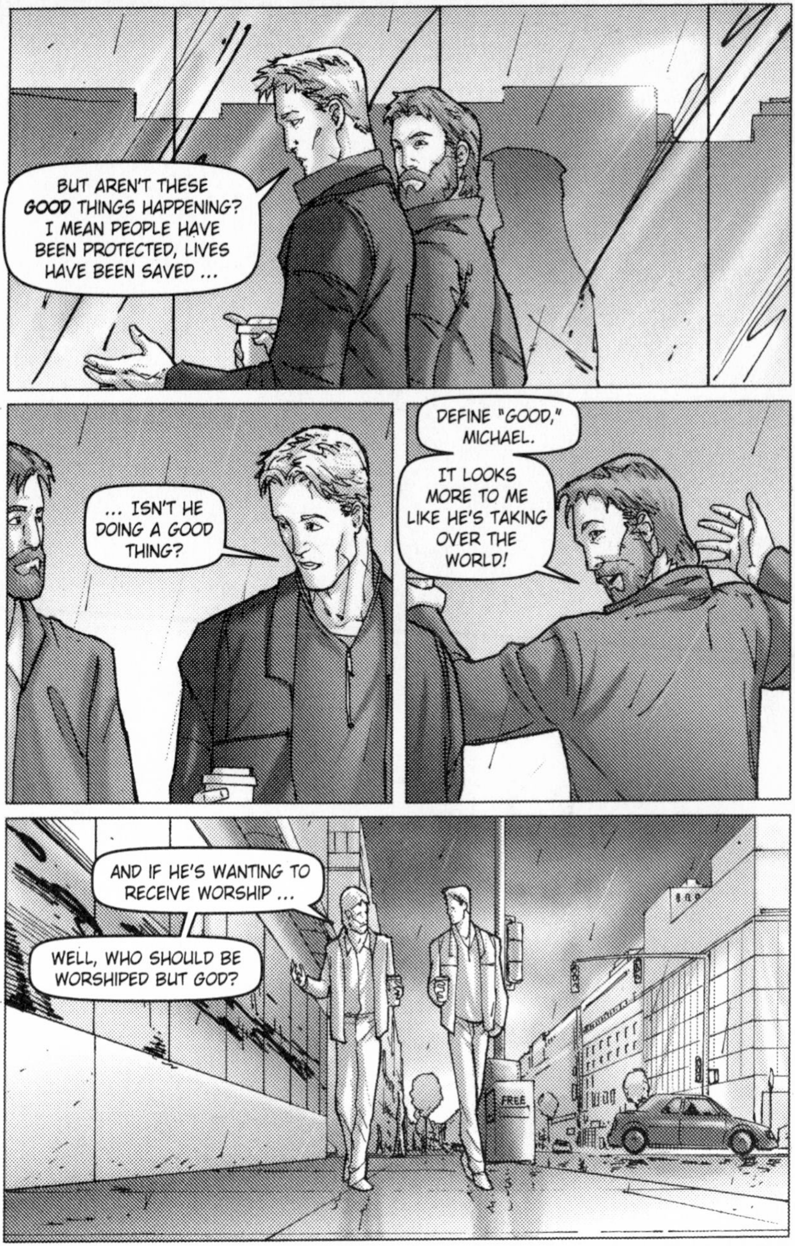
BUT AREN'T THESE **GOOD** THINGS HAPPENING? I MEAN PEOPLE HAVE BEEN PROTECTED, LIVES HAVE BEEN SAVED ...
... ISN'T HE DOING A GOOD THING?
DEFINE "GOOD," MICHAEL.
IT LOOKS MORE TO ME LIKE HE'S TAKING OVER THE WORLD!
AND IF HE'S WANTING TO RECEIVE WORSHIP ...
WELL, WHO SHOULD BE WORSHIPED BUT GOD?
FREE

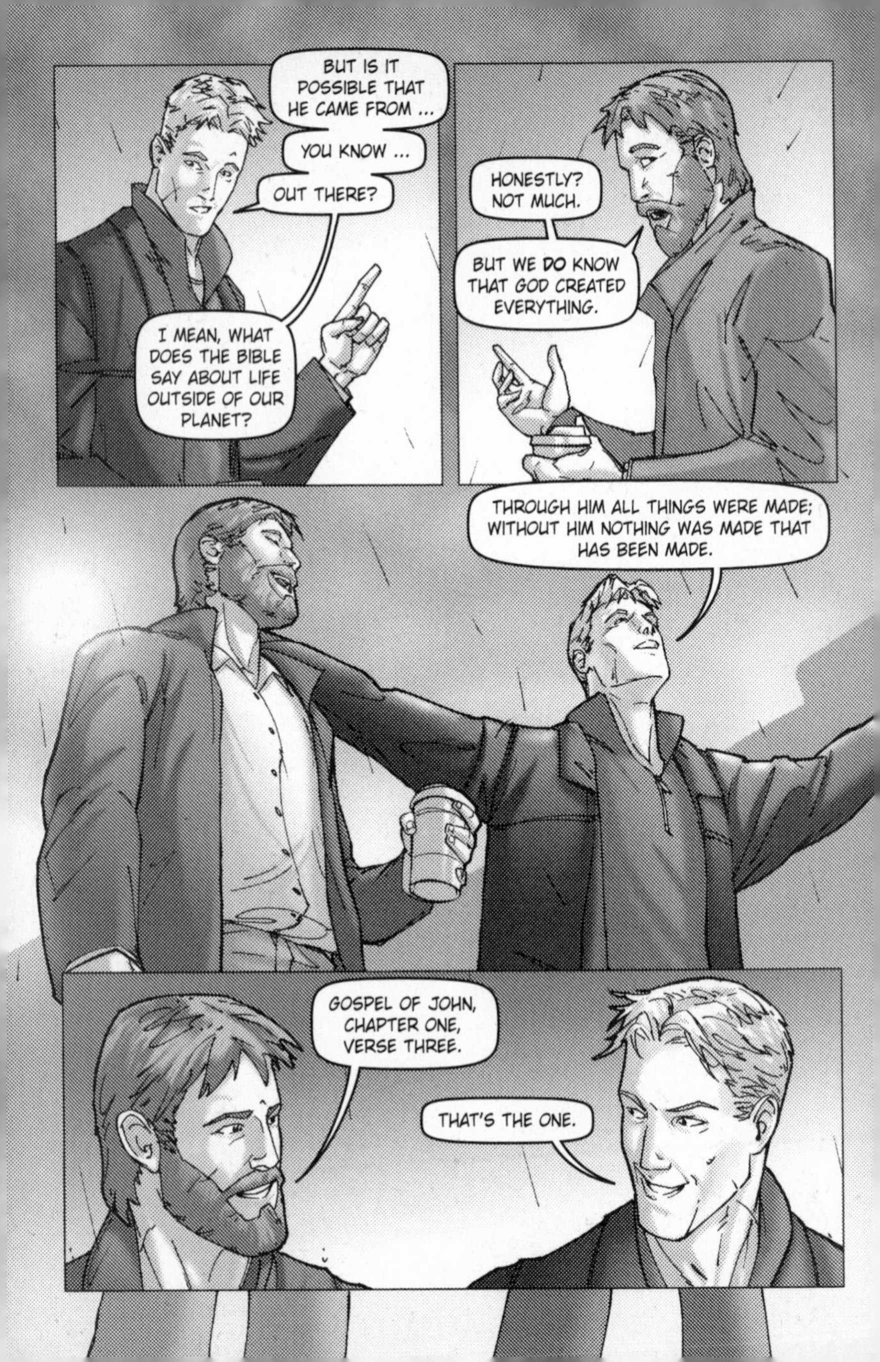
BUT IS IT POSSIBLE THAT HE CAME FROM ...
YOU KNOW ...
OUT THERE?
I MEAN, WHAT DOES THE BIBLE SAY ABOUT LIFE OUTSIDE OF OUR PLANET?
HONESTLY? NOT MUCH.
BUT WE DO KNOW THAT GOD CREATED EVERYTHING.
THROUGH HIM ALL THINGS WERE MADE; WITHOUT HIM NOTHING WAS MADE THAT HAS BEEN MADE.
GOSPEL OF JOHN, CHAPTER ONE, VERSE THREE.
THAT'S THE ONE.

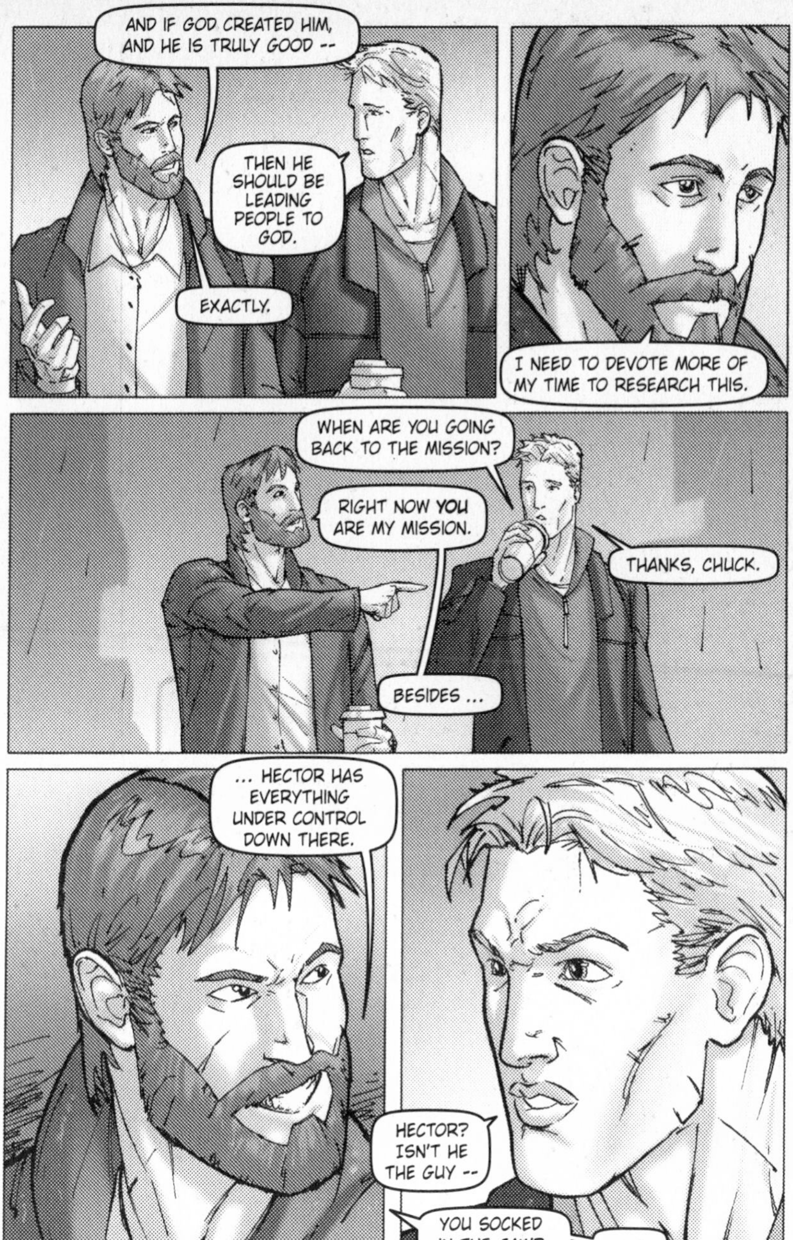
AND IF GOD CREATED HIM, AND HE IS TRULY GOOD --
THEN HE SHOULD BE LEADING PEOPLE TO GOD.
EXACTLY.
I NEED TO DEVOTE MORE OF MY TIME TO RESEARCH THIS.
WHEN ARE YOU GOING BACK TO THE MISSION?
RIGHT NOW **YOU** ARE MY MISSION.
THANKS, CHUCK.
BESIDES ...
... HECTOR HAS EVERYTHING UNDER CONTROL DOWN THERE.
HECTOR? ISN'T HE THE GUY --
YOU SOCKED IN THE JAW?
YUP.

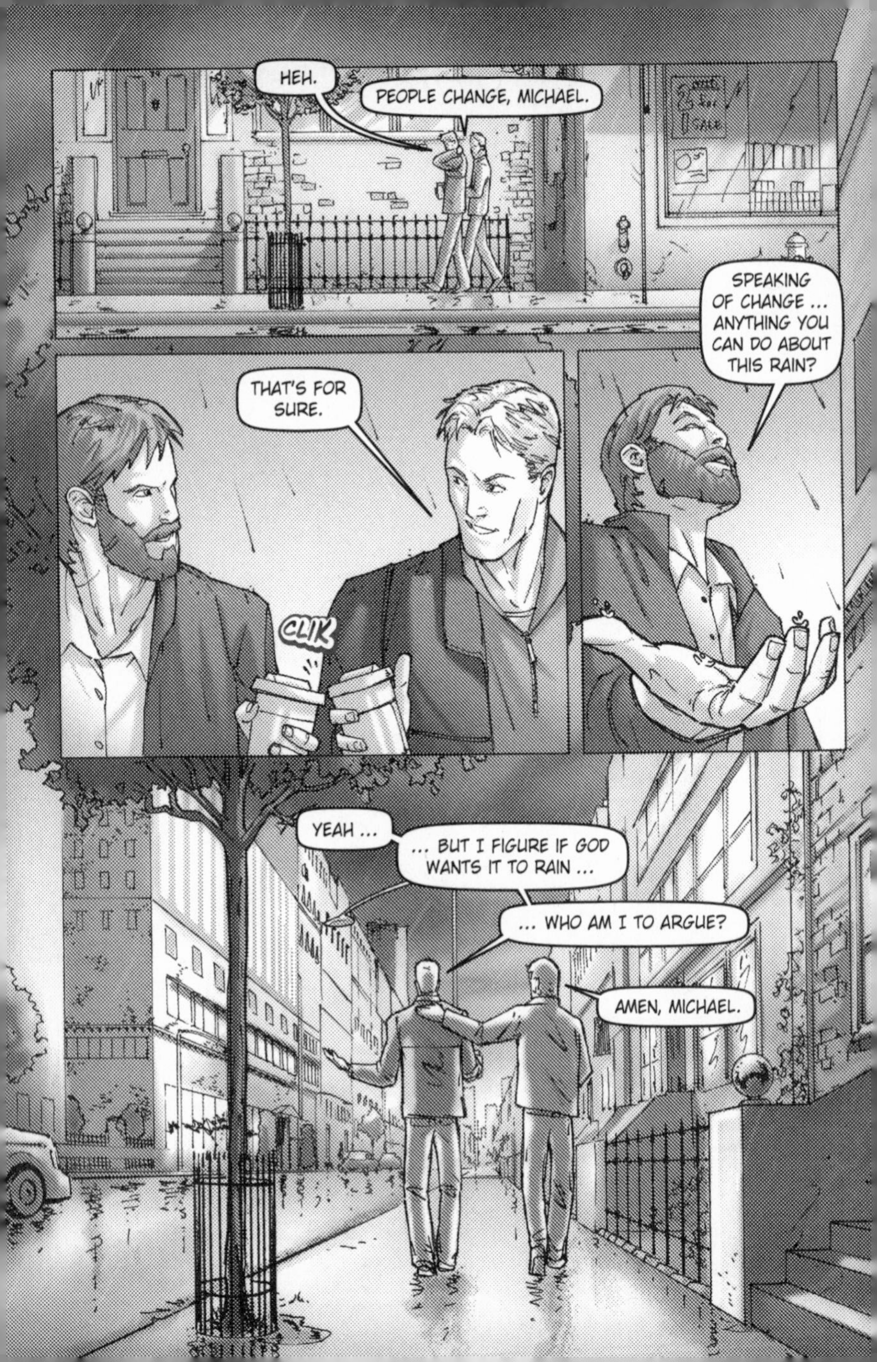
HEH.
PEOPLE CHANGE, MICHAEL.
THAT'S FOR SURE.
CLIK
SPEAKING OF CHANGE ... ANYTHING YOU CAN DO ABOUT THIS RAIN?
YEAH ...
... BUT I FIGURE IF GOD WANTS IT TO RAIN ...
... WHO AM I TO ARGUE?
AMEN, MICHAEL.

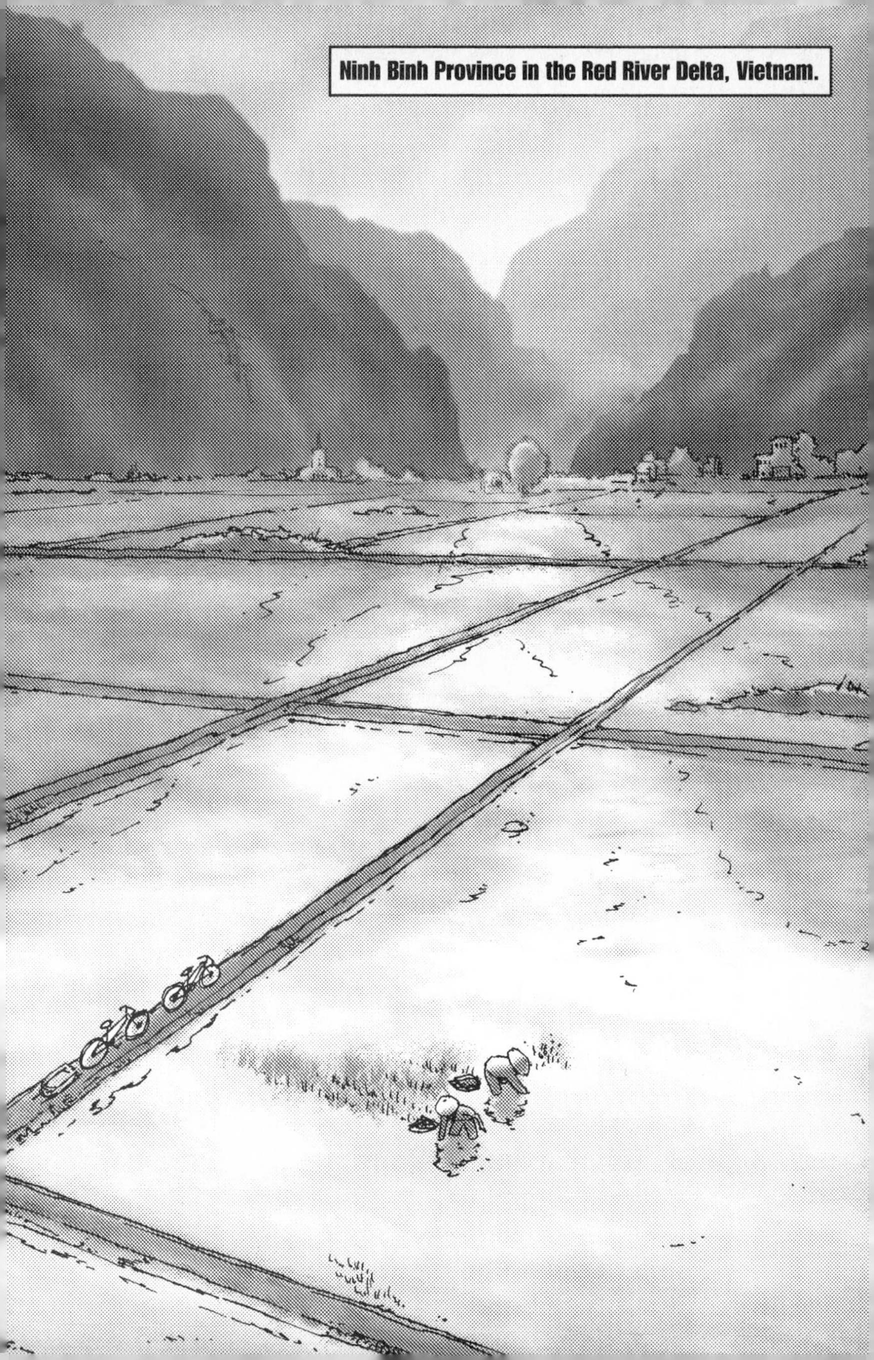
Ninh Binh Province in the Red River Delta, Vietnam.

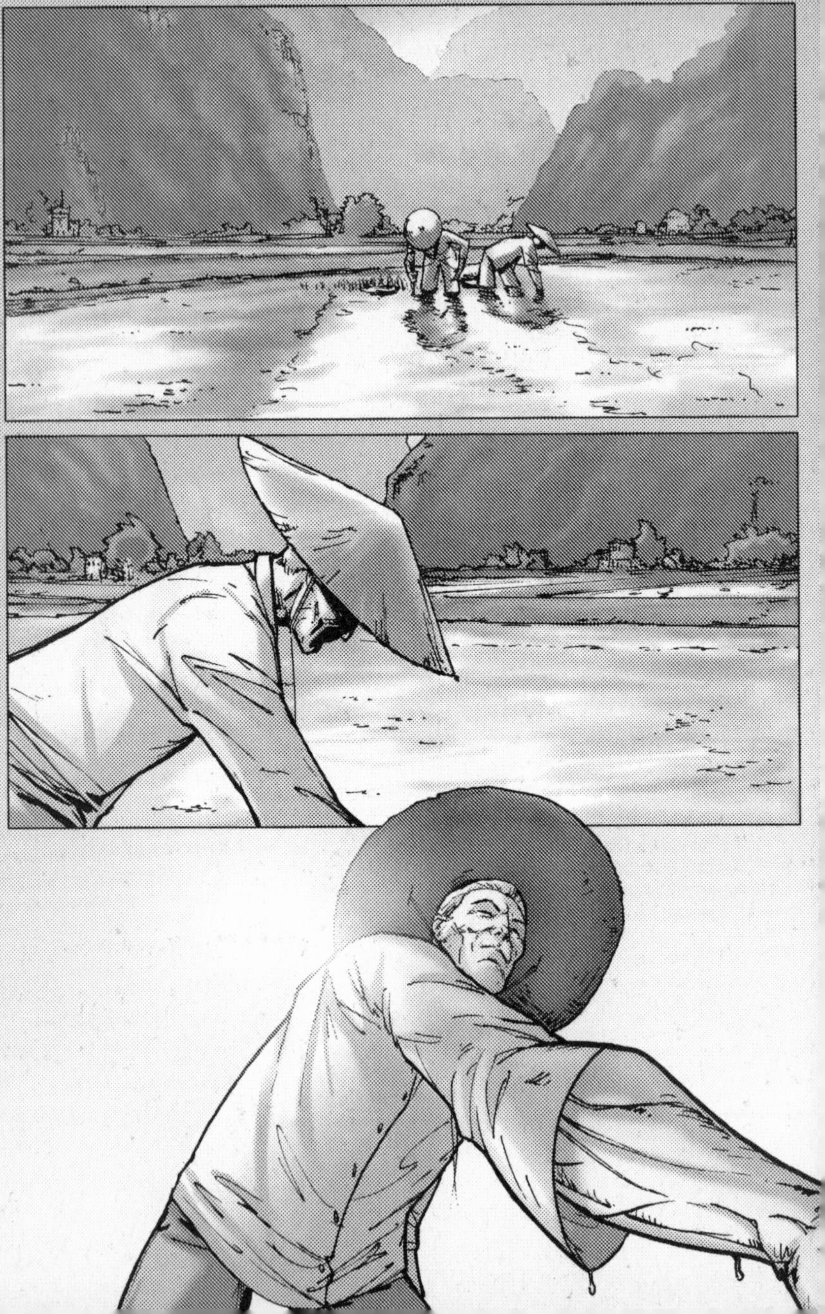

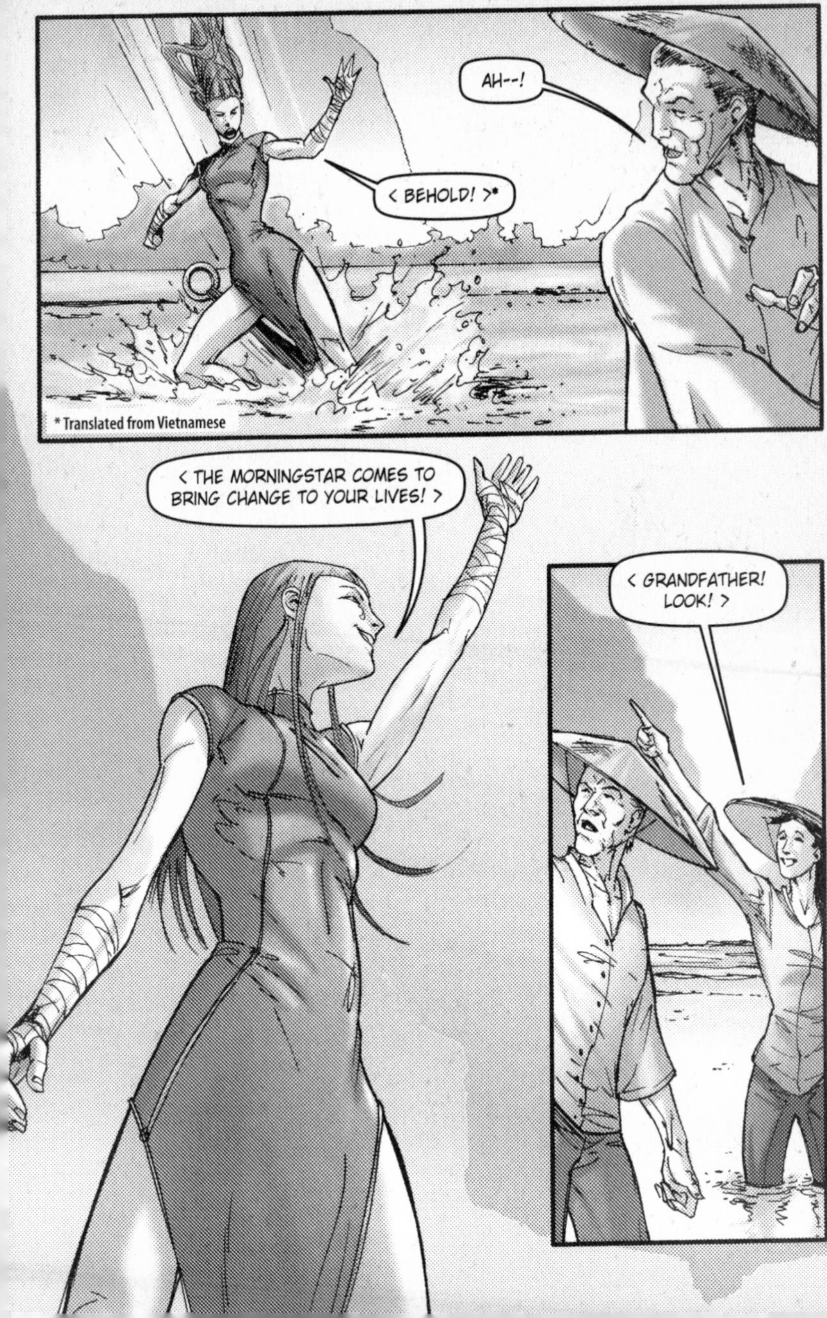
AH--!
< BEHOLD! >*
* Translated from Vietnamese
< THE MORNINGSTAR COMES TO BRING CHANGE TO YOUR LIVES! >
< GRANDFATHER! LOOK! >

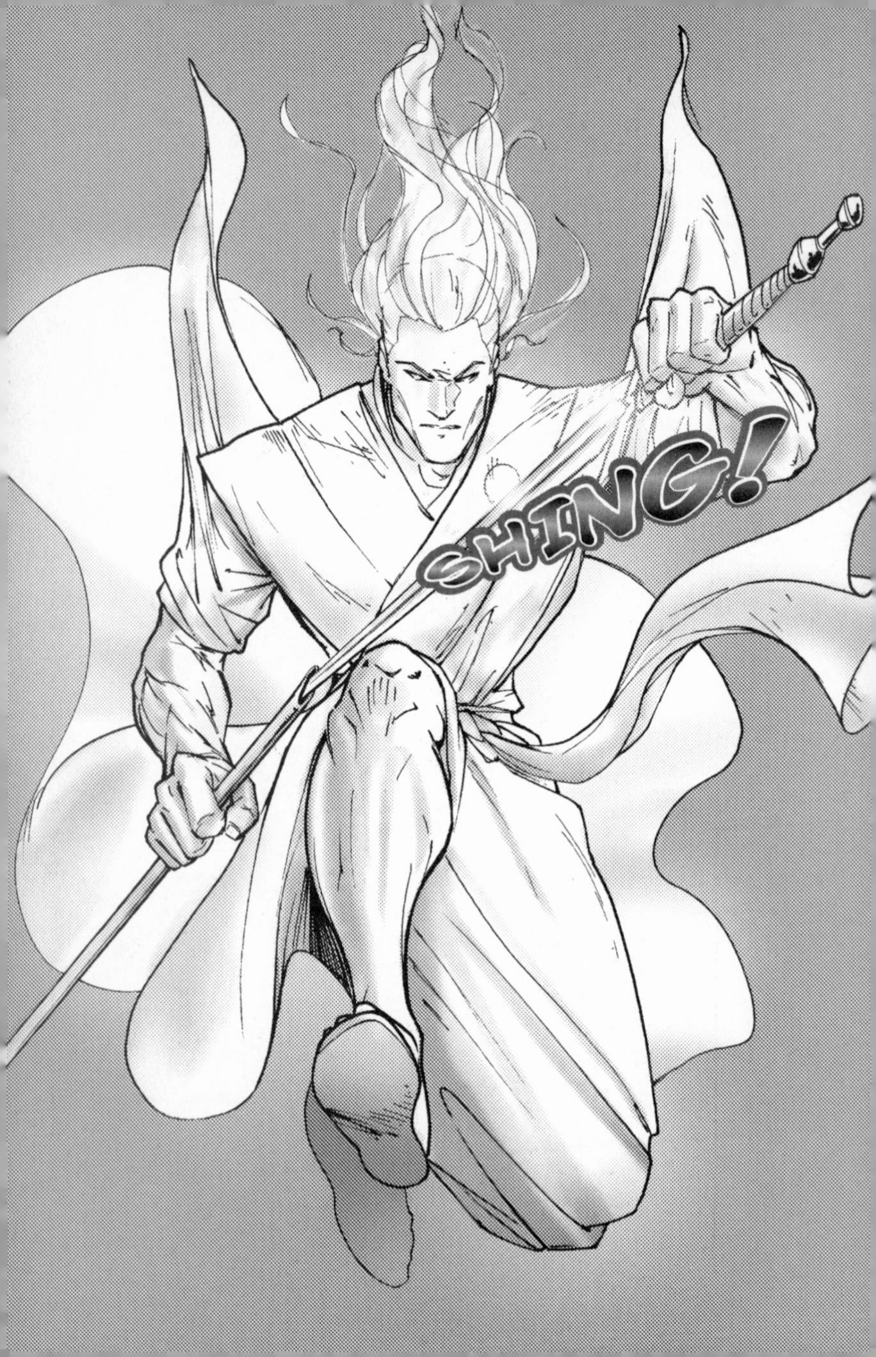
SHING!

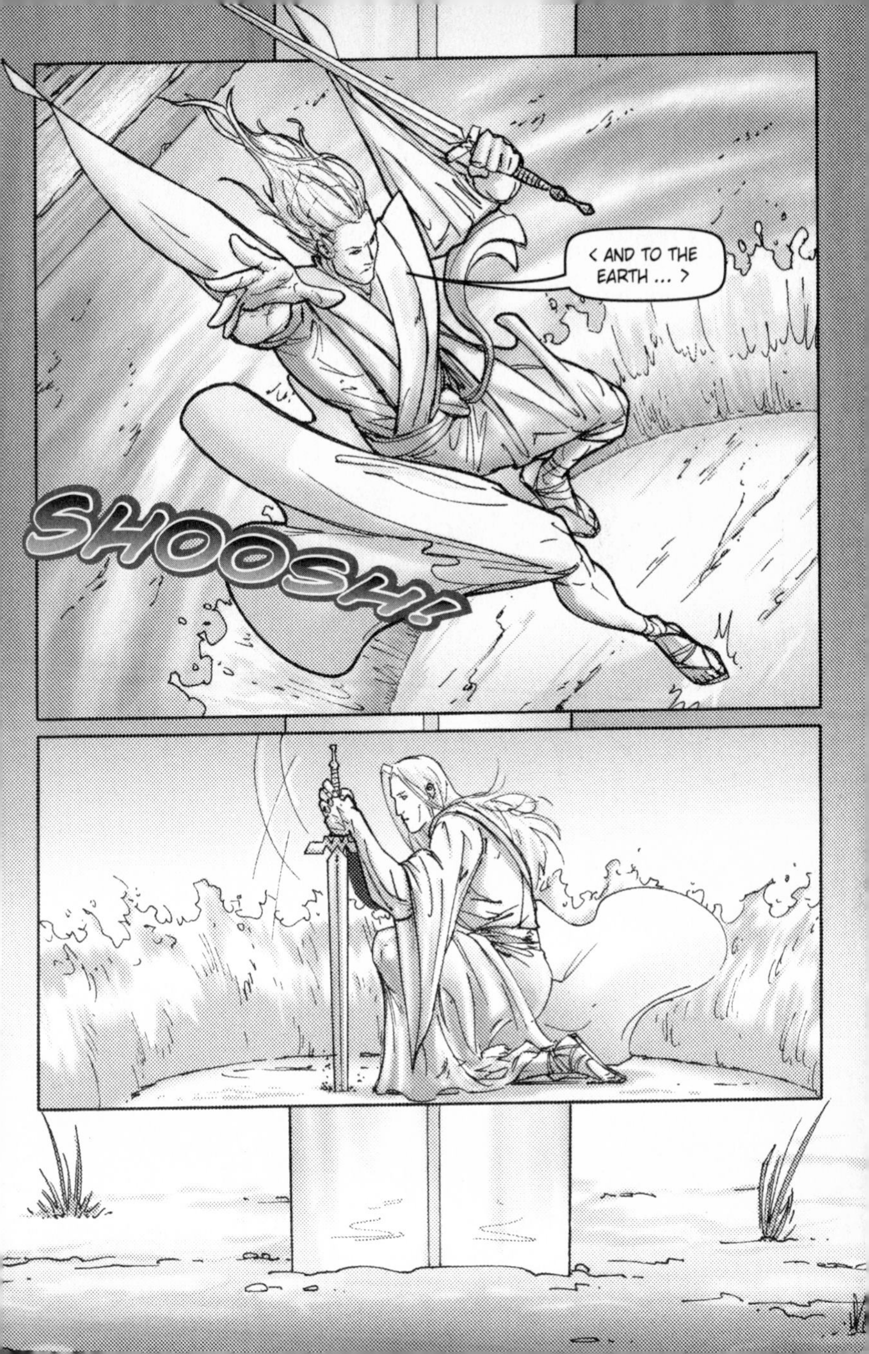
< AND TO THE EARTH ... >
SHOOSH!

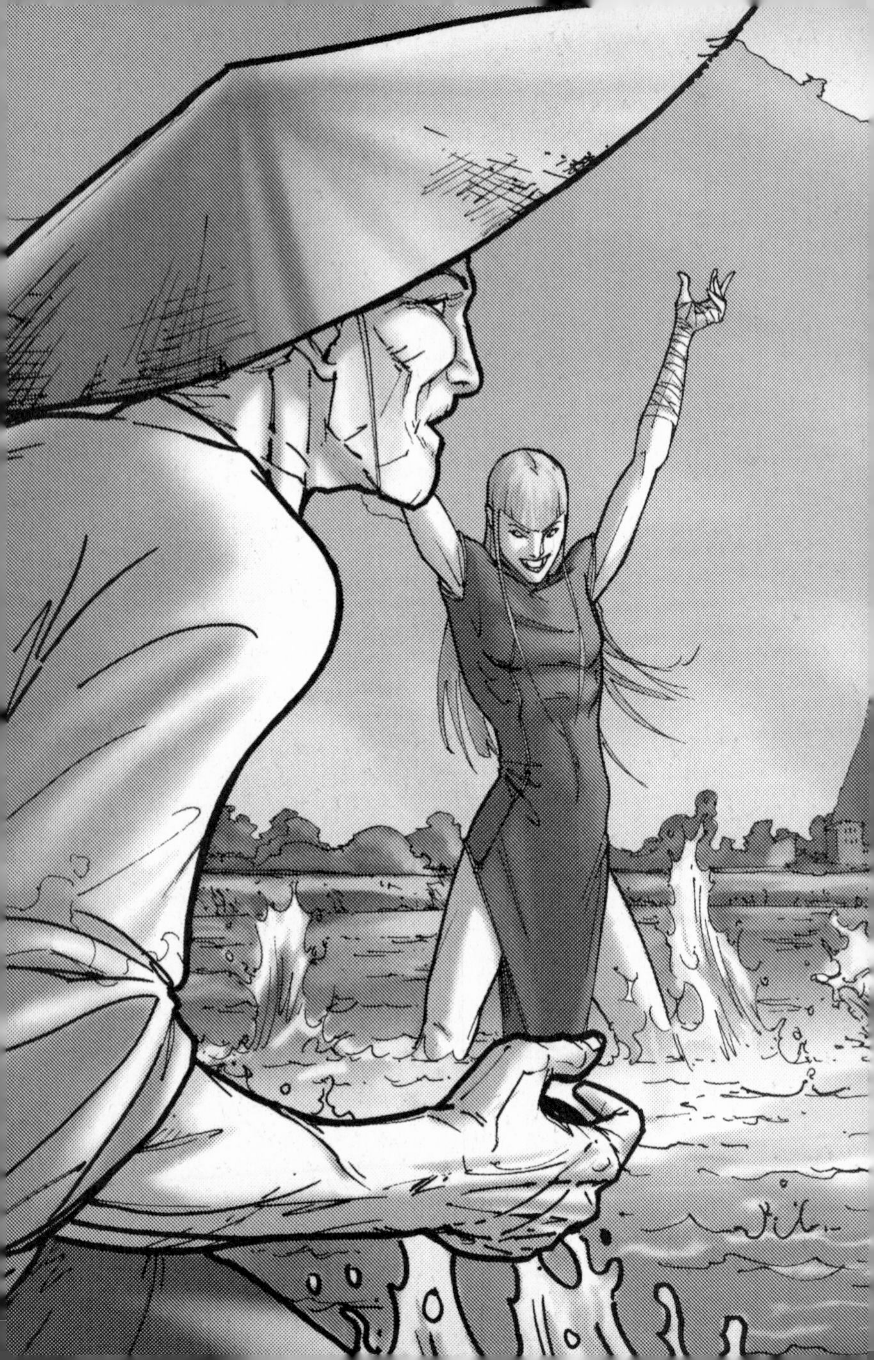

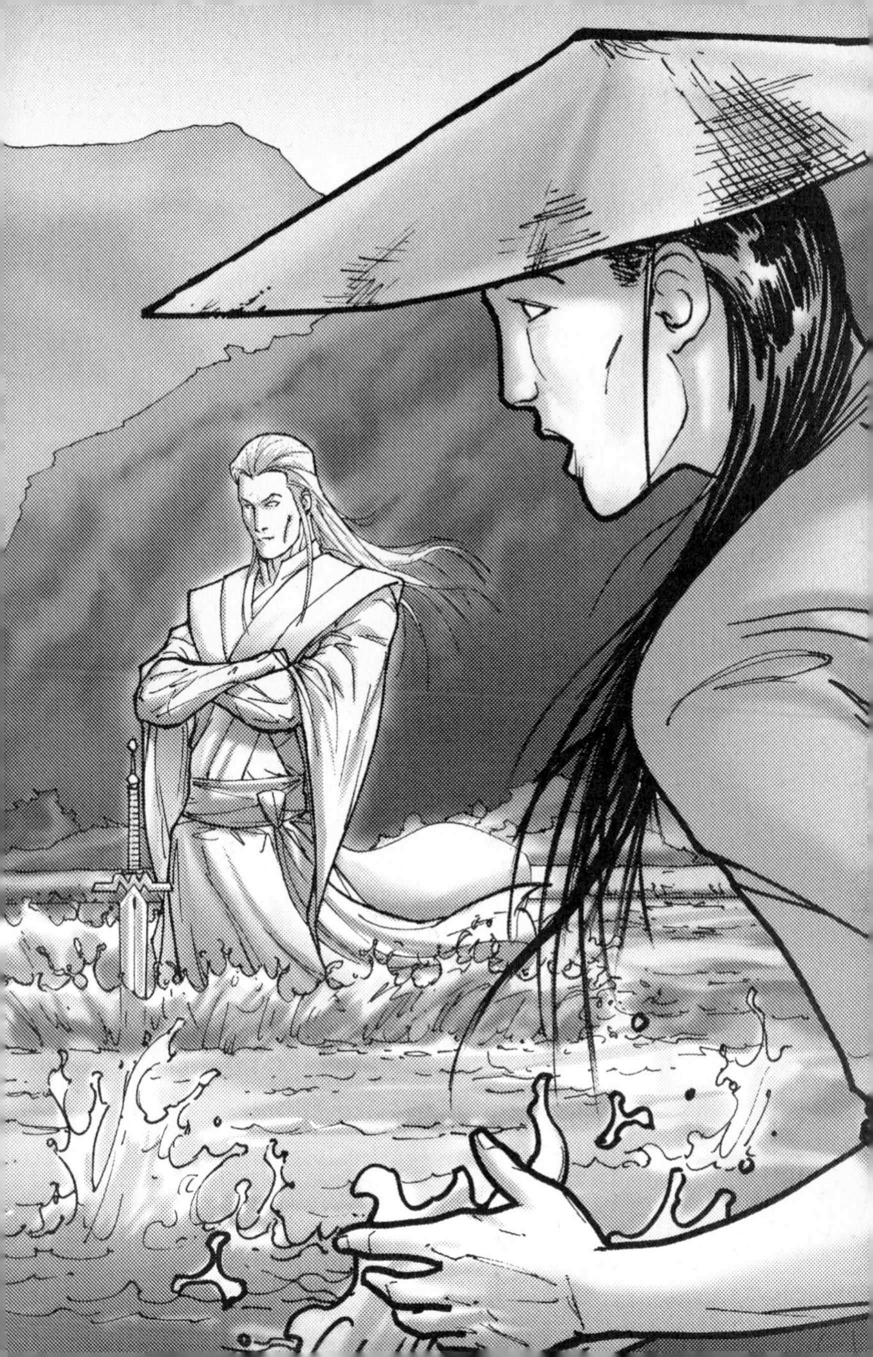

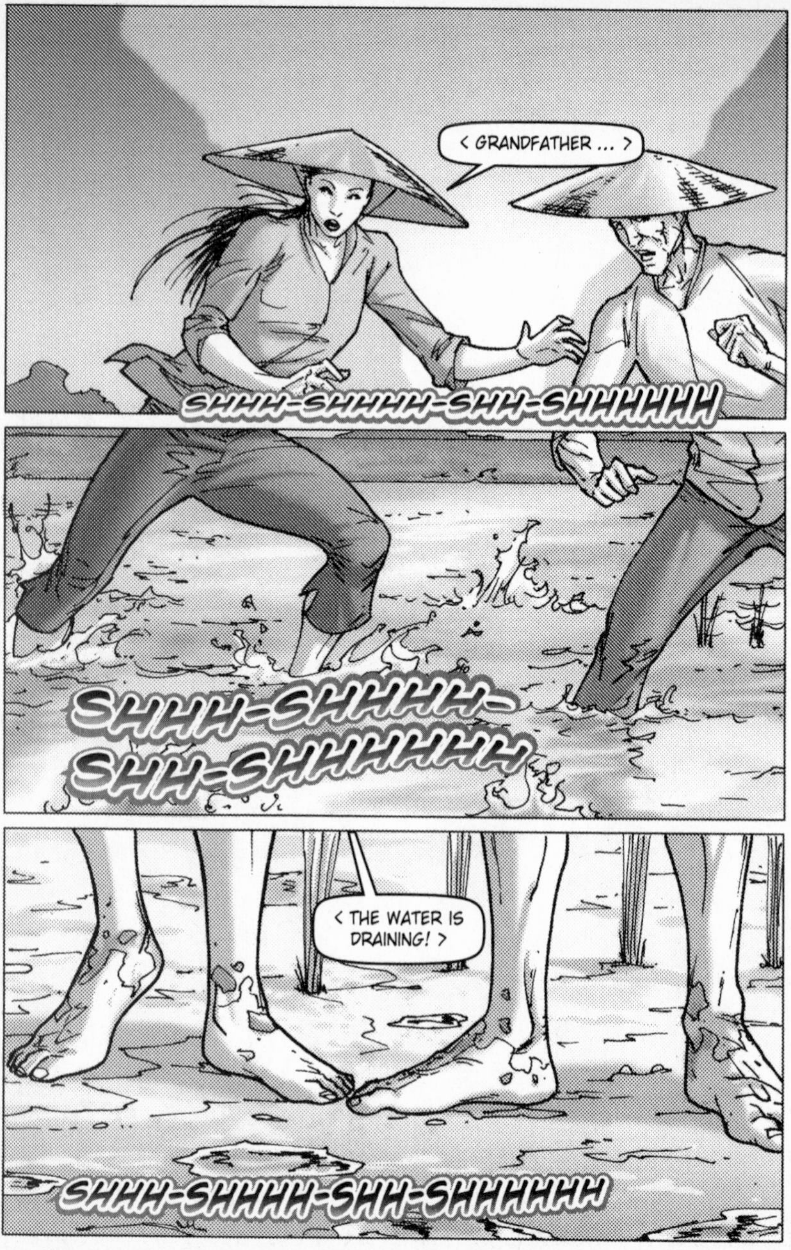
< GRANDFATHER ... >
SHHH-SHHHH-SHH-SHHHHHH
SHHH-SHHHH-
SHH-SHHHHHH
< THE WATER IS DRAINING! >
SHHH-SHHHH-SHH-SHHHHHH

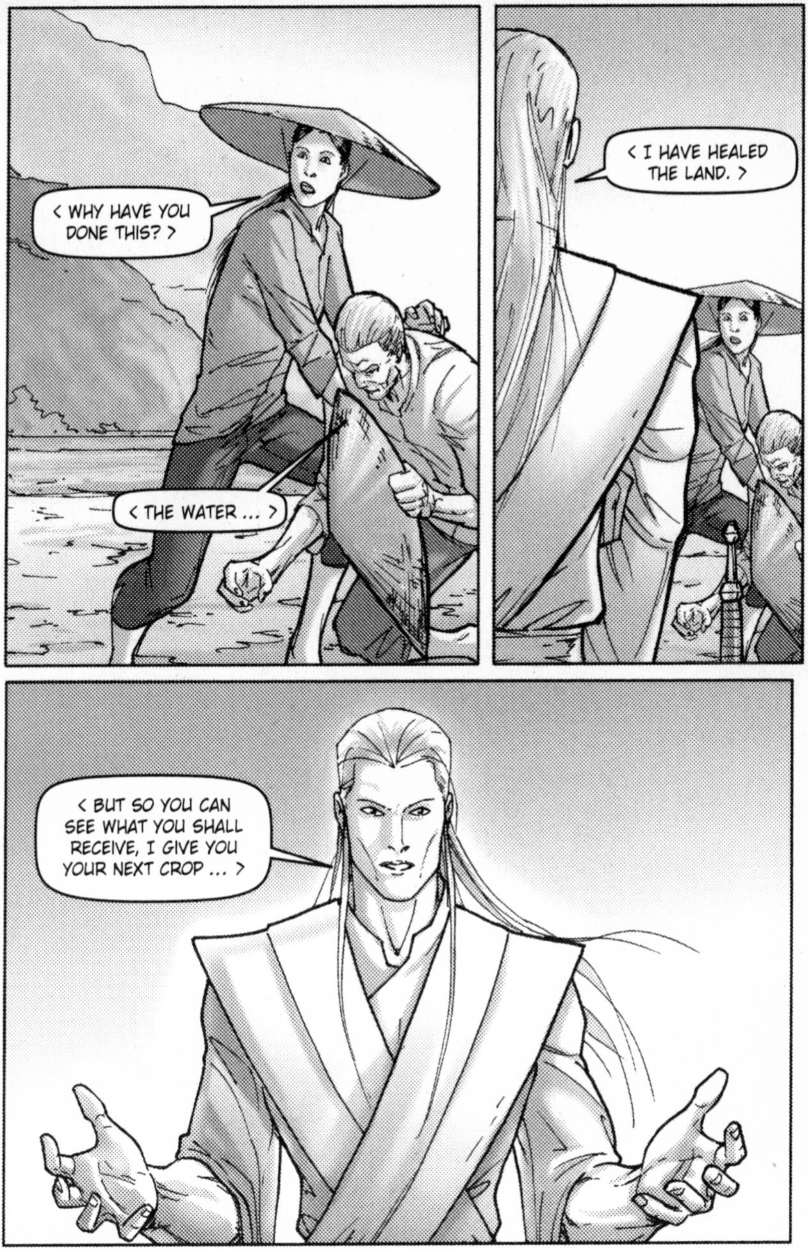
< WHY HAVE YOU DONE THIS? >
< THE WATER ... >
< I HAVE HEALED THE LAND. >
< BUT SO YOU CAN SEE WHAT YOU SHALL RECEIVE, I GIVE YOU YOUR NEXT CROP ... >

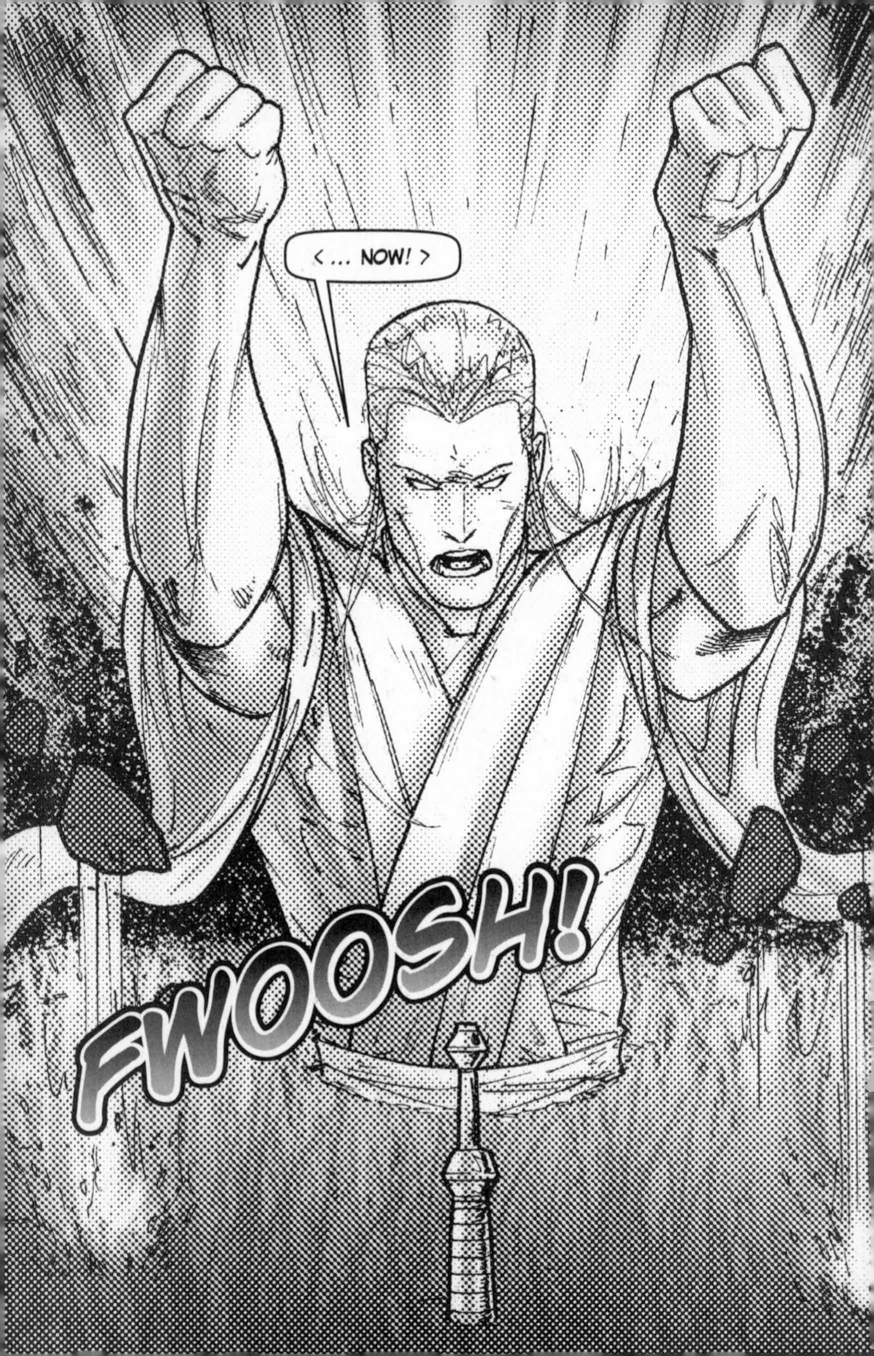
< ... NOW! >
FWOOSH!

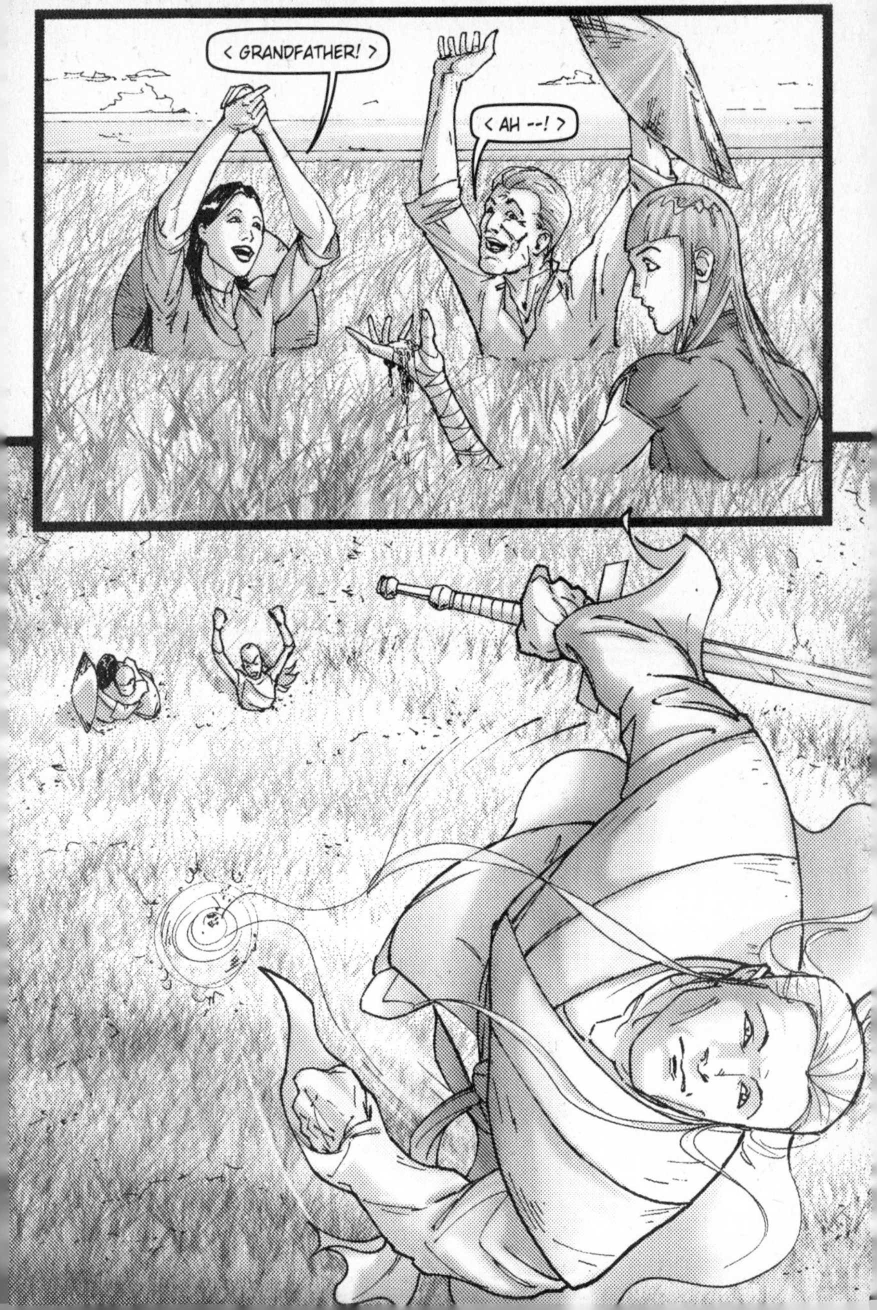
< GRANDFATHER! >
< AH --! >

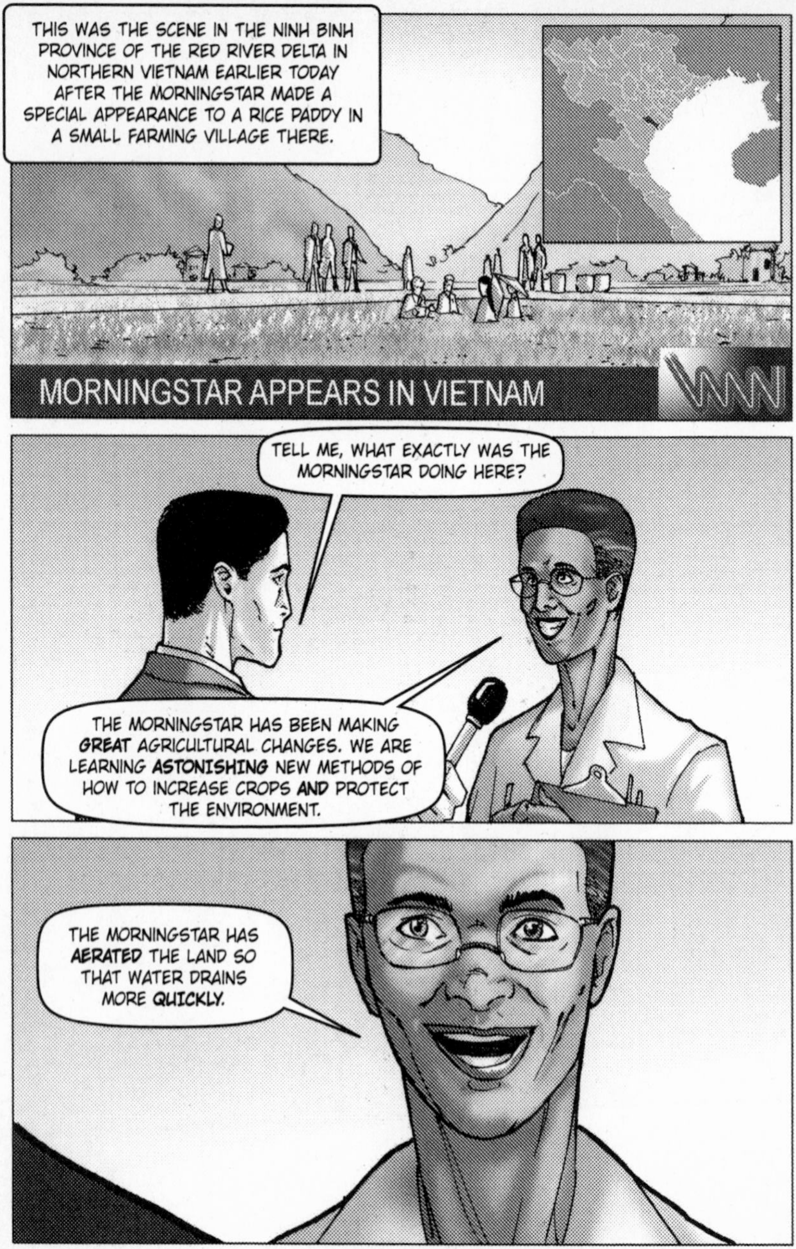
THIS WAS THE SCENE IN THE NINH BINH PROVINCE OF THE RED RIVER DELTA IN NORTHERN VIETNAM EARLIER TODAY AFTER THE MORNINGSTAR MADE A SPECIAL APPEARANCE TO A RICE PADDY IN A SMALL FARMING VILLAGE THERE.
MORNINGSTAR APPEARS IN VIETNAM
TELL ME, WHAT EXACTLY WAS THE MORNINGSTAR DOING HERE?
THE MORNINGSTAR HAS BEEN MAKING **GREAT** AGRICULTURAL CHANGES. WE ARE LEARNING **ASTONISHING** NEW METHODS OF HOW TO INCREASE CROPS **AND** PROTECT THE ENVIRONMENT.
THE MORNINGSTAR HAS **AERATED** THE LAND SO THAT WATER DRAINS MORE **QUICKLY**.

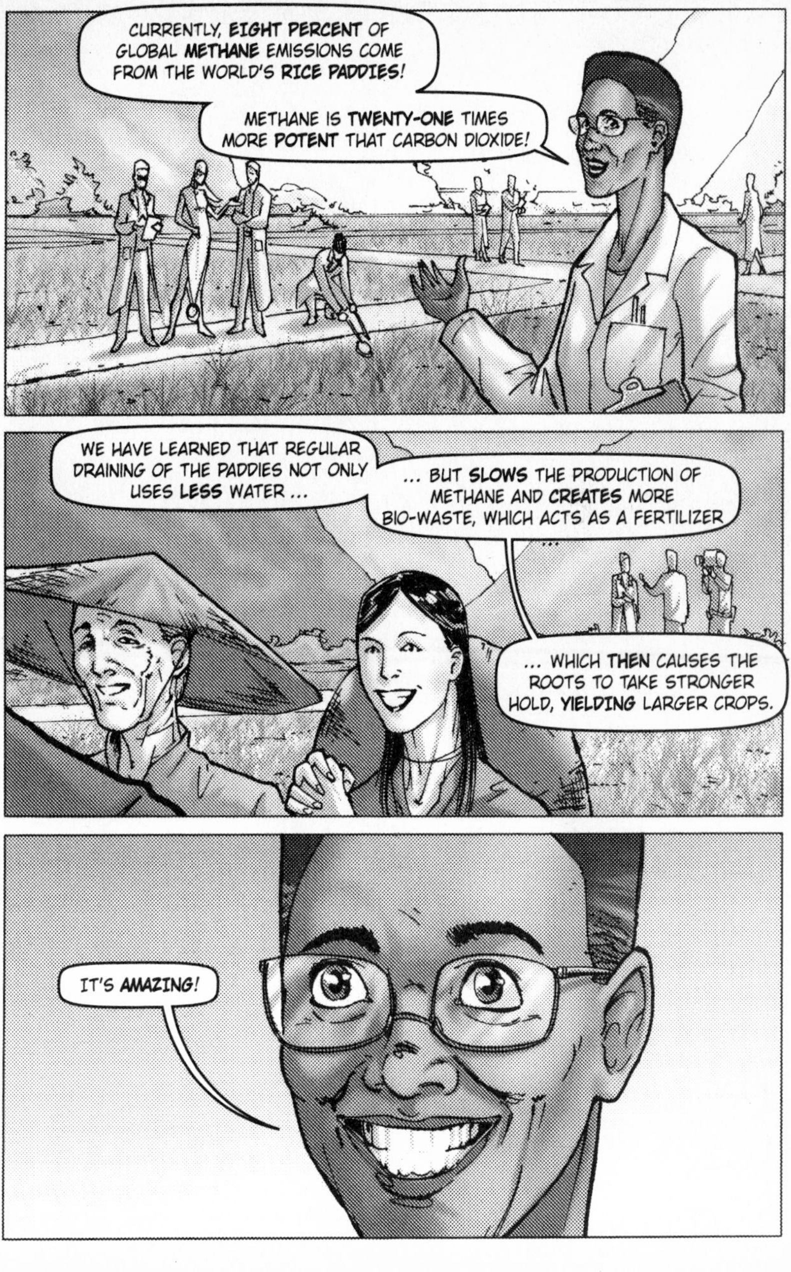
CURRENTLY, EIGHT PERCENT OF GLOBAL METHANE EMISSIONS COME FROM THE WORLD'S RICE PADDIES!
METHANE IS TWENTY-ONE TIMES MORE POTENT THAT CARBON DIOXIDE!
WE HAVE LEARNED THAT REGULAR DRAINING OF THE PADDIES NOT ONLY USES LESS WATER ...
... BUT SLOWS THE PRODUCTION OF METHANE AND CREATES MORE BIO-WASTE, WHICH ACTS AS A FERTILIZER ...
... WHICH THEN CAUSES THE ROOTS TO TAKE STRONGER HOLD, YIELDING LARGER CROPS.
IT'S AMAZING!

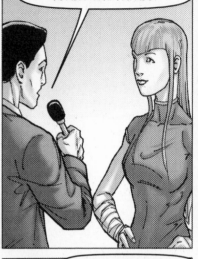

NOW, KWAN YIN WAS ALSO ON THE SCENE, AND WE HAVE HER HERE AS WELL.

KWAN YIN, IS IT TRUE THAT THE MORNINGSTAR'S ACTIONS HERE TODAY ARE BASED ON PREVIOUSLY RESEARCHED AGRICULTURAL FINDINGS?

YES, BUT **HE** MADE IT **HAPPEN!**

THE MORNINGSTAR INTENDS TO **ELIMINATE** FAMINE AND HUNGER!

THIS IS HOWARD PHAN REPORTING FROM THE RED RIVER DELTA IN VIETNAM.

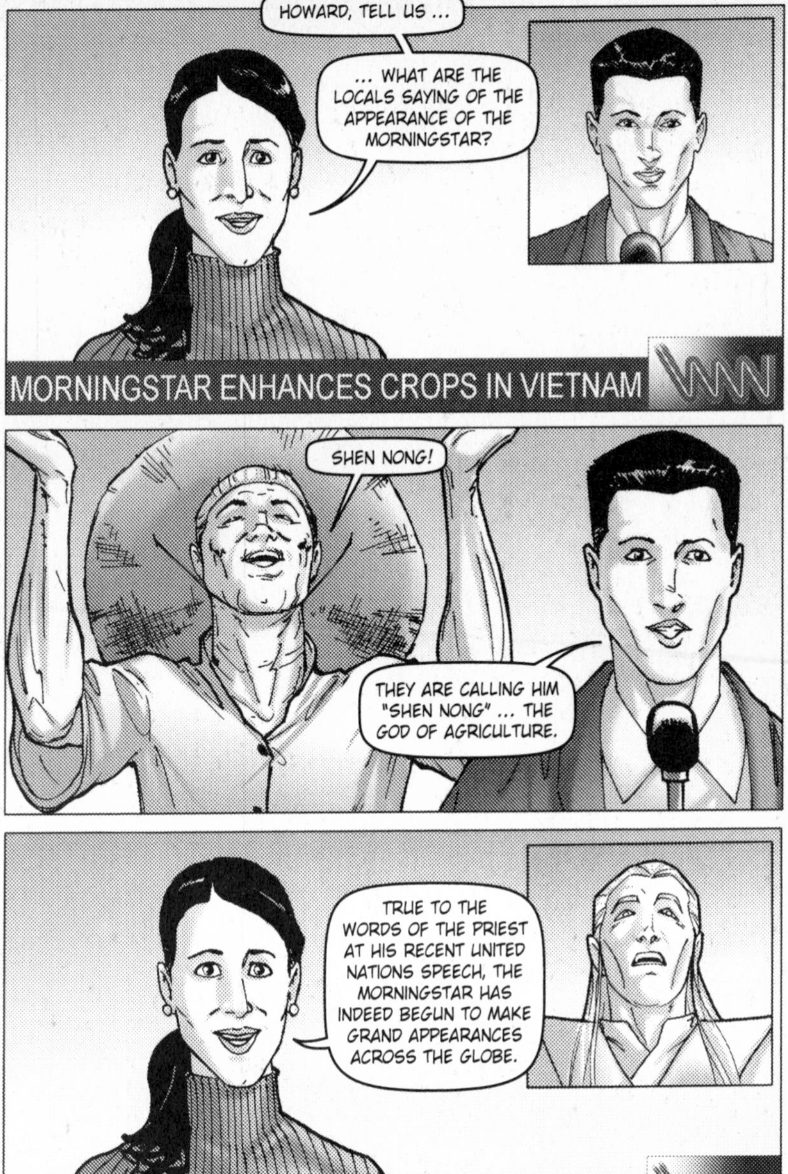
HOWARD, TELL US ...
... WHAT ARE THE LOCALS SAYING OF THE APPEARANCE OF THE MORNINGSTAR?
MORNINGSTAR ENHANCES CROPS IN VIETNAM
SHEN NONG!
THEY ARE CALLING HIM "SHEN NONG" ... THE GOD OF AGRICULTURE.
TRUE TO THE WORDS OF THE PRIEST AT HIS RECENT UNITED NATIONS SPEECH, THE MORNINGSTAR HAS INDEED BEGUN TO MAKE GRAND APPEARANCES ACROSS THE GLOBE.
MORNINGSTAR ENHANCES CROPS IN VIETNAM

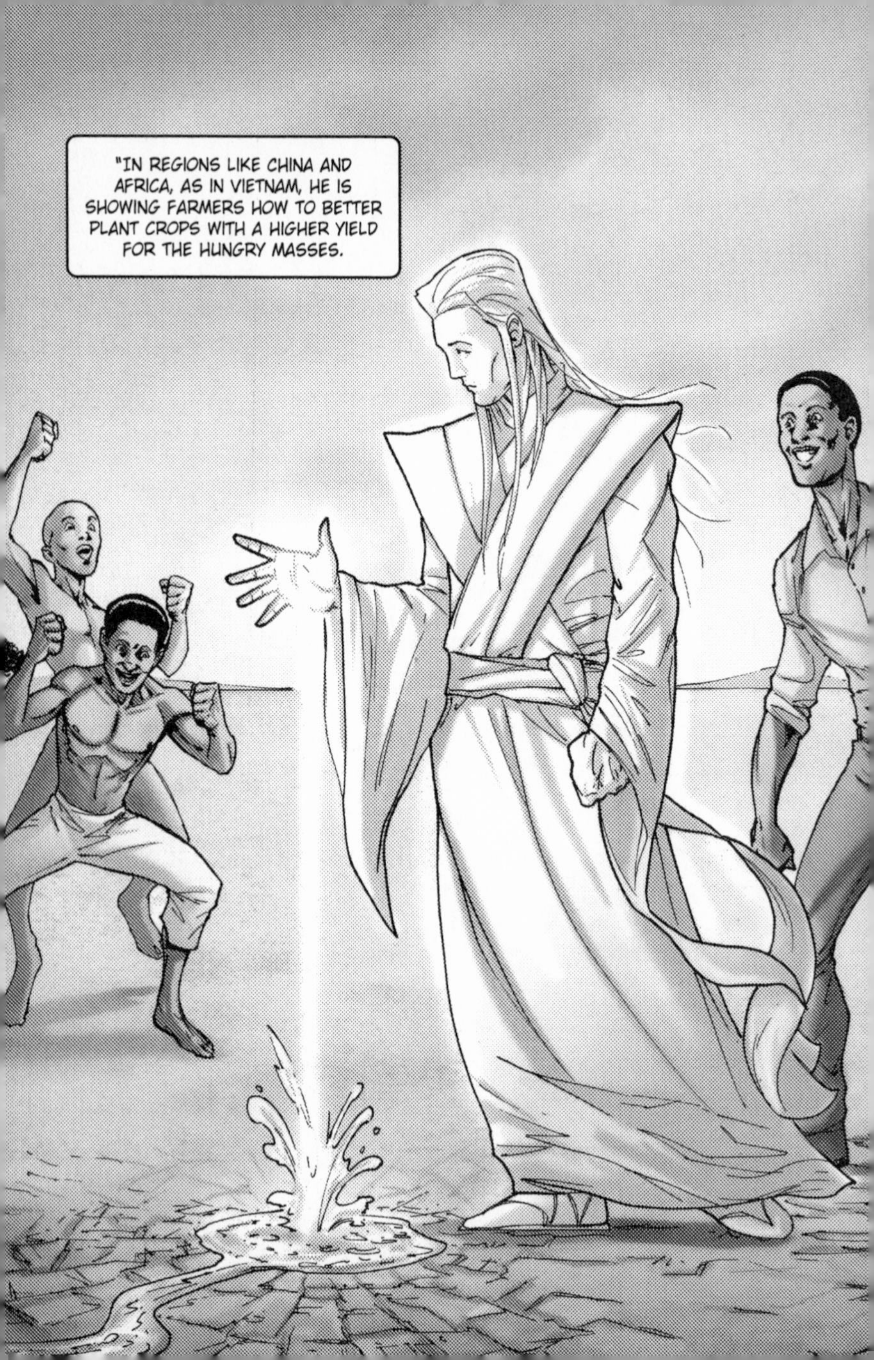
"IN REGIONS LIKE CHINA AND AFRICA, AS IN VIETNAM, HE IS SHOWING FARMERS HOW TO BETTER PLANT CROPS WITH A HIGHER YIELD FOR THE HUNGRY MASSES.

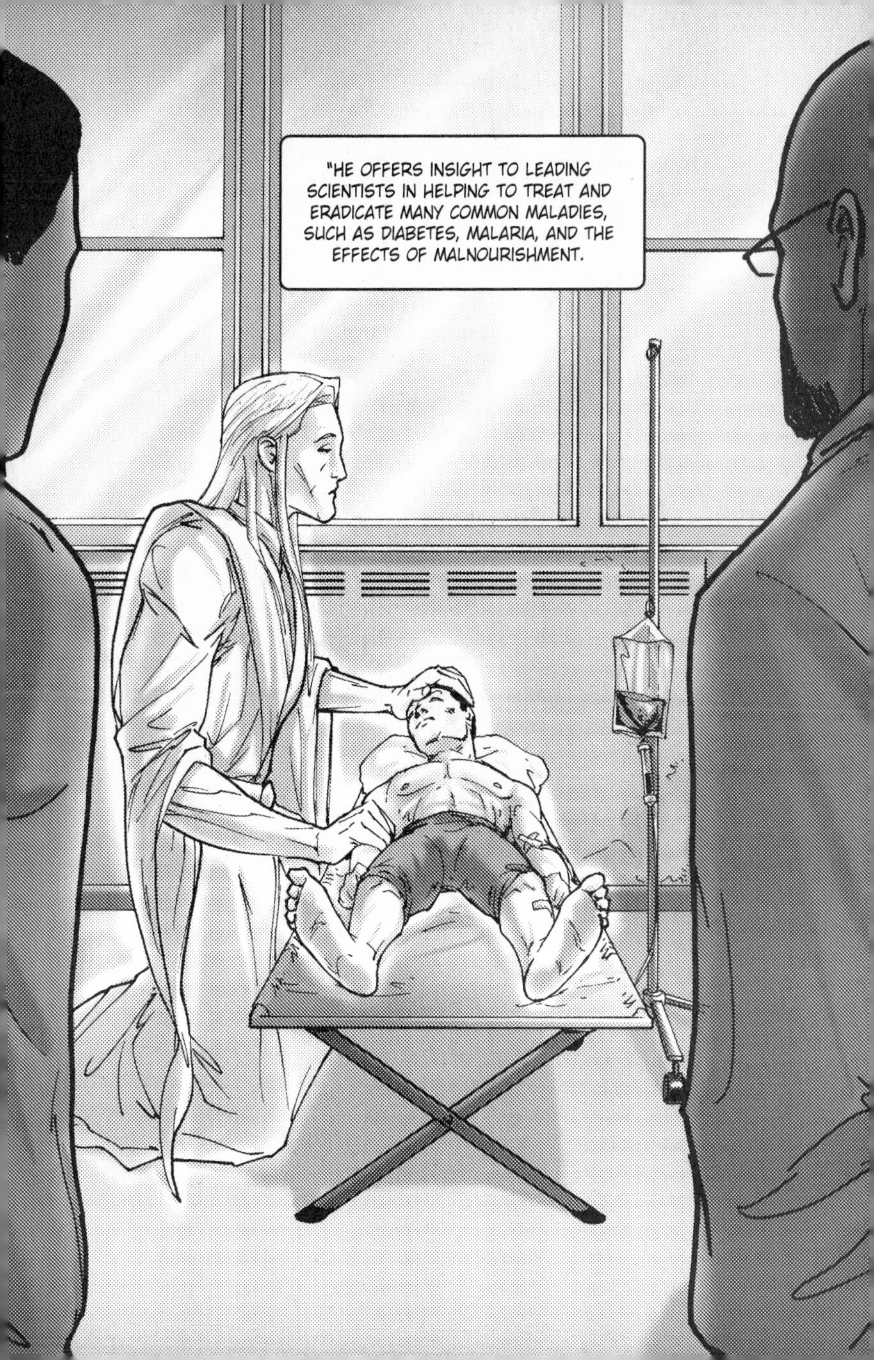
"HE OFFERS INSIGHT TO LEADING SCIENTISTS IN HELPING TO TREAT AND ERADICATE MANY COMMON MALADIES, SUCH AS DIABETES, MALARIA, AND THE EFFECTS OF MALNOURISHMENT.

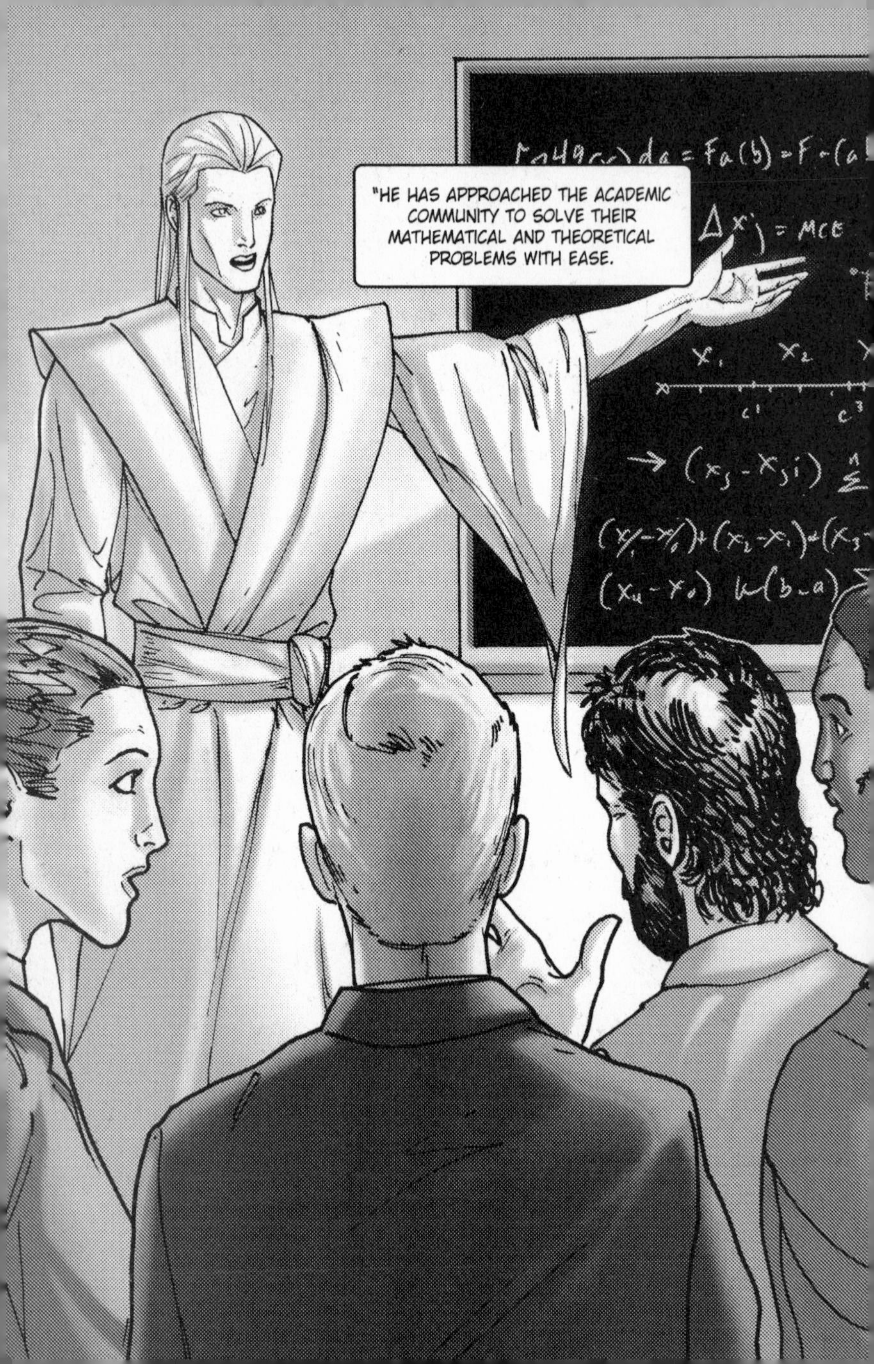
"HE HAS APPROACHED THE ACADEMIC COMMUNITY TO SOLVE THEIR MATHEMATICAL AND THEORETICAL PROBLEMS WITH EASE.

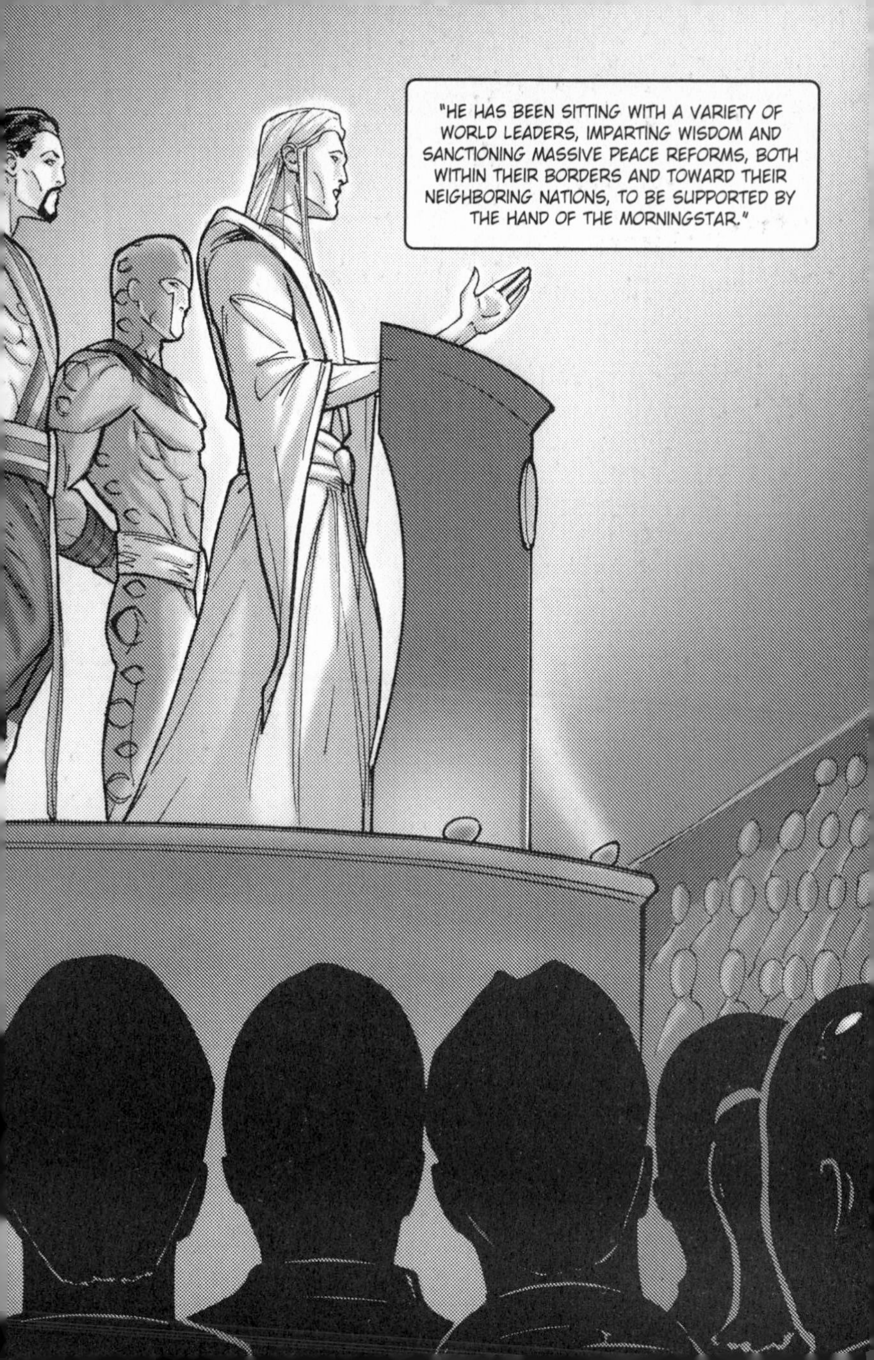
"HE HAS BEEN SITTING WITH A VARIETY OF WORLD LEADERS, IMPARTING WISDOM AND SANCTIONING MASSIVE PEACE REFORMS, BOTH WITHIN THEIR BORDERS AND TOWARD THEIR NEIGHBORING NATIONS, TO BE SUPPORTED BY THE HAND OF THE MORNINGSTAR."

THOUGH IT APPEARS THAT NOT **ALL** NATIONS HAVE EMBRACED THESE CHANGES WITH ENTHUSIASM.

MORNINGSTAR MAKES GLOBAL CHANGES

THE MORNINGSTAR PROPOSES GREAT CHANGES FOR OUR WORLD. HE SUGGESTS A UNIFYING BELIEF SYSTEM. HE HAS BEEN OF TREMENDOUS HELP TO THE THIRD WORLD.

HE HAS PLACED HIMSELF IN A LEADERSHIP ROLE OVER THE UNITED NATIONS, BUT ...

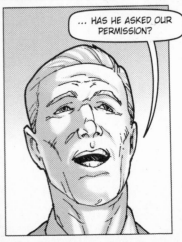

... HAS HE ASKED OUR PERMISSION?

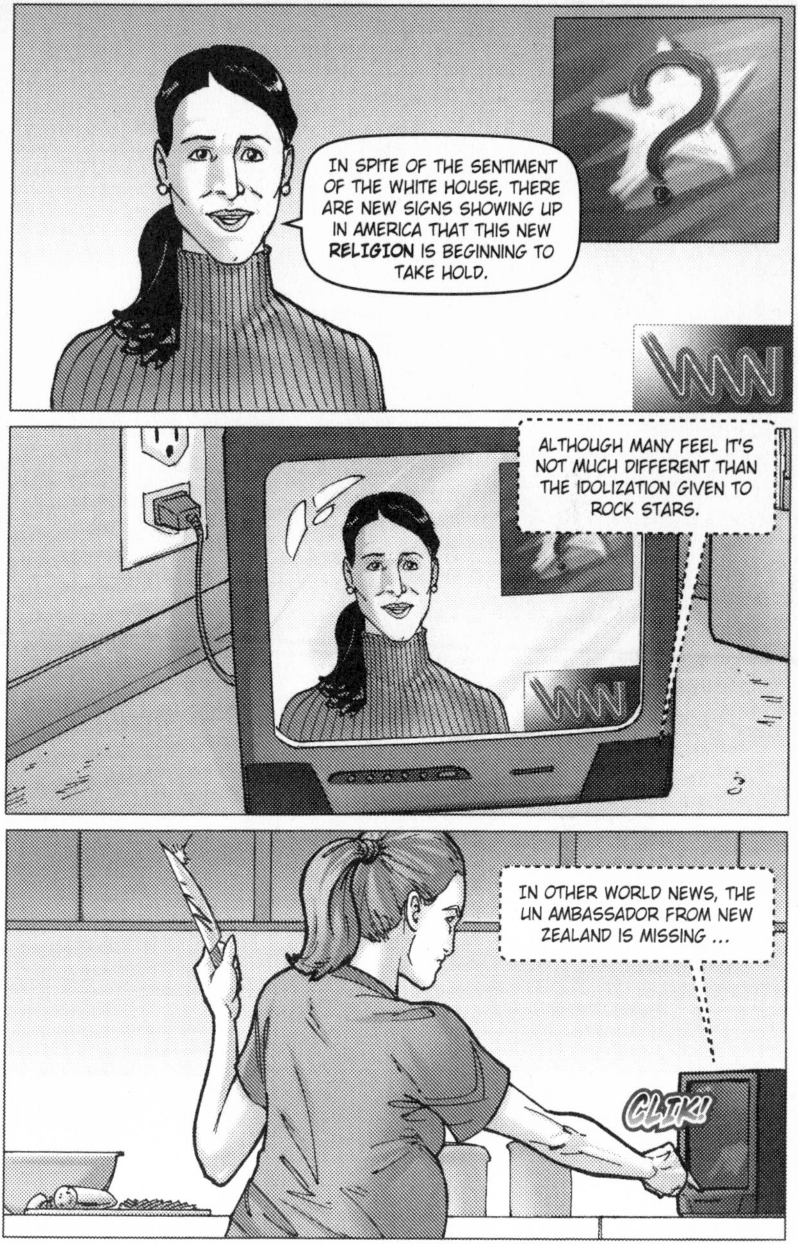
IN SPITE OF THE SENTIMENT OF THE WHITE HOUSE, THERE ARE NEW SIGNS SHOWING UP IN AMERICA THAT THIS NEW **RELIGION** IS BEGINNING TO TAKE HOLD.
ALTHOUGH MANY FEEL IT'S NOT MUCH DIFFERENT THAN THE IDOLIZATION GIVEN TO ROCK STARS.
IN OTHER WORLD NEWS, THE UN AMBASSADOR FROM NEW ZEALAND IS MISSING ...
CLIK!

SIGH ...

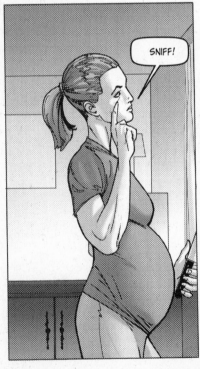

SNIFF!

SIGH ...
SNIFF!

CHOP-
CHOP--
CHOP

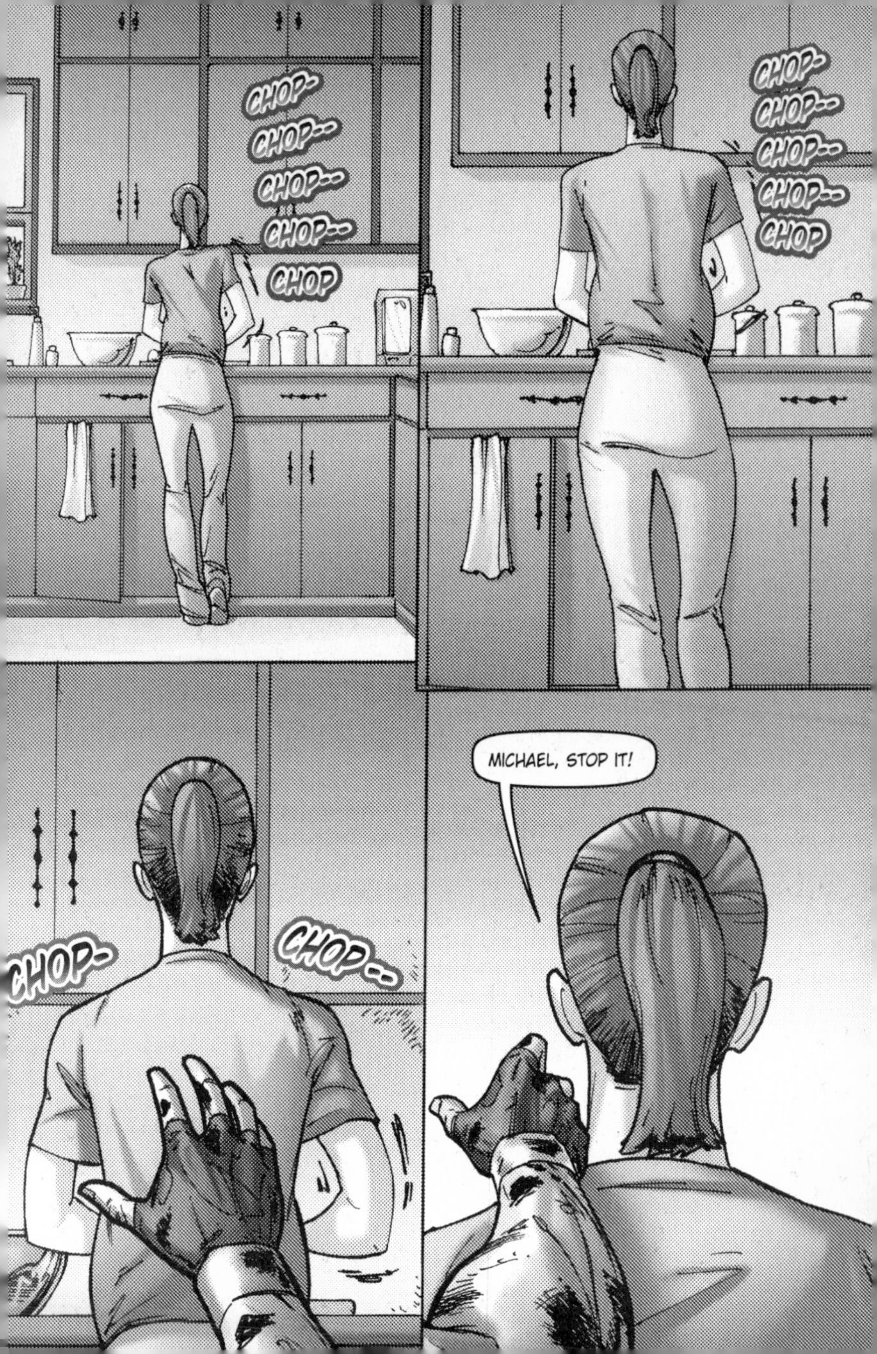
CHOP-
CHOP--
CHOP--
CHOP--
CHOP
CHOP-
CHOP--
CHOP--
CHOP--
CHOP
CHOP-
CHOP--
MICHAEL, STOP IT!

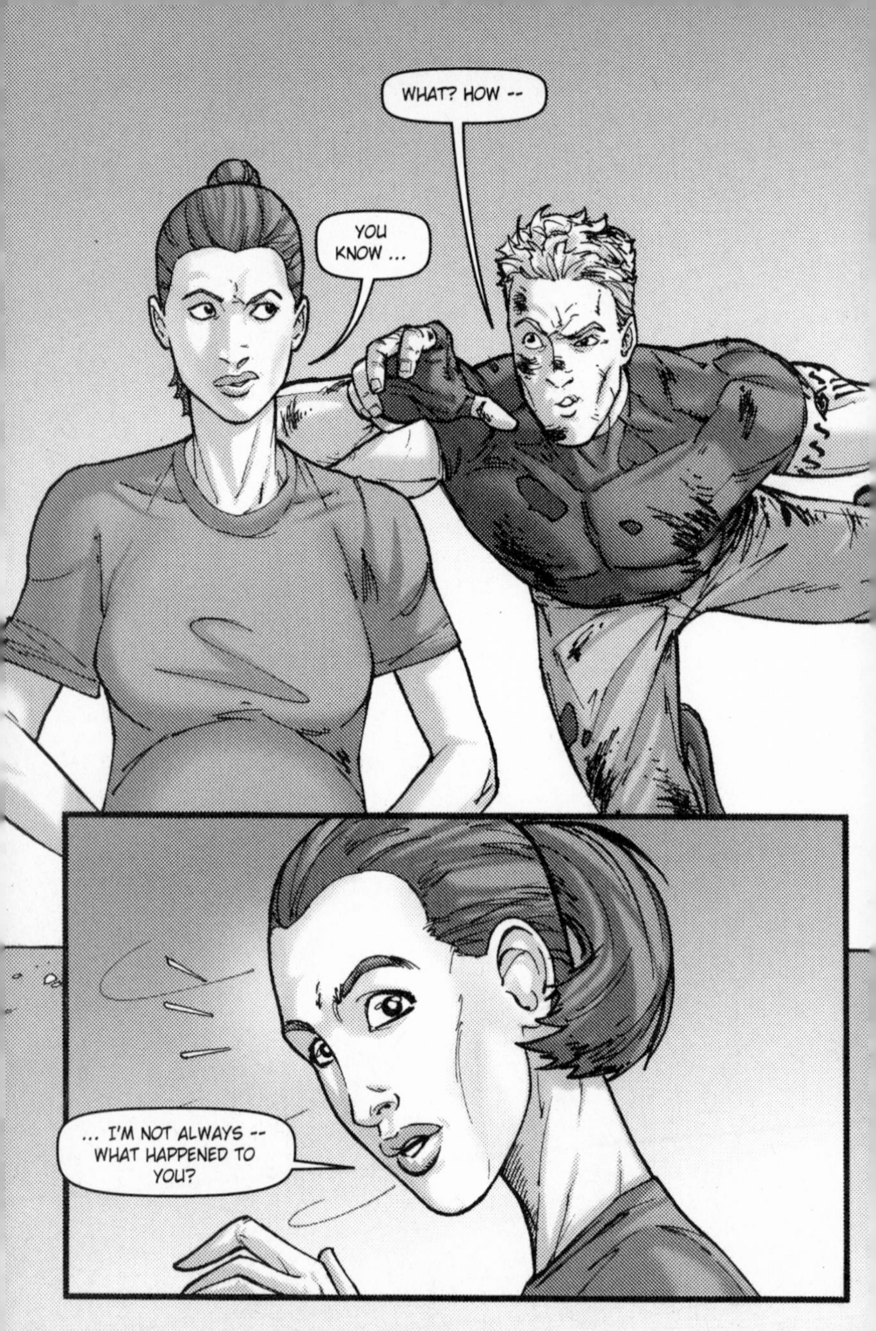
YOU KNOW ...
WHAT? HOW --
... I'M NOT ALWAYS -- WHAT HAPPENED TO YOU?

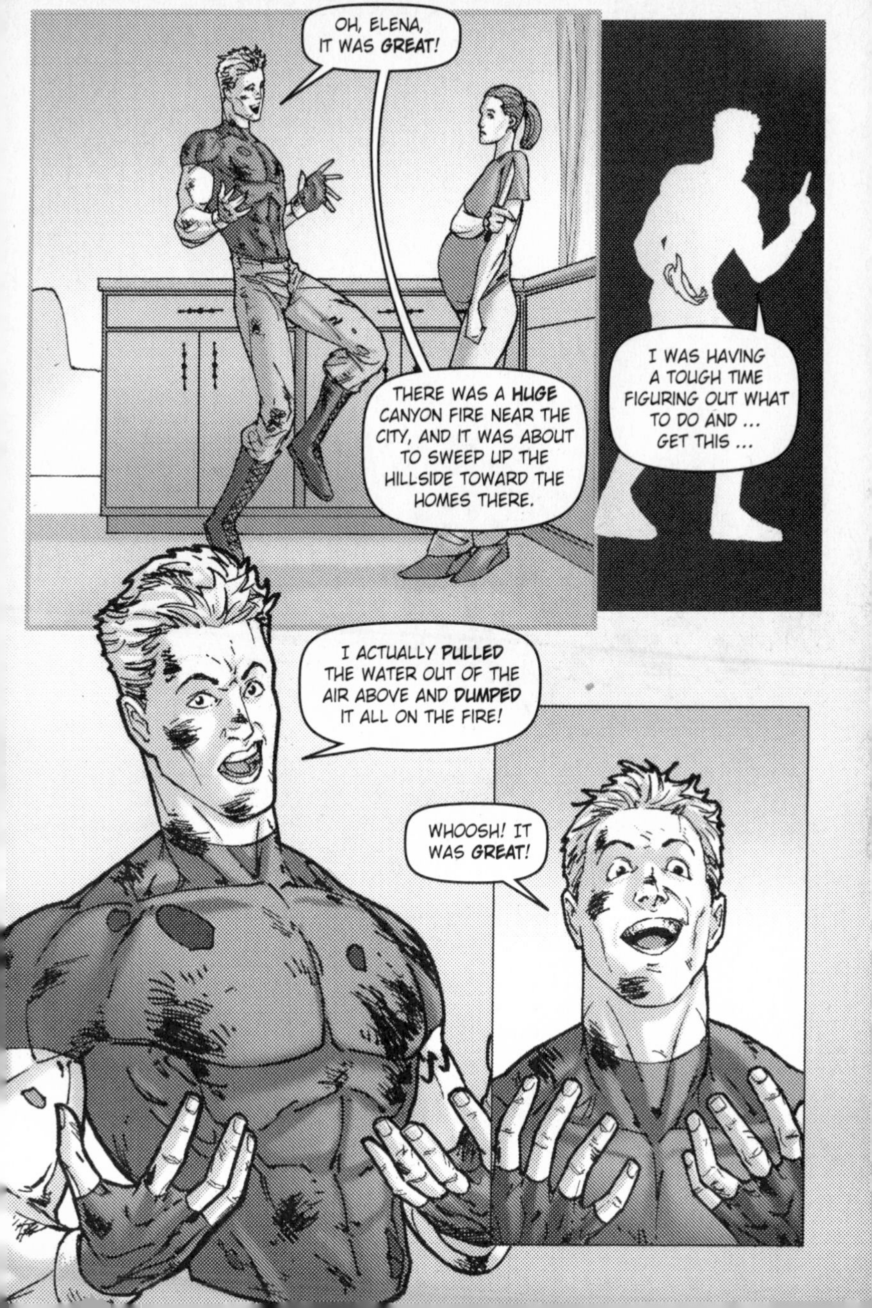
OH, ELENA, IT WAS **GREAT**!
THERE WAS A **HUGE** CANYON FIRE NEAR THE CITY, AND IT WAS ABOUT TO SWEEP UP THE HILLSIDE TOWARD THE HOMES THERE.
I WAS HAVING A TOUGH TIME FIGURING OUT WHAT TO DO AND ... GET THIS ...
I ACTUALLY **PULLED** THE WATER OUT OF THE AIR ABOVE AND **DUMPED** IT ALL ON THE FIRE!
WHOOSH! IT WAS **GREAT**!

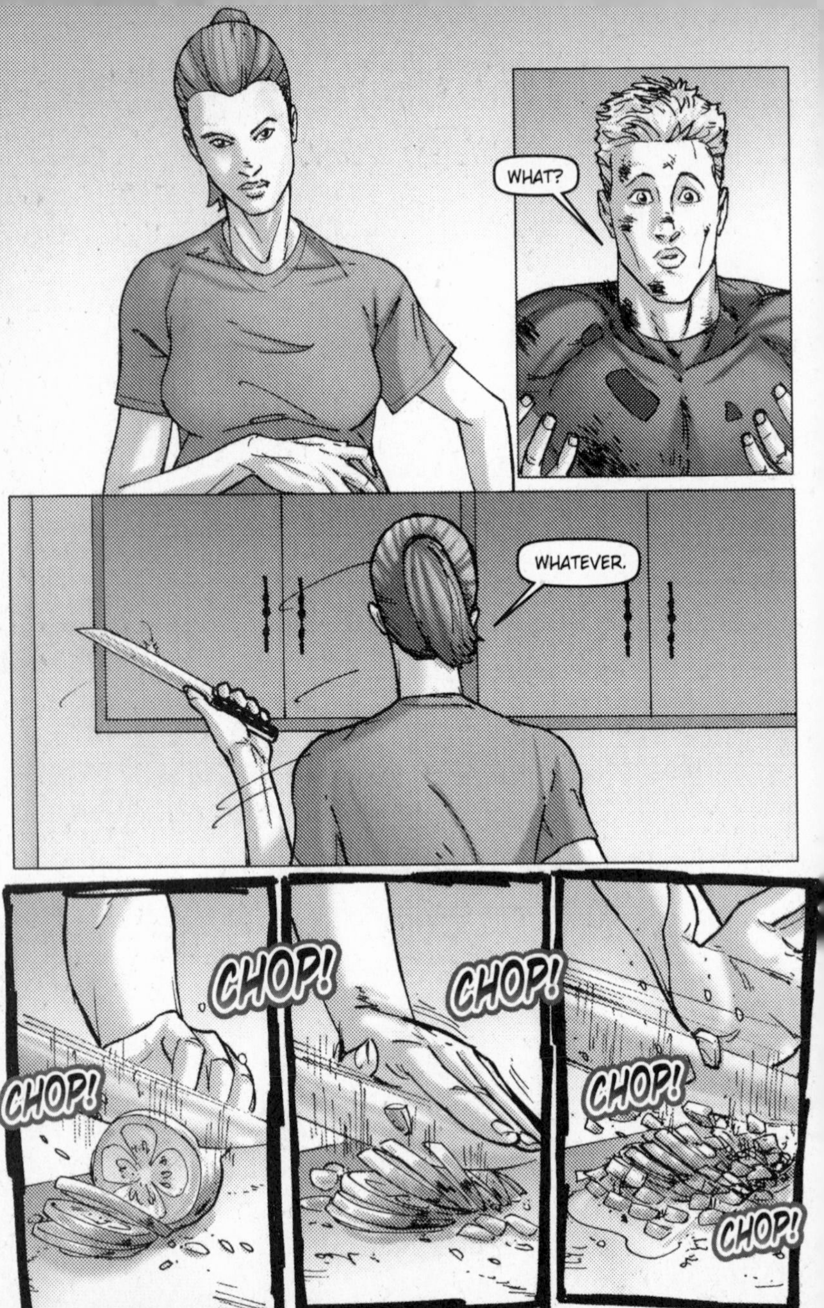
WHAT?
WHATEVER.
CHOP!
CHOP!
CHOP!
CHOP!
CHOP!
CHOP!

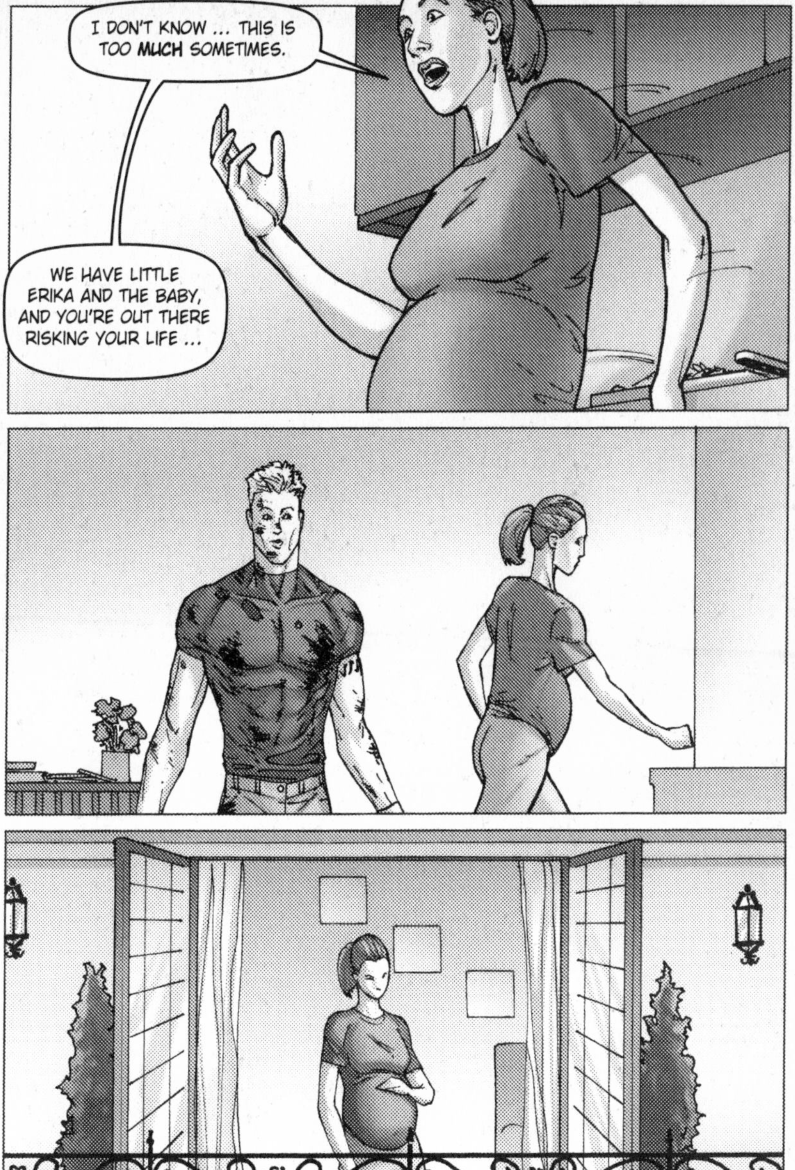
I DON'T KNOW ... THIS IS TOO **MUCH** SOMETIMES.
WE HAVE LITTLE ERIKA AND THE BABY, AND YOU'RE OUT THERE RISKING YOUR LIFE ...

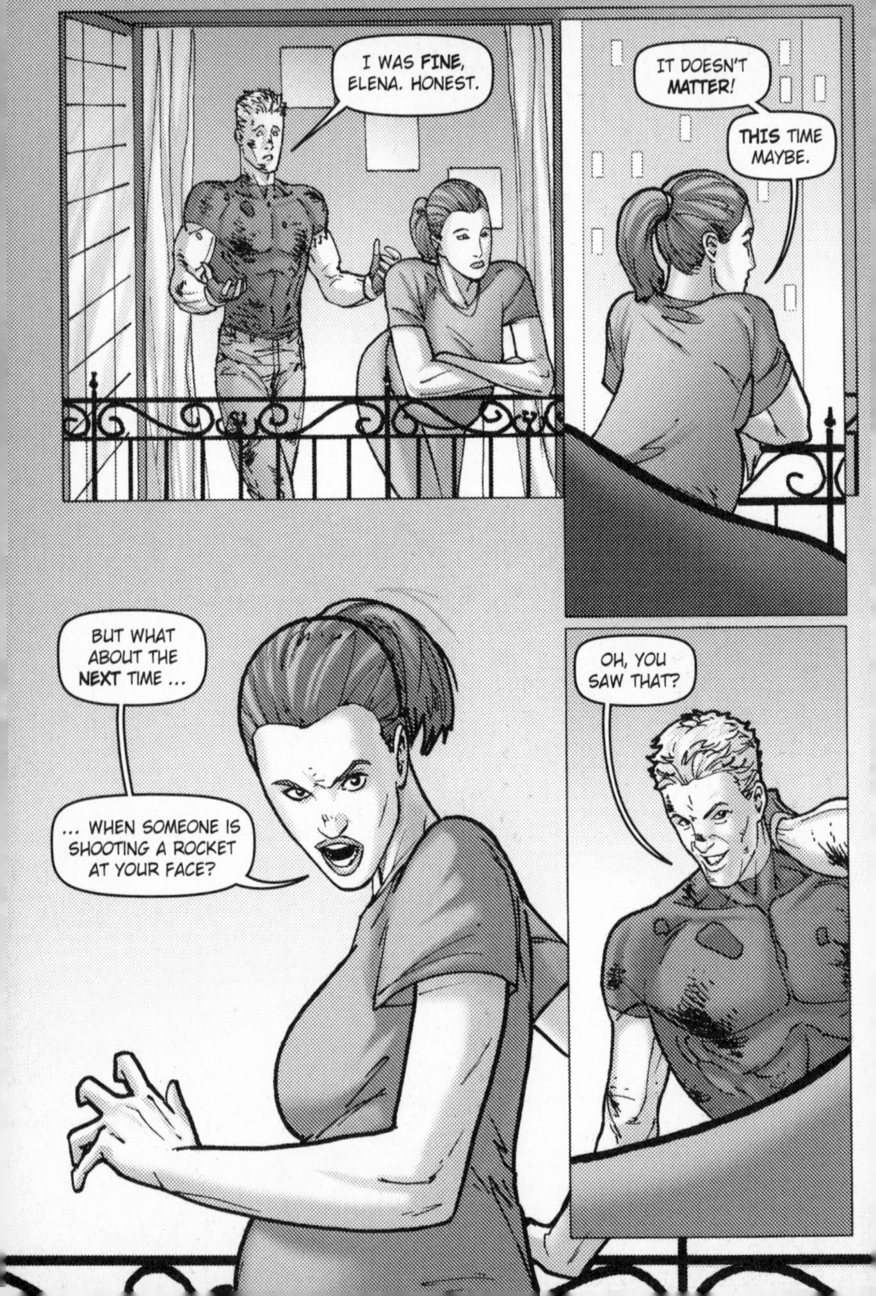
I WAS FINE, ELENA. HONEST.
IT DOESN'T MATTER!
THIS TIME MAYBE.
BUT WHAT ABOUT THE NEXT TIME ...
... WHEN SOMEONE IS SHOOTING A ROCKET AT YOUR FACE?
OH, YOU SAW THAT?

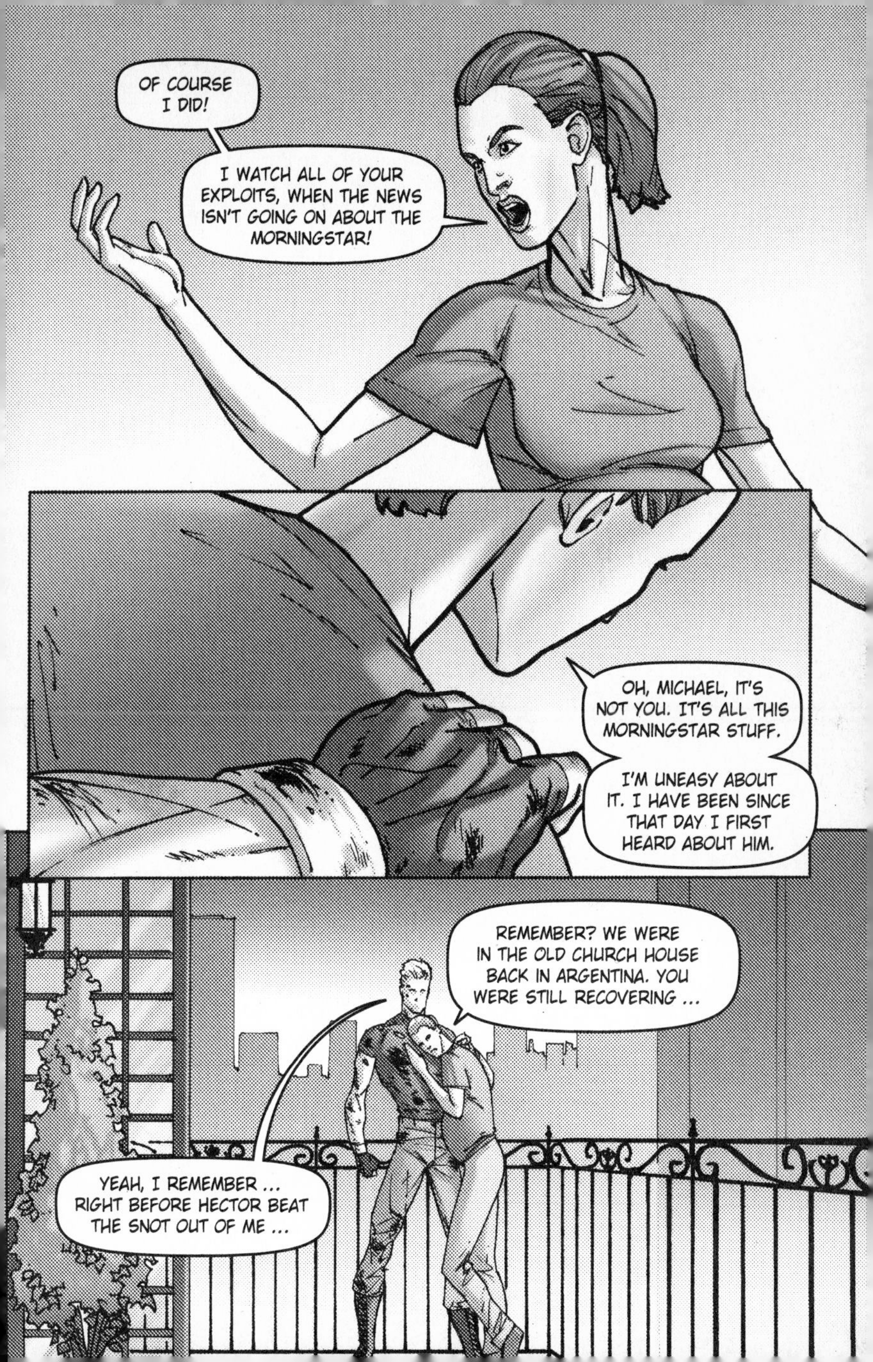
OF COURSE I DID!
I WATCH ALL OF YOUR EXPLOITS, WHEN THE NEWS ISN'T GOING ON ABOUT THE MORNINGSTAR!
OH, MICHAEL, IT'S NOT YOU. IT'S ALL THIS MORNINGSTAR STUFF.
I'M UNEASY ABOUT IT. I HAVE BEEN SINCE THAT DAY I FIRST HEARD ABOUT HIM.
YEAH, I REMEMBER ... RIGHT BEFORE HECTOR BEAT THE SNOT OUT OF ME ...
REMEMBER? WE WERE IN THE OLD CHURCH HOUSE BACK IN ARGENTINA. YOU WERE STILL RECOVERING ...

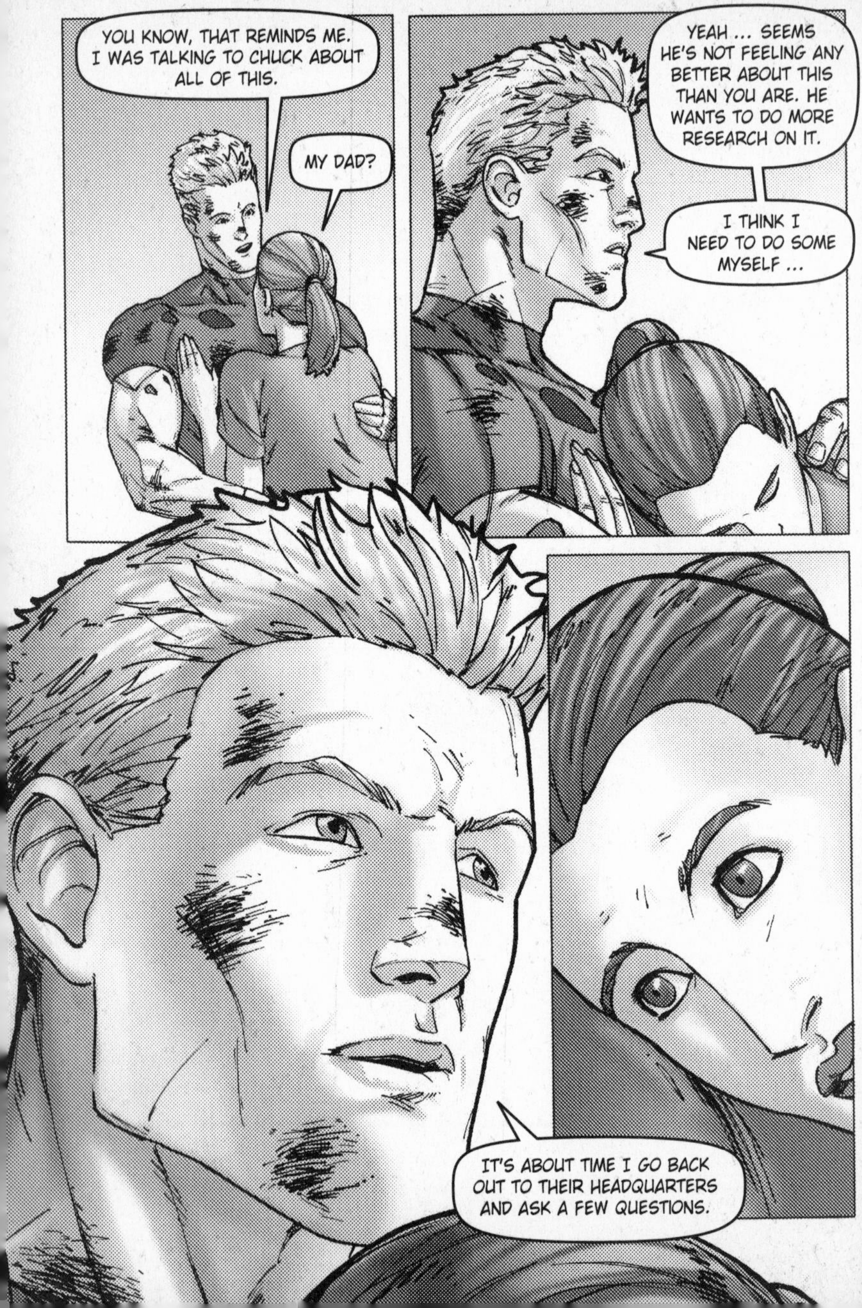
YOU KNOW, THAT REMINDS ME. I WAS TALKING TO CHUCK ABOUT ALL OF THIS.
MY DAD?
YEAH ... SEEMS HE'S NOT FEELING ANY BETTER ABOUT THIS THAN YOU ARE. HE WANTS TO DO MORE RESEARCH ON IT.
I THINK I NEED TO DO SOME MYSELF ...
IT'S ABOUT TIME I GO BACK OUT TO THEIR HEADQUARTERS AND ASK A FEW QUESTIONS.

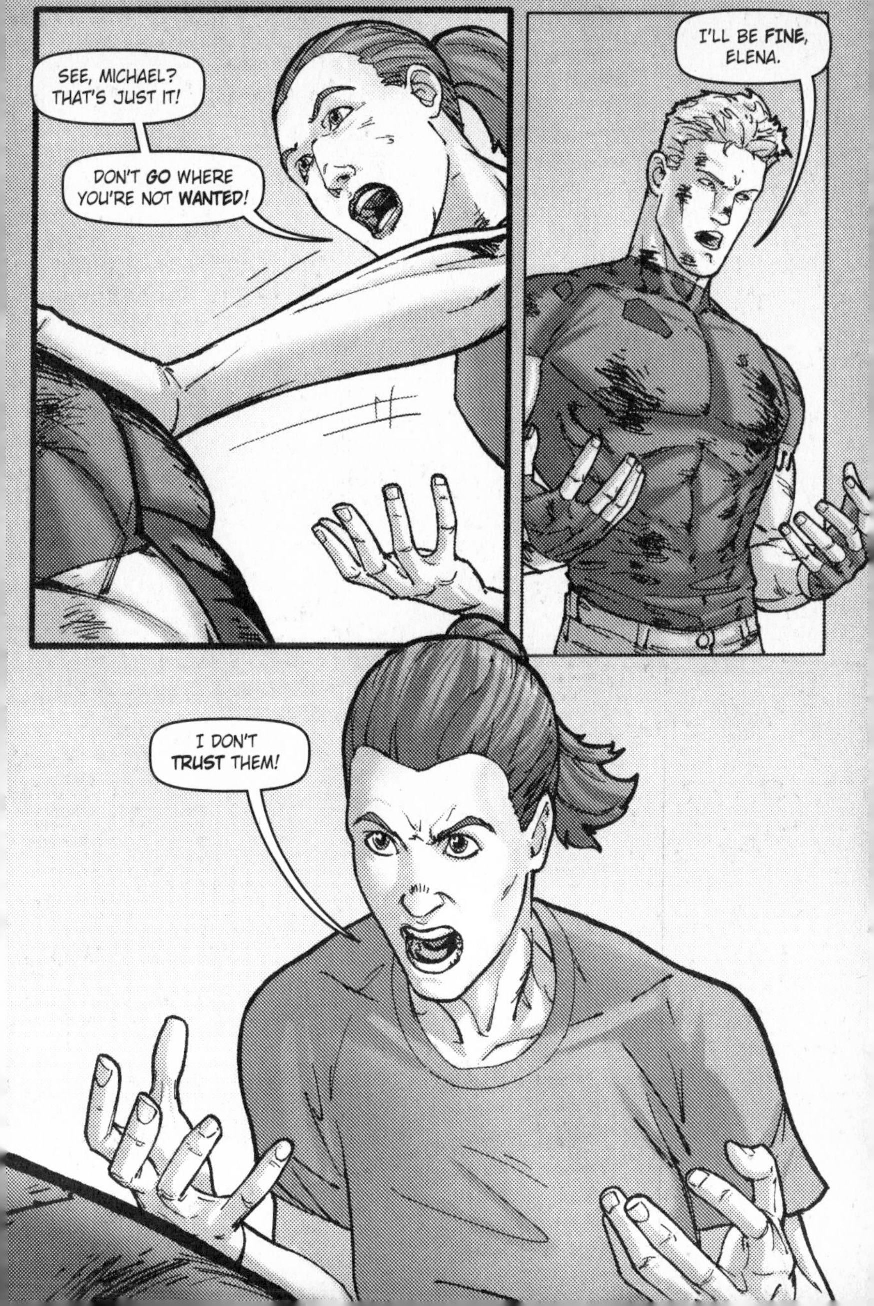
SEE, MICHAEL? THAT'S JUST IT!
DON'T GO WHERE YOU'RE NOT WANTED!
I'LL BE FINE, ELENA.
I DON'T TRUST THEM!

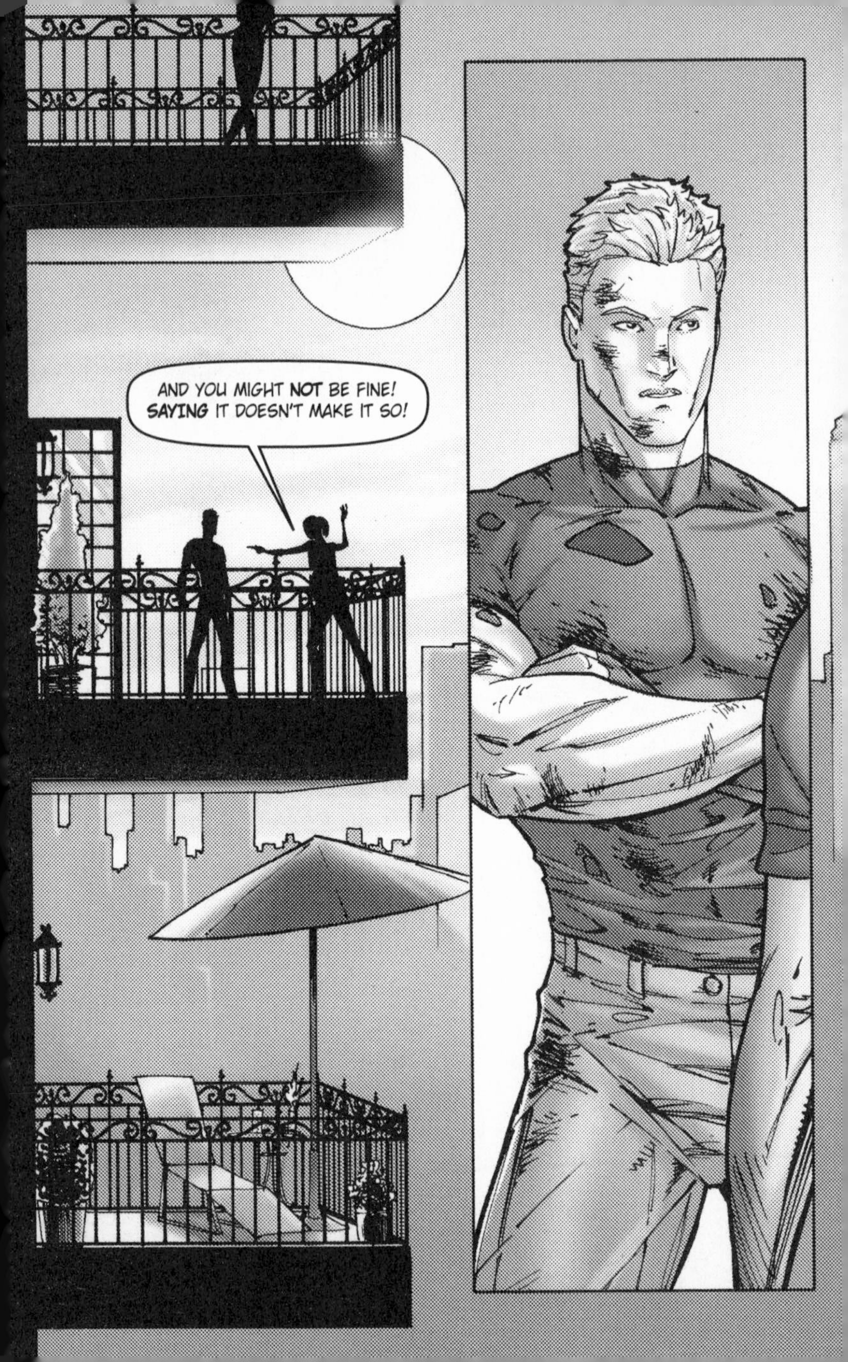
AND YOU MIGHT NOT BE FINE! SAYING IT DOESN'T MAKE IT SO!

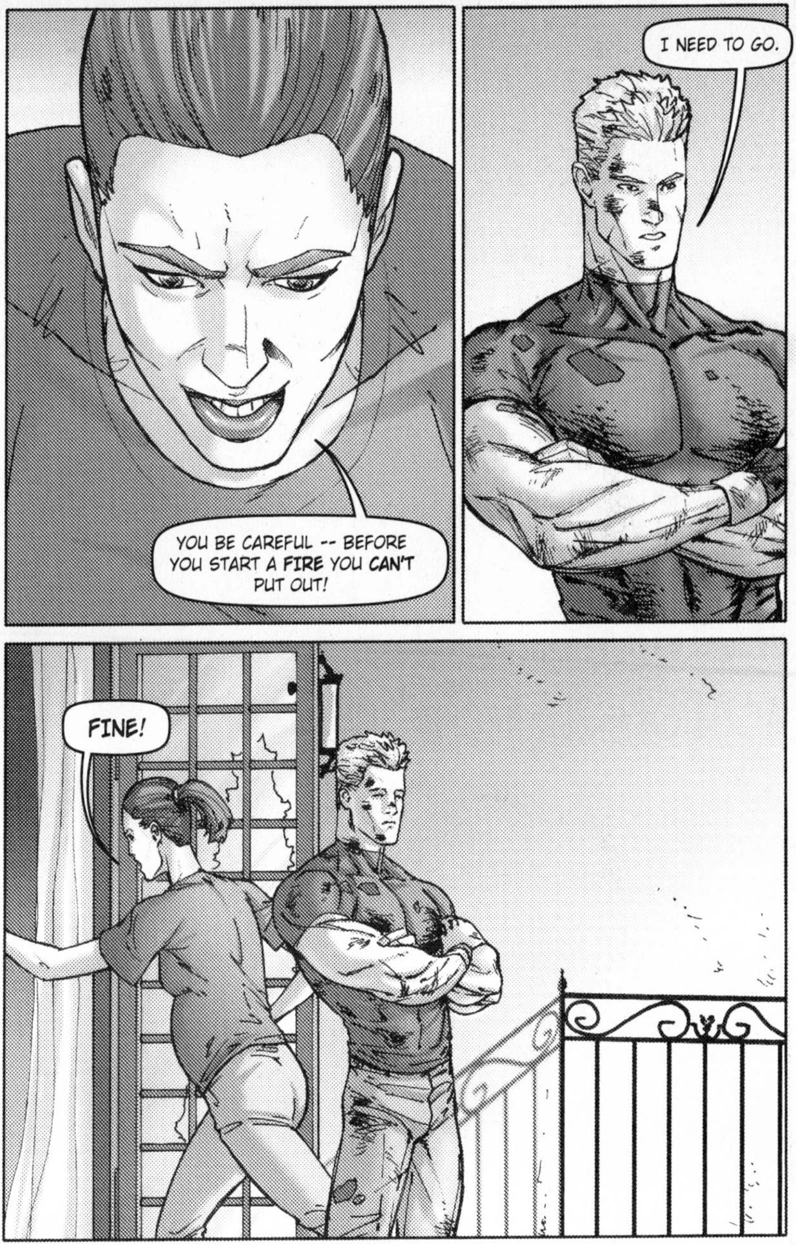
YOU BE CAREFUL -- BEFORE YOU START A FIRE YOU CAN'T PUT OUT!
I NEED TO GO.
FINE!

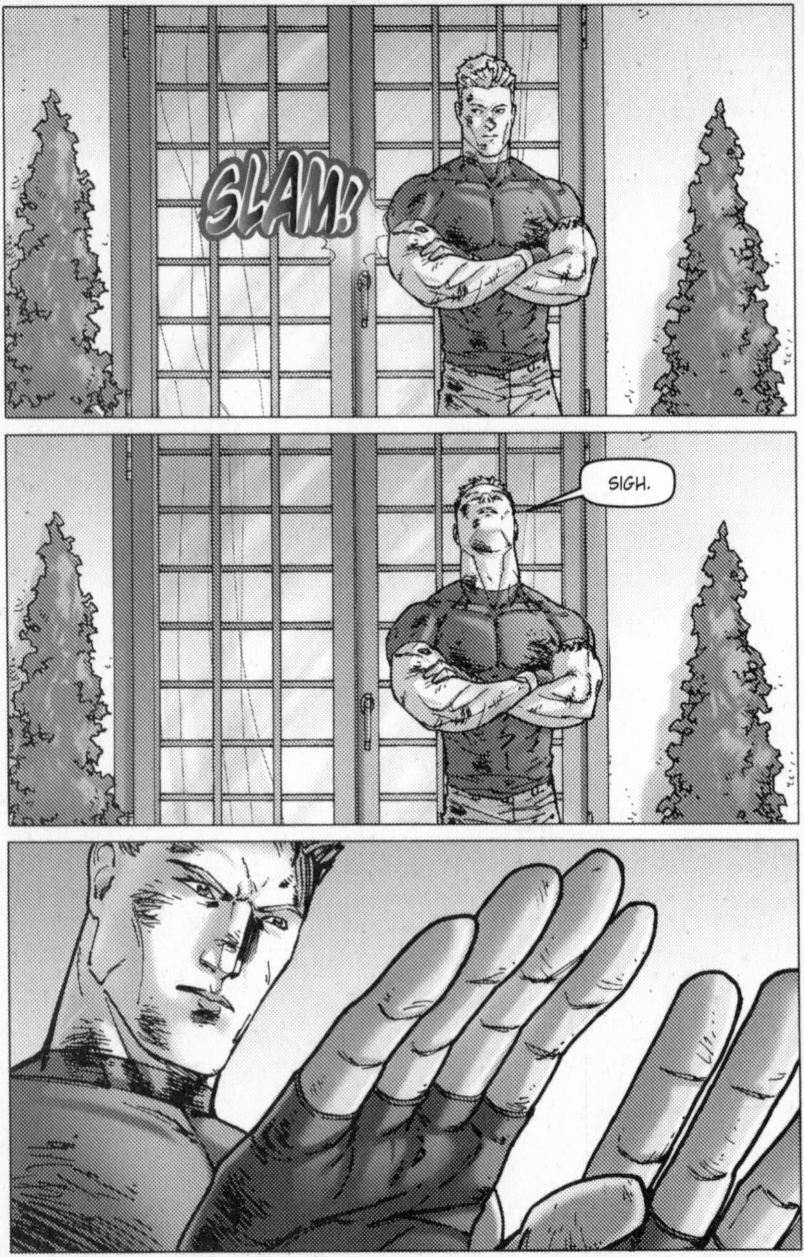
SLAM!
SIGH.

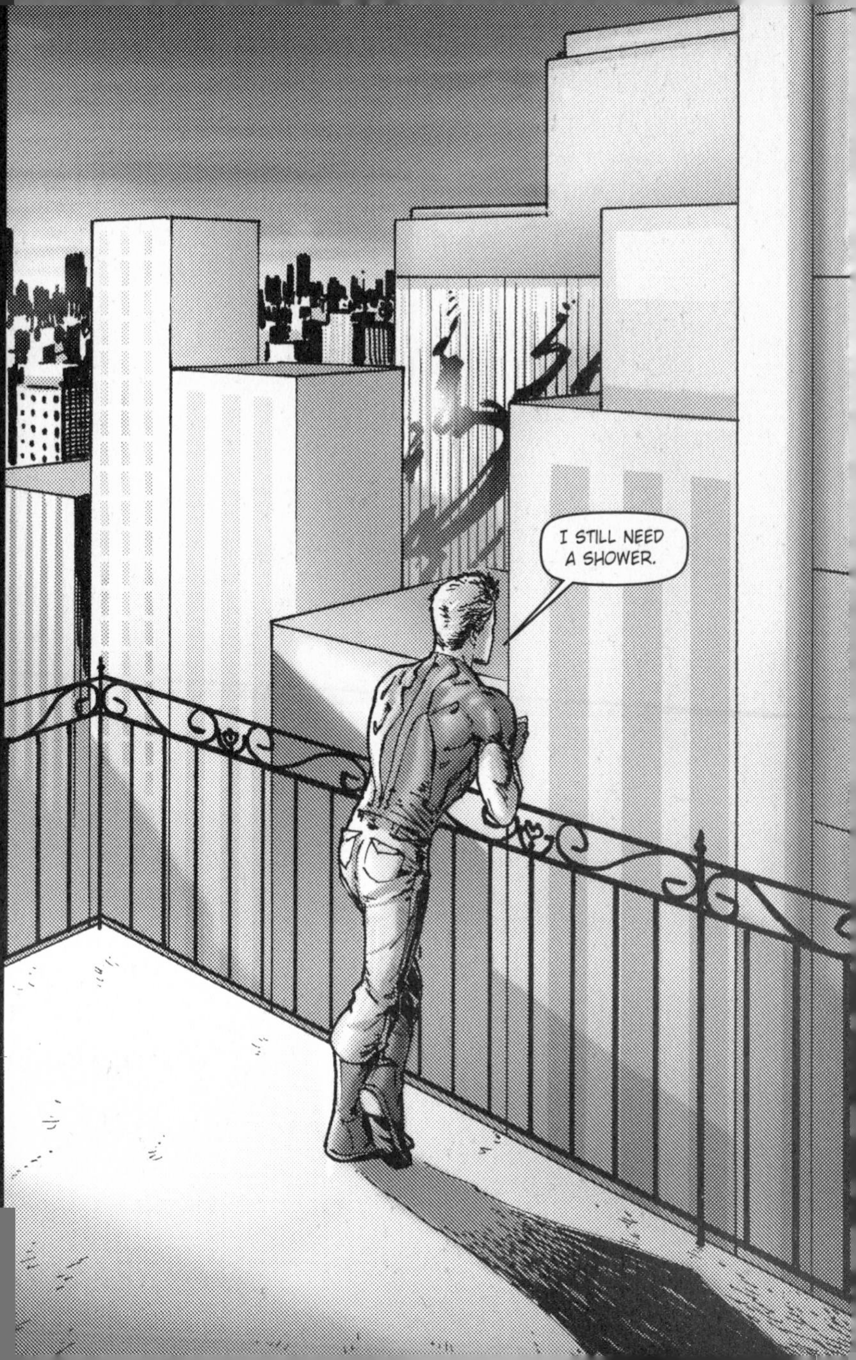
I STILL NEED A SHOWER.

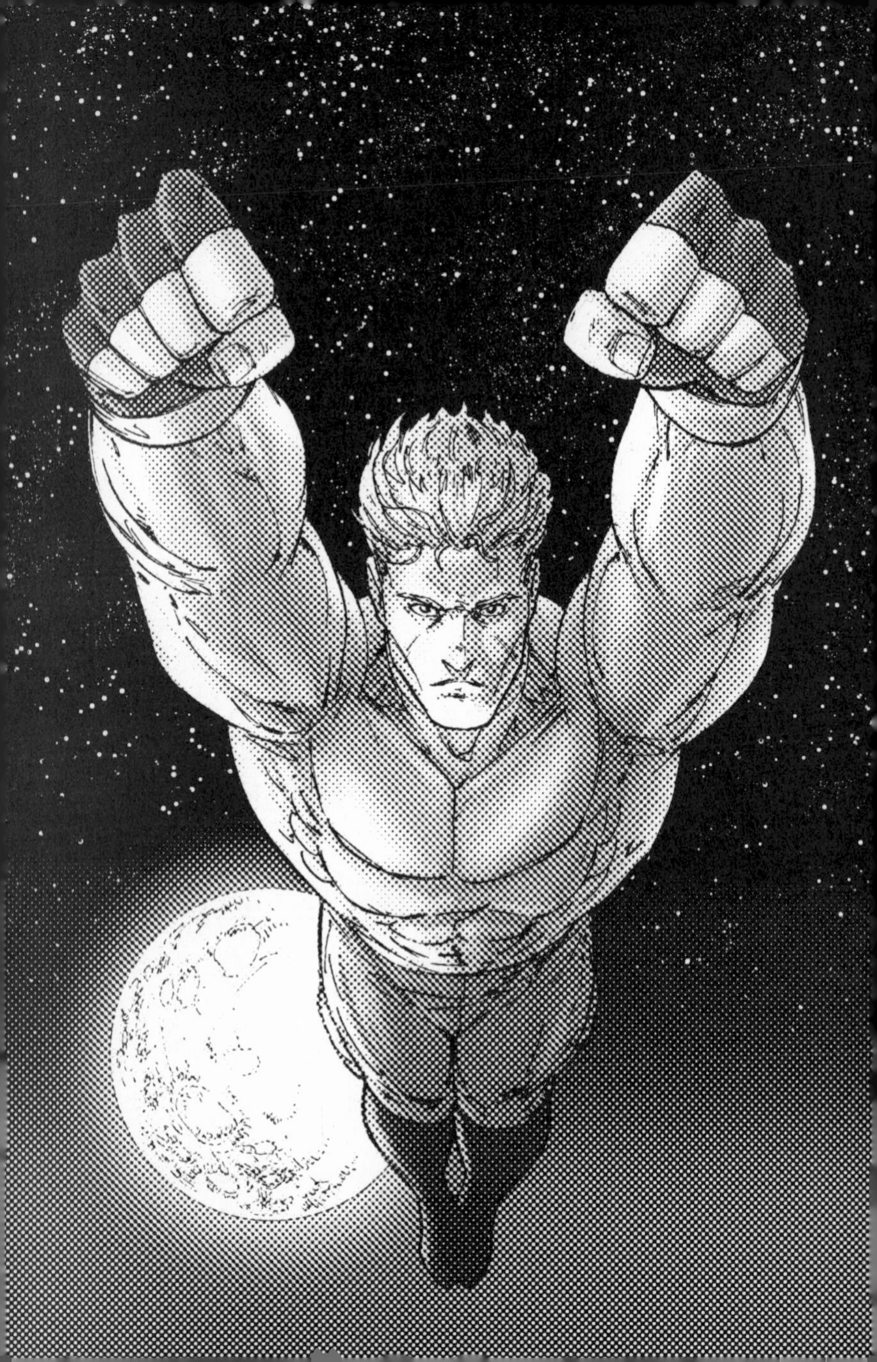

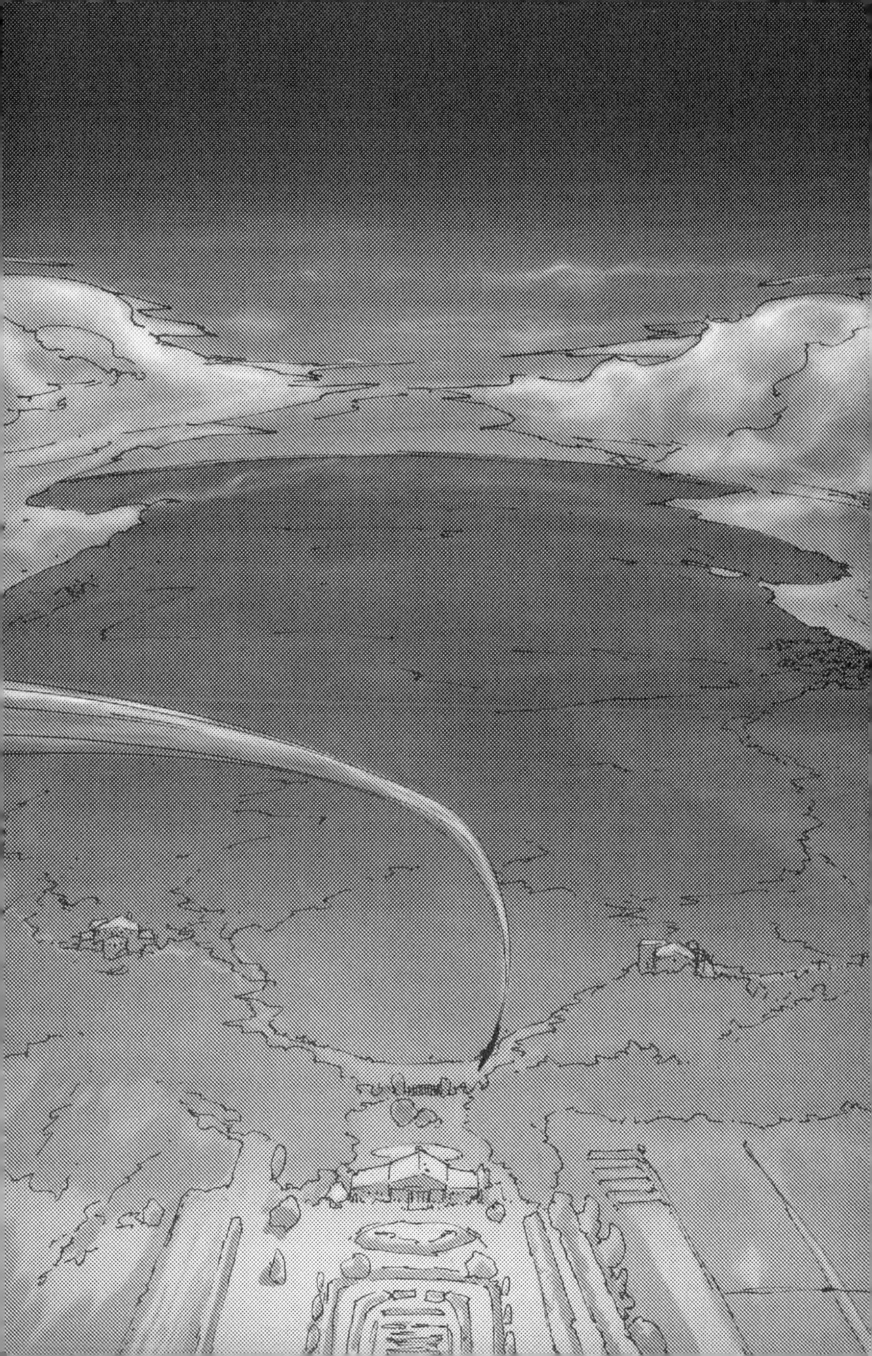

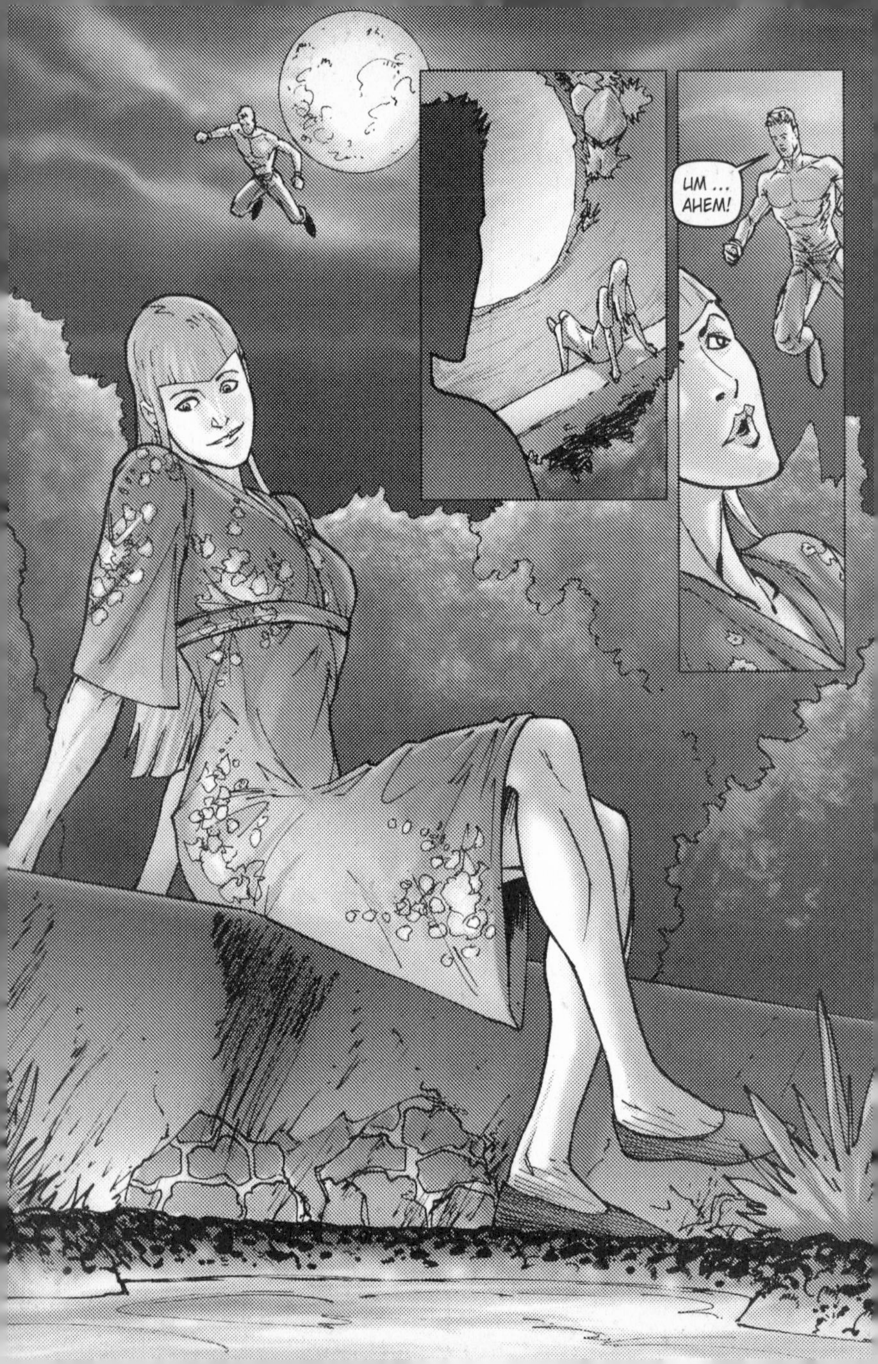
UM ... AHEM!

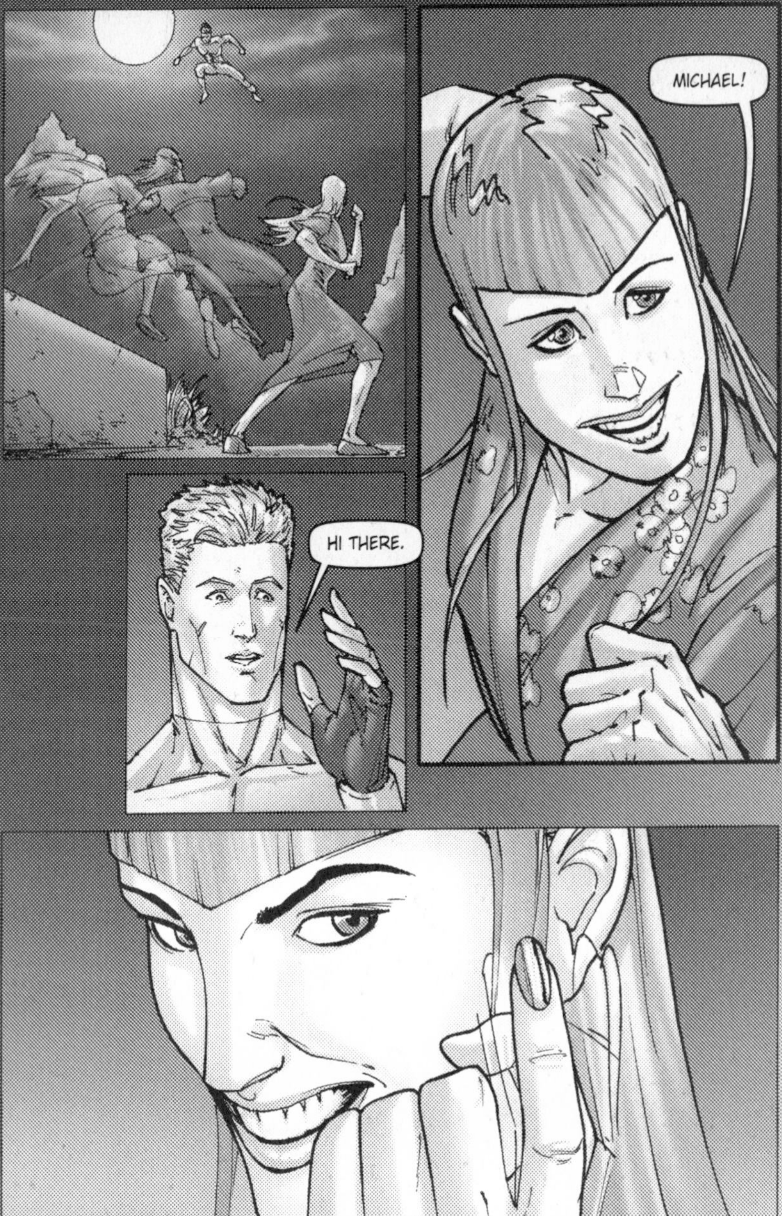
HI THERE.
MICHAEL!

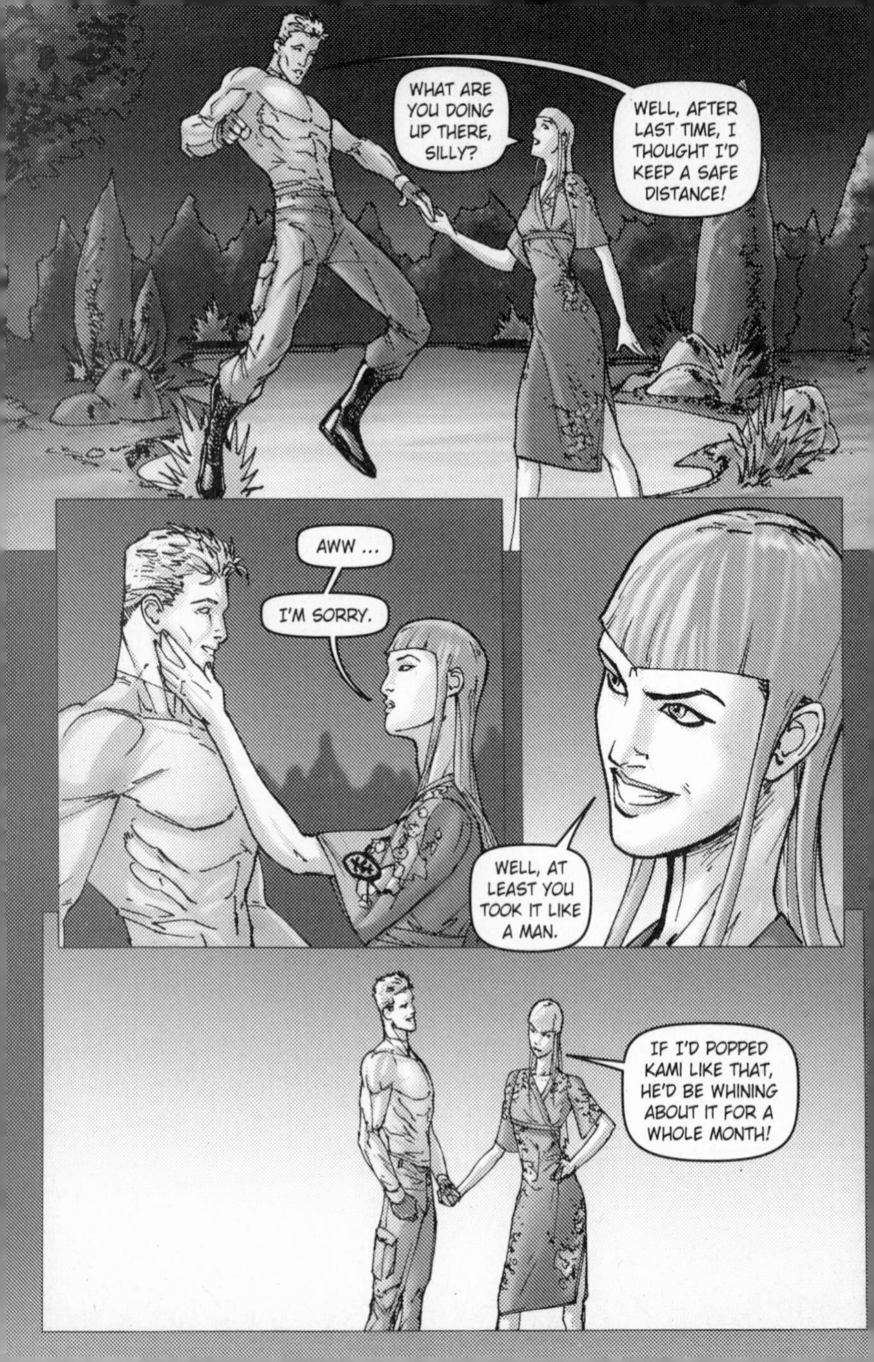
WHAT ARE YOU DOING UP THERE, SILLY?
WELL, AFTER LAST TIME, I THOUGHT I'D KEEP A SAFE DISTANCE!
AWW ...
I'M SORRY.
WELL, AT LEAST YOU TOOK IT LIKE A MAN.
IF I'D POPPED KAMI LIKE THAT, HE'D BE WHINING ABOUT IT FOR A WHOLE MONTH!

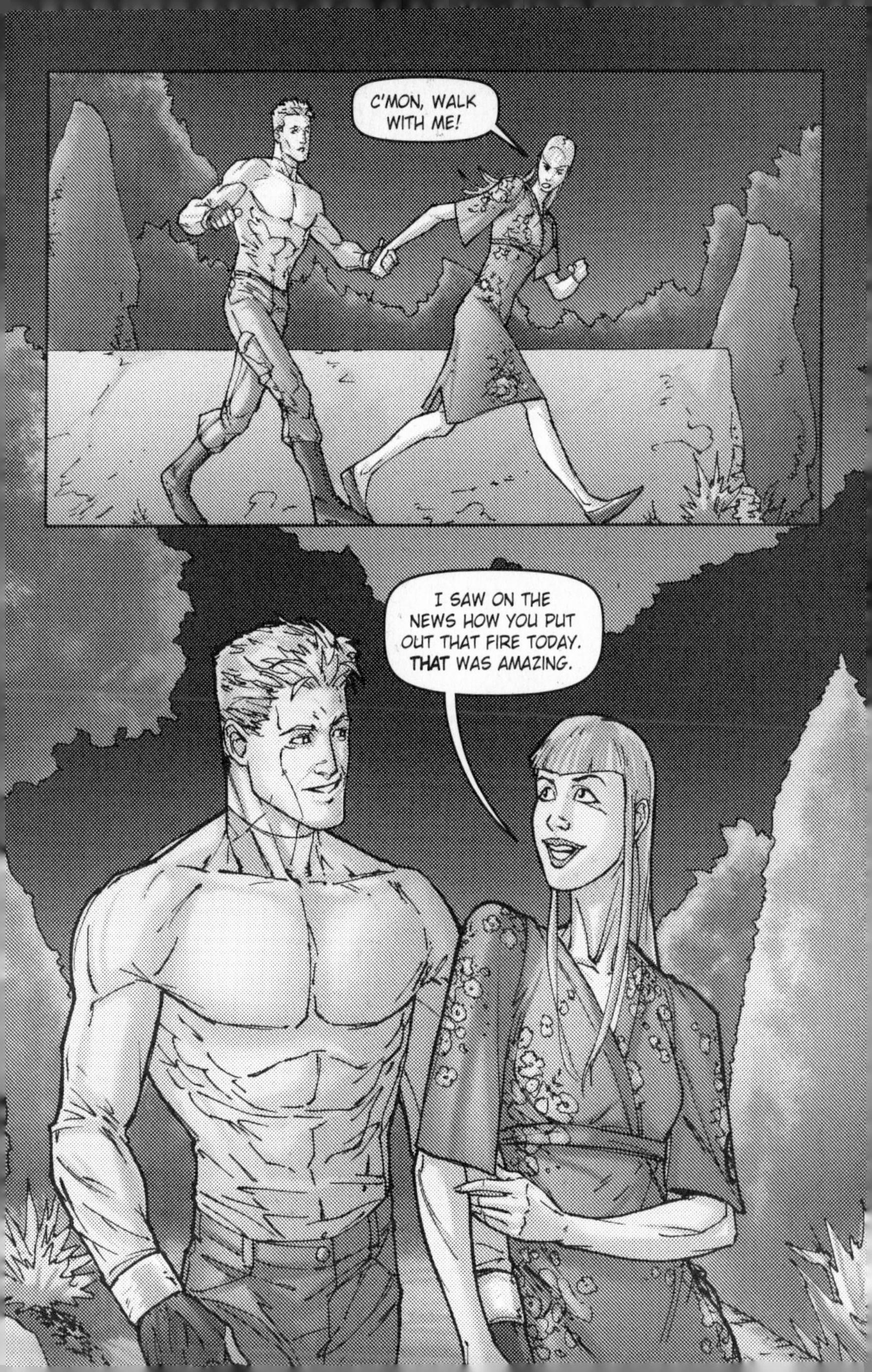
C'MON, WALK WITH ME!
I SAW ON THE NEWS HOW YOU PUT OUT THAT FIRE TODAY. **THAT** WAS AMAZING.

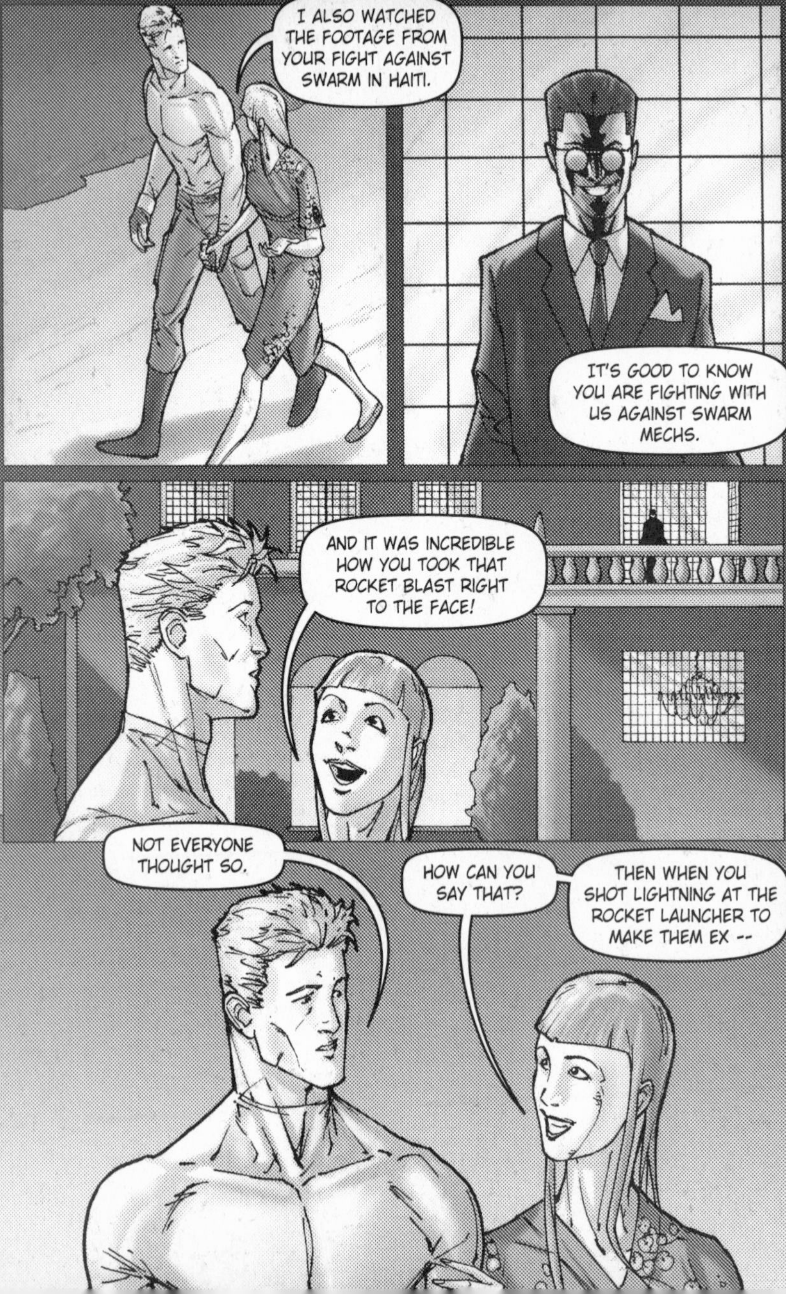
I ALSO WATCHED THE FOOTAGE FROM YOUR FIGHT AGAINST SWARM IN HAITI.
IT'S GOOD TO KNOW YOU ARE FIGHTING WITH US AGAINST SWARM MECHS.
AND IT WAS INCREDIBLE HOW YOU TOOK THAT ROCKET BLAST RIGHT TO THE FACE!
NOT EVERYONE THOUGHT SO.
HOW CAN YOU SAY THAT?
THEN WHEN YOU SHOT LIGHTNING AT THE ROCKET LAUNCHER TO MAKE THEM EX --

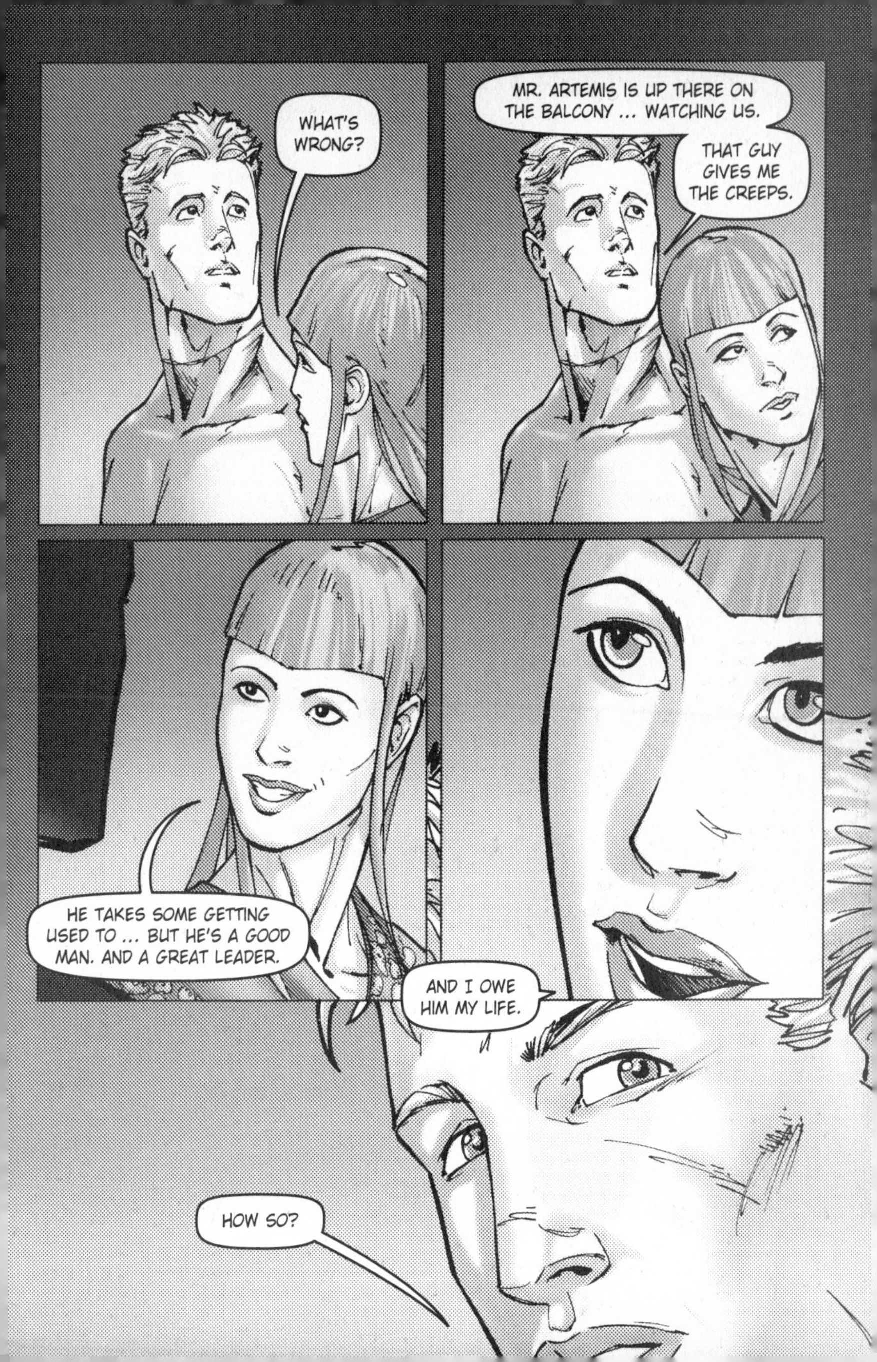
WHAT'S WRONG?
MR. ARTEMIS IS UP THERE ON THE BALCONY ... WATCHING US.
THAT GUY GIVES ME THE CREEPS.
HE TAKES SOME GETTING USED TO ... BUT HE'S A GOOD MAN. AND A GREAT LEADER.
AND I OWE HIM MY LIFE.
HOW SO?

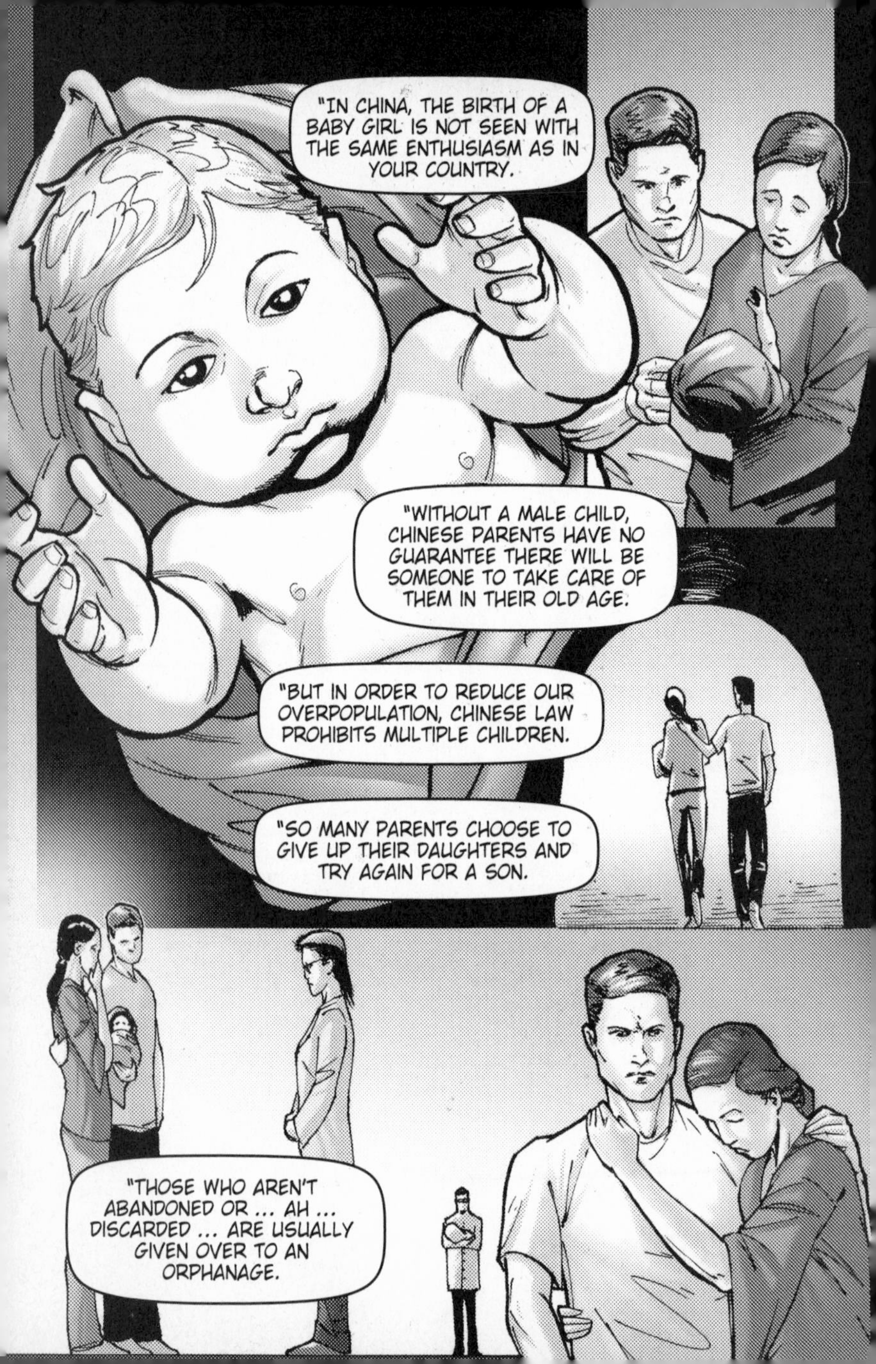
"IN CHINA, THE BIRTH OF A BABY GIRL IS NOT SEEN WITH THE SAME ENTHUSIASM AS IN YOUR COUNTRY.
"WITHOUT A MALE CHILD, CHINESE PARENTS HAVE NO GUARANTEE THERE WILL BE SOMEONE TO TAKE CARE OF THEM IN THEIR OLD AGE.
"BUT IN ORDER TO REDUCE OUR OVERPOPULATION, CHINESE LAW PROHIBITS MULTIPLE CHILDREN.
"SO MANY PARENTS CHOOSE TO GIVE UP THEIR DAUGHTERS AND TRY AGAIN FOR A SON.
"THOSE WHO AREN'T ABANDONED OR ... AH ... DISCARDED ... ARE USUALLY GIVEN OVER TO AN ORPHANAGE.

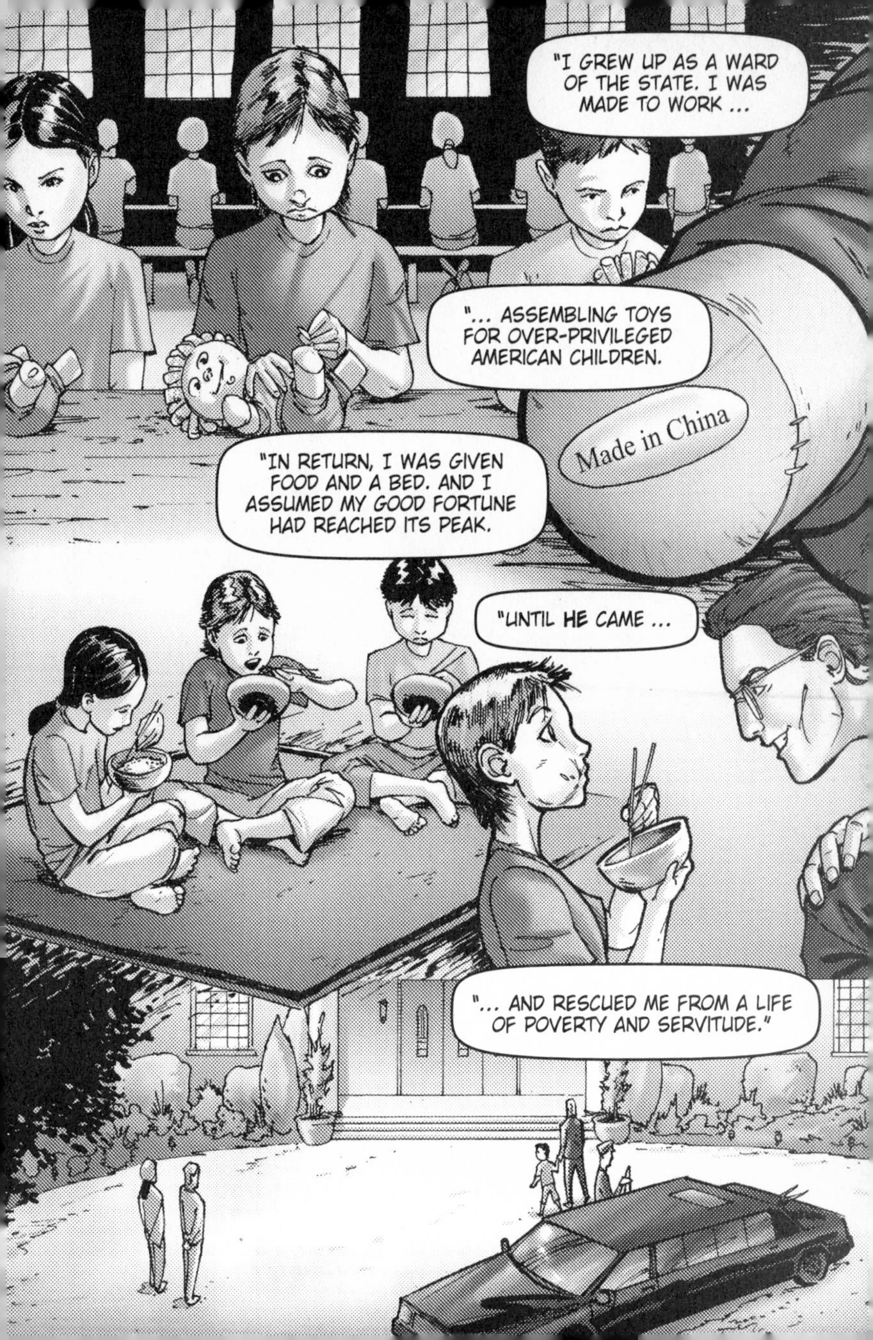
"I GREW UP AS A WARD OF THE STATE. I WAS MADE TO WORK ...
"... ASSEMBLING TOYS FOR OVER-PRIVILEGED AMERICAN CHILDREN.
Made in China
"IN RETURN, I WAS GIVEN FOOD AND A BED. AND I ASSUMED MY GOOD FORTUNE HAD REACHED ITS PEAK.
"UNTIL **HE** CAME ...
"... AND RESCUED ME FROM A LIFE OF POVERTY AND SERVITUDE."

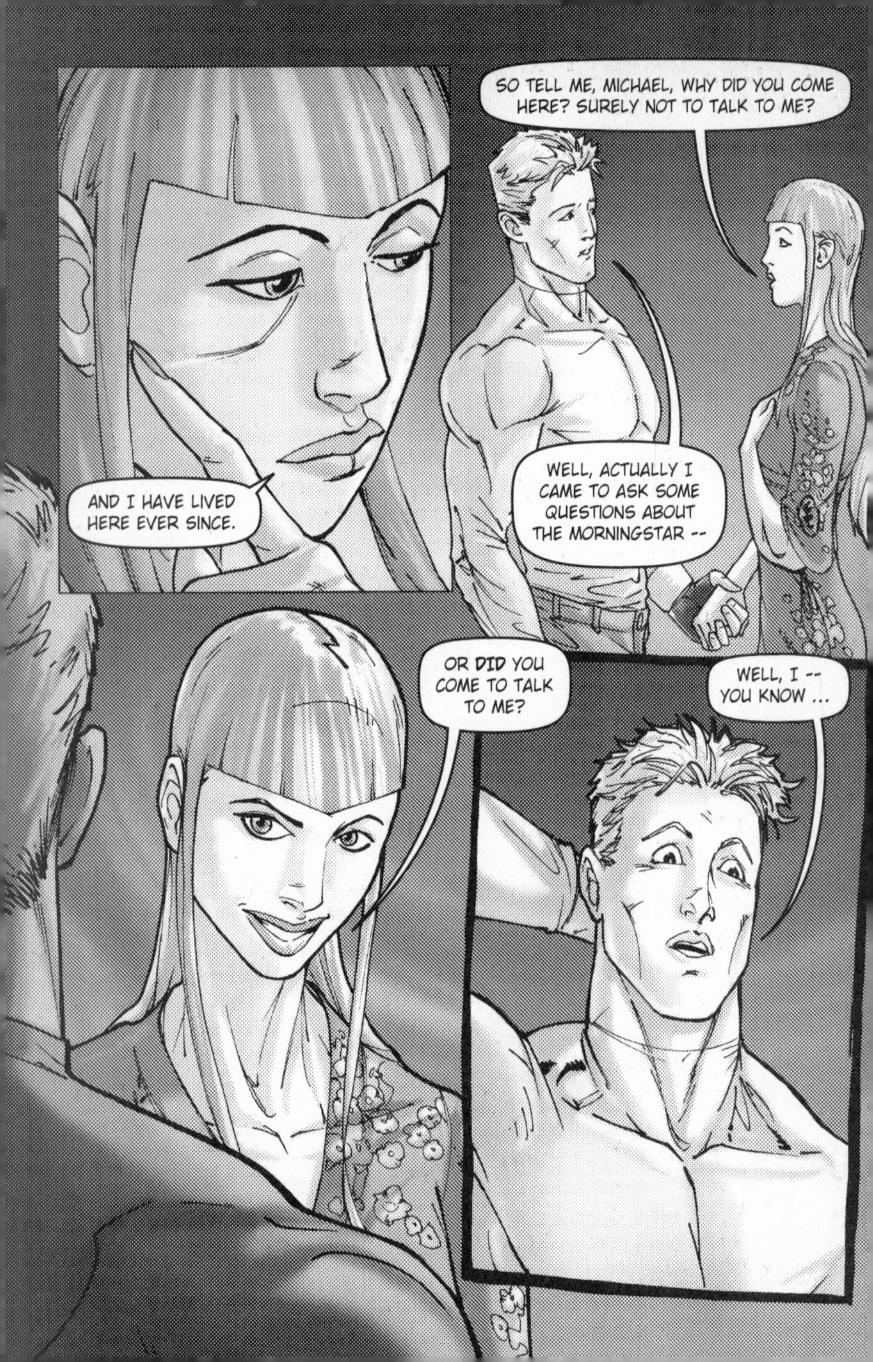
AND I HAVE LIVED HERE EVER SINCE.
SO TELL ME, MICHAEL, WHY DID YOU COME HERE? SURELY NOT TO TALK TO ME?
WELL, ACTUALLY I CAME TO ASK SOME QUESTIONS ABOUT THE MORNINGSTAR --
OR DID YOU COME TO TALK TO ME?
WELL, I -- YOU KNOW ...

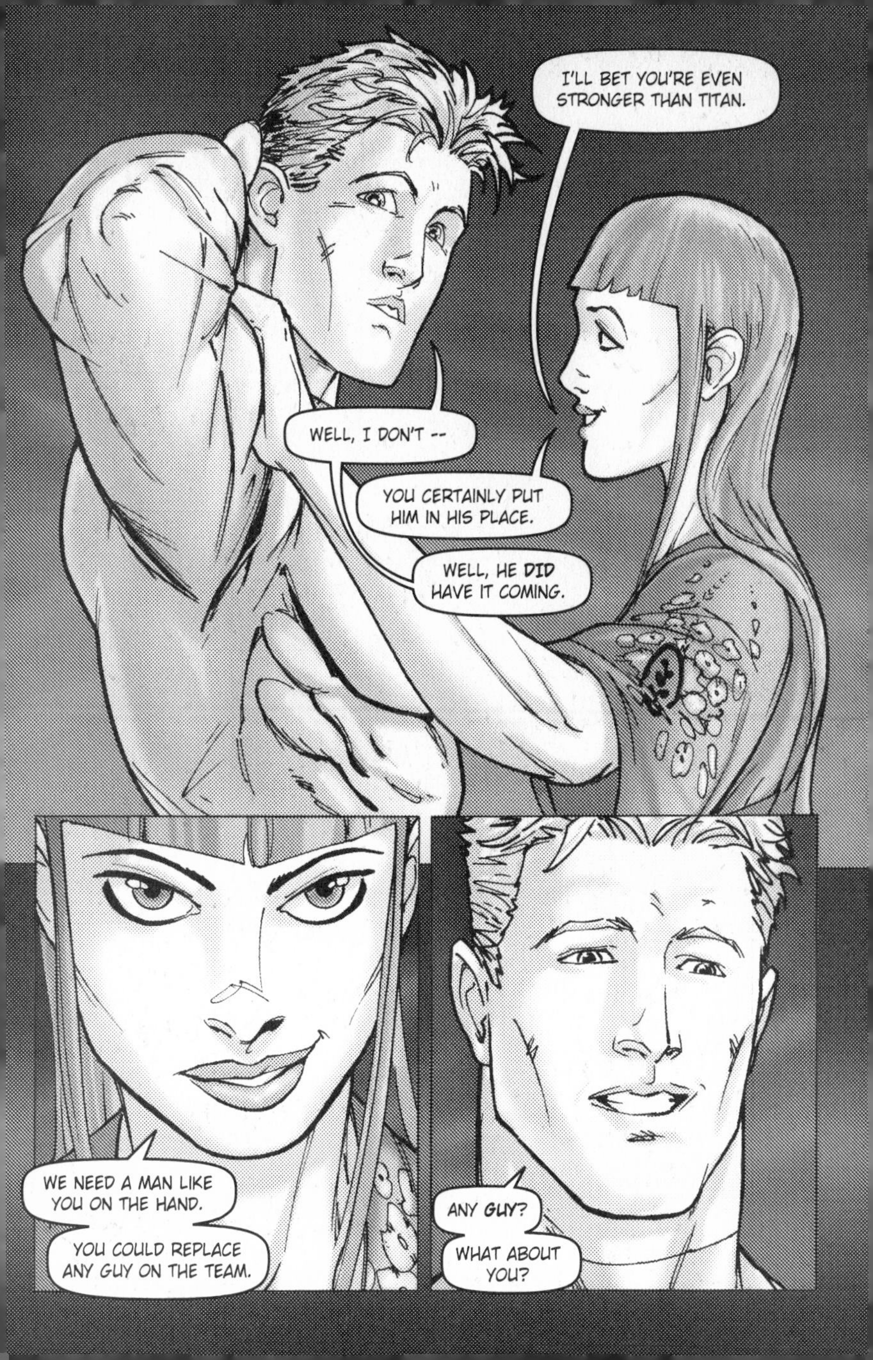
I'LL BET YOU'RE EVEN STRONGER THAN TITAN.
WELL, I DON'T --
YOU CERTAINLY PUT HIM IN HIS PLACE.
WELL, HE DID HAVE IT COMING.
WE NEED A MAN LIKE YOU ON THE HAND.
YOU COULD REPLACE ANY GUY ON THE TEAM.
ANY GUY?
WHAT ABOUT YOU?

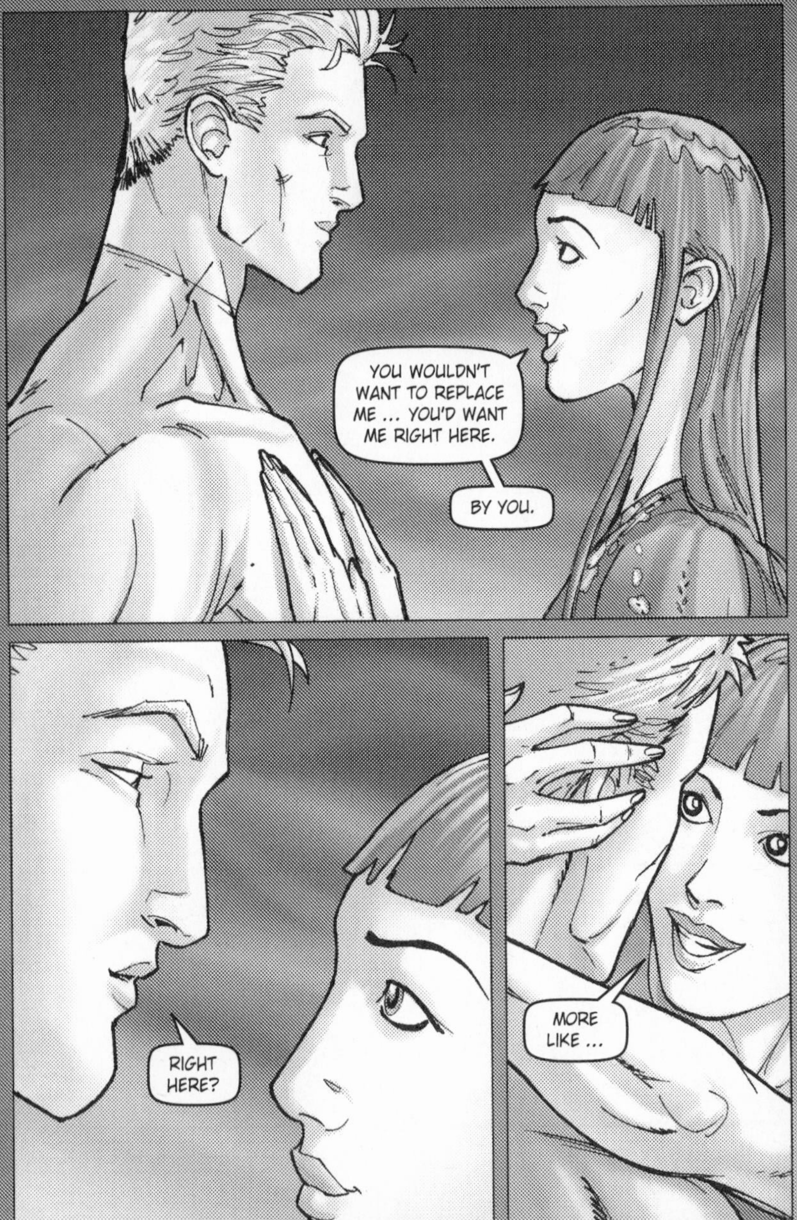
YOU WOULDN'T WANT TO REPLACE ME ... YOU'D WANT ME RIGHT HERE.
BY YOU.
RIGHT HERE?
MORE LIKE ...

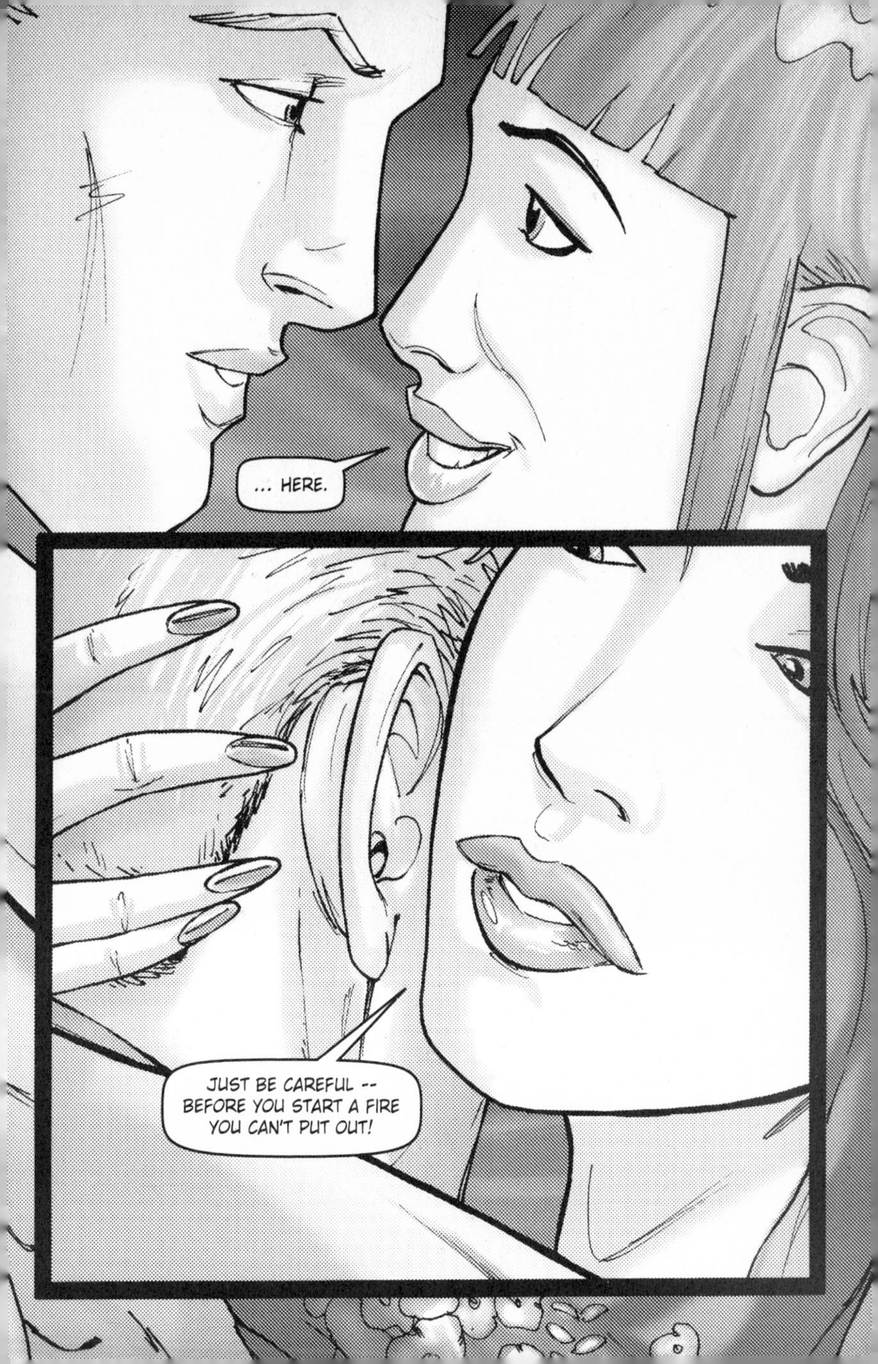
... HERE.
JUST BE CAREFUL -- BEFORE YOU START A FIRE YOU CAN'T PUT OUT!

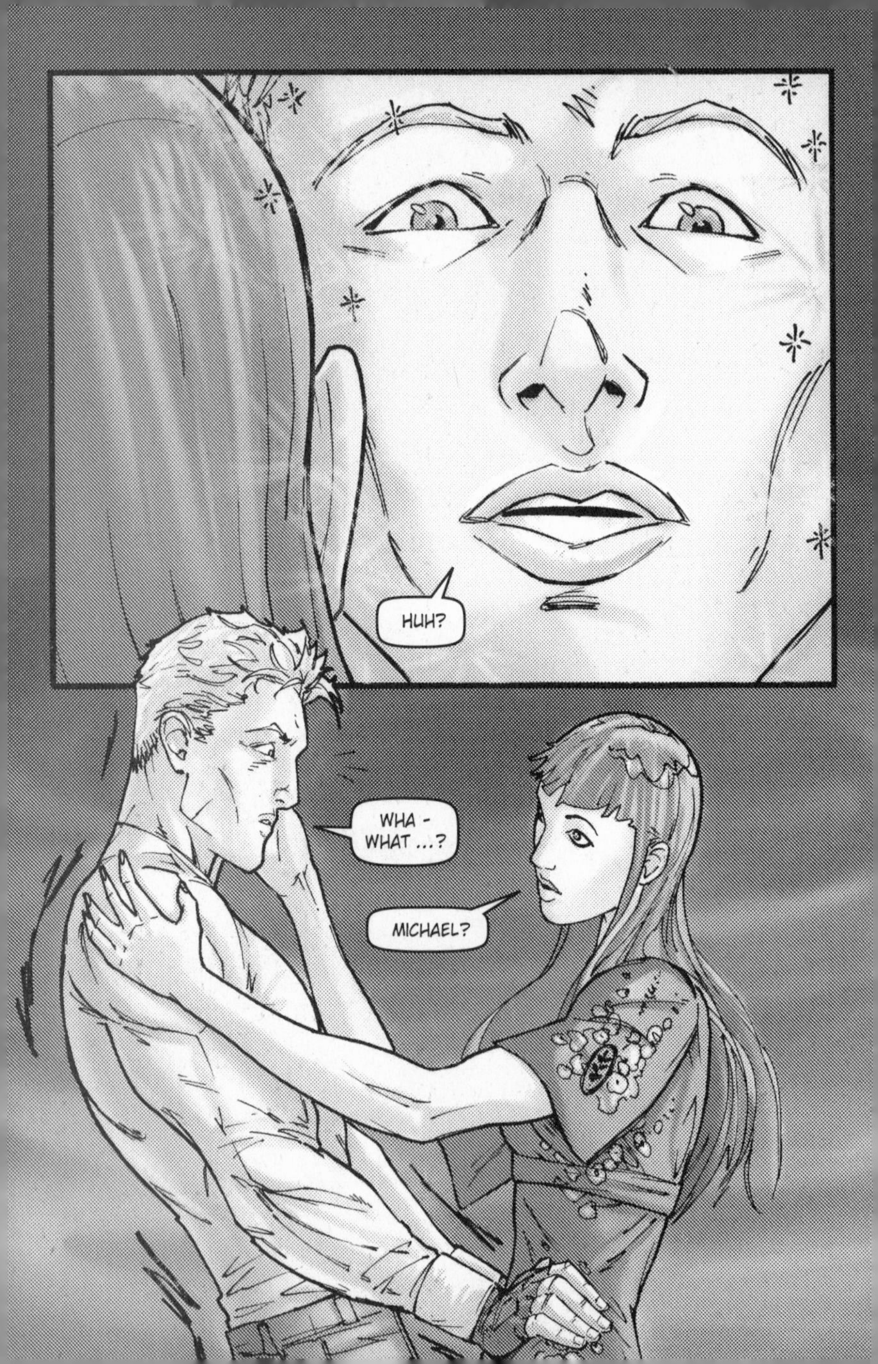
HUH?
WHA - WHAT ...?
MICHAEL?

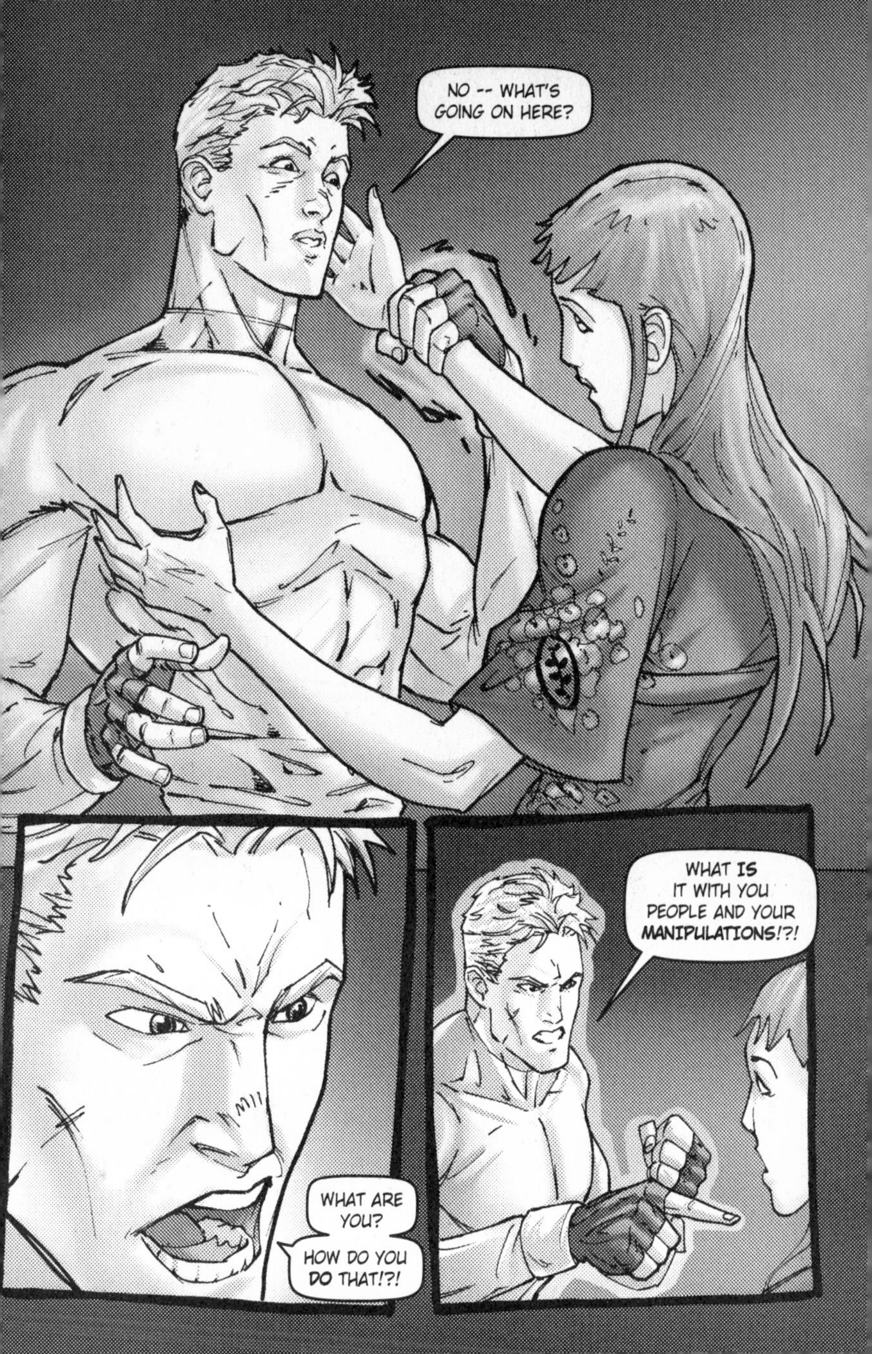
NO -- WHAT'S GOING ON HERE?
WHAT ARE YOU?
HOW DO YOU DO THAT!?!
WHAT **IS** IT WITH YOU PEOPLE AND YOUR **MANIPULATIONS**!?!

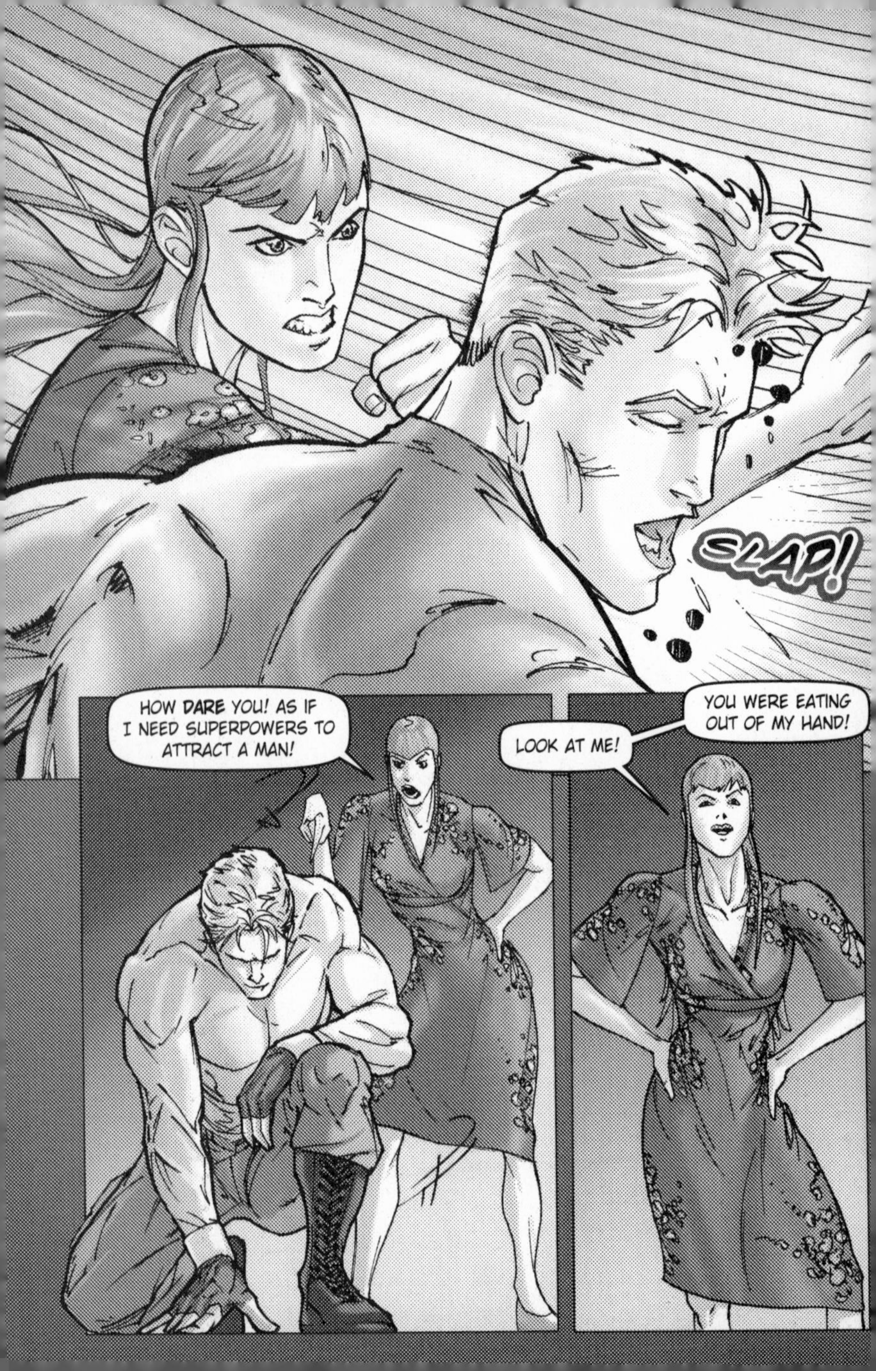
SLAP!
HOW DARE YOU! AS IF I NEED SUPERPOWERS TO ATTRACT A MAN!
LOOK AT ME!
YOU WERE EATING OUT OF MY HAND!

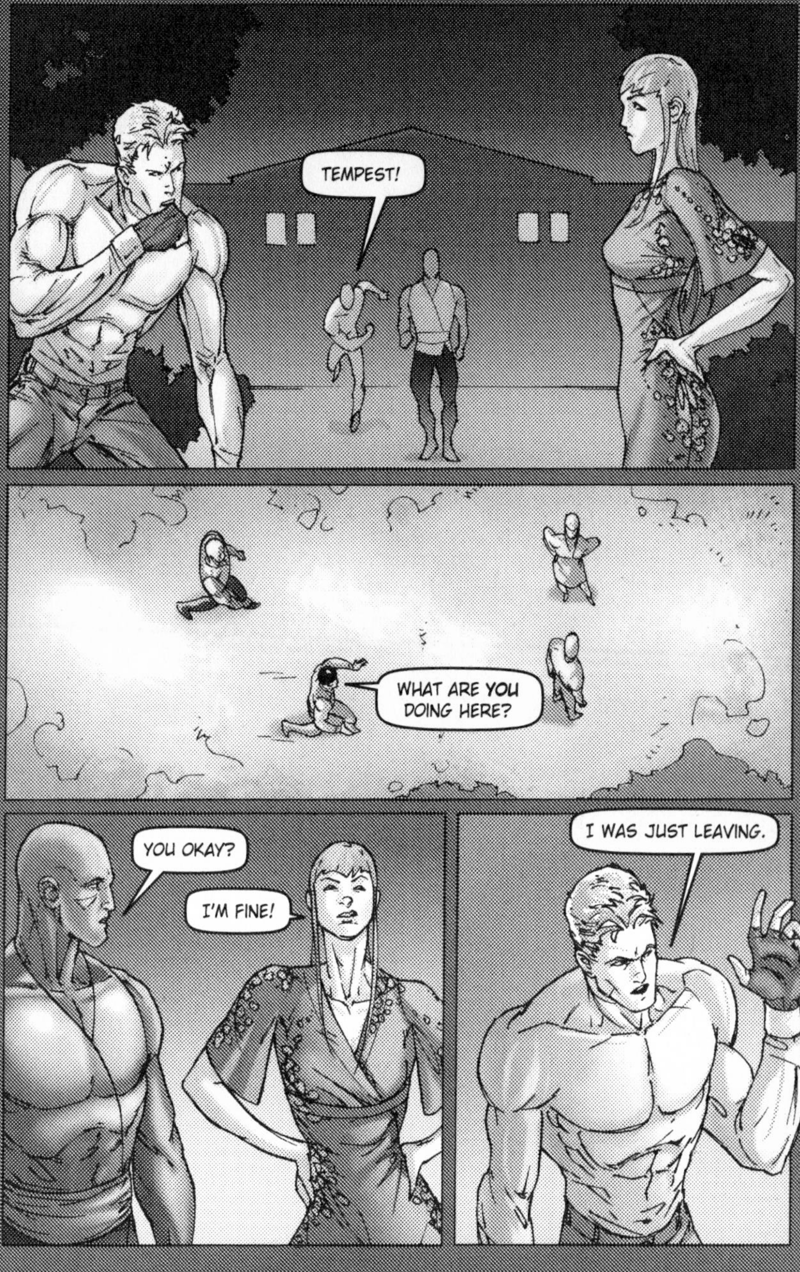
TEMPEST!
WHAT ARE YOU DOING HERE?
YOU OKAY?
I'M FINE!
I WAS JUST LEAVING.

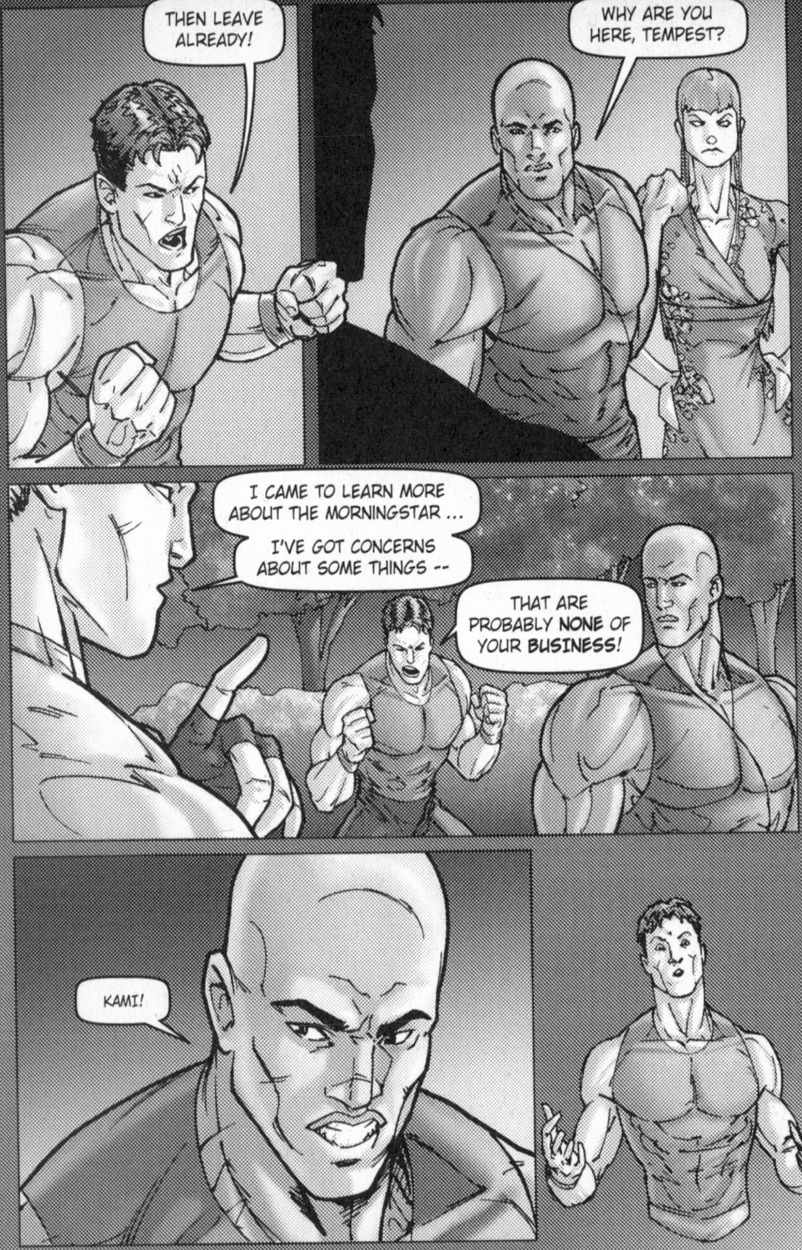
THEN LEAVE ALREADY!
WHY ARE YOU HERE, TEMPEST?
I CAME TO LEARN MORE ABOUT THE MORNINGSTAR ...
I'VE GOT CONCERNS ABOUT SOME THINGS --
THAT ARE PROBABLY NONE OF YOUR BUSINESS!
KAMI!

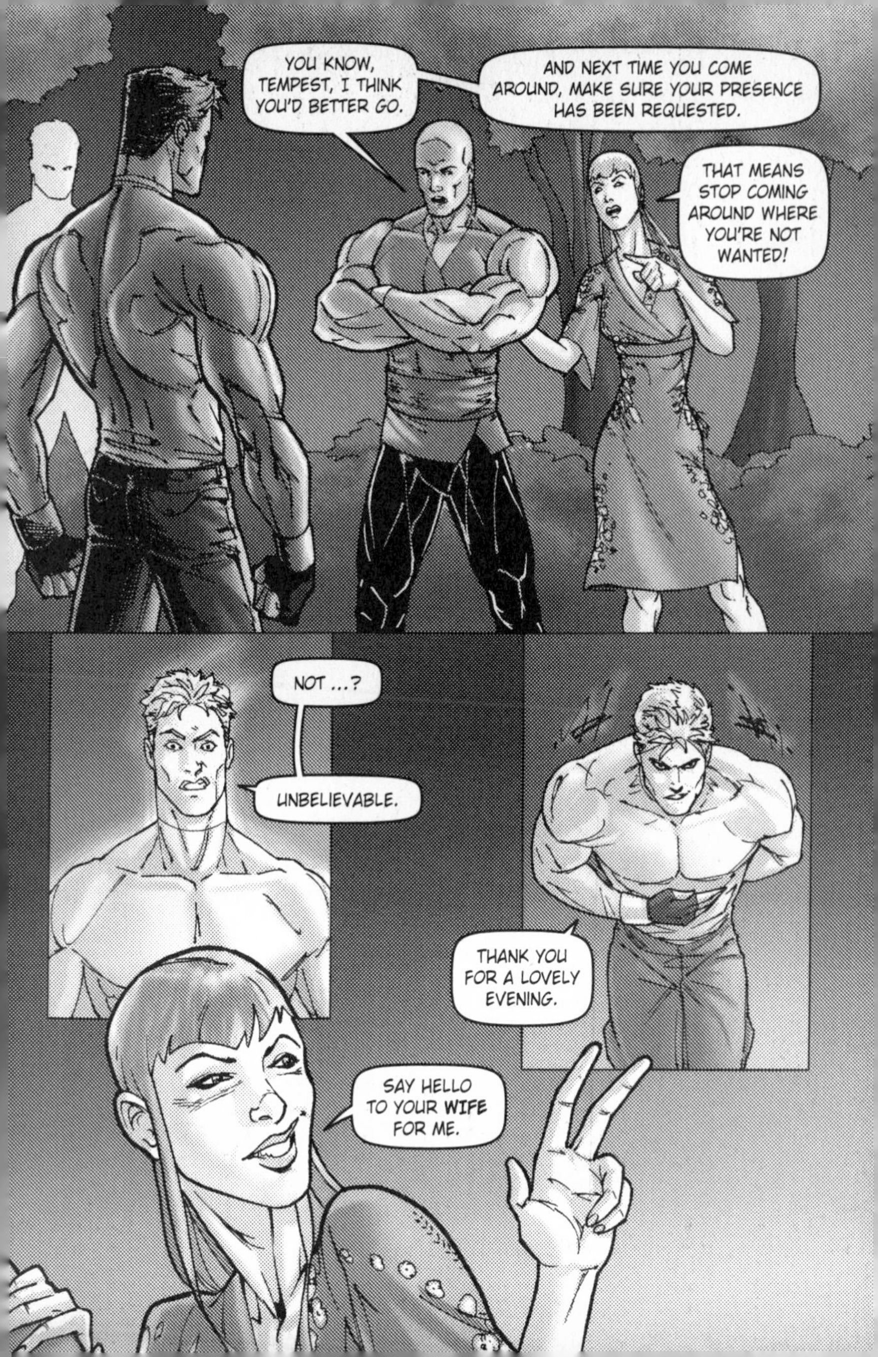
YOU KNOW, TEMPEST, I THINK YOU'D BETTER GO.
AND NEXT TIME YOU COME AROUND, MAKE SURE YOUR PRESENCE HAS BEEN REQUESTED.
THAT MEANS STOP COMING AROUND WHERE YOU'RE NOT WANTED!
NOT ...?
UNBELIEVABLE.
THANK YOU FOR A LOVELY EVENING.
SAY HELLO TO YOUR **WIFE** FOR ME.

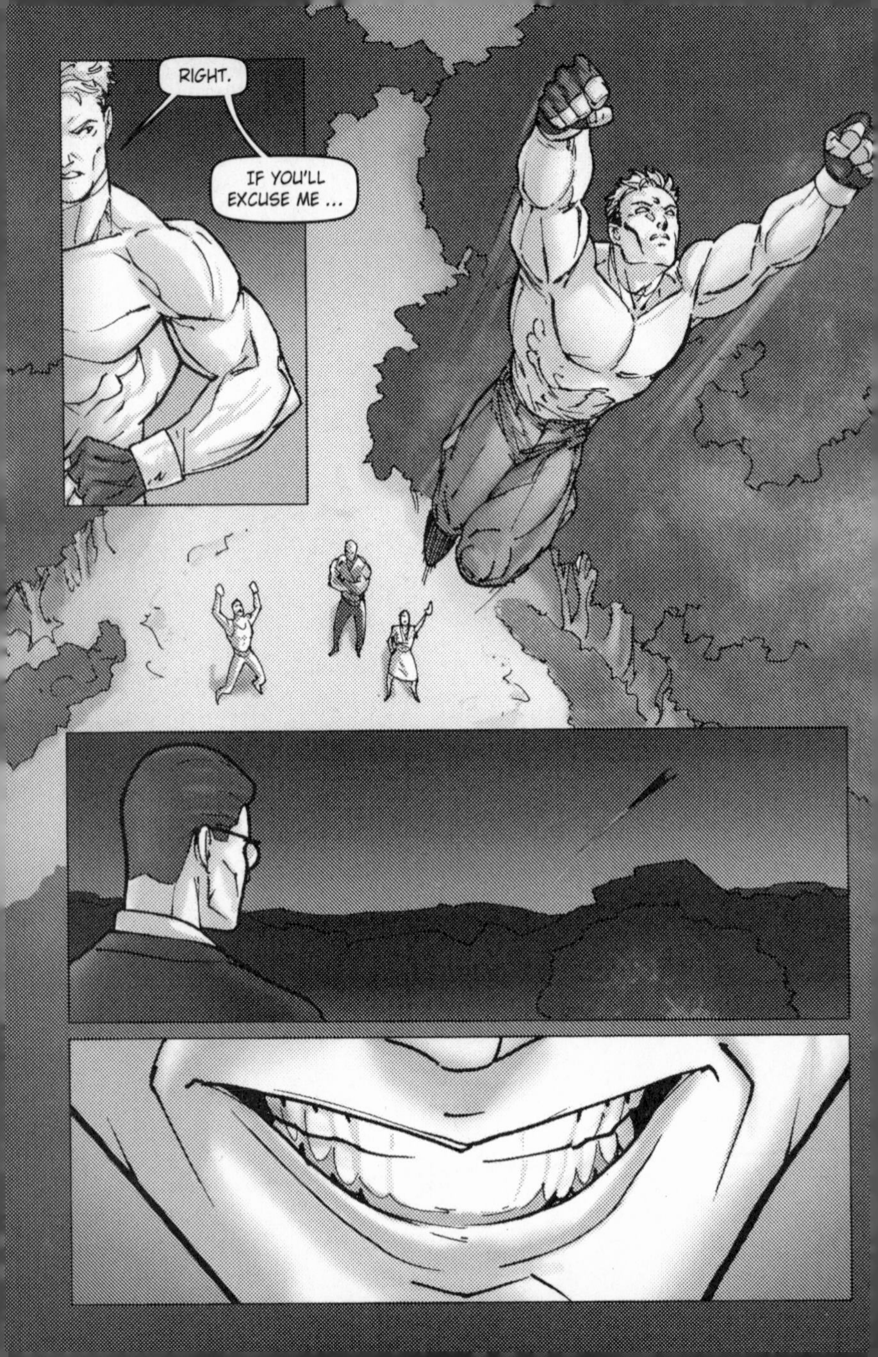

RIGHT.
IF YOU'LL EXCUSE ME ...

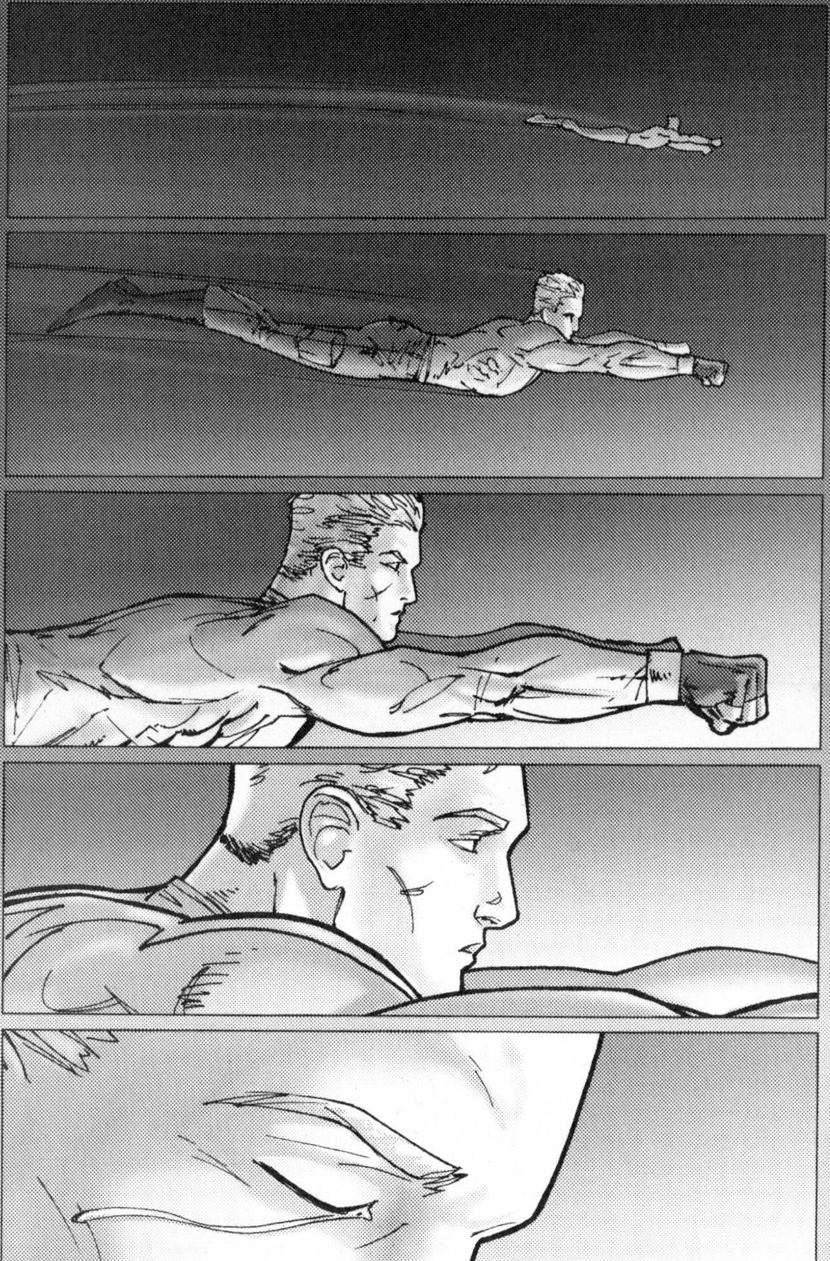

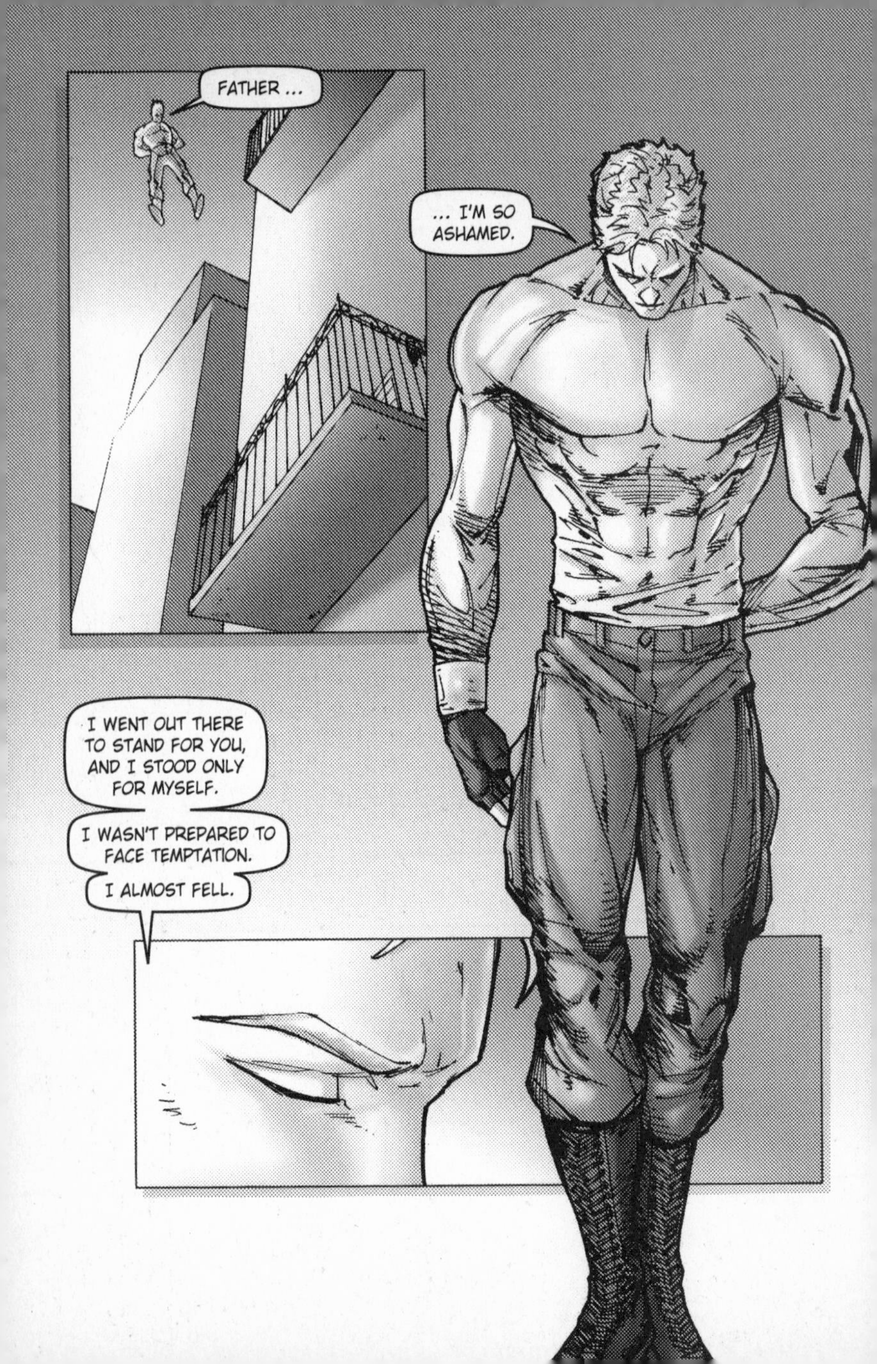
FATHER ...
... I'M SO ASHAMED.
I WENT OUT THERE TO STAND FOR YOU, AND I STOOD ONLY FOR MYSELF.
I WASN'T PREPARED TO FACE TEMPTATION.
I ALMOST FELL.

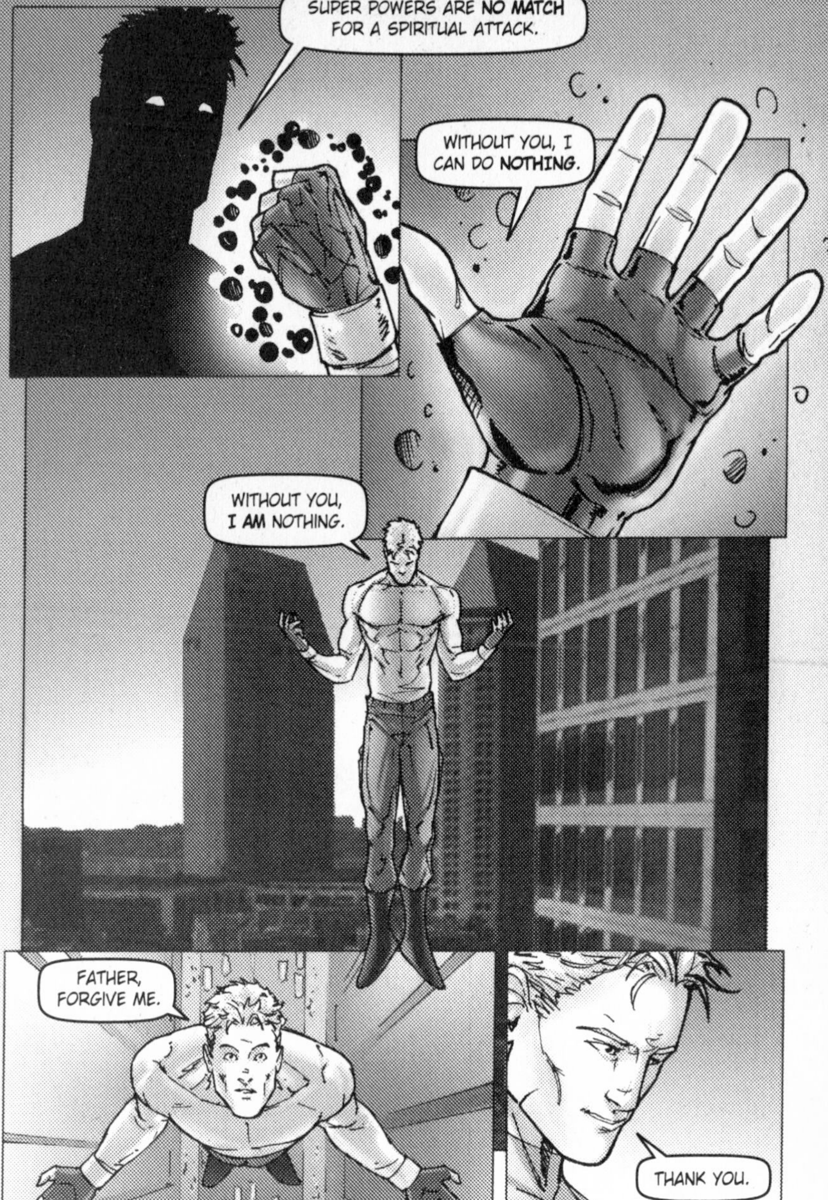
SUPER POWERS ARE NO MATCH FOR A SPIRITUAL ATTACK.
WITHOUT YOU, I CAN DO NOTHING.
WITHOUT YOU, I AM NOTHING.
FATHER, FORGIVE ME.
THANK YOU.

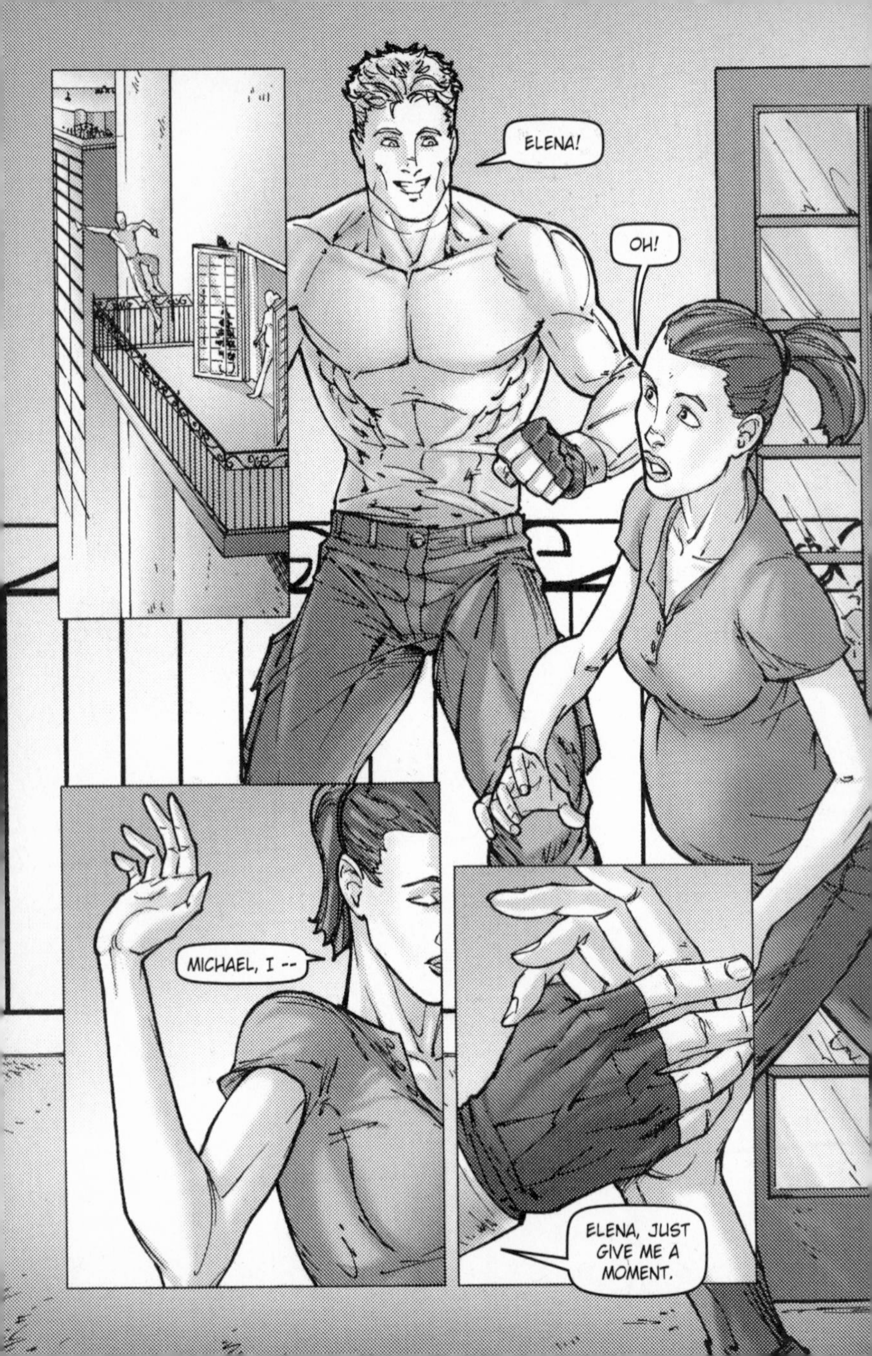
ELENA!
OH!
MICHAEL, I --
ELENA, JUST GIVE ME A MOMENT.

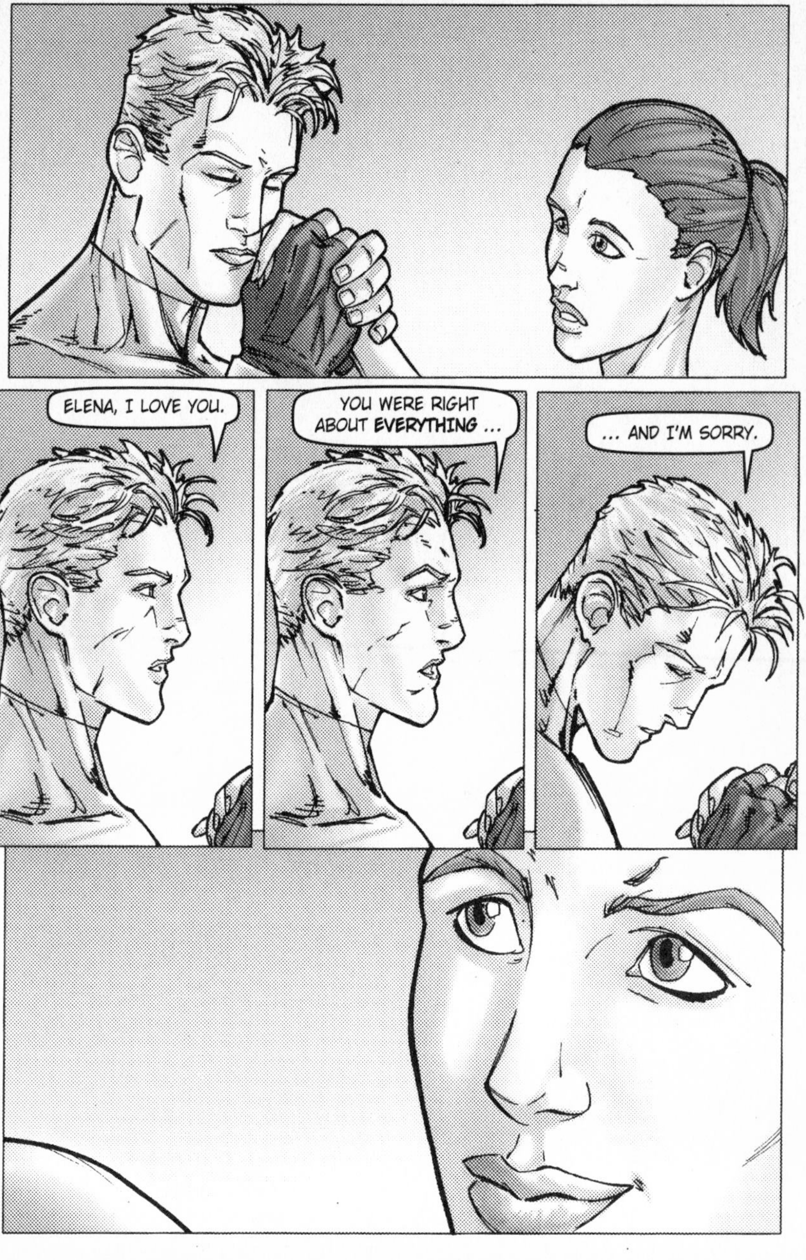
ELENA, I LOVE YOU.
YOU WERE RIGHT ABOUT **EVERYTHING** ...
... AND I'M SORRY.

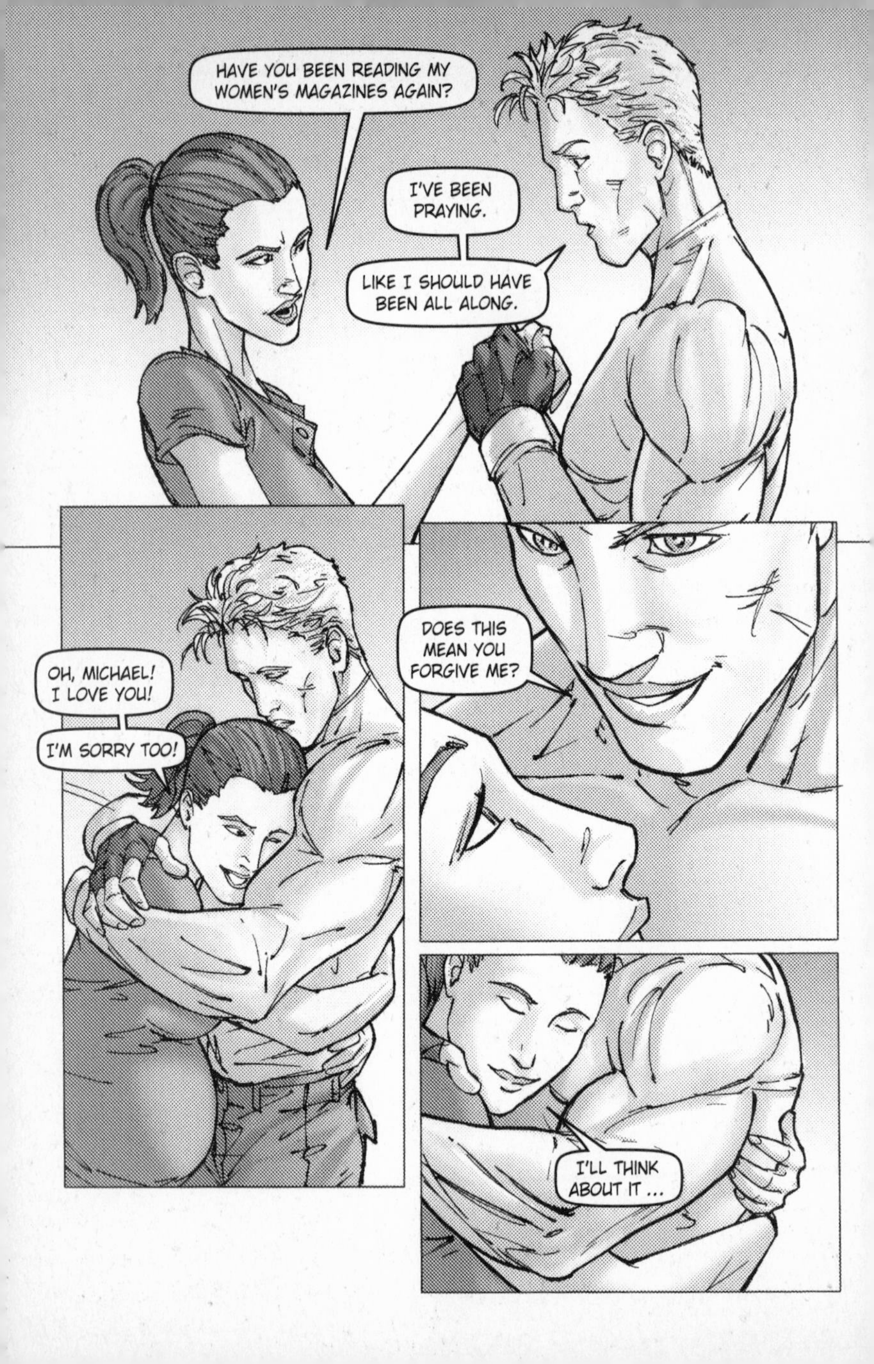
HAVE YOU BEEN READING MY WOMEN'S MAGAZINES AGAIN?
I'VE BEEN PRAYING.
LIKE I SHOULD HAVE BEEN ALL ALONG.
OH, MICHAEL! I LOVE YOU!
I'M SORRY TOO!
DOES THIS MEAN YOU FORGIVE ME?
I'LL THINK ABOUT IT ...

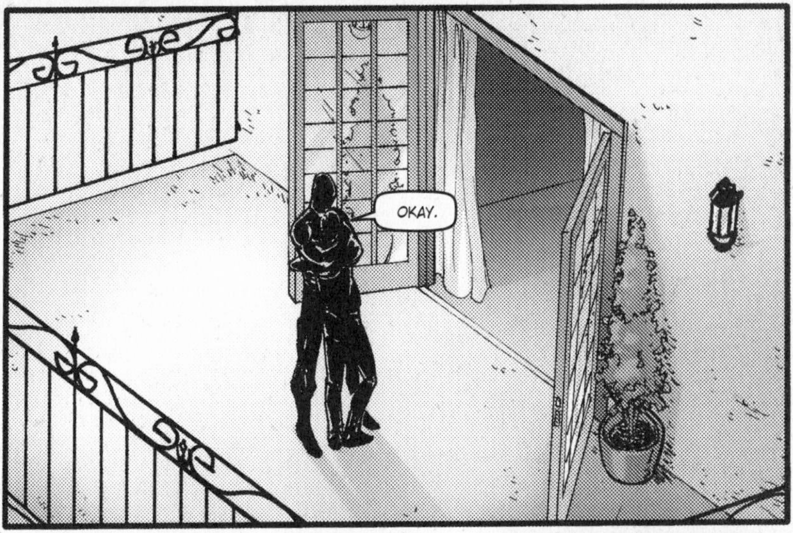
OKAY.

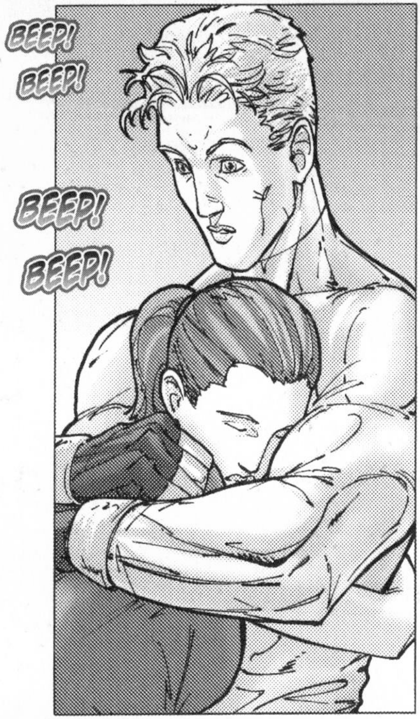
BEEP!
BEEP!
BEEP!
BEEP!

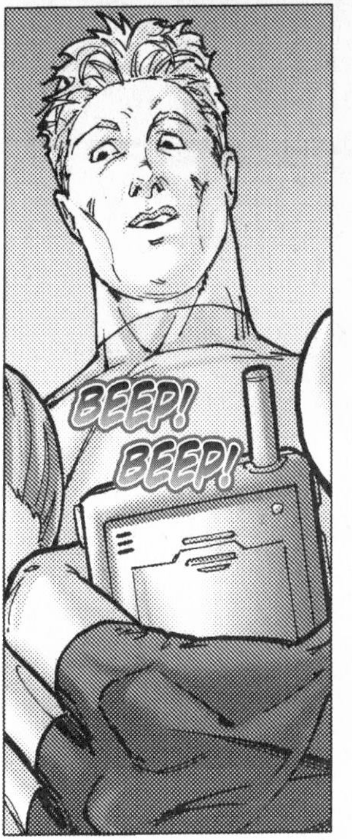
BEEP!
BEEP!

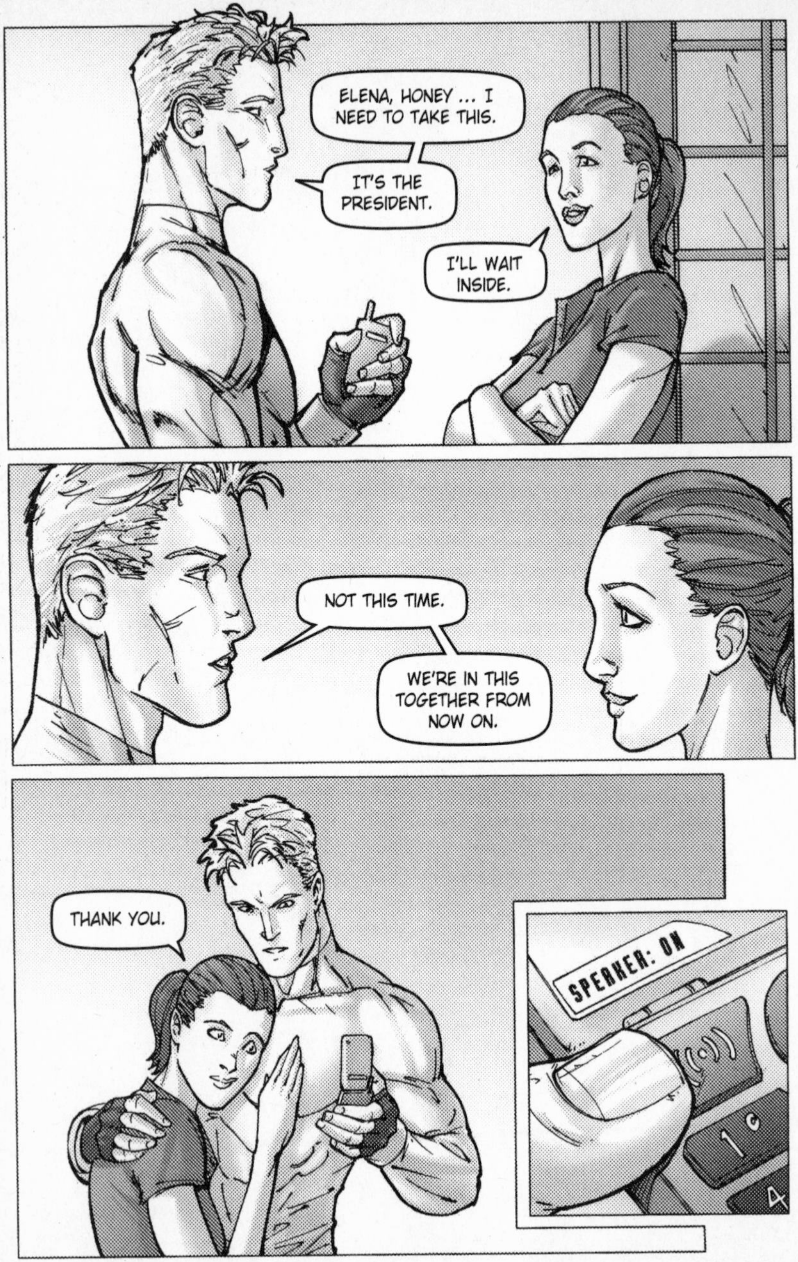
ELENA, HONEY ... I NEED TO TAKE THIS.
IT'S THE PRESIDENT.
I'LL WAIT INSIDE.
NOT THIS TIME.
WE'RE IN THIS TOGETHER FROM NOW ON.
THANK YOU.
SPEAKER: ON

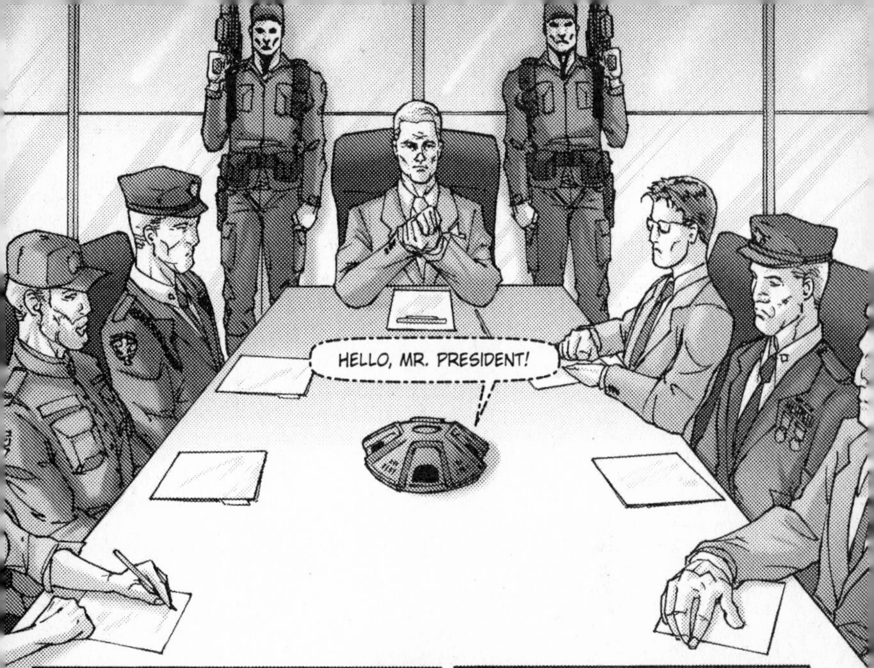
HELLO, MR. PRESIDENT!

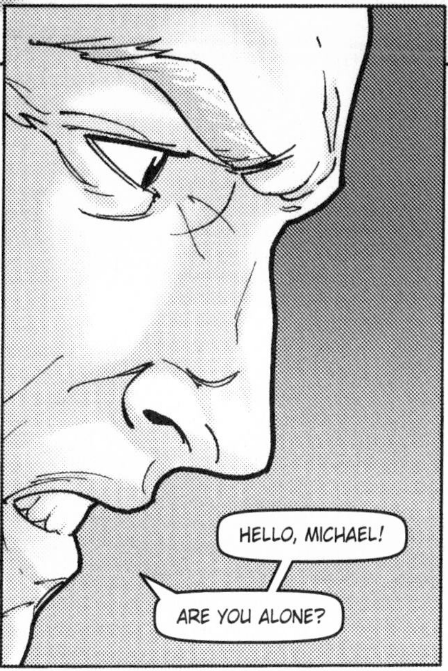
HELLO, MICHAEL!
ARE YOU ALONE?

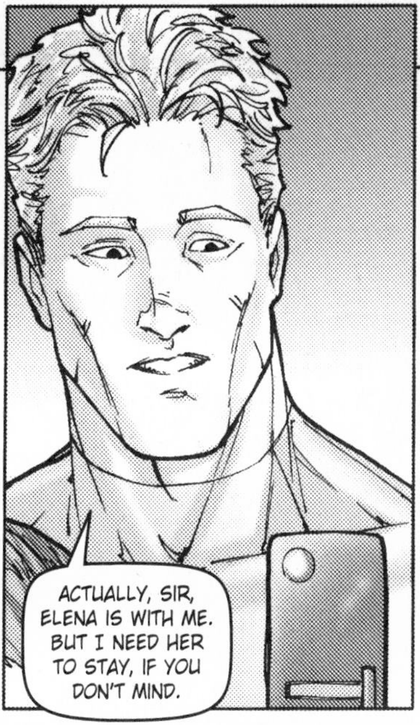
ACTUALLY, SIR, ELENA IS WITH ME. BUT I NEED HER TO STAY, IF YOU DON'T MIND.

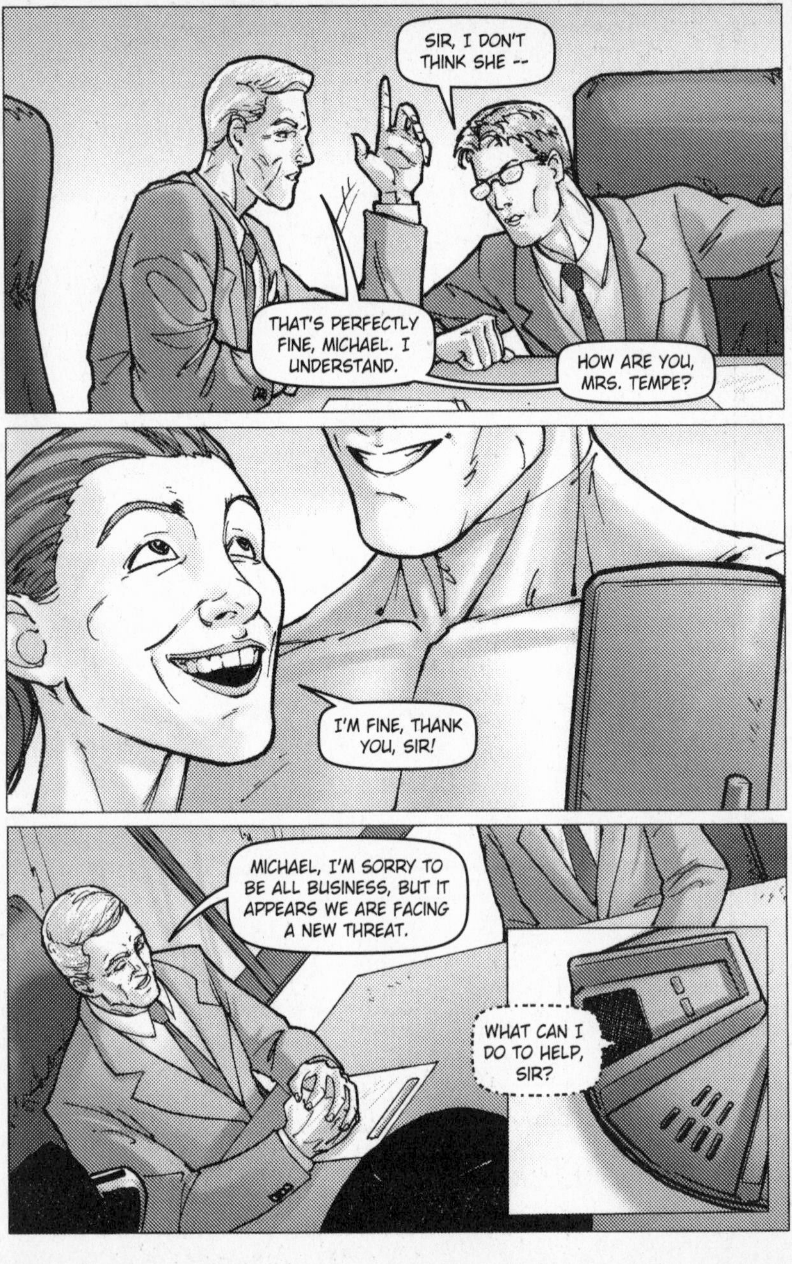
SIR, I DON'T THINK SHE --
THAT'S PERFECTLY FINE, MICHAEL. I UNDERSTAND.
HOW ARE YOU, MRS. TEMPE?
I'M FINE, THANK YOU, SIR!
MICHAEL, I'M SORRY TO BE ALL BUSINESS, BUT IT APPEARS WE ARE FACING A NEW THREAT.
WHAT CAN I DO TO HELP, SIR?

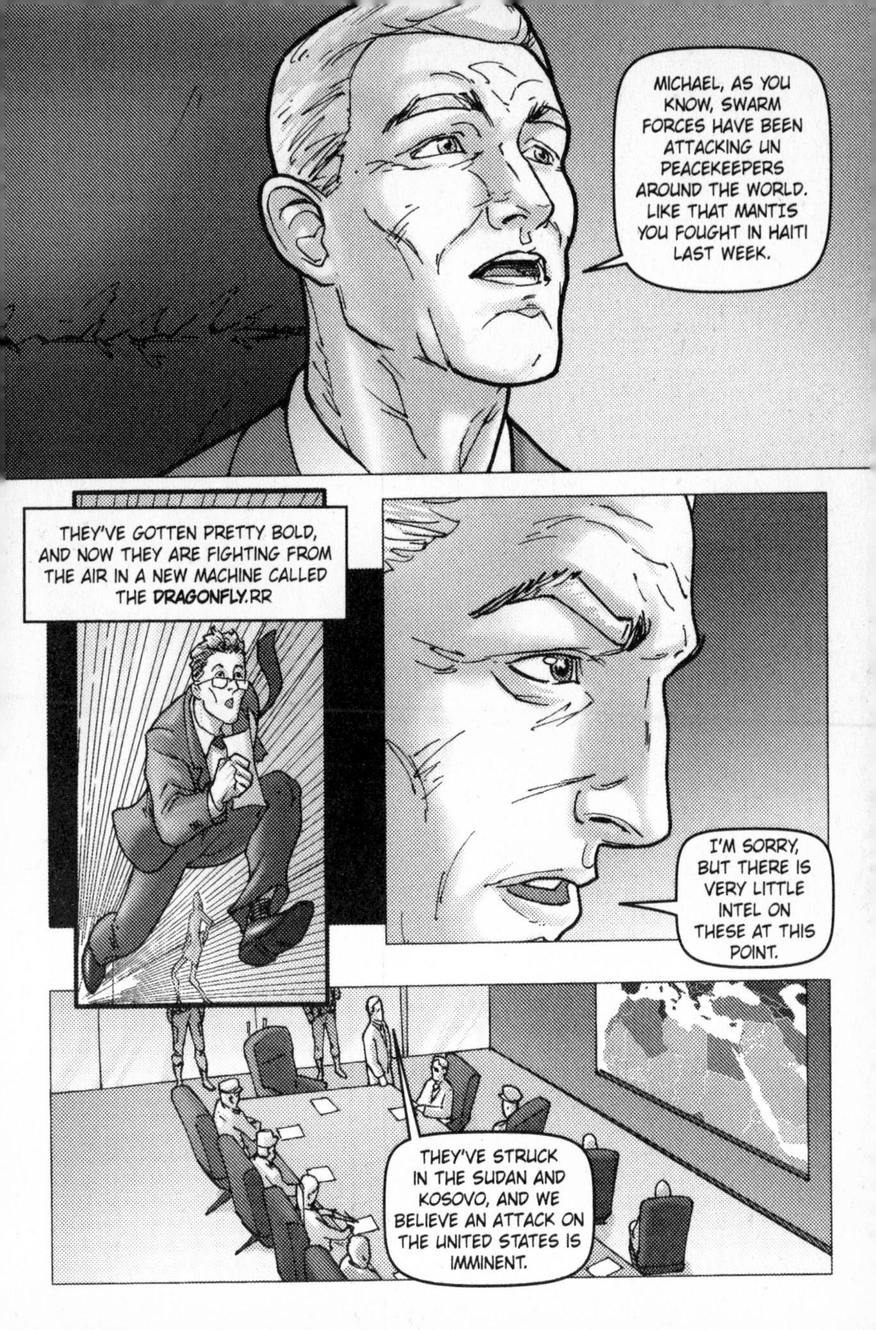
MICHAEL, AS YOU KNOW, SWARM FORCES HAVE BEEN ATTACKING UN PEACEKEEPERS AROUND THE WORLD. LIKE THAT MANTIS YOU FOUGHT IN HAITI LAST WEEK.
THEY'VE GOTTEN PRETTY BOLD, AND NOW THEY ARE FIGHTING FROM THE AIR IN A NEW MACHINE CALLED THE **DRAGONFLY.RR**
I'M SORRY, BUT THERE IS VERY LITTLE INTEL ON THESE AT THIS POINT.
THEY'VE STRUCK IN THE SUDAN AND KOSOVO, AND WE BELIEVE AN ATTACK ON THE UNITED STATES IS IMMINENT.

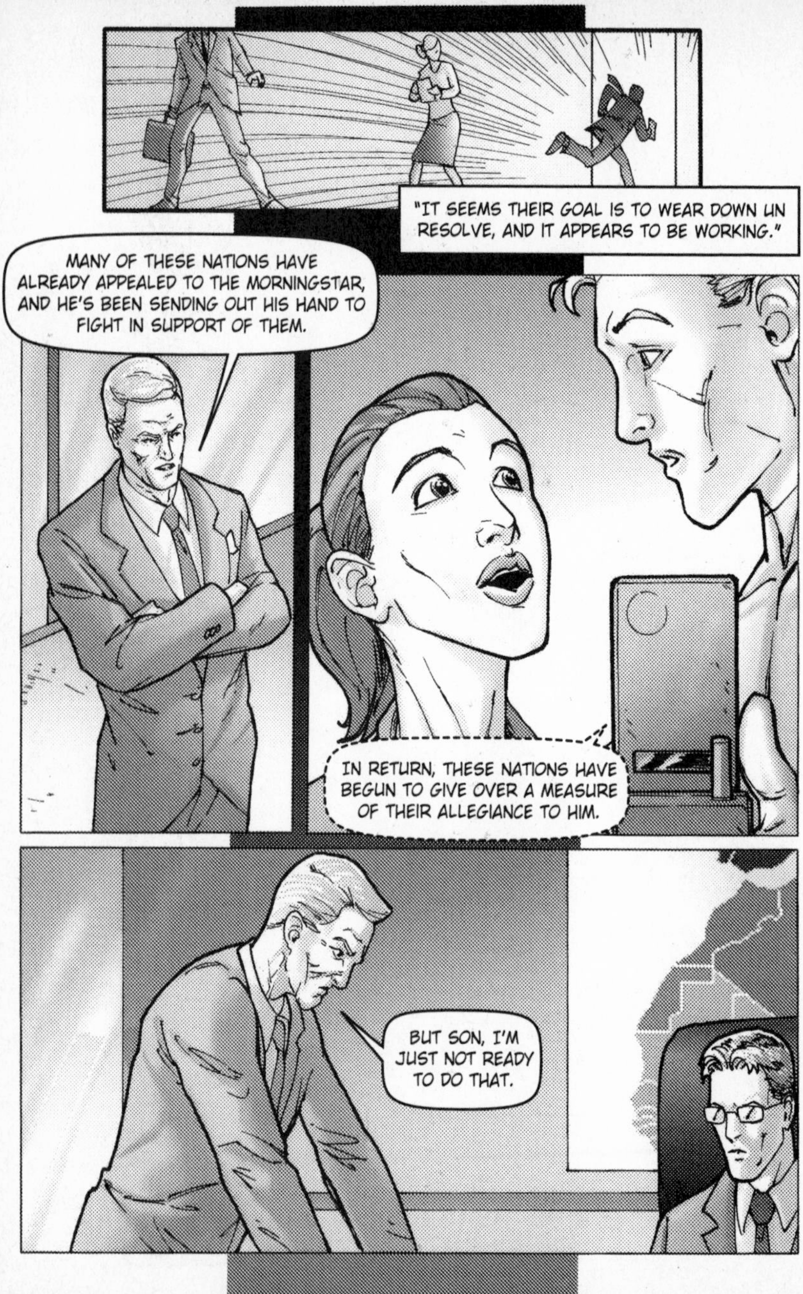
"IT SEEMS THEIR GOAL IS TO WEAR DOWN UN RESOLVE, AND IT APPEARS TO BE WORKING."
MANY OF THESE NATIONS HAVE ALREADY APPEALED TO THE MORNINGSTAR, AND HE'S BEEN SENDING OUT HIS HAND TO FIGHT IN SUPPORT OF THEM.
IN RETURN, THESE NATIONS HAVE BEGUN TO GIVE OVER A MEASURE OF THEIR ALLEGIANCE TO HIM.
BUT SON, I'M JUST NOT READY TO DO THAT.

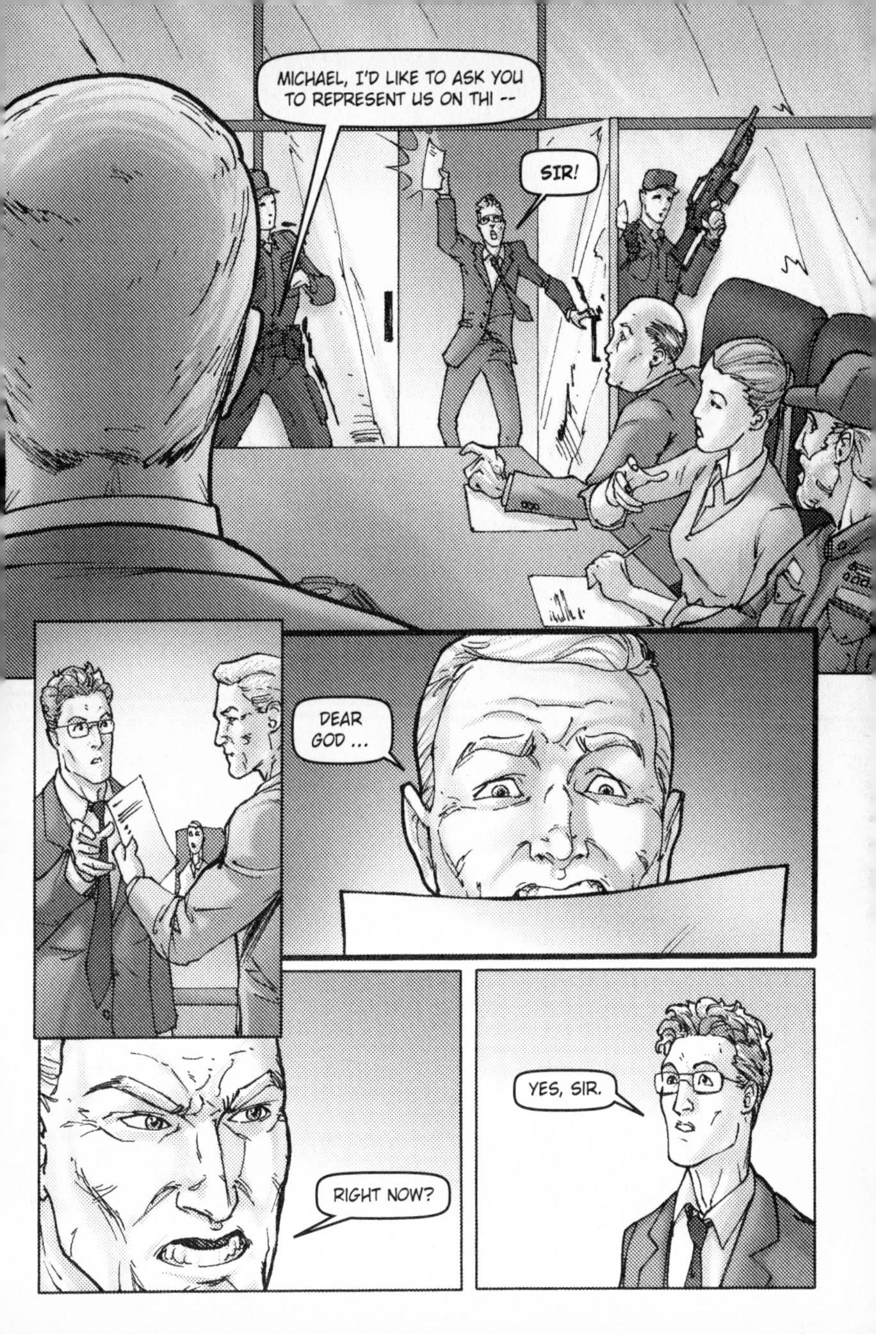
MICHAEL, I'D LIKE TO ASK YOU TO REPRESENT US ON THI --
SIR!
DEAR GOD ...
RIGHT NOW?
YES, SIR.

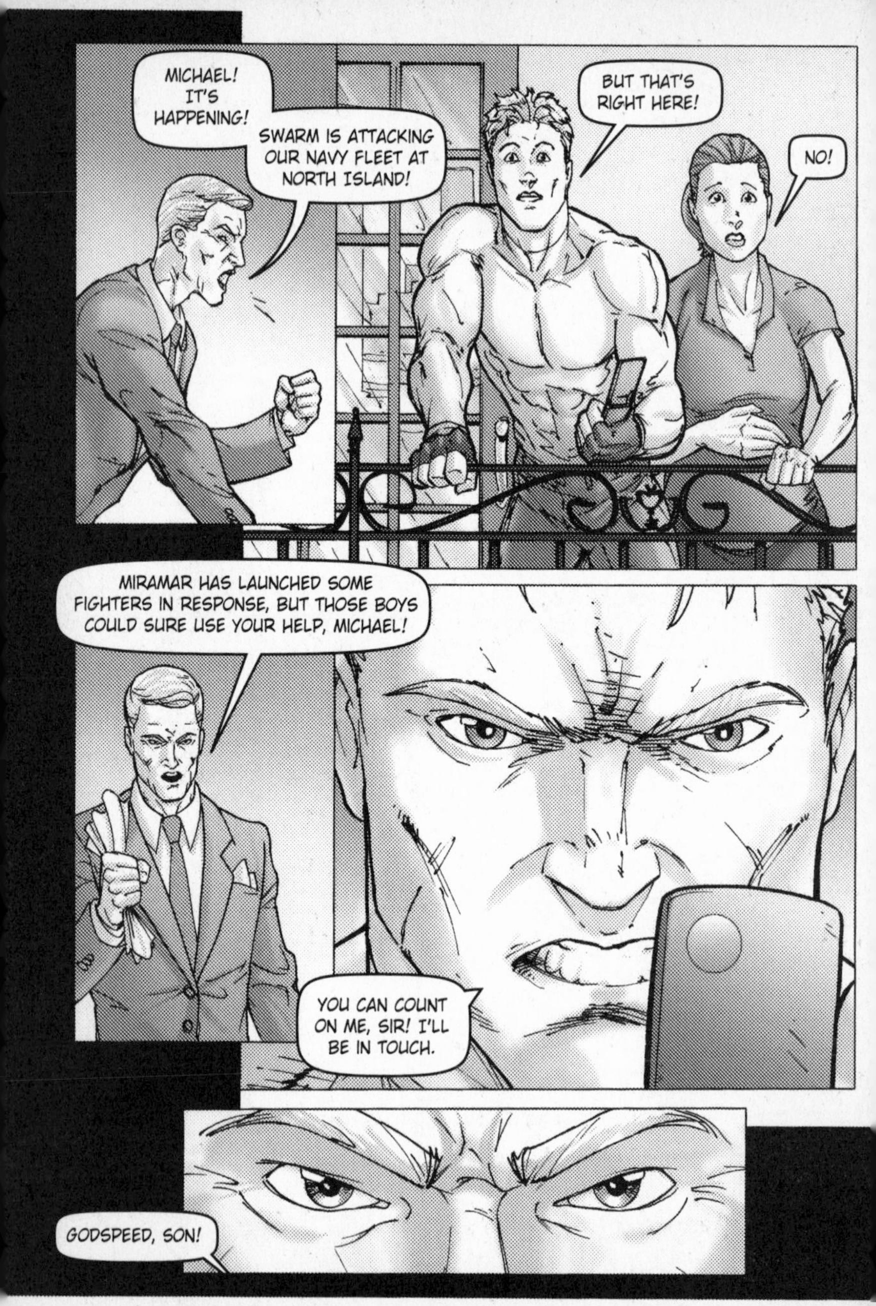

MICHAEL! IT'S HAPPENING!
SWARM IS ATTACKING OUR NAVY FLEET AT NORTH ISLAND!
BUT THAT'S RIGHT HERE!
NO!
MIRAMAR HAS LAUNCHED SOME FIGHTERS IN RESPONSE, BUT THOSE BOYS COULD SURE USE YOUR HELP, MICHAEL!
YOU CAN COUNT ON ME, SIR! I'LL BE IN TOUCH.
GODSPEED, SON!

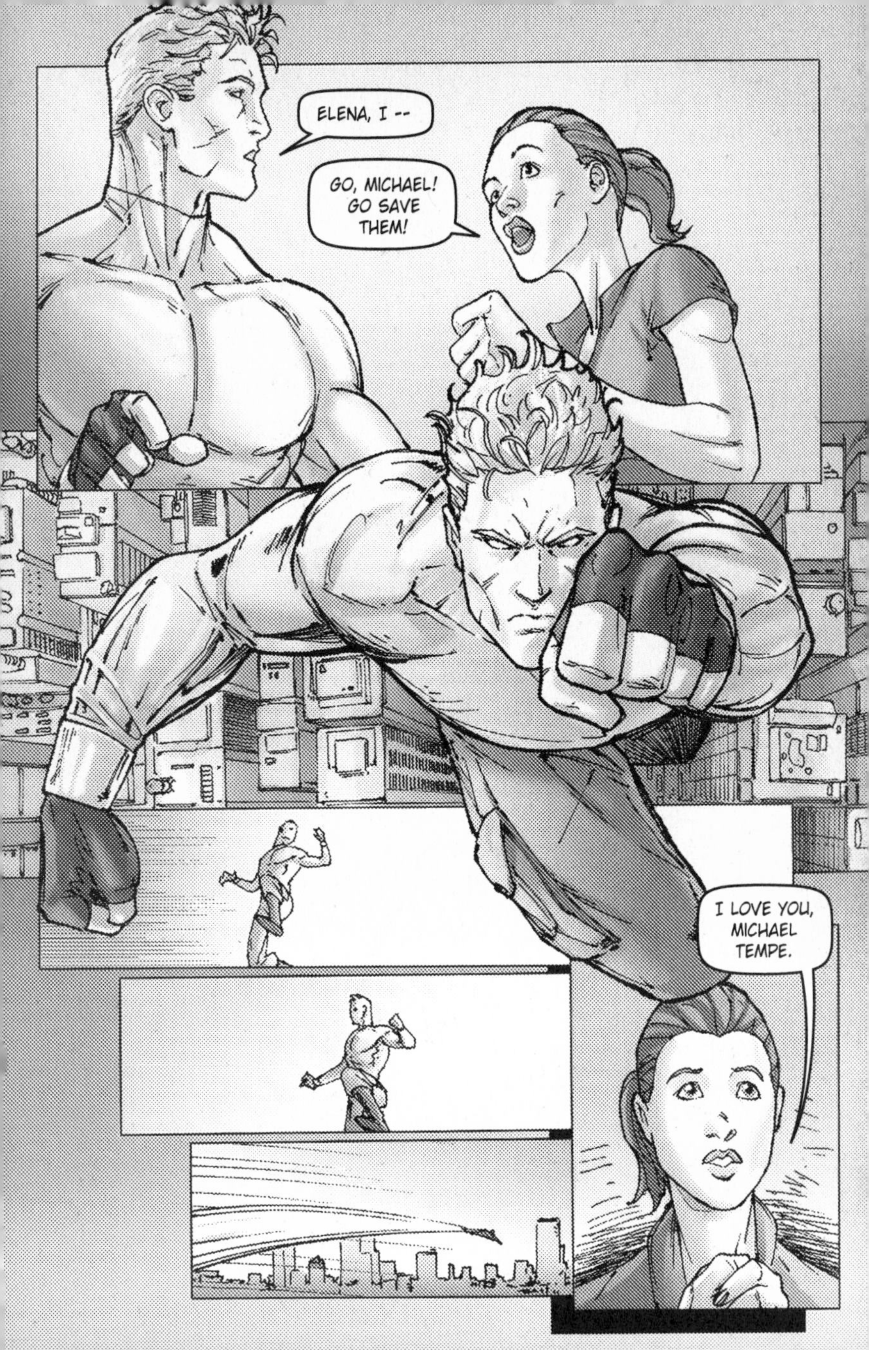
ELENA, I --
GO, MICHAEL! GO SAVE THEM!
I LOVE YOU, MICHAEL TEMPE.

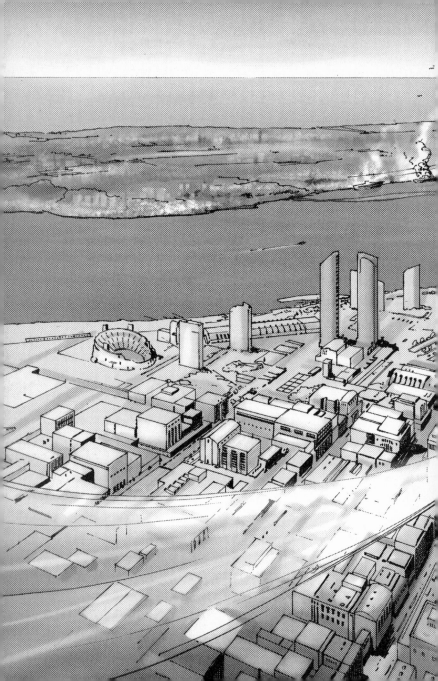

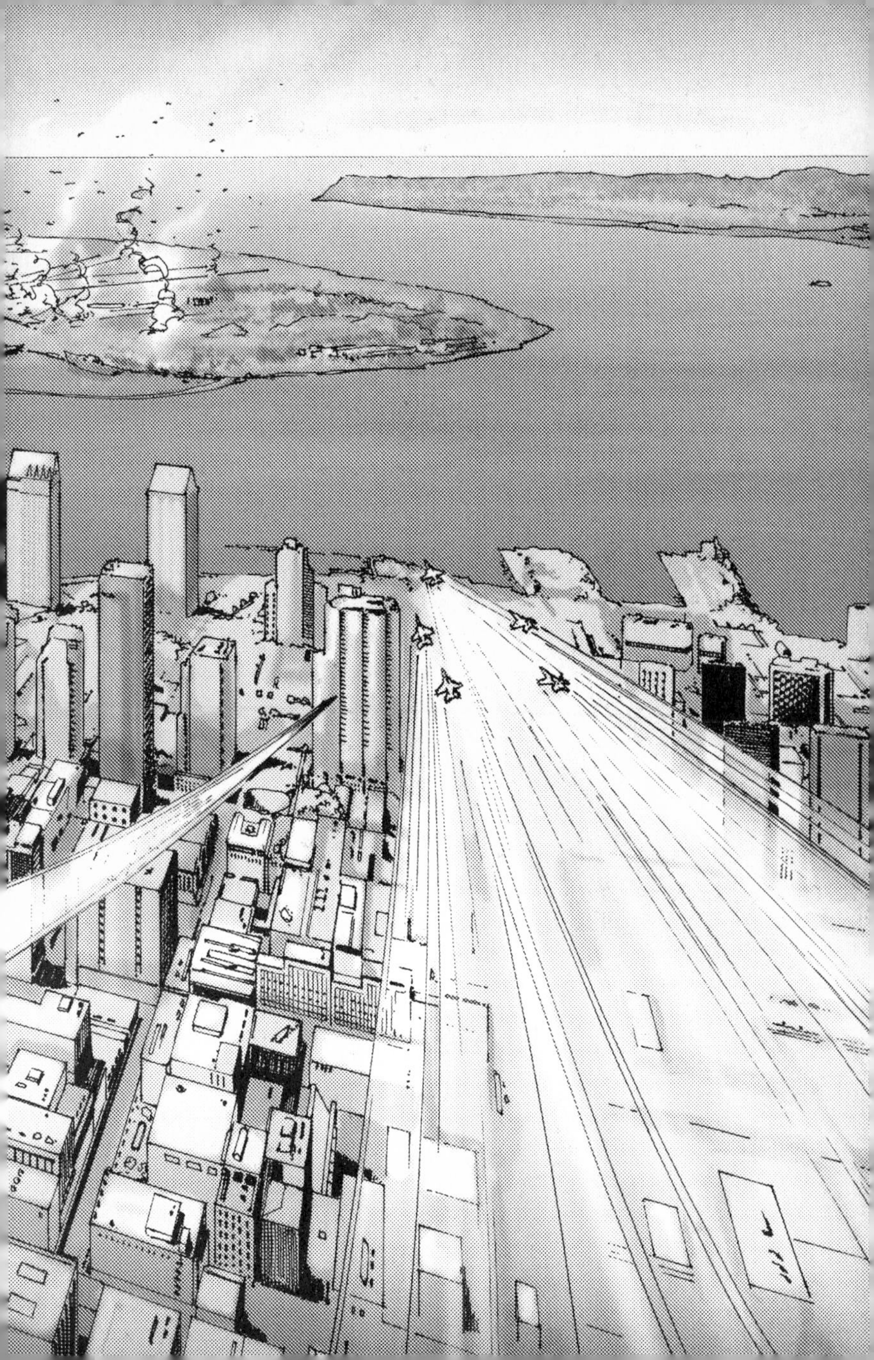

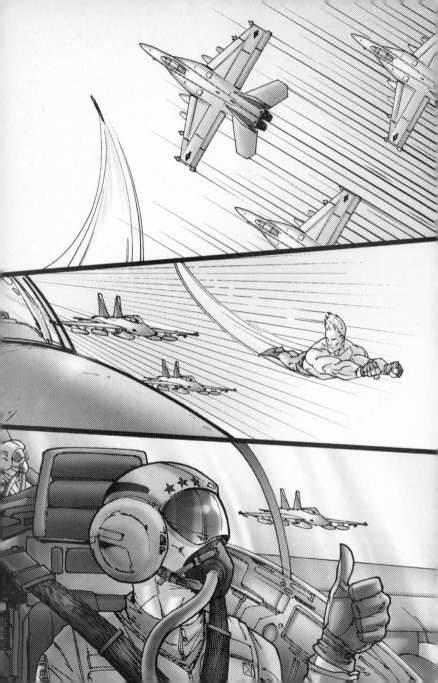

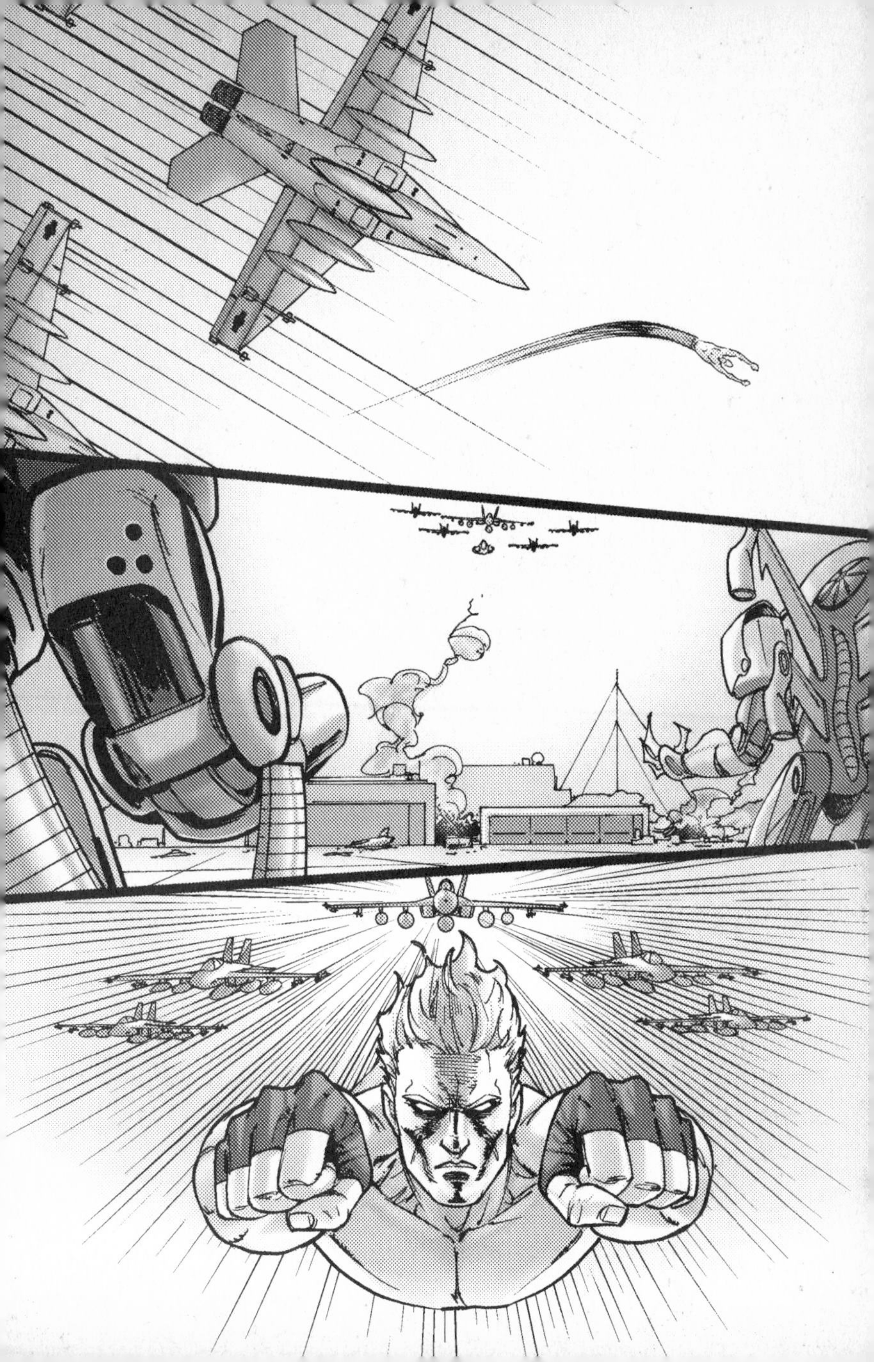

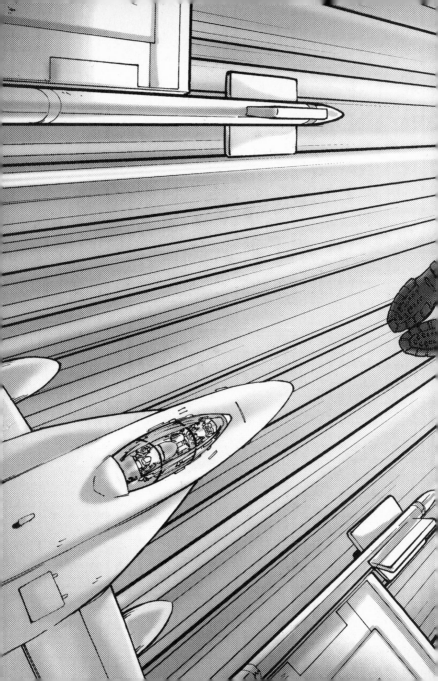

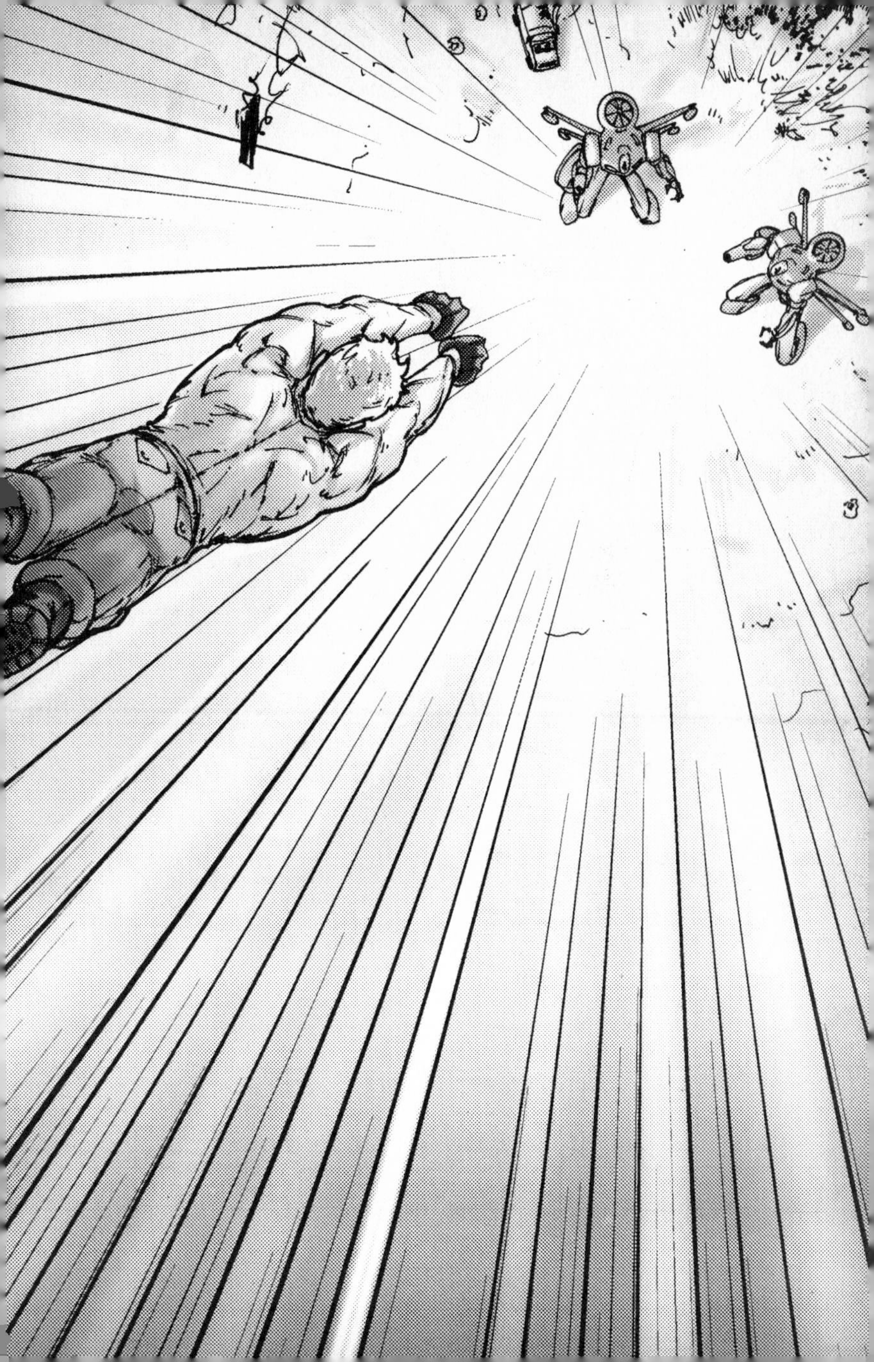

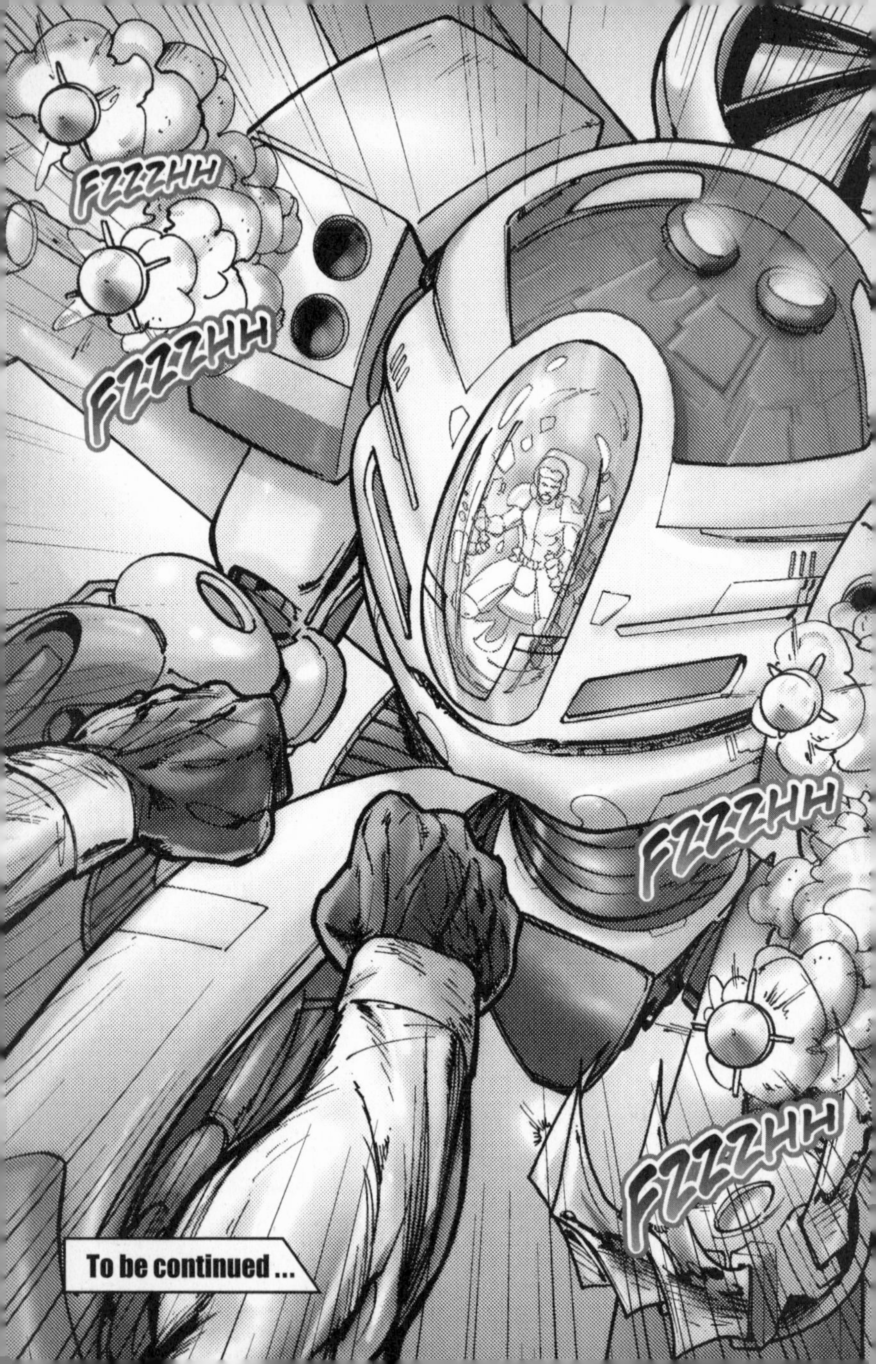
FZZZHH
FZZZZHH
FZZZHH
FZZZHH
To be continued ...

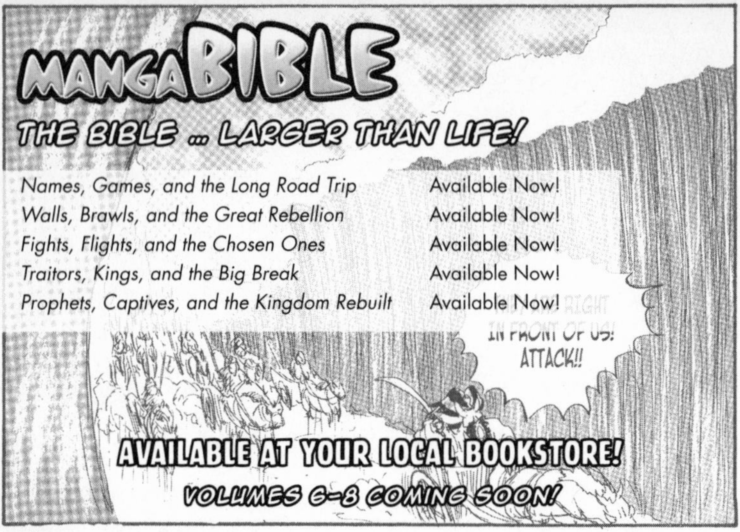
IN FRONT OF US!
ATTACK!!

MANGA BIBLE

THE BIBLE ... LARGER THAN LIFE!

Names, Games, and the Long Road Trip	Available Now!
Walls, Brawls, and the Great Rebellion	Available Now!
Fights, Flights, and the Chosen Ones	Available Now!
Traitors, Kings, and the Big Break	Available Now!
Prophets, Captives, and the Kingdom Rebuilt	Available Now!

AVAILABLE AT YOUR LOCAL BOOKSTORE!

VOLUMES 6–8 COMING SOON!

LAMP POST

TOMO

STUDENT BY DAY, NINJA AT NIGHT!

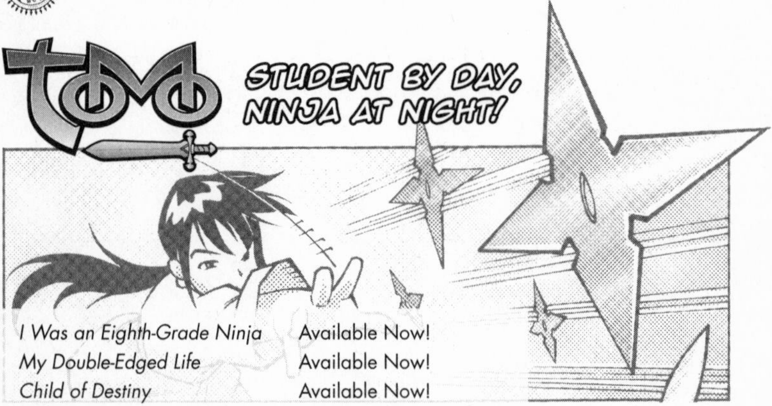

I Was an Eighth-Grade Ninja	Available Now!
My Double-Edged Life	Available Now!
Child of Destiny	Available Now!
The Argon Deception	Available Now!
Secret Alliance	Available Now!

AVAILABLE AT YOUR LOCAL BOOKSTORE!

VOLUMES 6–8 COMING SOON!

funnypages PRODUCTIONS

ZONDERVAN®

ZONDERVAN®

We want to hear from you. Please send your comments
about this book to us in care of zreview@zondervan.com. Thank you.

Grand Rapids, MI 49530
www.zonderkidz.com

ZONDERVAN.com/
AUTHORTRACKER
follow your favorite authors